FoR KEEPS

by

Chautona Havig

First Edition
ISBN 1453811850
EAN-13 is 9781453811856

Edited by Barbara Coyle Editing

Many thanks also to Christy for her hours of labor in editing. You helped me make Barbara's job so much less painful!

The events and people in this book, aside from the caveats in the first book, and Lorna with the picture frame (a true story my friend Crystal shared with me and used by permission) are purely fictional, and any resemblance to actual people is purely coincidental, although I'd love to meet them!

Visit me at **http://chautona.com** and **http://fairburytales.com**to meet more of my "imaginary friends."

For Carmen —

I can't imagine my life without memories of chocolate, cheesecake, the Olive Garden, and late night chats about fascinating things such as hammers, screwdrivers, and drills. Who knew we were such handywomen? Don't answer that. This book's for you. Your friendship is priceless to me. I already miss you more than I could ever say. That's sayin' something coming from a gal who can talk… a lot!

For Mom Havig —

You'll never know how blessed I feel to have you in my life. Thank you for being everything that I could have hoped for in a mother-in-law. Not all women have such a treasure.

Books by Chautona Havig

The Rockland Chronicles

Noble Pursuits
Argosy Junction

The Aggie Series

Ready or Not
For Keeps
Keep Away (coming 2011)

The Annals of Wynnewood

Shadows and Secrets
Cloaked in Secrets
Beneath the Cloak (coming 2011)

The Not-So-Fairy Tales

Princess Paisley (coming 2010)

A Rude Awakening

Chapter One

Monday, August 4th

Lost in dreams of term papers, finals, and job applications, Aggie rolled over, sliding further under the sheets in a futile attempt to drown out childish shrieks outside. "Lord, I am so grateful I decided against elementary education. Can't you prompt the mother of those kids to make them be quiet?" As the shrieks turned to wails, she groaned and added a pillow to her makeshift soundproofing. A new thought crossed her mind. "Lord, why are kids—"

Understanding dawned. Just as Aggie jumped from her bed and flew to the window to see if she could determine the cause and culprits of the banshee-like chaos outside, she heard Tina's no-nonsense voice. "All right, that's enough. You're making enough noise to wake the dead—or at least your aunt."

"A few seconds ago, those two were nearly synonymous," Aggie muttered dryly. "Besides, the way your voice carries, I'm sure Murphy is feeling properly chastised right now, and she hasn't done anything wrong. Yet."

The protests of the children, as Tina ordered them into the kitchen, told Aggie the woman might need backup. She hurried from her room and down the stairs, and was on the second floor before she looked at her knees peeking out of her summer nightgown. The last time she'd left her bedroom without getting dressed first, Luke had tried to avoid a snicker when she grabbed her keys to run to town for a gallon of milk. "Mibs," he'd said while strolling from the room, "wouldn't you rather put on something more appropriate for a trip to the store?"

She turned on her heel and scrambled up stairs. Naughty children could revel in their naughtiness for just a couple of minutes while she threw on a skirt and t-shirt. So obsessed was she with getting downstairs, Aggie didn't have time to glance in the mirror. It was a daily ritual. She woke up, brushed her teeth, got dressed, brushed her hair, frowned at her appearance, prayed that they'd be done with renovations soon, and then dreamed of the day she could take her faded, stained, holey clothes out to the fire pit she hoped to have and burn them.

Pandemonium reigned in the kitchen. Vannie held Kenzie in a chokehold as she argued with Laird who restrained a kicking, screaming Cari. The other children all spoke at once, while Tina repeatedly cried, "Just calm down and tell me what's going on!"

"Stop!" Silence descended instantly. Scowling faces threw nasty looks at each other, but all arguing ceased.

Tina raised an eyebrow. "Impressive."

"Just remember, 'stop.' It'll save your sanity, I promise you." Turning to the children, Aggie pointed at Cari. "Tell me what you did wrong."

"Kenzie—"

"I didn't ask what Kenzie did. I asked what Cari did. What did Cari do wrong?"

"She—"

Taking a deep breath while biting her tongue, Aggie led Cari to the corner. "Stand there. Not a word. You listen to how this works; I didn't ask what she did. I asked what you did. You'll get a turn in a minute."

A few mumbles began, but Aggie's stern face soon squelched them. "Kenzie. What did you do wrong?"

"Well, Cari—"

"Kenzie…" Aggie leaned against the island, crossing her arms.

"I wouldn't let Cari play with me."

"That isn't nice, but it isn't against the rules. Anything else?" A pointed look from Laird told Aggie all she needed to know. "I'm waiting."

"I pushed her."

"Hard, too!" Lorna's indignant tone nearly sent Aggie into a fit of giggles. "Cari just wanted to play."

"What did Lorna do?" Aggie's sigh wasn't lost on Vannie and Laird.

The pixie-eyed girl sniffled. "I kicked her."

"Kenzie?" Aggie's eyes flew to Kenzie's legs to see if there was any evidence.

"No, Vannie." Lorna's indignation had returned.

"You kicked Vannie." Trying to hide a smirk, Aggie rubbed her nose. "Ok, and why did you kick Vannie?"

"'Cause she slapped Cari's hands."

Aggie's eyes closed for a moment as she processed this information. What was she going to do now? As if inspired by genius, an idea formed rapidly in her mind. "Laird, who did *not* do something wrong this morning?"

"Ellie."

"Ellie," Aggie began, "did you do anything wrong this morning?"

"Probably. I wanted to do a lot of things that are wrong."

"Such as?"

"Knock some heads together," the child admitted. "Mommy would be so ashamed of us."

"Not you, Ellie," Tavish argued. "You tried to be a peacemaker."

"Not in my heart."

Before a new argument erupted, Aggie shook her head. "Ok, ok. For the record, Ellie, temptation isn't the sin. It's not a sin to feel like doing something wrong, as long as you turn around and do the right thing instead and don't dwell on the temptation." She tugged at Ellie's thick braid and sent her to pour herself a bowl of cereal.

"Ok, did anyone else here manage to avoid doing anything wrong before…" Aggie peeked at the clock. "Seven twenty-five?"

9

Laird shrugged. "Probably Vannie. She's always doing the right thing— even if it is obnoxiously bossy."

"Obnoxiously bossy isn't the right thing. Ok, so for the rest of you, I want you to go upstairs, put on your pajamas, and brush your teeth. Go!"

"But I'm hungwy!" Cari's wail from the corner prompted a few echoes, but Aggie silenced them with another order to "stop."

"If you want to eat at all today, I'd suggest you obey *without* arguing."

Fifteen minutes later, the only sounds in the Stuart-Milliken abode were those of Ellie rinsing her bowl and storing it in the dishwasher, and Ian giggling as Tina fed him his breakfast. Ellie danced upstairs for her sketchbook and pencil before racing outside. Aggie hardly noticed. Instead, she turned the page and finished her Proverb-du-jour, before closing the Bible. "'Avoid it, do not pass by it; Turn away from it and pass on,'" she whispered. "Now, how do I get that through their heads?"

Armed with a roll of metal screen-looking stuff, a tool belt, and bucket, Luke knocked and entered, glancing around to see where all of the children were hiding. Seeing Tina playing with Ian in the study, he raised his eyebrows and got a grin in response. "You should have seen it. She was—"

She glanced at the stairs, and his eyes followed as Aggie's familiar voice interrupted them. *"Awake! awake! and let your song of praise arise..."*[1]

"They aren't up yet?"

"They were. She woke up to a display of temper and ugliness that would give the GIL a run for her money." Tina rolled her eyes, remembering. "Honestly, Luke, I don't know how she does it. I'm going crazy, and there's an end in sight for me." She frowned and ducked her head. "I'm ashamed to admit it, but it's true. How is she going to survive eighteen more years of this?"

"One day at a time, I suppose. Don't tell her—"

"I don't," Tina assured him. "When we talk, I remind her that she can do all things through Christ. I assure her it's going to get easier every day."

"But you don't believe it." A frown accompanied his words.

"I've been here long enough to tell you it hasn't gotten any easier for me, and I don't bear the brunt of it like she does."

"Well, all I know is that if anyone can do it, Mibs can."

"Why do you call her that?" Tina had wanted to know since the first time she heard it.

"You'll have to ask her."

"I did. She said she didn't have the foggiest."

Smiling, more to himself than at her, Luke took another step forward and said, "She should know. She just has to think about it."

Luke passed Aggie in the hall as a group of subdued children slowly filed from their bedrooms, sending curious glances at their aunt. He smiled his encouragement and climbed the stairs to her little third floor retreat. It took several trips to carry up all the stones, mortar, trowel, and other tools into the room. With most jobs, he worked quickly. Aggie had once confessed that his prep work time drove her crazy, but she'd confessed that how swiftly he finished after that prep was impressive.

The fireplace wouldn't be one of those swift projects. She was bound to come upstairs in an hour and expect to find it almost complete, but he wouldn't have the stones planned out in that time. Tina's fireplace "makeover" was a time-consuming and difficult project for him. He didn't particularly like working with mortar. It wasn't as bad as yard work, but...

The house slowly filled with familiar sounds. The backdoor latched shut half a dozen times, the trash bag hit the dumpster with a satisfying clank of glass against metal, and then faint strains of Aggie's hymn occasionally drifted through the window. "… *would be my prayer, dear Lord, each day…*" He smiled. Her choice of hymns never ceased to amaze and amuse him. "…*hold my hand. I need Thee ev'ry hour. Through this pilgrim land, protect me by Thy **saving** pow'r!*"

Her emphasis on every and saving wasn't lost on him, nor was the realization that her voice grew clearer and stronger with each passing second. She wouldn't finish before she entered her room, which made him smile. He loved it when Aggie sang.

11

Though her voice grew quieter when she entered the room, she ended the song naturally as she watched his progress. Luke waited several seconds before he said, "You know, Mibs, you set the tone of this house with your hymns. I think that's why your children are so joyful most of the time."

"You missed our morning lack of joy, mister."

"Were you singing when whatever happened, happened?"

"I was sleeping."

His slight smile broke into a huge grin. "I rest my case."

"What's all that metal?" Aggie asked, deliberately trying to change the subject.

"Lath. You have to use it to hold the mortar."

"You don't sound thrilled." This was a first. Luke usually seemed invigorated by their projects.

"It's not my strong point. I'm just concentrating. I didn't mean to be short."

"You weren't." Aggie glanced around her. "This floor seems different than the other floors."

"It's newer. This room was once part of the attic. I bet it was remodeled in the sixties or seventies."

"So, the other side of that wall..." Aggie pointed to the wall behind her bed, "is the attic?" Somehow, she'd missed that connection.

"Yep. I think the infamous nail is right on the other side of it."

Luke nearly exploded with laughter at the treacherous look she gave the wall. "Well, if any nails poke me now, I should be good on the tetanus front."

She wandered into her bathroom and ran her fingers along the marble-topped cabinet. "I'm glad you talked me into this marble. It's just so pretty."

"It wasn't much more than the solid surface stuff, and it just seems to fit the room and the house better. I think you may have spent an extra hundred dollars at most." She jumped at his voice in the doorway.

"I even found a few green towels that match those leaves!"

She pointed to a few towels that did match well, but even to his inexperienced decorating eye, looked well-loved. "So, those are the colors you're going to buy?"

"No, I just thought I'd use these."

12

His arms crossed across his chest. A familiar stubborn look etched itself into Luke's features, while his eyebrows furrowed. She'd seen that look when she wanted to try to cut corners that he called "saving a dollar so you can spend five more to do it right later." Aggie hated that look, because it usually meant that he was right, and of course, she was wrong.

"What about window curtains?"

Aggie gulped. "I thought maybe I'd skip them since I'm so high. It's not like anyone could see in here…"

"And that's the look you want in here?"

The temptation to lie was nearly overpowering. Oh, how she wanted to spew a line of drivel about simple lines and uncluttered walls and surfaces in the bathroom to have a nice clean look to it. If she confessed that she was trying to avoid any more expenditures, she'd be on her way to buy bathroom décor and accessories inside an hour. It was how things worked when Luke got that look on his face. Truth triumphed over self, and Aggie shook her head. She couldn't bring herself to admit it aloud, but she had to be truthful.

"So, what are you going to do about that?"

"Change clothes?"

"Atta girl, Mibs."

At her closet, she paused. "Luke, why do you call me Mibs?"

"You know. You might not realize that you do, but you do."

"And you're not going to tell me?" As she spoke, a pile of t-shirts tumbled into her arms. Luke's forehead furrowed.

"Nope. By the way, I was thinking we should expand that closet to take up that whole corner. Then, you'd have a nice nook there for a little couch — what are they called?"

"I don't know." She frowned. "More closet space would probably be better for resale, wouldn't it?"

"Are you planning on moving?"

"Not for awhile, but —"

"Don't design your space how you think someone else wants it then. If you don't want that much closet, I can just bump the one side a bit, or you can buy a dresser or two. Your current set up is just a logistical nightmare."

With fresh clothes in hand, she returned to the bathroom, closing the door behind her. As she pulled on a fresh and unstained t-shirt, Aggie called, "Just do what you think is best. I've always drooled over those closets that could hold enough for a small boutique, but they are a bit of overkill."

She re-emerged looking a little bohemian in her many-tiered skirt and shaking out her hair as she removed her ponytail. "Well, let's just hope that Tina has decided on colors and that I know what she's talking about."

"Take her with you."

"I can't concentrate with all the kids, and with you up here…"

"You two go out. Since she's been here, you've hardly had a few minutes just to enjoy 'girl time.' I'll go cut down the grass in the back and measure off the grill area we discussed. This can wait. Maybe I'll send Laird and Tavish up and see what they come up with."

"You're going to let them put up rock?" The incredulity left an expression on her face that was priceless.

"No, but they can play with the layout. Who knows, maybe it'll be perfect or nearly so, and I can come in and start laying stone."

Once down the steps and in the second floor hallway, Luke's words finally registered. "Did he really say 'girl time?'"

"I have four sisters. I know about girl time."

Her eyes rolled heavenward, and she was thankful he couldn't see. "The way you sneak up on me like that is going to kill me someday. I should make a will and leave all the kids to you for scaring me like that."

"You should also overcome your habit of rolling your eyes at me when I do it."

Her head whipped around and she stopped, stunned at his words. "How did you—"

"You always do that when you get sarcastic with someone. Vannie is starting to pick it up." Before she could reply, he added, "And mentally beating yourself up about it isn't going to fix anything."

"It's scary how well you know me. Scary."

Libby says: I've been waiting for you!

Aggie says: Well, I was just admiring my new fireplace.

Aggie says: Tina was right. It does look better now.

Libby says: Luke said she made the right call. He wasn't sure why paint wouldn't have been good enough, but now he agrees that she chose the right solution.

Aggie says: Is he still speaking to us?

Libby says: I think so. He's already talking about painting walls tomorrow.

Aggie says: I was practicing my cutting in skills, but I'm still pretty pathetic. I do better with roller work.

Libby says: That'll save him a bunch of time. He said he got the fire pit and the patio all marked off today.

Aggie says: Yep. It's going to be perfect.

Libby says: You don't seem yourself tonight. Are you tired?

Aggie says: Hard day. It started by putting the kids back to bed this morning and then early to bed tonight. I haven't had this much trouble with them in a long time.

Libby says: I remember those days. Oh, my. There were times that I wondered who was inhabiting my children's bodies!"

Aggie says: Off topic. Why does Luke call me Mibs? Tina says she asked him today, I asked him today, and he told both of us that I should know.

Libby says: If Luke won't tell you; I'm not going to! I don't relish the idea of having my head bitten off!

Aggie says: *shrugs* I think he likes being all mysterious.

Libby says: He's a man. Of course he does.

Aggie says: *giggles*

Aggie says: Tina is going to take Vannie school shopping tomorrow. If I can manage, I think I'll convince her to take the other kids one at a time. It'll be good for them to have some focused attention. I haven't figured out how to incorporate that yet.

Libby says: That's a lovely idea! I think you'll find that having one child help you each day in the kitchen will be a nice way to have some one-on-one interaction. You'll have to figure out what to do with Ian when he gets old enough for his turn, but with seven days a week, it gives you ample opportunity…

Aggie says: Do I sound like a terrible person for confessing that the last thing I want to do is add work to an already distasteful task? I am already such a lousy cook. Why would I subject the kids to an even more unskilled culinary example?

Aggie says: Never mind, you're right. I'm just being selfish.

Libby says: Children can chop vegetables, crush breadcrumbs, set tables, and all kinds of things. They don't have to start with crème brûlée.

Libby says: Oh, you beat me to it. I would say that you're being a tired mommy. Being a mother is hard work, but having a helper in the kitchen isn't the only way to do a one-on-one time. It's just one that was easy for me.

Aggie says: Well, I'm going to try it anyway. I need to do something.

Libby says: Aggie, you are the most teachable young woman I think I've ever met.

Aggie says: You mean desperate, don't you?

Libby says: Possibly. I'm at my most teachable when I'm desperate.

Aggie says: Touché. Oh well, I need to do the whole face-washing, tooth-brushing bit. It's my last night in my bedroom. Until it's done, it's back to the library for me.

Libby says: Goodnight, Aggie. I can't wait to see your room. Luke says it's either going to be a work of genius or a work of Genie-ous.

Aggie says: Night. And if he's still there, tell him I said I'll get him for that.

Libby says: He's pretending to quake in fear—or is that laughter?

Aggie says: *shuffles downstairs to rig a bucket of water for Luke's grand entrance in the morning*

Libby says: LOL. Now he's rubbing his palms together in a most fiendish fashion. I would be worried if I were you.

Aggie says: You should be—for him.

Libby says: The Sullivans bid you goodnight!

Aggie says: Goodnight all… both… whatever.

Un-Fashion Able

Chapter Two

Tuesday, August 5th

Ian, ineffectively corralled in a playpen, greeted Luke when he arrived to work on Aggie's room. Plopped in the middle of the room, Aggie worked around it, throwing frowns in the child's direction every time he hiked one of his little knees toward the top. At the sight of Luke, the baby squealed and threw his hands up for Luke to rescue him from his prison. Luke dropped his water bottle and tool belt and pulled the little tyke into his arms. "Mornin', squirt. Are you causing trouble already?"

"See those footprints?" Aggie's disgust was nearly palpable.

"Did you think a curious toddler would ignore a lovely chance to finger paint?"

"I put him on that blanket," she jerked her roller in the direction of a blanket that now was bunched under the playpen and flung a stream of paint that splattered across Luke's chest. Her look of horror faded into amusement before she erupted in a fit of giggles.

"If you thought I needed a makeover, you could have just told me." Luke punctuated his comment with a swipe at his nose where a drop of paint threatened to fall at any second.

" — and told him to stay."

"He didn't." Feeling like the master of stating the obvious, Luke couldn't repress a smirk.

"Well, I've heard of other mothers doing it…"

"And you think that moms just put a child on a blanket, tell them once not to get off, and that's all it takes?"

The moment he spoke, Aggie flushed with embarrassment. "I've become too dependent on Vannie as an extra pair of eyes." Shoulders slumped, she continued. "I've made finishing more important than being the mother that he needs."

Several seconds dragged as Aggie contemplated her words, staring at the paint roller in disgust. Her face fell, the corners of her eyes filling with pain. She dropped the roller in the tray, took the paint-splattered Ian from Luke, gave him a forced smile, and carried the baby out of the room. Her wavering voice wrenched his heart further when it floated up the stairs seconds later, "…*Fill Thou my life, O Lord my God…*"[2]

Hesitant, Luke's eyes flitted back and forth between the abandoned paint tray and the open doorway. He turned to follow Aggie and on the second floor, heard sniffles punctuating the next verse. *"Praise in the common words I speak, life's common looks, and tones. In fellowship in hearth and board with my beloved ones…"* A hiccough set his resolve. Some things were more important than finishing a room.

Down in the kitchen, Aggie had already strapped Ian into the high chair, and with fistfuls of baby wipes, she scrubbed the paint from his hands, face, and leg. The bottom of both feet bore traces of dried-on paint, which she now scrubbed at ineffectually in an attempt to finish the clean up in one try. "Laird, will you go get Ian some clean clothes?" she asked without looking his way.

Luke turned and went to retrieve the desired clothing. When he returned, he set them on the counter at Aggie's right, and smiled. "Will these work?"

"Why didn't Laird —"

"He didn't hear you; I did. So, I got them."

"Oh, sorry." Aggie pulled the t-shirt over Ian's head, ignoring his protests, and wiggled the shorts over his knees, hips and around the child's waist, before setting him on the floor where she knew he'd be off in search for the kitten. "There. At least you're clean again."

18

She grabbed the paint-splattered romper and carried it to the sink. "Thanks, Luke."

"Aggie?"

The weary young woman sighed. "Is something wrong?"

"I don't know." He leaned against the counters and tried to meet her eyes as she attempted to scrub the paint out of Ian's outfit. "Is there?"

She nearly slammed her head into his nose as she whipped her head around to meet his gaze. "What are you talking about?"

"You've got that look on your face, Mibs. I know that look."

"What look?"

Luke heard a squeal from the kitten and rescued it from Ian's overeager hands, and then returned to answer the question. "That look that says, 'I'm not qualified for this job, but come what may, I'm going to do it right if I die trying— even if it kills me."

"If I died trying, wouldn't that be evidence that it killed me?"

"You'd think."

"Qualified or not, I have to get the paint out of this thing."

Luke took the wad of sodden fabric from her hands, opened the trash cupboard, and dumped it in the bag. "There."

"Hey, I was—"

"Wasting your time."

"It just seems so wasteful," she admitted.

"Will you put it on him if it's stained?"

"No, but..."

His laughter surprised her. "You're dodging the subject! It actually worked. We were discussing your propensity to expect too much from yourself."

Before Aggie could respond, the twins came tearing through the kitchen in search of something, but Aggie sent them back to the door to walk. "Again." Cari sent her a dirty look but retraced her steps outside for a third time. The defiance on the child's face wasn't lost on Aggie. "And again..."

"But—"

"And again..." With almost exaggerated nonchalance, Aggie shrugged at Luke, fighting to keep her expression curious, interested, even bored—anything but irritated or angry.

Scowling with every step, Cari stomped back and forth from the island to the screen door, until Luke was sure that Aggie would give in, but the young woman surprised him. She saved the DVD collection from Ian's curious hands, wiped up the counter, found Tupperware for the baby to play with, and carried on a conversation about floor finishes, all while repeating "again" to Lorna and Cari.

After half a dozen trips, Lorna, who hadn't shown a nasty attitude, was sent to play again, but Cari marched back and forth with a vehemence that would have terrified Aggie six months earlier. "You should just behave, Cari. I want to play."

"I am behaving! I'm coming in and out just wike Aunt Aggie says. It's not *faiw!*"

"I said to come in quietly. Your stomping isn't quiet."

For a few seconds, it looked like Cari was cooperating. She opened the door with the sweetest expression that anyone had seen from the child. However, when Aggie sent her back for one last round, the child stomped to the back door, opened it, and slammed it shut. She then opened it again, quietly shut it, and walked sedately across the floor as if incapable of creating such a nasty display of temper as she'd just exhibited.

"If you think that you will get away with any bad attitude at all, you're mistaken. I did say you had to come in quietly. I did not say you had to leave quietly, it's true, but," Aggie's voice grew very quiet and her tone was carefully measured. "You know that it is always against the rules to throw a tantrum, and that is what your stomping is. It's a nasty temper tantrum."

It took half a dozen more trips that were quiet, but with a sullen face, before Cari relaxed her features and threw herself into Aggie's arms. "I's sowwy, Aunt Aggie. I'll walk nice now." Without being told, she turned and strolled to the back door, opened it, stepped through, closed it, and then reopened it with a genuinely contrite look on her face. At Aggie's side, she asked, "Do I pwactice again?"

Visibly sagging with relief, Aggie sent the girl to follow her sister and sank to one of the barstools that she kept near the island. She laid her head onto her arms, leaning onto the smooth cool countertop, and sobbed. "I can't do this, Luke. I am such a failure. Everything I do is wrong. I—"

"Mibs—"

"Stop calling me that! I don't even know what it means. I've got out of control children, a house that is more than I can handle, no where to hide, and that's probably a good thing, because if I do hide, chaos erupts, and — "

Tavish burst into the kitchen, oblivious to the pity party in full swing, and announced, "There's a wasp's nest out there! Can you believe it! I've got to get my book and see what kind they are!"

Before Aggie could process Tavish's alarming information, the boy was thundering up the stairs in search of his encyclopedia of insects. Luke started out the back door and down the steps. Just as his foot stepped onto the grass, he heard Aggie's voice, cracked, wavering, and off-key, sing, *"The Lord is in His holy temple. Let all the earth keep silence before Him — "*[3] The song ended abruptly with a sniffle and a hiccough.

One glance at the combination summerhouse-carport, and Luke saw that Tavish was correct. He shooed the children away, insisting that they play in the front yard until they'd eradicated the pests. How he was going to do it, he didn't know. Whatever he did, it needed to be before Aggie's nerves snapped.

By dinnertime, the nest was a bitter memory in Tavish's budding-entomologist's heart. As was a frequent custom in Aggie's house, the children trooped into the kitchen, like clockwork, begging for a dinner that she hadn't even considered yet. After a debate between "leftover buffet" and pizza, Aggie grabbed the phone. The moment the pizzeria answered, they placed her on hold, and Tina and Vannie entered the house bearing buckets of KFC.

Grateful for a break from pizza rescues, Aggie allowed Vannie to take the baby while she pulled out plates, loading each as swiftly as possible. "Luke, it looks like there's plenty here. Why don't you take a shower and join us? You left those jeans and t-shirt here the other day. They're in the mudroom in the cabinet to the left of the dryer — top shelf."

She watched him hesitate and then nod. As she listened to the children fill Vannie in on the great wasp eradication, she relaxed for the first time all day. With all of her failures, she hadn't managed to destroy the close and loving relationship that the children had with one another.

Dinner was always a noisy affair, and that night was no exception. By the time Luke rejoined them, the children were laughing at the dance he'd done with the bellows he'd used to try to smoke the wasps into a stupor. "And then he rushed to bomb the nest and tried to run away without being stung. He almost did it too," Tavish raved. "He's good with pests."

Cari's little voice piped up importantly. "Of couwse he is! I heawd Aunt Aggie tell Aunt Tina that he's vewy good wif me!"

"Aw, Cari. You're a pest all right, but a nice pest," Tavish reassured her, unaware that his compliment was quite backhanded.

Eager to diffuse the situation before it became one, Aggie said, "Vannie, I can't wait to see what you and Tina found today. You'll have to show me right after dinner. I know what good taste Tina has. Whenever I need something new, I always ask her what she suggests."

"We only found one shirt and a pair of saddle shoes. The shirt will go with anything, but I'm not sure about the shoes. I just loved them, and since we hadn't found anything else, I decided to get them." Dejection, exhaustion, and irritation laced Vannie's voice.

Aggie glanced at Tina, confused. "It was ridiculous, Aggie. Everything in the stores that fit was either too mature for her or too indecent for anyone. I took her to every store in the Eastbrook Mall and half a dozen down by Boutique Row, and the only one down there that had anything was Boho Chic, but you have to order from them. Since I wasn't sure, I didn't buy anything there, but I did write down the styles and sizes we liked in case you decide to go for it." With a look of utter disgust, she added, "Don't even get me started on the jeans. I thought the low-slung, squeeze your rear into an odd shape fad was grotesque. Skinny jeans are a million times worse."

Aggie frowned. "Tina, you own about a million pairs of them!"

"Well, they're going in the garbage. It's amazing how you see things in a new light when you see them on other people."

Shrugging, Aggie turned to Vannie. "Where did Allie buy your clothes? Didn't those stores have anything?"

Vannie shook her head. "Mom usually just bought fabric and made them or had Mrs. Gansky make them when she couldn't do it herself." A new look brightened Vannie's eyes. "Last summer, I made a couple of skirts at Mrs. Gansky's house. Those were fun."

"I didn't know Allie knew how to sew," Aggie mused thoughtfully. It wasn't the first time she'd learned something about her sister and wondered how she hadn't known. She'd spoken to or instant messaged Allie every day for years. How had she missed so much of her sister's life? "I guess we should call Boho. Did they say how long the clothes take?"

"They have a six week backlog right now…"

Tina's news wasn't what Aggie needed to hear. "Great, now what do I do?"

Luke grinned. "It seems to me, you have one solution. You'll have to learn to sew." A roguish twist to his grin gave him a taunting look as he added, "Or, should I say *seams*? S-e-a—"

"Ha, ha. Very funny," Aggie retorted. "If you're so clever, you make the girl's wardrobe."

Aggie's threat was lost amid Tina's titters and Laird's guffaw, and even Vannie cracked a smile that seemed to draw her out of her clothing misery. Seeing that Aggie wasn't amused, Tina tried to mollify her friend a bit. "We did manage to find her underthings and a pair of athletic shoes. She said hers were too small, and she'd need them for gym."

"I just need clothes, Aunt Aggie. Everything is too short, too tight, and what Mom called 'seedy.'"

Shoulders slumped, Aggie turned to Vannie and asked, "Did we bring the sewing machine, Vannie? Do you know how to run it?"

"Wha—" Tina looked stunned and then shook her head.

The transformation in Vannie amazed the three adults at the table. It was evident that the child not only knew something about sewing, but she actually enjoyed it. "The sewing machine and serger are in my closet. I also have a few of the pieces of fabric Mom was going to make up for me before…" For the first time in weeks, when Vannie mentioned something her mother would never do again, the child didn't dissolve into a fit of weeping. Instead, through unshed tears, her eyes shone with budding excitement.

"Ok, do you know enough about sewing to prevent me from ruining your clothes? Can you operate that thing? Show me how?"

Vannie nodded as Luke interjected, "You know, if you need help, Mom sews nearly everything for her, the girls, and their girls."

"She does?" Aggie tried to remember what she'd seen Libby wear. Whatever it was, it hadn't screamed "homemade," so that had to be a good sign — she hoped.

"Yep. She's pretty handy with a machine. Whenever she wants to go somewhere or buy something special, she takes in a little sewing—usually around school formal times. Those girls always want something unique. I guess it's social suicide to arrive at a prom wearing a dress that some other girl at the prom is wearing."

"Well, duh!" Tina insisted. "That's a cardinal rule of surviving the American educational system. Be individual or die."

"Just make sure you're individually exactly the same as everyone else," Aggie added.

Laird's voice, laced with disgust, interrupted the social commentary around him. "I'm so glad I am not a girl."

"Why is that, Laird?" Luke was sure the boy would comment on the pressures of modern society on young women, the expectations regarding beauty, or something equally lofty.

He laughed with the rest of them, mostly at his own folly in expecting so much out of an eleven-year-old boy, when Laird said, "Because we just go to a store, buy jeans, a few shirts, and we're done. Girls have to get all fussy with their clothes."

"Spoken like a man," Aggie said, disgustedly.

Luke punched a fist in Laird's direction, and nodded. "Welcome to manhood, son."

As Tina soaked in the tub, resting her aching feet, Vannie and Aggie flipped through boxes of patterns that Vannie carried down from her closet. The boxes were full of everything from basic tops, skirts, and dresses, to vintage classics and more recent trendy options. At one time, they seemed to have been sorted by size, but now several odd sizes were tucked into groups, requiring a resorting of the lot. As they sorted, Aggie watched Vannie pull a few favorites out of the stacks.

By the time Tina joined them, the living and dining room seemed carpeted in patterns. Aggie stacked patterns by age and then by degree of perceived difficulty. Her mind was engrossed in trying to plan wardrobes for her five girls. So focused was she on her task that the idea of being able to purchase something appropriate for the younger girls didn't even occur to her. Instead, she plowed through her ideas, making lists as she went.

"So, do I keep the Boho information, or…"

"Can you call tomorrow and order four outfits? I'm not confident that this will all look ok. Knowing that something is coming would help keep me from freaking out when I sew a sleeve to a skirt or something."

"Remember your half inside-out pillow with the seams on the outside?"

"Don't remind me. Ms. Slade hung it in her class all week as a 'testimony to the futility of some people trying to learn anything of practical use.'"

When Tina's cell phone rang, she waved goodnight and closed herself into the library, talking to her father about plans and developments at the Milliken-Stuart household. Vannie yawned and said goodnight as well, but Aggie returned to her stacks of patterns and tried to find reasonably cute options that looked the least work-intensive. Lost in her own world of fabric, notion, and trim requirements, she jumped when hands closed over her eyes, and a voice said, "Working hard?"

"Aaak! William! You scared me!"

A glance over the back of the couch proved that he wasn't in the least bit contrite. "What are you doing now, Naggie Aggie?"

"Learning to sew. Want to teach me?" She whacked him with a pattern for emphasis.

"I think I'll pass." He moved a stack of patterns from one section of the couch and sank into the cushions. "Um, Aggie, on second thought, do you think it's safe?"

"Do I think what is safe?" Confusion made her nose wrinkle.

"You and a sewing machine."

"Very funny, Mr. Markenson. If you're not nice to me, I'll sic a nice social worker I know on you."

William widened his eyes in mock despair. "Oh, save me from the evil neighbor who, by the way, is having a very difficult time living down your nickname for her."

"She earned it," Aggie retorted dryly. "Anyway, I bet she could teach you some manners."

He didn't respond other than to smile at her silliness. Aggie watched as he leaned back against the back of the couch, ankle resting on his knee, and his hands laced together behind his head. As each second passed, she saw him visibly relax until he looked as at home and comfortable as any man could desire, and she wondered how long it would be before he no longer had to work to feel comfortable in her home without painful memories of his past intruding into his present.

"You've done a good job with this house, Aggie," he said at last. "I mean, I know it's not done, but from here, it looks better than I've ever seen it. That kitchen is amazing! Well, I'd want something that matched better — cherry wood and dark granite or something, but — "

"Hey, no knocking my cool cabinets. They're exactly what I've always dreamed of." Her eyes roamed over the outline of her new kitchen. The lights were off, but she could still see the island, the upper cabinets, and the corner of her favorite piece, the hoosier. "I still can't believe that Luke spent all that time making each cabinet so unique! You'd never know they were all one piece and made at the same time."

Changing the subject, she held up two patterns and asked, "Button holes or zipper? Which is easier? Do you know?"

"Well, you should ask someone who has actual experience with a machine, but look at the picture. The zipper has two long rows of straight stitches. Just up and down. The buttonhole one has about five. That's like five mini zippers, and you have to be sure they're equally spaced. Zippers look easier to me." He studied the pattern jackets closely again. "Yeah, I'd go for the zippers. There's less mending with them too. You don't have buttons to lose and replace."

"It sounds like someone has problems keeping his buttons on his shirts."

"It's a tough job, but someone's gotta do it," he admitted with a smirk.

Aggie flipped through the pile of patterns on her lap, while occasionally pulling one out and stacking it in a new pile next to her. One dress with a row of tiny buttons down the front caught her eye. She stared wistfully at it for a few seconds, and then dropped it in the reject pile. "Well, I guess this one is definitely out."

26

William grabbed a small box of patterns near him and flipped through them. From time to time, he pulled one out and piled it next to him, before continuing his perusal. Curious, she reached over him and snagged his pile. Almost every single one was one of the vintage patterns that Aggie had been warned to avoid. Vannie insisted that the sizing was "off" and she didn't know how to fix it.

"Oh, you have excellent taste! I think they're just beautiful. All those full skirts and fitted bodices. They remind me of the party dresses that are in that *Madeline* movie."

"After that one dress, I had you pegged as a prairie muffin type." William's statement was nearly a question.

"I don't think I have a type. I'm no Alexa Hartfield, but I love pretty, feminine clothes that accent a person rather than overpowering them. I'd look like a freak in most of what she wears, but I love how beautiful they are!" The pensive tone in her voice wasn't lost on him.

As he listened, it occurred to William that Aggie hadn't had many opportunities to dress up in her nicer clothes. She practically lived in denim and t-shirts, and most of what she wore was stained, holey, and almost threadbare in spots. "Actually, that's almost what I came here about. I thought you might like a change of clothing for a while."

Her brow furrowed. "My clothes aren't feminine enough for you or they're too feminine? And," she added with a frown, "since when is it any of your business what I wear?"

"I didn't say your clothes weren't perfect for what you're doing around here, but then I'm no expert on women's clothing." He winked before he continued. "I just thought —" He shrugged. "Well, we'd talked about getting to know each other. You know, see if there was any chance for a relationship. I thought maybe Friday…"

Something in William's tone made Aggie wonder if he was more attracted to the idea of a relationship, a relationship with her specifically, or if it had more to do with some fascination with her family or her home. Whatever it was, she was nearly as determined as he to discover what it was. "I think I'd like that."

"Good."

"Since clothes brought up the subject, what do I wear? Casual? Dressy? White House Formal style dressy?" She grinned. "Pick your fashion poison."

27

As he stood, William passed her the stack of patterns he'd been holding. "Wear something special. I promise it won't be another dinner of despair."

"I'll be ready. It'll be nice to eat without having to refill plates, cups, wipe up spills, and replace dropped forks every one point nine seconds."

She listened to the screen door shut with a whoosh, the sound of his footsteps on the porch, and the gentle whack of his car door as he prepared to drive home. How had she missed his arrival? The sounds of night seemed to press around her as she listened to see what else she might have missed.

As time passed, the realization that she was going on yet another date with William washed over her. Tina would be excited that she was going out at all. For a moment, she grew nervous as memories of the last fiasco, otherwise known as her first date, flooded her mind. She shook herself. Surely, nothing could be as truly horrifying as their last attempt.

Luke says: You're up late, Aggie.

Aggie says: Well, I was hoping to get your mom. I made a list of girls, patterns for each, and stuff to buy, but I was curious about buttonholes vs. zippers.

Luke says: What about them?

Aggie says: Well, which one is easier? A buttonhole or a zipper. William says zippers. What are your thoughts? If your mom was online, I'd ask, but…

Luke says: Well, I can only tell you what I think I remember, but I'm pretty sure that my sister hates zippers with an unparalleled passion.

Aggie says: Oh, great! I remade my lists only to include zippers. That was a waste of time.

Luke says: Don't worry about it. Mom will tell you which is easier and then show you how to cut whatever you want out for either thing.

Aggie says: She can DO THAT?

Luke says: *chuckles* Aggie, Mom doesn't use patterns half the time. She knows what she's doing, and, fortunately for Vannie, she's fast.

Aggie says: WOW! Ok, well do you think she can help me find affordable fabric? I spent a while on Google looking, but so much of it is over eight dollars a yard!

Luke says: I think she has favorite sites bookmarked.

Aggie says: Oh good! These patterns seem to take two to three yards of fabric. That's eighteen to twenty-seven dollars just in fabric for one outfit. Who knows what buttons and zippers and thread and...

Aggie says: *looks at pattern jacket* elastic and bias tape—what is bias tape?

Luke says: Strips of fabric, cut on the diagonal, and then sewn together and pressed. I don't remember what it's FOR, but I've bought enough of that stuff and ironed enough of it when my "fingers needed employment" to keep me out of trouble, that I'll never forget WHAT it is.

Aggie says: Well good. You'll be the official bias man. Hey, does that make you biased?

Luke says: Probably.

Aggie says: Anyway, I have to find fabric. The stuff Vannie has... it seems so juvenile for a girl going into the eighth grade.

Luke says: Um, Mom probably has that covered. She loaded my truck with two totes of fabric, her button box, zipper basket, thread and bobbin boxes, notions basket, both sewing machines, and her serger. Interfacing blew off the notions basket, so she's digging more of that out now. It was across the road and in a gutter before we could save it.

Aggie says: Hmm...

Luke says? What?

Aggie says: Does what you just said make sense to you?

Luke says: LOL Yep!

Aggie says: Well, I got sewing machine, thread, buttons, zippers, and fabric, but the rest... scary.

Luke says: Scary how?

Aggie says: Did you ever take Home Ec in school?

Luke says: In school, no.

Aggie says: That's how scary. I did. Those things should mean something to me, I assume. They don't. I know what lath is now, thanks to yesterday's project, but I have no idea what...

Aggie says: Sorry, had to scroll up to find the right word. Interfacing is and why you'd want a face on your inters in the first place.

Luke says: LOL. Well, it doesn't have anything to do with faces…

Aggie says: Luke?

Luke says: Yes, Mibs?

Luke says: Oh, sorry.

Aggie says: For what?

Luke says: You don't like that nickname.

Aggie says: I don't?

Luke says: You told me to stop calling you that.

Aggie says: I did?

Luke says: *chuckles* Just before Tavish derailed your room's paint job.

Aggie says: Oh, during my emotional collapse. Ignore me.

Luke says: Now, or then.

Aggie says: Smart question. Then. I don't hate it. It's nice to have a nickname again. Well, one other than Naggie Aggie. How did William pick the exact thing that Doug used to call me? It stings every time he says it.

Luke says: If you told him, he'd stop.

Aggie says: And feel bad for something that isn't his fault. I just have to hope he finds a better one.

Aggie says: Well, it's really late, and if I don't beat the kids up in the morning, I have to beat them when I get up in the morning.

Luke says: LOL

Aggie says: JUST KIDDING. I think. No, seriously…

Luke says: You can pretend all you like, but no one would believe for a second that you'd do it.

Aggie says: Shh! Don't let the kids hear you. They'll revolt en masse.

Luke says: Nah, just Cari… and on a bad day, Kenzie.

Luke says: You were amazing with her today. I was impressed. Mom says you have a natural way with children when you don't second-guess yourself. She says you're your own worst enemy.

Aggie says: Probably. I can't think about it right now, or I'll never get to sleep for wondering.

Luke says: Goodnight, Mibs

Aggie says: ☺ Goodnight, Luke. Thanks.

Twists of Life

Chapter Three

Wednesday, August 6th

Aggie's library looked like a scraggly yard sale by the time Luke and Libby were done dragging in all of the supplies the scout-like woman brought with her. To make room for what Tina called "the sweatshop," Aggie's bed, otherwise known as the couch, was shoved to one end of the room. Long banquet tables, obviously borrowed from their church, were set up in the center of the room, and piled with sewing machines, fabric totes, boxes of notions, and things that looked too technical for Aggie's blood.

While Luke ran power strips to the table for the machines and Libby's "killer iron," Libby and Vannie unpacked the fabric, stacking it in piles by amount. Curious about the impending clothing factory in her home, Ellie crept in, climbed up into the window seat with her sketchbook, and watched everyone with an interested eye. Baby Ian was already proving to be a problem. Every item placed within reach became a temptation he found impossible to ignore. Much to Aggie's surprise, Kenzie, Cari, and Lorna stepped into the room, wrinkled their foreheads at the strange contraptions, and went in search of their "babies."

Once Aggie, Libby, and Vannie set up shop in the library, Tina grabbed Laird and Tavish and took off for Rockland on a masculine clothing-finding mission. They were instructed not to return without church clothes, jeans, shorts, shirts, underclothes, and two pairs of new shoes. The boys looked terrified, but Tina took it in stride. "No worries, guys. I know right where to go, and with any luck, we'll be done in time to check out the batting cages before we come home."

The moment the screen door shut with its soft "whap," Libby rubbed her hands together as if hatching a diabolical plot to ruin Aggie's life. "All right. Vannie comes first, is that right?"

"I think so. I don't know what Tina will find for Ellie or the little girls, but we know there wasn't anything for Vannie."

"Ok, well I'm going to give you a list of stores to try when you need something for her. There are places that sell exactly what I think Vannie likes, based upon the patterns she's hoarding, but you have to know what they are and how to find them. Boho isn't the only place in Rockland to buy decent clothes for young teens."

Aggie sank to the couch in relief. "Really? You mean, we don't have to do this! Oh, Libby! That is the best —" The crestfallen look on Vannie's face changed her words. " — news I've heard in a long time. It's good to know that if we need to buy something, we can."

"The list is in my purse. I can get it now —"

"Well, I was hoping you'd still be willing to do some sewing with us. I know how Vannie has been looking forward to it, and it's probably a good thing for me to learn..."

Libby glanced at Vannie as the girl shuffled through her stack of patterns. A look of frustration clouded her face until it looked as if she'd like to throw them at something. "Is something wrong, Vannie?"

"Well, it's just that patterns are always *almost* what I want, but not quite. I wish someone could see into my head and make patterns from that."

"Show me, Vannie." Ellie's quiet voice from the window seat made all three of them jump with surprise.

While Aggie and Libby discussed needs, Vannie tried to explain to Ellie what was wrong with each pattern and what she'd like changed. The child sketched, erased, sketched some more, listened, erased, made a few more adjustments, and then handed over the sketchpad. "Is that what you wanted?"

"Wow! It's almost exactly what I wanted!"

As Ellie asked questions and made a few more alterations to her picture, Aggie and Libby went to see the drawing. "Oh, I see what you are after, Vannie. That's very clever."

"I like that style, but they're all cut too low or too short. This way it's still in style, but it isn't immodest. Mommy—"

"Your mom taught you well, Vannie. Once you take that first step into 'well it's not *too* bad,' it's hard to know when you've crossed the line. You managed that beautifully!"

The girl beamed, reminding Aggie that she needed to ensure that she didn't slight the children in the praise department. Everything that she needed to do crowded in her mind, threatening to overwhelm her, until she muttered, "Just what is in front of you, Aggie Milliken! Just what is in front of you."

"What did you say?"

Her face flushed as she raised her eyes to meet Libby's. Luke's mother stood holding Ian, his fists full of zippers, and stared at her. "I just reminded myself to focus on what was in front of me. I have a tendency to look ahead, and ahead, and ahead, until I get so overwhelmed I don't know what to do next. My mom taught me to just reach out for what I can touch right now, and start there."

"She's a very wise mother."

"Mrs. Sullivan, do you think we could use this fabric for this dress? Can we make these adjustments, or is it too much?"

"Oh, we can handle those alterations with no problem." Taking the fabric, Libby began measuring, comparing to the pattern requirements, did some mental calculations, and nodded. "There's plenty enough for that and then some. Do you know how to lay it out?"

Vannie nodded and started unfolding the fabric. "You'll have to show me what to change, but—"

"Get it laid out and put just one or two pins in to hold it in place. I'll shift it when I get there and then you can pin it properly."

At the horrified look on Aggie's face, Libby shook her finger, teasing her. "Young woman, you need to learn to trust people."

"What if she messes it up?" Aggie whispered out of earshot.

"So what? She learns and moves on. You must quit expecting everything to go right the first time."

Those words, familiar ones at that, pierced Aggie's heart. Libby was right, of course. Before she could respond, the phone rang. Distracted by the sight of Vannie pinning pieces to the fabric with a confidence she couldn't fathom, Aggie's voice chirped, "Hello?"

"Agathena Milliken, how do you expect to teach those children anything, if you cannot even answer a phone properly?"

"Good morning, Mrs. Stuart. What can I do for you?"

"I am calling to let you know that my lawyer will be visiting you. With your ridiculous restraining order, I'm forced to work through him. He'll be bringing papers for you to sign. I'd appreciate your swift cooperation."

"Sign for what?"

"They're just finalization of property transfers and things like that. I don't have time to explain everything. He is doing us a great favor by going all the way out there, so please do not take any more of his time than absolutely necessary."

"That won't be necessary, Mrs. Stuart. Simply have the papers sent to Mr. Moss. He'll bring them out after reviewing them, or I'll go in and sign them there if necessary."

"I don't have time to play games, young lady. Your irrational and emotionally manipulative games have caused this problem, so you'll have to suffer the consequences. He'll be there in an hour."

Even the phone's disconnect click sounded abrupt and unpleasant. Aggie stared at the handset as if mesmerized by it. Libby watched for a moment and then asked, "Aggie, are you ok?"

"Yes. The children's grandmother is sending papers for me to sign, and she thinks I'll just put my signature anywhere she wants it and without my lawyer looking at it. I've always known she thought I was unqualified to be the children's guardian, but I had no idea she thought I was an idiot."

"Mom said that Grandma Stuart seemed to think people weren't very intelligent, but it was because she always assumed they'd defer to her wishes rather than because she ever actually considered their intelligence."

With a shrug, Aggie agreed. "That's possible, I suppose. I'd better call Mr. Moss." As she suspected, her lawyer assured her there should be no papers necessary for her to sign. He promised to come to the house as soon as possible, but was sure it'd be at least two hours. "Keep a copy of everything, but sign nothing. If the lawyer brings only one copy, take them and lock them up. I'll look them over when I get there."

"Can I do that? Is it legal?"

"I think it's imperative. We'll deal with any accusations or trumped-up charges if they come. I know Mrs. Stuart's lawyer. He's an excellent attorney, working on a very large retainer, but he won't risk being disbarred even for Geraldine Stuart."

The filing cabinet had a lock, but Aggie had no idea where to find the key. After several minutes of searching, Luke stopped her. "Just take them upstairs to Vannie's room and put them on the shelf over her door. I'll block the lawyer's access to the stairs. He can't go up without physically assaulting me, and he knows it."

With the plan in place, everyone went back to work, but Aggie was jittery. She tried to pay attention to the instructions Libby gave Vannie, but it was hopeless. Instead, she swept the porch, vacuumed the living room, made sure the little girls' hair was all brushed, and put the remaining breakfast dishes in the dishwasher. Yes, the library was a mess, but anyone could see they were in the middle of a project.

"I can close the doors if you like, Aggie." Libby's face showed concern.

"I'm just being ridiculous. Don't worry about me."

Ian began to protest as she tried to corral him and his toys into one very small part of the living room. Frustrated, she gave up and carried him upstairs. Luke was rolling paint onto her walls, and the result was exactly what she'd hoped it'd be. The tan paint was so creamy; it almost had a golden glow to it. Aggie inhaled the scent of fresh paint and announced, "It's going to be beautiful."

Startled, Luke jumped and rolled the paint at an awkward angle. "You enjoyed that much too much."

"I did," she agreed.

"So, is he here?"

"No, that's what I came to talk to you about. I was wondering if you can take Ian when you come downstairs. I try to keep the toys from ending up all over the place, but you know how he is. Everything will be everywhere if I give the kid half a chance. Keeping him in arms with that man here is probably best, but I don't want to risk the papers near the baby either." Aggie squeezed the baby and held him close, as if it'd ward off evil lawyers with their mountains of paperwork.

"I'd be happy to."

Luke put the roller back in the pan and wiped his hands carefully on a rag. Once certain he was free of paint, he began showing her his plans for her room. It took her until the end of his demonstration to realize what he'd done. "Thanks, Luke."

"What for?"

"I appreciate the distraction."

With a cheeky grin, he picked up the roller once more and loaded it with paint. "Hey, it's not every day a guy finds out he's a distraction."

Aggie watched him pick up where he'd stopped, checked the window a couple of times, and then ambled out of the room and toward the stairs. Just as she reached the second floor, she heard Luke calling for her. Once inside the room again, she giggled. "Oh, you are so silly."

"I got a smile out of you. It's worth it for that."

She started to make a retort, but tires crunched on the gravel. "Oh, no! I forgot to call the little ones in!" Without another word, she dashed down the stairs calling for Cari, Kenzie, and Lorna.

After stuffing the paint roller in a zip lock bag and zipping the top as far closed as it would go, Luke scrubbed his hands in the bathroom sink, and then went to do his part in "Operation Thwart Geraldine... Again." The walls he left behind still sported their unusual paint job. Instead of solid blocks of creamy tan, it looked like a graffiti artist with a preference for minimalist modern art had attacked the walls. In huge block letters, they read, "MIBS' ROOM. KEEP OUT!"

Gordon Steiner was a very distinguished-looking man. Still unsettled by the nature of his visit, Aggie was unable to think coherently. She welcomed the man into the living room, offered him a chair and a glass of water, and then blurted out, much to her mortification, "You're too handsome to be a lawyer."

Before she could recover her wits, Luke snickered, Vannie gasped, and Libby closed the pocket doors, shutting off the library entirely. "Why, thank you, I think." Mr. Steiner folded his hands and glanced around him. "You have a lovely home." What he didn't say spoke volumes. It was evident, just from his reaction to everything, that he'd heard only the worst of her.

"Before I look at your papers, would you like me to give you a tour? We've worked almost non-stop to make this place into a home. How we accomplished so much, I'll never know."

"I'd like that."

The slicing motions Luke made across his throat were never seen by Aggie. Instead, he followed her into the kitchen, listened with evident pride as she raved about his handiwork, apologized for the mess in the library, and then room by room, explained what they'd done and how it had been accomplished. "The wiring was really the worst. Well, that and the cabinets, I imagine. He got those done in a week! How—"

"Um, Aggie?"

She turned to Luke expectantly. "Hmm?"

"I worked on those from the day we talked about what you wanted in your kitchen. I just finished them up that week." To the lawyer, he added, "I didn't want to leave a false impression. I don't think anyone could pull that off in a week— even with help."

Aggie filed that information away for later discussion, and led the man outside to see how the yard and house had progressed. "There's still a lot to do out here, but we're getting there."

"It's truly amazing. I'm very impressed." There was a hint of disbelief in the man's voice. "I assume most of the rooms just needed a fresh coat of paint?"

"Well, that and the floors needed to be refinished. That's what took the longest. After we did the first and knew what to do, we worked on several rooms at once almost assembly line style." Aggie went on to explain how she painted the trim, Luke painted the walls, then sanded floors , and how they went in a circle, room by room adding coats of urethane to finish the wood. "The floors would have needed more work if we wanted to make them perfect— without scratches or anything, but I decided to let the house keep its character. We sanded and then what was left, as long as it wouldn't splinter, we left alone."

The confused expression on Gordon Steiner's face was priceless. She thought about letting him remain lost and confused, but Aggie couldn't bring herself to do it. "It was truly horrible when we moved in. Broken lattice out front, paint peeling everywhere, this room and the dining room were both loaded with beds, and no matter how hard I tried, it was always a mess. Oh, man, and the kitchen..."

As suspected, the bewildered look dissolved as she spoke. "Well, with so much to do, it's a wonder that you manage to keep it as nice as it is right now."

"I have a lot of helpers, Mr. Steiner."

"And a lot of mess makers. Some would say—" He stopped mid sentence and shook his head. "I have another appointment— much sooner than I'd like so if we could take care of the paperwork..." As the man dug them from his briefcase, he looked up at Aggie curiously. "Are you sure—" Again, his head wagged reminding her of a puppy with wet ears.

"Is this my copy or yours?" The question was delivered sounding much calmer than her quaking insides felt.

"I thought—" Once more, the man closed his mouth abruptly, and this time leveled steady eyes on her. "No. This is the only copy, as requested."

It took every ounce of her self-control not to fling the papers at him and demand he leave her property. She was furious— livid. How dare he come into her home, make pleasant small talk, inspect it like a judge and jury, and then act like she was some kind of lunatic for asking questions that anyone with a lick of common sense should!

Papers in hand, she rose from her chair and walked to the stairs. "I'll be back in a minute."

"I—" Mr. Steiner, once more, shook his head as Aggie's legs disappeared upstairs. He glanced at Luke who stood in front of the bottom step, baby Ian struggling in his arms. "She isn't bringing the papers back down, is she?"

"No."

"She didn't request the papers, did she?"

"No."

"She doesn't know what they contain?"

Luke's eyes answered for him long before he quietly answered, "No."

Gordon Steiner stood, snapped his briefcase shut, and crossed the room to shake Luke's hand. "Tell her to read them carefully or hand them over to a lawyer. I will tell my client that she accepted them but did not sign or return them." At the screen door, the man turned back once more. "Oh, and when you warn her to remain

38

alert—and you should—thank her for her compliment. It made my day."

Before the man's car started, Luke heard the beginning strains of *God Will Take Care of You* struggling to be heard over the obvious sobs that accompanied them. "Be not dismayed," a choke drowned out the next words, " —tide. God will take care of you." A hiccough followed next. " —His loving wings…"

Luke hurried into the library, deposited Ian in Libby's arms, and took the stairs two at a time. He found her, eyes closed, face turned toward heaven, forcing the words through clenched teeth. "Heee… wiiillll… take caaarrree.."

"Mibs?"

Without even opening her eyes, Aggie thrust the papers toward the sound of his voice. " —of yoooouuu. God will take care of you."[4]

The papers clearly stated in the first paragraph that Aggie was petitioning the court to make Geraldine Stuart the legal guardian of the children. "Oh, Mibs."

"I am so furious, I could think and say many sinful things right now. Every curse word I've ever heard is fighting every other one for preeminence in my heart. I want to go through them alphabetically, categorically, and finally by which one comes to mind first, just for the sheer joy of letting all the ugliness that just filled my heart out again."

"You won't like how you feel when it's over…"

"Yeah, that was the rub." Her carefully measured tone told him she wasn't over her anger.

He handed her the papers and suggested she put them in a safe place until Mr. Moss arrived. "I'll go uncorral the girls and Ian." Before he turned to leave, Luke brushed a single angry tear from her cheek. "The lawyer said to tell you to read them carefully, turn them over to a lawyer, and thanks for the compliment."

"Compliment?" The blank look on her face was mirrored in her mind. "What compliment?"

"You did say he was too handsome —"

"Oh. That. Ugh." She tried to push the embarrassing moment aside, but couldn't. "Well, didn't you think he was awfully handsome for someone in such a nasty profession?"

"Well," Luke began, trying to hide the amusement struggling to surface at the corners of his mouth. "I am not in the habit of noticing if men are or are not attractive. Women, I confess, I cannot help but notice sometimes, but I just don't—"

"All right, all right. I get it."

"But," Luke continued as if she hadn't interrupted, "I do think you are taking out your frustration with Geraldine's abuse of a profession on an innocent bystander. Gordon Steiner didn't know you weren't aware of the contents of those papers. He was just as stunned as you are, but for different reasons."

"Then he's not despicable as a person, but I still don't care for his job."

"Be prepared for at least one of your children to be a lawyer."

"Why!"

Laughing, Luke hurried toward the steps and out of range as he replied, "Murphy's Law, of course!"

Tina arrived with the boys around four o'clock, with bags of clothes and a couple of bags of groceries. "We're grilling tonight. Hamburgers!"

"I see bags. Tell me you scored for the boys and not for you." Something in Aggie's voice told Luke she was only partially teasing.

"I didn't buy a thing for me, but I did find a couple of cute tops and at least one skirt for Vannie while I was out."

The slow rise in Tina's volume did nothing to distract the girl in question from her task. Peeking into the library, Tina saw Vannie hard at work sewing long seams together on a machine that looked familiar. "Is that a serger?"

Vannie jumped but kept sewing. "Yes. I'm just cleaning up the seams now that we know it fits right."

"I like the fabric; it's going to look great on you."

Aggie saw Vannie flush with pleasure at the compliment, and sighed. She'd already forgotten her resolve to encourage the children and find things in their lives to praise. If it wouldn't be likely to cheapen her words in the children's eyes, she'd have made a note for herself and pasted on the fridge right then. Instead, she turned to Luke and asked, "Will you and your mom stay and eat with us?"

He shook his head. "Can't. Aunt Martha expects us tonight. We'll be over in the morning, though. I can tell Mom is engrossed." A tender look filled Luke's eyes as he watched his mother leave instructions for Vannie. "I bet she cuts out a few things before she goes to bed tonight."

As she wiped perspiration from her forehead, Aggie recalled Luke's face as he watched and spoke of his mother and wondered if she'd ever become the sort of mother that would evoke that kind of caring in her nephews' hearts. Would they ever know how fiercely she loved them? Would she ever become half as worthy a person as women like Libby and her mother were?

Shaking off the morose mood that tried to implant itself in her heart, she flipped the burgers and called for Laird to bring her the buns. It wasn't the time to grow too introspective. The natives were restless — able to be soothed only by hamburgers, salad, and root beer floats. Aggie made another mental note. *Ask the Lord to add another star to Tina's crown.*

After dinner, the dishes, a sweet time of singing, and then pajamas and teeth brushing rituals, Vannie, Tina, and Aggie sat around the living room, flipping through the patterns Libby had left for them. Each of them had their own method of perusing the choices. Tina worked quickly, each pattern receiving only seconds of her time before she moved onto the next. Vannie occasionally pulled one from a pile, sorted through past ones for something she remembered, and piled both, and sometimes a third, on the floor around her. Aggie's style was predictable. She looked at every pattern from all angles. Frequently, she called the others' attention to some detail or lack there of. Few patterns left the original pile, but she'd only weeded through a small fraction of the number Tina and Vannie had.

"Hey Tina," Aggie held up a pattern of a pinafore and dress set. "Wouldn't it be adorable to have matching dresses for the twins? We could even use two different colors. Then we'd be able to tell them apart with or without funky hairstyles."

After a surreptitious wink at Vannie, Tina turned a poker face, one Aggie always envied, to her friend and said, "Well, I don't know about that style on Tavish — I never pictured him in something that length, but Ellie would be charming. I wonder if she'd think it too babyish..."

41

Before she finished teasing, Aggie grabbed the closest throw pillow and helped it live up to its name, tossing it at Tina's head. Tina caught it and threw it back at Aggie, joking about "throwing like a girl" and needing "a sharper implement for beheading than a simple accent pillow." After watching several volleys with much interest, Vannie inched a pillow from behind her back and lobbed it at her aunt, ducking as it hit Aggie square in the face.

A massive pillow fight commenced. After a pile of patterns were sent skittering across the floor by a rogue pillow, the fight escalated — on the lawn. Twilight faded into dusk as they pummeled one another with the pillows, occasionally whacking fireflies instead of the intended target. Anyone looking at the second floor of "The Shambles" would have seen rows of faces watching the melee in the yard below.

Aggie's neighbor watched the craziness for a couple of minutes before she grabbed the pillow from her bed, crept across the yard, through the fence, tiptoed up to Aggie, and walloped her upside the head. "That's for calling me Murphy."

Howls of laughter erupted as Aggie dashed around the others playing an improvised version of duck, duck, goose, whacking each one on the head with the pillow as she passed. Grinning mischievously, she bopped Ellene on the head and screeched, "Goose!" before dashing away again.

Though having a reputation of being stern and a little stuffy, Ellene retorted, "Not goose, Murphy!" as she swung the pillow at Aggie's legs with every ounce of strength she could muster.

The force wasn't strong enough to trip her, but trying to avoid it sent Aggie's feet stumbling for balance. Her attempts to right herself were futile, and she went down hard on her ankle. Eyes smarting, she tried to pull herself up but failed. "Aaak. I think I need some ice."

Tina groaned. "That's your weak one, isn't it?"

"That was three months ago!" she gasped, trying to swallow the tears of pain that threatened. "It's been fine for ages."

"They're always weaker after they've been sprained, Aggie." Tina sent Ellene signals requesting backup and added in her firmest schoolteacher voice, "You'll need to get it checked."

"Come on, it's not that big of a deal, right Ellene? I just go to bed, sleep it off, and it'll be fine. Right?"

"Even if you put ice on it," Ellene began, examining Aggie's foot gently, "it's swelling fast. It's probably just a mild sprain, but you could have broken something." The woman's eyes clouded with concern. "I'm so sorry, Aggie."

"It wasn't your fault. Accidents happen."

While Tina ran for a bag of frozen veggies to double as an ice pack, Ellene whipped out her cell phone and dialed the clinic. An impudent grin accompanied her voice as she spoke to the person on the other end. "Hello? This is Murphy Howard over on Last Street, and we have a woman with an ankle injury. We're bringing her in, but I wanted to make sure someone who can run the x-ray is on hand." A few nods, an "mmm hmm" followed and then she spoke again. "She twisted it in a killer pillow fight. Yes, that's correct, a pillow fight. Murphy Howard. H-o-w-a-r-d." Ellene gave an exaggerated roll of her eyes and covered her mouth to stifle giggles. "I think you might know me better as Ellene."

Fresh tears smarted as Aggie tried not to laugh and failed. Each shake of her shoulders seemed to travel through her torso, into her leg, and jostle her ankle. Even with the pain she felt, it was obvious to her that this sprain wasn't nearly as severe as the last one. She didn't feel faint, sick, the blackness didn't even threaten to appear—nope. It just hurt and would for a day or two.

Luke says: Aggie? Is it you?
Aggie says: No, it's Tina. Aggie is asleep on the couch.
Luke says: Uncle Zeke listens to the police scanner and heard that Aggie went to the clinic with an injury. Is she ok?
Aggie says: Argh! I have to change the settings on this thing.
Aggie says: I can't be Aggie. It just doesn't work.
Luke says: I can understand that.
Tina says: Aaah… now that's better.
Luke says: Well, hello Tina. So, can you tell me what happened? Is she ok? Did they send her home?
Luke says: Of course they sent her home if she's sleeping on the couch. I assume that means it isn't very serious.
Tina says: Whoa, boy. Hold on. .

Tina says: Ok, we were having a pillow fight, and she fell and twisted her ankle. The doctor said it isn't too bad. He thinks she'll be walking normally in a few days.

Luke says: That's good to know. But it looked bad, right? I mean, that's why you took her in. He's sure it isn't serious?

Tina says: We were just over cautious. She sprained it terribly a few months ago.

Luke says: Ouch! That sounds painful. I remember that time. ☺

Tina says: You do? That was before she moved here. I thought you met her when Zeke sent you to fix the electrical nightmare.

Luke says: I did. But, when she lived in Rockland, Uncle Zeke had me install an intercom system for her. She slept through it, but I remember how she winced, even in her sleep, if she shifted at all.

Tina says: You were Mr. Sandwich!? I didn't know that!

Luke says: Well, come to think of it, I don't know if Aggie does. It all depends on if Uncle Zeke ever said anything.

Tina says: I'll have to ask. How funny is that?

Luke says: Do you think she'll have trouble sleeping this time? The last thing she needs is a bad case of sleep deprivation.

Tina says: Well, she's resting right now. That doctor was a little over-zealous and loaded her up on Vicodin. She's out.

Luke says: Well, it's late, and I should be getting home.

Tina says: You're not home?

Luke says: I'm at my mother's house helping her with a few things.

Tina says: I'm very tempted to don my matchmaker's shawl.

Luke says: Why?

Tina says: I just can't help wonder what your "intentions" are concerning my friend.

Luke says: I haven't figured those out for myself yet.

Tina says: Is that a polite way of telling me to mind my own business?

Luke says: No. I just don't know…

Luke says: What I mean is that I haven't given enough thought to it.

Tina says: Hee hee.

Tina says: Ok, ok. Don't kill yourself. I didn't expect an in depth answer. I have what I need to know.

Luke says: Uh, oh. I think I just stuck my neck out there. Are you going to put it in a noose?

Tina says: Nah. Aggie would loop one over MY head if I tried.

Luke says: Well, that's a relief. You know what they say… no noose is good noose.

Tina says: Good one.

Luke says: It's not mine. I got it from one of those old musicals.

Luke says: Mom says to tell you she's making a pot of soup and some bread to bring over tomorrow.

Tina says: That'll help a lot. Thank her for us. I know the kids love it when they get what Laird calls "real food."

Luke says: That boy is a riot sometimes.

Tina says: Well, it's time to check on Aggie again. I'd better go.

Luke says: The whole Sullivan family is praying for her. Will you tell her that? Oh, and tell her to feel free to send us back home tomorrow if it's too much to have us there.

Tina says: Sure thing! I think it'll be a welcome distraction to have your mom there teaching her how to ruin fabric, notions, and trims.

Luke says: Thank you, Tina. I know how much it means to Aggie that you're here. We would have helped, but an old friend is much better.

Tina says: I see your point, but I'm not sure how much I like being called old. I guess it's just one more proof that the Lord knows what He's doing—especially when we don't.

Tina says: Ok, gotta go. Nighters, Luke. You're a good friend to her too.

Luke says: Goodnight, Tina and thanks.

Sew What?

Chapter Four

Thursday, August 7th

Aggie awoke cotton-headed and exhausted—a great contrast to Tina's chipper exuberance, despite getting up in the middle of the night to wake Aggie for her pain medication. The sun shone through the living room window, the birds sang outside, and even the geraniums hanging in their pots from the porch railing fluttered their petals in the wind as if to greet her. The scent of freshly baked blueberry muffins lingered in the air, making her stomach growl.

"How did you have time to bake muffins? The kids aren't even awake yet!"

"I got up to get you your medication, so I decided to bake while there weren't any fingers to lick the bowl clean. Around here, if you give anyone a lick or two, there isn't enough left to bake!"

Tina arrived with orange juice, a buttered muffin, and another Vicodin. "Time for the next dose."

"Are you sure? It seems like you just woke me up for the last one."

"The bottle says," Tina began, hands on her hips and a stubborn expression on her face, "to take one tablet every six hours as needed for pain. You're in pain, so take the tablet."

"But it's not that bad." Even as she spoke, Aggie knew she'd lose the battle. Her foot was aching already. It wasn't unbearable, but if the full force of the medication wore off, it would probably become nightmarish again.

A squeal and then a screech pierced the morning air. Without another word, Aggie reached for the tablet and the glass of juice Tina offered. "You're right. My head is starting to throb."

Aggie despised how fuzzy-headed the pills made her feel, but fuzz trumped pain any day. If she hadn't yet convinced herself of the wisdom in taking the medication, the sight of Ian making a beeline for her would have. The child squealed at the sight of "Gaggie" and tried to rush her, but Tina scooped him up before he could attack the ankle.

Vannie's apologies began before Tina could settle Ian in his aunt's arms, but Aggie stopped her. "Vannie, it's ok. You expect too much of yourself." She gestured for the girl to come closer. "You do so much around here to help me. It's not your fault that Ian is fast, and you didn't anticipate his every move."

"I just don't want to see you hurt anymore. I try to help, but sometimes I think I make things worse."

Before Aggie could reply, Tina draped an arm around the girl's shoulders and steered her toward the front door, calling for the children to pour juice, grab the grapes from the fridge, and the hard-boiled eggs on the counter. "You know what to do; get food on the table. We'll be back in a few minutes."

From where she sat, Aggie couldn't hear what Tina said to Vannie, but she watched the girl's face change from troubled to nearly beaming. Squabbles started in the kitchen, but Aggie put an immediate stop to them. "Ok, Ellie, come get Ian and put him in his chair. Laird, peel the eggs, Tavish, rinse the grapes, Kenzie, put plates on the island, and Cari and Lorna, go sit down. When Vannie entered again, Aggie forced herself to send her to help. "I need you to go pour the juice and make plates for Cari and Lorna. Oh, and tell Laird to cut up grapes and feed them and bites of muffin to Ian."

Vannie agreed happily, entering the kitchen with that confidence and sense of purpose that only comes from knowing

48

you're appreciated *and* needed. Tina shook her head. "How do you do it? I would never have thought of asking her to do more after she was just taking on too much responsibility."

"It's something Libby said the other day. She said that we tend to overcompensate when children react poorly to a situation and that creates new problems."

"Wasn't she talking about kids manipulating you after getting in trouble?" Tina stood, hands on hips, and frowned. "I think that medication is affecting your thinking."

"Well, I just thought it applied the other way too. We can make a kid feel unneeded just because they don't *have* to take on responsibilities that aren't theirs to assume."

"Well, it was obviously the right thing to do, but I know I wouldn't have done it—" Her eyes caught movement on the street, and she smiled. "The world's steadiest handyman and his gem of a mother have arrived. Is he going to finish your closet today? I swear, he's taking more time on that one room than it took him to do the rest of the bedrooms."

"He's building the taj-ma-closet in there."

"You've got the room for it, and once this work is done, just think about how cool it'll be shopping to fill it with new clothes."

Aggie shook her head. "You know I can't afford to do that. I will start buying more, though. I can't wait to wear something remotely attractive again."

Before she could continue, Luke knocked softly on the screen, and then opened the door for his mother. "Good morning. How's the invalid?"

As she stepped in the door, carrying a large pot of soup, Libby rolled her eyes and jerked her head toward Luke. "Ignore my Luke. He likes to tease."

"I learned from the best, mother mine. Oh, I forgot the bread." With that, he disappeared outside and away from the onslaught of joking sure to commence.

"There are two casseroles in that box behind your seat. Don't forget them!"

It seemed that Libby's spiritual gift of service was out in full force, making Aggie feel like a princess. When he returned from his third trip to the truck, he dumped a pillow and blanket on one of the chairs and helped Aggie to the other while he and Libby worked to

49

make the couch as comfortable as possible. As they worked, he talked almost non-stop and without the usual pauses. "Mom always said that a couch is only as comfortable as the quilt that covers it when you're sick."

"But I'm not sick..." Aggie couldn't resist reminding him.

"Well, it's the same thing. You need to be as comfortable as possible so you'll stay put and let that ankle heal."

A protest erupted before she could stop and consider how ungracious it might sound. "I'm not that injured. It was just a little wrench. Look! The thing is hardly swollen. The doctor just wants to be a little cautious since I sprained it a few months ago."

Libby gestured for Luke to help Aggie back to the couch. "That's well and good, but he still said to rest it, didn't he?"

"He said I could probably handle crutches just fine —"

"In this house, with all the stairs getting inside, upstairs, up to your room, down to the basement, even down to the mudroom, you think crutches are going to help? Rest it." Luke's voice held a firmness she'd only heard him use with Cari.

"But I've got so much to do —"

He fluffed an enormous pillow and helped her sink back against it. Settling her ankle ever so gently on another pillow, Luke waited for her to meet his eyes before he said in that same firm tone, "Aggie, lay down. You can fight doctors and friends, but you cannot fight my mother. She's going to help you plan a million charming little wardrobes right here." His jaw worked as he took his time formulating what he wanted to say next. "It needs to be done, and you can do that reclining on the couch just as well as you could standing at the table."

Aggie hesitated. "I —"

Leaning over her, his eyes locked on hers and with a voice so soft and earnest that the others could only hear the tone instead of the words, he added, "Please, Mibs. Rest."

Libby, returning from the kitchen with water and a bowl of grapes, stopped in the doorway of the living room, eyes wide. Tina stifled a giggle, and Vannie, watching everyone from the stairs, furrowed her brow, clearly lost as to what was so interesting to the other two women. Luke, unaware that he was the object of much speculation, didn't move until he heard her agreement.

50

All throughout the morning and into the afternoon, Luke, Libby, Tina, and the children worked to keep Aggie sitting. When Mr. Moss called about the paperwork he'd retrieved the previous day, Aggie tried to get up to grab her clipboard and found it thrust into her hands by Laird who looked very severe for the usually happy-go-lucky boy. When her glass was empty, before she could move her good leg off the couch, Ellie whisked it away and returned with a fresh glass of water. Luke brought snacks every time he went through the kitchen, which amused her greatly. It was impossible to eat all the food he brought, but thanks to the help of ravenous twins, a steady grazer like Ian, and the kitten who managed to snatch bites of anything left unattended, nothing went to waste.

Libby and Tina, sensing Aggie's growing irritability with immobility and the constant noise, called for the children to don their swimsuits and get in the van. Libby set up the pack 'n' play in the mudroom and put Ian down for a nap in there, leaving strict instructions for Aggie to get Luke's help instead of trying to lift the boy. "We'll be back by six." Libby stuck her head up the stairs and called, "Luke!" She waited for him to jog down the stairs before she continued, "Please put the casserole in the oven at five o'clock."

"Yes, ma'am. Can Aggie come supervise construction?" Luke's wheedlesome voice sounded like a little boy who brought home a dog that "followed" him and begged to keep it.

"How do you plan for her to get up two flights of stairs?" Libby's tone made Aggie's heart sink. The woman would say no; she was sure of it. Even as she thought it, Aggie realized how ridiculous she was. If she wanted to go upstairs, she didn't have to get Libby's permission. The whole thing was ridiculous, yet, she felt obligated to follow Libby's advice.

"I thought I'd throw her over my shoulder like a continental soldier."

"But her ears don't hang low. She's a girl, not a basset hound." Libby threw Aggie a look that clearly said, "that boy," and sighed loud enough for him to hear two floors above her. "If you can get her up there without whacking her foot on something or letting her put pressure on it, more power to both of you. Take Tina's air mattress up there so she's comfortable, though."

"Yes'm." Luke's feet thundered down the steps.

While Tina and crew drove away from the house and toward the pool in Brunswick, Luke tried to find a way to safely carry Aggie upstairs. "I'd throw you over my back and use your arms, but I think I'd pull them out of their sockets."

"You don't need to carry me. Just help me to the steps and I'll go up backwards on my bum."

"What if you bang your foot? Mom'd thrash what's left of me when I got done beating myself to a pulp."

Laughter rang out through the house, echoing against empty walls. It sounded strange to her—lonely. "I'll be careful. I've done it before, you know."

With him hovering like a mother hen, Aggie scooted up each step. It took her longer than she'd expected, and by the time she limped to the air mattress, she was drenched in sweat and completely drained. "Wow. That second floor is a killer."

"Just rest. I'll go get your water and a bowl of grapes or something."

"No more grapes. You have enough in me to ferment and get me drunk already."

"How about cookies," he suggested on his way out the door. "I happen to know Mom brought a whole container that she has hiding in the truck. I could bring a few in..."

"Done."

Luke ambled down the stairs, out to his truck, and snagged four cookies. In the kitchen, he put a napkin on a plate, set the cookies on it, and covered them with another napkin. He hesitated over water vs. milk, and then reached for the water pitcher in the fridge. Milk would get too warm too quickly, and Luke considered nothing more disgusting than warm milk. After a quick peek to ensure that Ian was snoozing happily, Luke climbed the stairs, humming a hymn he'd heard Aggie sing, but didn't know.

She was already asleep when he stepped into her bedroom. Beads of perspiration formed on her forehead and upper lip, but she slept as soundly as her nephew. Luke stood watching her for a moment, before he put the plate and glass on the floor next to her, set up an oscillating fan to cool her, and shuffled back downstairs again.

He wandered from room to room, looking at every change they'd made. Luke observed the difference in how she'd decorated some parts of the house as he noticed others that looked like they needed something to make it feel homier.

With her asleep upstairs, Luke couldn't work on the closet, which left the back yard or the basement. He knew she had specific plans for differing areas of the yard, so he opened the door to the basement, flipped on the switch, and started downstairs. There was enough trash, junk, and filth in the basement to keep him busy for days. It was truly the worst part of the house.

An hour passed, two. Luke had hardly cleared the area at the foot of the stairs. Old paint cans, an ancient toaster, piles of rotting newspapers, and boxes of old mayonnaise jars made their way upstairs and into the dumpster as Luke worked his way through the trash. He wrinkled his nose at the musty dank scent that came with an old abandoned basement. Just as he was ready to grab a broom and sweep that one area, he heard the bubbly sounds of a fully awakened Ian calling, "Gaaa — gieee."

Luke abandoned the basement, hurrying upstairs to change his shirt and wash his hands and arms before he went to retrieve the baby. As he pulled the child from the pack 'n' play, he said, "Boy, your aunt is never going to live down being called 'Gaggie.' That's priceless. Absolutely priceless."

Friday, August 8th

"Ok, Aggie. For Vannie, we have four skirts, four dresses, and two skorts. Is that everything? Does she need nightgowns?" No one could say that Libby Sullivan was a slacker.

"Oh, Aunt Aggie. All of my winter ones were at my knees and elbows by the end of spring. My summer ones are so short and thin they're indecent. Can I make a new summer one and a couple of winter ones?"

Absently, Aggie nodded as she continued to look through boxes of fabric. Lost in an eclectic pile of fabric, Aggie didn't hear Vannie's excited squeal. Instead, she held up a piece of fabric for Libby's inspection. "What about this? The kittens are so cute."

Luke's mother smiled indulgently. "Well, it looks like there's about a yard and a half at most. It'd be enough for a jumper for one of the twins…" Her voice trailed off as she thought of something new. "Aggie, I have an idea. Why don't we go get a few t-shirts, and you can start with t-shirt dresses. They're an easy way to start, and it's so encouraging to have something finished in a very short amount of time." As she spoke, Libby dug through the boxes and piles, pulling out some of the smaller pieces of fabric.

"If you think that's best, I'm for it. I thought t-shirt fabric was hard to sew, though?" Aggie watched, fascinated, as Libby cut snips of fabric from each piece, glued it to a piece of paper, and wrote shirt sizes next to each piece. "How do you know what size shirt to do?"

"Aggie, I have granddaughters. I had daughters. It just comes automatic for me." She held up a finished list. "Do you think Tina would mind a trip into Brunswick?"

"Tina will go wherever my liege sends her."

Aggie thrust Libby's list at her friend, and waved her out the door. "Get out of here and don't come back until you have shirts and a chocolate caramel crunch cone. You're grumpy."

"Look who's talking."

"Point taken. Now go." As Aggie returned to her work, Libby's and Vannie's eyes met across the room, and each shook her head.

The idea that she could create something worth wearing, even for sleeping or playing, was a bit incomprehensible to her. No matter how hard she tried to feel confident in Libby's ability to teach her everything she needed to know, Aggie's experience had taught her that machines with needles and she didn't mix. Oil and water had a better chance of homogenizing naturally.

Libby picked up the beloved kitten fabric, and ignoring Aggie's agape jaw, found the middle, and tore the fabric in half. Before the would-be seamstress could protest, Libby snipped several inches from one side of the fabric and tore it again. Aggie cringed.

"Doesn't that hurt the fabric?"

"Not this kind of fabric. It's the easiest way to ensure you have a nice straight line," Libby mumbled as she worked.

"Can I work on my dress?"

Before Aggie could answer, Libby nodded. "Of course. If you need any help, just let me know."

Amazed, Aggie watched as Vannie pulled out what was obviously a skirt to a dress, odd shaped pieces of fabric that turned out to be the bodice, and a length of uncut fabric and a pattern. The confidence with which Vannie laid the fabric on the table, adjusted the pattern to exactly where she wanted it, and then laid butter knives all around the perimeter and center of it was astounding. The girl cut the weird looking piece out and folded scraps, leftover fabric, and all, dropping them back in the plastic work bin.

Libby nodded her approval as she continued to tear fabric into what were supposed to become the skirts to Aggie's t-shirt dresses. It appeared to her as if she could learn a lot from her niece. Vannie wasn't as fluid and confident as Libby was, of course, but for a girl not yet thirteen, it was quite impressive.

As Libby explained what she was doing, talked about different aspects of construction, and tried to infuse a little general knowledge into her uncertain pupil, Aggie realized that sewing had its own strange language. She was certain that even Ms. Slade had never said anything about things like cross-grain, selvedges, or rotary cutters. In her understanding, bias was a preference and a facing had little to do with clothing and much to do with courage.

To everyone's surprise, Tina burst through the door shouting, "Success!" The door slammed shut with a bang as she almost skipped into the library with two Wal-Mart bags on her arm. She found Libby's fabric piles and pulled shirts from each bag, matching it with the fabric and comparing it with the list she still had in hand. "There. Now what do we do?"

Libby glanced at Aggie. "How's the ankle?"

"I haven't had a pain pill in twelve hours and it only throbs if I put more than a little pressure on it. It's fine."

"Good. Have you ever used a machine?"

Aggie tossed an annoyed look at Tina's clearly audible snort. "Tina remembers my futile attempts in junior high. She would be wise," Aggie added, determined not to look any more foolish than necessary, "to remember that she wasn't exactly Martha Stewart herself."

Disappointment washed over Aggie as she sat at the machine, her left foot trying to work the foot pedal. Minutes ticked by as she "familiarized herself with the machine" and "tested the tension." Her foot felt awkward when she tried to press down on the foot pedal, and controlling speed was nearly impossible, but she kept working with every part of the machine until she knew that a presser foot had nothing to do with ironing. It took her even longer to remember how to turn it off. After thirty minutes, Libby declared her ready to sew her first seam—exactly at the moment Laird ambled into the room carrying Ian and asking for lunch.

"Is it noon already? Arrgh! I wanted to *do* something. I've been in here all morning, and I haven't *done* anything." Seeing the look on Laird's face, she hurried to add, as she rose from the table, "So, what are we having for lunch anyway?" Despite her forced cheerfulness, her frustration was evident to all.

"Well, I don't know what you're having, but I intend to have whatever casserole I smell cooking. I can almost taste it, and I assure you, it tastes heavenly." Tina gave an exaggerated sniff and reached over to rub Ian's pudgy little belly. "You want some too, don't you little man?"

As if it appeared on command, the aroma of a chicken and broccoli casserole tantalized Aggie's senses. "Oh, what is that? It smells so good." She glanced around her. "Where are the girls?"

"Which ones? You have five, you know." Tina's mockery answered the question. Wherever the girls were, Tina not only knew their location but also what they'd been doing.

"Very funny. Ok, so you know the kids are safe. That's good. I guess we go dish up our mystery dish."

"It's not much of a mystery, Aggie," Libby insisted. I just pulled a frozen casserole from my freezer this morning and had Luke pop it in while we worked. I suspected he'd be serving it for us while we sewed, but this'll give him a break. He's been playing hard."

"Playing?" Aggie hobbled into the kitchen and pulled the large pan of bubbling chicken and broccoli out of the oven and placed it on the stove.

"He's not going to get much done today. He played hide and seek, tag, red light-green light, Mother, may I, and what I think is an improvisation of steal the bacon all morning."

Before Aggie could respond, Tina's cell phone began playing Heartland's *I Loved Her First*. Sliding her phone open, Tina greeted her father, asking how things were at home. Her delight in hearing from him dissipated visibly as she listened, and at last she closed her eyes, took a deep breath, and promised to be home by Saturday evening. The near-curt goodbye sealed Aggie's opinion.

"Well, Aggie, it looks like I'm going home for another 'dinner' tomorrow. I'll probably leave before you're even up in the morning."

"Lance?" Tina's parents regularly scheduled "dinners" in order to give Tina and Lance, a young ambitious junior vice president of Tina's father's company, a chance to get "better acquainted." As far as Tina was concerned, they'd been sufficiently acquainted since thirty seconds after the initial introductions.

"I'll miss church on Sunday, but I'll be back by dinnertime."

Stitch by agonizing stitch, Aggie worked diligently on the two little t-shirt dresses. Before she ever lowered the presser foot, she asked Libby, sometimes twice, if she was doing things correctly. She'd made several jump starts at the beginning; her foot seeming to consider the pedal as a car brake, so she tended to slam her foot against it sending the needle flying across fabric and nearly into her fingers. As a result, she over compensated and managed to keep the machine sewing at a pace usually reserved for garden slugs.

However, after ripping and sewing more seams than she'd ever imagined and asking more questions than she'd ever before asked in the space of three hours, she proudly hung the two little dresses on hangers in the doorway where she could see and admire them. To her disgust, while she'd plugged away at her two little dresses, Libby had cut out at least half a dozen garments, and Vannie had completed her dress and had almost finished cutting out a skirt.

"It took me three hours to sew eight seams. Is there something wrong with this picture?" The stifled amusement on the others' faces was less than hilarious.

"I think we can blame this one on the gathering threads," Libby assured her. "You forgot to count those. Gathering threads are the worst part of any garment, particularly for a beginner. They almost always break." A twinkle appeared in Libby's eyes as she winked at Vannie. "Particularly when you make your stitch length *smaller* than normal rather than larger…"

Luke, hearing giggles erupting from the library on his way to rinse the primer from his paint roller, stepped into the room and leaned against the doorjamb. "It looks like she did a good job! Those are very pretty little dresses. I think the girls are going to like them."

Libby, nodding agreeably, chuckled. "Well, I don't want to stomp on Aggie's triumph, but adding a skirt to a premade t-shirt isn't exactly difficult. It took her two hours to sew two seams, gathering threads, pull the threads, and then sew the skirt to a premade top and hem it. Most of the girls in my classes manage to do their first one in forty-five minutes to an hour. I can do it in fifteen minutes."

Stunned by Libby's words, Aggie's forehead wrinkled, and she pressed her lips together to keep them from quivering. She felt childish and foolish, but her feelings were a little bruised. Before she could become too upset, Libby continued. "She stressed about every step—second guessing herself all the way. I think she's actually a natural, but she made everything twice as hard as it really was. Will you tell her to relax and trust her instincts? The world won't implode if she doesn't produce a perfectly finished garment. It just needs to be presentable."

Laughing, Luke winked at Aggie and said, "Did you get all that, or should I repeat?"

"Got it." Though the words still smarted a bit, she tried to take Libby's gentle teasing as the encouragement she knew Luke's mother meant it to be.

"Aggie?" Libby waited for Aggie to meet her gaze. "I forgot to tell you my sewing motto. 'Perfect isn't without flaw. Perfect is finished.'"

Now Aggie's smile was genuine. A look, one Aggie hadn't yet categorized yet, settled over Luke's face. Grinning like a Cheshire cat, he hurried out of the house, and after climbing into the truck, he drove toward town. At a loss, Aggie turned to the others and threw up her hands in exaggerated disgust. "Is it so terrible to be slow? I'm now beneath his company because I tried to do a good job? Oy!"

Tina picked up Aggie's sarcasm and ran with it. "Well, you know, had you finished in say two hours and fifty-eight minutes, he might have been able to tolerate your existence, but those two minutes are a bit excessive, don't you think?"

"Oh, you girls are so silly. I know my Luke. He's planning a prank of some sort; we'd better be on our guard. In some ways, my Luke is still a little boy; he enjoys teasing people a little too much."

The women tried to guess his plot and plan a defense, but before they could come up with a plausible idea, Lorna came dancing past on her way to the bathroom singing, "I will *salt* Him. I will *saaaallllt* Him. I will, I will, *salt* you, oh Lord!"

"Hmm," Aggie remarked dryly, "I thought the Lord was supposed to 'salt' us so we could season our conversation with grace."

"Well," Libby said, still stifling back chuckles, "I guess it proves that the Lord's words apply to all of us. 'Give and it shall be given unto you.'" Lorna danced past still salting the Lord with her song of praise, prompting Libby to add, "However, it might be good to explain the difference between salt and exalt. Just in case."

"I would say," Tina added, "that usually salt is bad if you over-indulge. I just don't think that there's any way that child could raise the Lord's blood pressure with her version of 'salting' Him."

By the time they'd cleaned up their sewing mess, Luke returned with a wrapped box. It looked like it'd been professionally wrapped, and had the women asked, he would have confessed that it was wrapped by the woman at the local hardware store. As Aggie unwrapped her new "mending basket," as he called it, the room reverberated with laughter. Slowly, and with great fanfare, she pulled duct tape, super glue, stapler and staples, and a tube of liquid nails from the box. Aggie, between fresh fits of giggles, managed to gasp, "So, now we know Luke's mending secrets!"

Martha says: Aggie, honey? Are you there?

Aggie says: Hey, Mom!

Martha says: I was wondering how you are feeling these days? Is the ankle bothering you much?

Aggie says: Not really. I mean, it isn't perfect, but the way everyone keeps forcing me to rest, it can't help but heal.

Martha says: I am glad to hear it. So, it's not as bad as last time?

Aggie says: No. The doctor said that he wouldn't be concerned about it at all if it hadn't had a good wrench at the old house. He said he thought I would have been walking normally by the next morning.

Martha says: That's good.

Martha says: I was wondering if you thought this month would be a good time to come visit. I miss the children.

Aggie says: Of course! I keep meaning to bring everyone up, but I don't know how to prepare for something like that, and Luke still needs a lot of input on what to do around here. My room is almost done though, so then it won't be so bad.

Martha says: I think you have enough on your plate without trying to make a trip like that yet.

Aggie says: Allie did.

Martha says: Yes, and Allie learned to do it one child at a time. It's a little like juggling. You don't usually throw all the balls you can in the air and expect everything to run smoothly.

Aggie says: I guess. Anyway, regardless, of course I want you to come. Come anytime.

Martha says: Is it ok if we don't give much notice? We'll bring food and such. You don't have to worry about that.

Aggie says: Mom, if I know you're coming days or weeks in advance, I'm going to stress out trying to keep everything great for you, and we both know that's unrealistic. Just call when you know, or when you're on the road. Either one works.

Martha says: I'll see when your father can get away. He's been helping the youth clean up lots on the east side. He'll probably want to wait until that is all finished.

Aggie says: Makes sense to me. It'd be nice if you could come before the kids start school though.

Martha says: We'll try.

Aggie says: Oh, drat. There is that maintenance warning. I wanted to tell you a few things. Anyway, I'll talk to you soon. Give Dad a hug for me. I love you.

Martha says: We love you too. We're so proud of all you're doing.

Aggie says: Mom, I can't imagine doing anything else now. It's still all so new, but it's the new norm.

Martha says: I knew Allie made a good decision. We're praying for you still. See you soon.

Mibs and Co

Chapter Five

Saturday, August 9th

Aggie tossed her book, scaring the kitten and making it yowl as if attacked. She tried to feel sufficiently guilty, but instead she just felt further irritated. Her foot was fine. In her opinion, she didn't even need the crutches anymore, but Tina, Luke, and Libby had all demanded that she keep it up for the morning. After sitting and sewing all day, her ankle had ached, and as a result, she'd spent a restless night. So she'd been resting on the couch all morning, and was bored to tears — literal ones.

With Tina gone, Vannie and Libby sewed in the library while Luke and the boys added the trim to her new closet and painted it. Ellie, Laird, and Tavish took turns reporting on the activities of Kenzie, Cari, and Lorna while Ian slept. On a trip to rinse brushes, Luke noticed how fidgety Aggie was, and said, "Do you feel like taking a drive? I saw some bookcases on sale in Brunswick and thought you might want to see if they'll work for that west wall."

"Oh! That's a great idea. I'll be right out. I need to change."

"Aggie, you're—" he rolled his eyes, "...aaand she's gone."

Minutes later, she emerged from the bathroom wearing a fresh and fun skirt, matching top, and with her hair down from its customary ponytail. Even Luke had to admit the transformation was a pleasant one. He needed to get the work on the house completed enough that Aggie no longer felt the need to help. Though he hadn't previously noticed, her entire demeanor changed with a fresh set of clothing. She'd overworked herself in the past months. It was time to do what he could to put a stop to that. She had enough work in being a mother without adding a fulltime job as house renovator. Even as he thought it, Luke realized he was mentally doing the thing that drove Aggie crazy most— making decisions for her.

Libby nodded approvingly at Aggie's change of clothes. "Get my Luke to keep you out until after lunch. We'll be fine here. You should try that Italian place in Brunswick, look at the bookcases, and you should try to find new cushions for that wicker. It's still just as hideous as ever, and I'm afraid your house will revolt if you don't do something fast."

As he helped her into his truck, Luke asked where she wanted to go first. "Let's look for cushions first. If my ankle gets sore, I can always just have you decide on the bookcases for me. I'm going to be picky about the cushions."

The first three stores were a bust, but at a home goods store, stuffed in a clearance bin in the back corner of the outdoor living department, were the exact cushions she'd dreamed of owning. Bold crimson and white cabana stripes had black pinstripes to combat the candy cane thoughts that tend to accompany stripes of red and white. "I can't believe we found them! Hey, can you reach those red throw pillows? I'd like um..." She thought carefully for a few seconds and then shrugged. "Two is probably fine."

"Mom always suggests two for each couch or loveseat and one for each chair. You need six, don't you?"

"They're five dollars a piece. Can I really justify thirty dollars for something so unessential? I won't even be using them in the house! It's just for outdoors."

Unwilling to push for something that wasn't essential or any of his business, Luke pulled two from the shelves above them. He started to bop her with it, and then pulled back in mock horror. "I forgot; no more pillow fights for you!"

"I fully intend," she insisted as she pulled the sizes she needed from the shelves, trying desperately not to lose control of her crutches, "to be a successful pillow fighter again— just as soon as my ankle is fully healed that is."

Even as she spoke, Aggie rubbed her ankle against her calf. It protested against so much use. "Come on, Mibs. Let me get what you need. If you go home exhausted and in pain, Mom will thrash me, Tina will drive back from Yorktown, and I'm afraid to think of what she'll do!"

"Oooh, he's skeered of Tiinnaaa…"

"Absolutely."

"Smart man." Aggie sighed, and pointed to the pieces she needed to replace the hideous ones that now ensured her porch was a nightmare of wicker proportions.

"Ok, so now that we've settled these, what do you think about lunch?" Luke wheeled the cart to his truck, settling Aggie in her seat before he leaned his own side forward and stuffed the pillows behind the seats.

"Sounds delicious."

"So you know where you want to go?"

"It's food. I'm starving, ergo, it's delicious."

"You're easy to please," Luke teased as he pulled out of the parking lot and onto one of Brunswick's main streets. "Mom suggested Italian…"

"Oh, pasta. Lovely properly cooked pasta that doesn't stick together in a clump or require a knife! I think it's a brilliant idea."

The heat was oppressive. Twice, Aggie reached up to pull her hair into a bun, but had nothing to hold it in place. Not for the first time, she seriously considered having it cut off in a chin-length bob. "How do you think my hair would look if it was short—say maybe around my chin?"

Luke, in one of his customary silences, turned onto another street and then pulled into one of the parking spaces in front of a small restaurant. With the truck still running, he hung his left arm over the steering wheel, and pushed himself into the corner of the truck to get a better look at her. "Well, it'd probably look very nice."

"You don't *sound* like you think it would look very nice."

"You asked how I thought it'd look," he protested, turning off the vehicle and opening his door. "I gave you my honest opinion. I

63

think it'd probably look very nice." He shut the door and took his time walking around the truck bed to help Aggie. She was already struggling to stand up without putting weight on her ankle.

"You may mean that, but something about the idea is distasteful to you. I can see it in your eyes and hear it in your voice."

Seconds passed into minutes. He walked her to the door, opened it for her, and waited until they were seated and their drink order taken before Luke said, "I just think you look nice as you are."

"I keep thinking about how cool shorter hair would be—"

"We don't live in the desert, Aggie. It gets cold too, you know."

"I know. I also thought about how convenient it'd be. Wash and go. No snarls, tangles, or braiding it to avoid snarls and tangles."

"It sounds like," he said with an obvious attempt at agreeability, "you'd be very pleased with it." Then as if making a significant concession, he added, "And, if you don't like it, you can always let it grow again."

"True. I might do it. Well, if I ever find time to make an appointment I think I can actually keep." She fingered the ends thoughtfully. "How hard do you think it'd be to cut it myself?"

Before Luke could answer, the waiter brought their drinks and asked if they'd like to order. Once Luke gave their orders, Aggie requested a chair. "I really need to elevate my foot. It's fine, but I want to keep it that way."

As they sat waiting for their food, Luke asked Aggie to plan her basement. On napkins, she drew out the things she thought she'd want or need, including a storage room with shelving. "I thought if I started with things organized, I might be able to keep them organized."

"What about the swings and slide and such? Does it matter which section we use for them, or do you really want them that close to the stairs?"

"I just thought that if their things were the first thing they saw, I'd be able to keep them from roaming the rest of the space and getting into things they shouldn't." Aggie's eyes sought his, looking for answers. "Why do you ask?"

"Well, I assumed there'd be a slew of toys strewn all over the bottom of the stairs, people getting hit by the swings or children careening down the slide. It seemed a little dangerous."

"So what would you do?"

Luke flipped over the napkin and started sketching again. The improvement in layout was evident almost immediately. With the new plans, the stairs opened into the family room, which flowed naturally into the indoor play area. Her storage area would hold out of season clothing, toys, decorations, and keepsakes. There was even a place to store bicycles out of season. Luke thought of everything.

The food, much more delicious than either had expected, distracted them from the house plans. They didn't talk; instead, they enjoyed their meals—lost in their thoughts. Aggie had realized as Luke sketched plans for the basement that once he was done, there'd be no reason for him to come again. Sure, he was a friend now and would spend time with them on occasion, but the easy camaraderie would be gone. That saddened her. She was just about to mention it, when a goofy grin spread across Luke's face.

From behind, a chorus of "Happy Birthday," startled her, nearly causing her to drop her fork in her lap. She peeked over her shoulder and found her parents, Tina, Libby, and all the children crowding around the table singing lustily. Each child held a gift; some were wrapped beautifully, obviously Vannie's handiwork, while others were a little more unique in their presentation.

Their waiter, aided by a waitress, scooted tables together, placed chairs, and took drink orders, while another waitress cleared room in front of Aggie for the cake Libby carried. She stood to hug her parents, and held onto her mother a little longer than she ever had. "Thank you for coming, Mom. You don't know how much it means to me—or do you?"

"Well, even a delicate little thing like me won't let anything get in the way of eating cake with my daughter!"

"I forgot all about it being my birthday." She slid her eyes sideways and frowned at Luke. "How did you know?"

"Tina."

Remembering, Aggie nudged Tina's shoulder before returning to her seat. "How did you get here? I thought you had a dinner party with Lance!"

"I called Dad and asked him to call me home so I could be honest. I want you to know, that little deception is costing me a real dinner with the dude."

"Happy Birthday to me. It's a wonderful gift." To the table, she made a grand sweeping gesture. "You all can see how loved I am for her to sacrifice herself in order to surprise me. She wouldn't do that for just anyone."

"If you keep this up, I'll bring him to *your* house for the dinner and spend the entire evening convincing him why you'd be the perfect little wife."

Aggie laughed. "That threat won't work on me anymore."

"Why not?" Tina's mock affronted attitude did hold a twinge of curiosity.

"Because. Now that I'm the mother of eight, no one is going to take your matchmaking schemes seriously, and we both know it. I'm safe now."

"Safe?" Luke frowned. "Safe from what?"

"Tina regularly threatens to sic the men her father finds her on me as a means of blackmail. Well, I was just saying that it won't work anymore." Sticking her tongue out at Tina, Aggie continued. "See, I've always thought that with Tina in the offing, no one would take a second glance at me, but she likes to swear that I have the 'girl next door' appeal, and that men always choose that over petite, gorgeous, and obscenely wealthy." Aggie snickered.

"And your point?" There was a hint of an edge to Luke's tone that she brushed off as dry mouth when he immediately grabbed his drink.

"Well, even if every up and coming junior executive in Mr. Warden's company was on the prowl for a simple girl with eclectic tastes, they'd go running now, wouldn't they?"

Under his breath, Luke growled, "Mibs, stop it!"

"Wha—"

"I think it's time for presents," Martha Milliken announced. "How about we go alphabetically this time? Let's see, I think that puts Cari first."

The children each gave her gifts that they'd made, some with Tina's help. Both Cari and Lorna gave her a refrigerator magnet made from clay. Ellie's gift was the picture of Ian that she'd drawn at the children's museum. Tina had taken it to be professionally framed, and Aggie knew exactly where she'd put it. Her little bookworm, Tavish, gave her a handmade bookmark, and Laird had found a small shelf in the attic that he'd sanded and spray painted for her bathroom. To her astonishment, the skirt Vannie had cut out, presumably for herself, was wrapped in Vannie's distinctive style. Another bookmark from Kenzie completed the children's pile.

"Well, I am overwhelmed. Everything is so special, particularly since you each made it for me. Thank you so much."

"Don't forget mine," Tina pushed a small gift bag across the table.

"Let me guess, perfume?"

"Would it be anything else?"

"It better not be," Aggie teased. "I am almost to the point that it isn't a waste to try to wear it."

Curious, Luke took the bottle from the table and sniffed the lid. A hint of fragrance, one he obviously recognized made him smile. "That's Aggie all right. I'd recognize that scent anywhere."

"Here's ours..." Martha passed a boxy-looking package to her. "I hope I got them right."

Vannie squealed when she saw the collection of Gene Kelly movies, and Aggie nodded happily at the sight of her favorite author's name on the cover of two books. "Perfect. If I just find time to read them —"

"We'll make sure of that," Libby assured her. "Here, my turn."

As Aggie pulled tissue paper away from the contents of the box, she expected to find another garment, but instead, cheerful geranium valances peeked out at her. "Oh! You made me the curtains! How did I never see you measure for them or anything?"

"I didn't have to. Luke had all the measurements in his notebook."

"That would explain it." She opened gifts from Mrs. Dyke, Murphy, and William, and added them to the enormous pile on the table. "I want to thank —"

"Wait, Aggie. You're missing one." Libby fumbled with the wrapping paper piles, searching for something. "Luke, where is your gift? You worked so hard on it!"

"I couldn't very well bring it in when we came in, could I? Laird, would you go get the thing wrapped in newspaper behind my seat in the truck?" He tossed the keys at Laird and grinned.

When they returned with the gift, Aggie wasn't surprised to see it wrapped in newspaper; after all, Luke had said it was. However, the blue painter's tape strategically placed as ribbon and the blue tape folded bow was an interesting touch. "How did you do that?"

"You can do anything with a little tape and a staple or two. I thought you would have realized that after your gift last night."

Carefully, so as not to ruin it, Aggie peeled the perfect little bow from the package and set it aside. Ian reached for it, but Aggie moved out of his reach. Amused, Tina snagged a strip of tape from the wrappings that Aggie discarded, and used it to tape the bow to Aggie's purse. "There, now it's protected, and you won't forget it."

Tina's words never registered. Aggie was transfixed as she pulled the last layer of tissue paper away and gasped, "Oh! Oh, Luke!"

Everyone crowded around her and watched as she traced the hand carved letters in the wood. "What does it say, Aunt Aggie?" Lorna's little voice interrupted the collective appreciative silence.

"It says, 'Welcome. *He settles the barren woman in her home and makes her the joyful mother of children. Praise the Lord.* Psalm 113:9.' Then it says Milliken-Stuart."

"What is a milkin' Stuart? We're just regular ones. We don't have cows."

"Aunt Aggie's last name isn't Stuart, though, Lorna. Her last name is Milliken."

"I think it should be Stuart. She's our Auntie Mom now, so we should *all* be Stuarts."

Laird tried again. "Aunt Aggie can't change her last name until she gets married. Then her last name will be the same as her husband's last name."

"I think it should be ours." A stubbornness, unfamiliar in Lorna, crept over the child's features.

"I think," Aggie began cautiously, "this is something we should discuss some other time. Right now, I want to admire all of my lovely gifts at home. Besides, we need Luke to hang this, and he can't do that here."

"I'm riding next to Aunt Aggie!"

Kenzie's claim almost gained Aggie's acquiescence, but a brief flash of disappointment in Luke's eyes prompted Aggie to change her mind. "I would, sweetie, I would, but I can't. You see, Luke brought me here and bought me lunch. It's rude to go somewhere with a friend and leave with someone else. I'll see you at home, and we can sit together on the settee and watch as Luke hangs the sign for me."

They were pulling out of the parking lot, before Luke seemed to realize what she'd said. "Are you going to hang the sign outside?"

"Yep. Right next to the front door over the doorbell. I want it to be a reminder to everyone who comes in just how blessed I am. Maybe that way, I won't get so many pitying looks."

"Pity?"

"People feel sorry for me. I'm just a poor overburdened, inexperienced ninny of a girl who is saddled with too much responsibility. Normal people have half the number of children or less, and most have husbands. I was 'forced' by circumstance to have to take on more than anyone should have to handle... You know the drill. That word joyful, the way you put it larger than the rest of the words and in a different font all together. That was genius. It really is a perfect reminder. By the doorbell, they'll *have* to see it."

"It was going to be a housewarming gift, but I didn't finish it in time. The trees took longer than I expected."

"How did you do that?" Her fingertips traced the finely detailed trees on either side of the welcome and verse.

"A wood burning tool. I ruined the first one. Then I got smart and burned first and carved last."

She laid a hand on his upper arm. "Did I thank you? I don't think I did. It's beautiful. I don't think I've ever received a nicer gift."

"It was my pleasure, Mibs. Truly."

"I still haven't discovered why you call me Mibs."

Luke's laughter filled the cab. "You're over-thinking it. It's really so simple." Nearly passing the turn off, Luke jerked the wheel, throwing his hand in front of her instinctively. "I think it fits you just perfectly."

Aggie says: Libby? Ohhhhhhhhh Liiiiiibbbyyyyyyy

Libby says: Mom had to run over to Corinne's. Rodney hit his head and then started vomiting, so she's going to help Corinne decide whether to go in or not.

Aggie says: Oh, no! I'll be praying. I'm surprised we haven't had more accidents with the children.

Libby says: No, you are just a self-sacrificing "auntie mommy" and take the hits yourself.

Aggie says: Tee hee. Wasn't that adorable?

Libby says: Yup. Almost as adorable as a little pantomime I saw once where someone called herself "Aggie Milly-Mommie."

Aggie says: Ugh. Yeah. Not one of my more mature moments.

Libby says: Maybe not, but it made me smile.

Aggie says: Well, I aim to please.

Libby says: How'd your date go with William?

Aggie says: He had to postpone 'til tomorrow. He got called in to cover for Megan. Her father had a heart attack.

Libby says: I'll be praying for both of them.

Aggie says: It is weird reading "Libby says" when Luke is doing all the "talking."

Luke says: Is that better?

Aggie says: Yep. You didn't have to do it though. I shouldn't keep you. I just wanted to thank your mom for the curtains and the cake.

Luke says: If I recall correctly, and I do, you did.

Aggie says: Well, I wanted to thank her again. I guess, instead, I'll have to thank you again for my plaque. It's just beautiful. I keep seeing Tavish out there running his fingers over the wood.

Luke says: How would you feel about him playing around with a wood burning pen?

Aggie says: Hmm… I don't know. That is so out of my element.

Luke says: It was just a thought.

Aggie says: If he was your son, would you let him do that?

Luke says: I had a whole kit at his age. All my fingers are present and accounted for, and I never burned down the house…

Aggie says: Will you show him how to use it and take care of it so he doesn't destroy the house or his hands?

Luke says: Definitely.

Aggie says: Well then, I say let's go for it. Where do I get one?

Luke says: I have a spare at home. I'll give him mine. He can work on trim scraps and stuff for a while until he decides if he likes it. Then we can buy him plaques and such to work on.

Aggie says: Thanks. You don't know how much it means to me that you take an interest in the boys. I don't know anything about being a boy.

Luke says: Well, I'd say that's a common problem for all mothers.

Aggie says: Yeah, but most mothers have fathers around to make up the slack. I have to rely on you and Zeke and William for that.

Luke says: And all of us are happy to do it. Chad wanted to take Laird and Tavish fishing over at Willow's sometime too.

Aggie says: Fishing as in worms, hooks, and flies? Hey, how do they capture those flies?

Luke says: Haven't you ever seen a picture of a hook with feathers and string and stuff tied to it?

Aggie says: Yeah, tied flies… oh! They actually USE those? I thought it was jut a hobby for looks. I didn't realize fish would fall for something so inedible.

Luke says: Didn't you take biology? Have you seen the brains on fish? Not much there, Mibs.

Aggie says: Just a minute. I want to do something.

Luke says: 'K

Mibs says: How's that?

Luke says: LOL. I like it.

Mibs says: Good, I think I'll keep it. Maybe my mom will figure it out.

Luke says: I'm sorry we didn't get that room next to the mudroom finished for them. I keep forgetting it's there.

Mibs says: That's ok. We can do it after my room. It's awfully small now that we expanded the mudroom. It'll barely fit a bed and a chest of drawers.

Luke says: I wouldn't put drawers in there. They'll just need the closet and we can add some shelves in it for their things.

Mibs says: Do you think we could find a comfortable futon or sofa bed? It'd take up less room during the day and give Mom a quiet place to go rest or read a book alone with just one child at a time.

Luke says: I'll ask Mom. She knows about that stuff. The good thing about that is that most of those are smaller than a queen-sized bed, so you could put an end table in there for a glass of water, glasses, and things like that.

Mibs says: If the closet wasn't there, the room would be so much bigger, but then we'd have to put a piece of furniture in there, so that wouldn't work.

Luke says: Well, actually, you know, there is enough room in the mudroom in that one bank of cabinets to hang a rod and remove the lower shelves. It's close enough not to be a pain for them.

Mibs says: You're right. That's a great idea! Can we do it?

Luke says: Just as soon as your room is done.

Mibs says: I wonder if we shouldn't do it first, so Mom and Dad know they can come back sooner. If you were working on it before they left...

Luke says: They'd worry that you were putting too much before you and neglecting yourself. Just talk it up when we're working on it or get your mom's input on colors or something. That'll let them know that they're important without making them feel guilty for taking away from work on your space.

Mibs says: You're right. Again. You're making a very bad habit of that.

Luke says: I'll put being wrong more often on my "to do" list.

Mibs says: You're so accommodating. Thank you.

Luke says: Anytime.

Mibs says: Uh oh. I think Kenzie is starting another nightmare. I better go.

Luke says: Oh, I didn't know she did that. I'll be praying for her.

Mibs says: Maybe not. Must have been a cat.

Luke says: Maybe your cat. So, does she have many nightmares?

Mibs says: Every now and then. Some kid at church gave her a very detailed description of what probably happened in her parents' accident, and now she has these nightmares every now and then.

Luke says: I'd like to give that kid a piece of my mind. Who does something that cruel?

Mibs says: Haven't you noticed how horribly cruel children can be?

Luke says: I suppose. That poor little girl. Have you ever asked her exactly what he said?

Mibs says: No, I was afraid it'd reinforce it and make things worse.

Luke says: Or, maybe it'd be so out there that you could tell her it isn't true. Kids also exaggerate. For all you know, this kid told her that their heads were cut off or something equally revolting.

Mibs says: I hadn't thought of that. You have a point. Maybe I'll do it.

Mibs says: Nope, I was right. She's starting up. Gotta go. Bye.
Luke says: Bye. Praying…

FIZZLED DATES

Chapter Six

Sunday, August 10th

Frustration built as William drove Aggie home from their date. Though she'd enjoyed the delicious dinner and the conversation had been interesting, there had also been an awkwardness and formality that she found miserable. With each block that whizzed past, she became more upset and agitated. A glance at William showed her that he was oblivious to the turmoil whirling in her mind which, irrationally, irritated her further.

As he pulled up to her door, Aggie nearly jumped from the car before he could turn off the engine. "Thanks for dinner. It was delicious. Don't bother to ask me out again, though. I'm determined to remain a happy and *single* mommy of eight. *Forever*." She smiled at him as she pushed the door shut. A glance at one of the upstairs windows showed Vannie watching them. She turned back to William once more. "Thank you again, William. Goodnight."

The bewildered look on William's face troubled her. In his mind, everything had probably been just fine. They'd gone to eat, had a nice conversation, driven past the lake to see the lights of the houses reflecting on the water, and then come home. If he had kissed her, it would have been the perfect romantic date, but she felt like a fraud. The thought of being kissed made her shudder. It wasn't that William was repulsive; he most certainly wasn't. However, the idea of something so intimate, with anyone, felt revolting.

Inside the house, she picked up the phone and dialed his home phone. Once the machine picked up, she spoke. "Officer Markenson, this is Aggie Milliken at 101 Last Street. I would like to report a domestic disturbance." She thought for a moment before continuing. "It appears that the lady of the house was just insufferably rude to her most dashing and gracious date tonight, and she would like to apologize in person. She will arrange for her handyman to watch the children and will be waiting at Espresso Yourself at eight o'clock tomorrow morning. She will understand if you choose to decline her invitation."

Her thumb hovered over the buttons on her phone. This was a call she dreaded making. If she asked his help, she knew she'd need to explain. Well, she *felt* obligated to explain even if it wasn't technically necessary. With a deep sigh, she punched the familiar numbers and waited, but to her disappointment, his voice mail picked up. It seemed like life was growing more complicated every second. If Luke would just come early the next morning, she could go and try to explain her irrational behavior to William over a cup of coffee. If only it was that simple.

The beep came, but she left no message. Instead, she clicked off the phone and flipped up her laptop. Maybe he'd be online. Even Iris or Libby would work. She glanced at the couch and smiled at a snoozing Mrs. Dyke. The dear old woman needed to go home.

"Mrs. Dyke?" Aggie shook the woman's arm gently. "I'm home. Would you like me to walk you home?"

"I'll do it, Aunt Aggie." Vannie stood at the bottom of the stairs with a hopeful smile on her face.

Their neighbor fought to open her eyes and pulled herself to her feet. "That'd be very thoughtful of you, Vannie." To Aggie she added, "You have a gem of a girl here. I don't think I was really necessary tonight."

"Of course, you were, Mrs. Dyke. You made Cari go to bed when she didn't want to listen to me, and you stopped Kenzie from putting the kitty in the microwave to dry him off."

All the way out the door and down the steps, Aggie listened as Vannie chattered about the fun she'd had with the elderly woman. To listen to her talk, Aggie would have assumed Vannie had the time of her life watching Mrs. Dyke play with the kitten, rock Ian, and sing Lawrence Welk songs to the little guys from the hallway.

Luke popped up on the messenger just as Vannie returned, so Aggie typed a quick, "I need to talk to you, bbiab," meaning be back in a bit, and turned to her niece.

"Thanks for helping with the children."

"She really did a lot more than she said."

Aggie followed her to the stairs, giving the girl a hug. "Thanks anyway." She waited for Vannie to go back upstairs, and then returned to the kitchen. Just as she started to grab the laptop and carry it to her favorite spot on the couch, she heard the shuffle of feet on the hardwood floor. Vannie stood in the kitchen doorway, her red hair curling into tight ringlets, and hanging down around her shoulders. "You know, "You could pass for Anne Shirley wearing that gown with your hair like that."

"Did she have frizzy hair or was it just red?"

"Who knows? I just think it's beautiful." Aggie sighed. "So, do you need something?"

"You looked upset when you came home. Is everything ok?"

She stifled another sigh, slid her laptop back onto the counter, and pulled two bowls from the cupboard. In the freezer, she found Rocky Road and Mint Chip ice cream. "Which one?"

"Rocky Road."

With heaping bowls of ice cream in each hand, Aggie led the way to the living room couch, and passed one to Vannie. "Eat up."

"Ice cream this late? What would grandmother say?"

It took every ounce of self-control, but she did manage not to say, "Hopefully something horrible." Instead, she shrugged. "I guess that's why Allie and Doug asked me to take care of you guys. They knew I'd know when it was best to sleep and when you need ice cream to sweeten your dreams."

"What's wrong, Aunt Aggie? Didn't you have fun with William?" The girl's disappointment was evident from the sad eyes to the droopy lips that should have been enjoying the ice cream.

"Nothing is really wrong, sweetie. I just learned tonight that I don't ever want to go on another date again."

Perplexed, Vannie asked the expected questions. "Don't you like Mr. Markenson? Didn't you have fun? I thought that's why people went on dates—to have fun."

"Well," Aggie began, praying for wisdom in how to explain her new thoughts to her niece. "Yes, some people do go on dates to have fun. Others do it as a way to get to know someone they think might be a good candidate for marriage, and others do it because that's what they think you're supposed to do when you get to be a certain age." She shrugged. "I think that's the only reason I went tonight, and it's just not a very good one."

"You don't like Mr. Markenson then." It wasn't a question.

"No, actually, I think he's a very interesting and kind man. I like him quite a lot, actually."

"So why not go because you want to get to know him better? Why isn't he a good choice for marriage?"

"I don't know that he isn't. I just know that this way of determining that isn't going to work for me. It was so—" Aggie searched for the right word. "Artificial."

After another bite of ice cream, Vannie set her bowl on the coffee table, pulled her legs up against her chest, and rested her head on her knees. "What is artificial about going out to dinner with a nice man? Doesn't everyone have to eat? You've had dinner with him here…"

As she thought about how to respond, Aggie grabbed their bowls, carried them to the kitchen, and then returned with an idea. "Ok, let me try to explain it like this. Tonight we went out to eat, right?" Vannie nodded. "Well, when William picked me up, he was wearing his best casual clothes, freshly shaved and showered, and this time," she winked, "he had on his best manners too."

"He told me he was an 'insufferable bore' on your other date."

"That about sums it up. It doesn't sound like him though."

The girl giggled as she pushed her hair from her face. "I was reading one of those old books that Mommy collected and asked what someone would have to do today to be one. He said, 'Take a woman out to dinner and make the meal miserable because you're embarrassed at what someone else did."

"Well, I want to be gracious and say it was understandable, but frankly, it wasn't. I was very upset that he took it all out on me." Forcing the memory from her mind, Aggie redirected her thoughts to the example she wanted to share. "Anyway, I wore my favorite dress, a little perfume, and made sure I looked my absolute best."

The girl looked more confused than ever. "I don't understand. Shouldn't you look your best? Mommy always dressed up when she went out with Daddy." Vannie swallowed hard. "She was all dressed up that night—" Though she didn't collapse in tears, the bereft girl couldn't continue.

"I know, but your mother was dressing to please her husband—to make him feel special by looking as attractive to him as she could. I don't like the feeling I got dressing up for a man that wasn't 'my' man. Does that make sense?"

"I guess…"

It seemed as if she'd never be able to explain her heart. "Well, when we got to the restaurant, the waitress led us to an amazing table that overlooks the lake. There were candles, on the tables, soft music played around us, and some couples danced out on the terrace. We talked about the menu, the music, and the stars…"

"That sounds so romantic." Vannie's sigh made her sound as if she were lost in a dream.

"Vannie," Aggie laughed, "it was like we were acting out lines from a movie or a book or something. There's nothing wrong with candlelight dinners, beautiful music, and flowers. Yes, they *can* be romantic, but—" She struggled to find the right words to express how awkward it had all felt. "I guess what I'm trying to say is that tonight I learned that most of what we call 'romance' is not real life—or at least it's not *my* real life."

"But isn't your real life whatever you make of it? If you aren't something and you want to be, you start doing it and then you are." A stubborn look flooded Vannie's eyes. Aggie knew that look; it was the exact one she'd always seen in Allie when someone criticized the number of children they had, the lifestyle they led, or commented on the "waste" of Allie's degree. "Mommy always said that if we don't grow and embrace the new things the Lord brings into our lives, we become pathetic… no, apathetic."

"I suppose you could argue that, in this instance, it's the same thing."

"Is it apathetic if I don't want to squeeze that into my life? To me, it felt fake. You know, your dad used to bring your mom flowers whenever he came home from a trip."

"I remember those flowers. Usually, they were red roses." Only a slight sniffle told Aggie how much the memories pained her sensitive niece.

"Well, in the traditional sense, that is what people consider romantic. Flowers, chocolate, nice dinners, concerts, and movies — those are some of the things that people think of when they think of romance. Do you know what your mom thought was the most romantic thing your father ever did for her?"

Vannie shook her head. It seemed almost wrong to share things with Allie's child that Allie hadn't chosen to share herself, but at last, she decided that if Allie felt free to share with *her*, Aggie could pass the story on to Vannie. "Did you know that your father used to hold your mother's head when she would vomit? Every pregnancy was hard on Allie." She swallowed hard before continuing. "She would get so horribly ill with each baby; do you remember?"

For a moment, the girl's face was blank, but slowly she nodded, remembering. Clearly, Allie had managed to do an excellent job of hiding her morning sickness. "Well, she did. She was horribly sick every time for weeks. Your father would take sick days off work, stay home, and hold her hair out of the way while she threw up everything she tried to eat." Her lip quivered as she tried to smile at the memory. "That's what your mother found most romantic of everything your father ever did for her."

"That sounds so gross!" Vannie's nose wrinkled in distaste. "Daddy couldn't stand being around sick people. He always threw up if he even heard one of us getting sick."

"That's exactly what Allie said. While he held her head and kept her hair out of the way, she'd throw up in a bowl, and he'd gag and sometimes get sick in the sink." Aggie waited until she had Vannie's full attention. "That's my idea of real romance, Vannie. It's someone caring enough about someone else that they will do anything to make that person feel special — even when the other person is getting sick."

"And you didn't feel special when you were out to dinner; is that it?"

"Well, it's more like I didn't think that kind of —" The talk seemed to be failing. "I didn't feel like me. William didn't feel like him. It all seemed like we were acting out lines because that is what books, movies, music, and magazines tell us you do on a date instead of it being what we naturally would do."

Several minutes passed as Vannie tried to process her aunt's words. There were so many things that Aggie wanted to interject, many things she hoped she'd be able to say to make the girl understand, but her heart told her to wait. At last, the girl lifted troubled eyes to meet hers and asked, "Aunt Aggie, if you don't date someone, how will you ever get married?"

"I don't know. Maybe I'm not supposed to get married, or maybe it's just that I'll need to find another way. I just know that tonight I saw something I've never seen before." Her niece's eyes reminded her of old cartoons with question marks for pupils. "I saw that I don't want to force a friendship into becoming something else, and that's what that date tonight felt like. It seemed as if I was working to turn our friendship into something deeper and more intimate rather than waiting for God to change it with us and for us." She rubbed her temple while searching and praying for words that would make Vannie understand and think about her own life as she grew into a young woman. "I don't know how to explain it, Vannie. I am just not 'going there' again. I'd rather play a good game of Monopoly with you guys, inviting William to join us, than sit through another dinner like that."

"You don't think you'd get used to it?" Disappointment dripped from every word.

"I don't want to get used to it, sweetie. I don't ever want to get used to acting like someone I'm not, and that's exactly what I did tonight. I'm actually quite ashamed of myself."

For some time after Vannie dragged herself up the stairs, disappointed and a little disillusioned after their frank discussion, Aggie sat on the couch lost in her own thoughts. Had she made the right decision to share that information with her niece? Was the girl too young to understand? Was it right to plant seeds that might grow into weeds of disappointment? Of course, those thoughts came after it was too late to change anything.

The mantle clock chimed on the half hour and startled her. "Luke!" Dismayed, she raced for her laptop and carried it back to the couch, hoping he hadn't waited for her all that time, and yet, illogically, praying he did. When she saw his status as "online," her fingers flew across the keys.

Mibs says: Luke? Are you still there? I can't believe I kept you waiting.

Luke says: Sure am! How did your date go?"

Mibs says: Flopped. I am NOT doing that again.

Luke says: Really? I'm sorry. Was it bad like last time or...

Mibs says: No, not at all. It was just so artificial. I've decided that dating and I don't mix. *waits to hear the earth shake as Luke falls to the floor, stunned*

Luke says: LOL. Nope, you won't hear that from me. I decided the same thing back in high school after watching what Corinne went through.

Mibs says: You've never dated either?

Luke says: Nope.

Mibs says: Well, Vannie would say, "No wonder you're not married." She asked how I'd ever get married if I didn't date.

Mibs says: That's what took me so long. She came in, needed to talk it through. She's very disappointed. I think I crushed her dreams of romance and stuff.

Luke says: Melanie got married without ever entering the dating scene. I liked what I saw. And, if she can con a great guy like Ryan into marrying her, then surely anyone can.

Mibs says: Is that your other sister?

Luke says: Yep. Olivia, Corinne, me, Cassie, then Melanie.

Mibs says: Well, all I know is that I don't ever want to sit through another fake meal again. BLECH.

Luke says: You know what I never understood?

Mibs says: What's that?

Luke says: Well, if you ask people why they date, they usually say something like, "it is a way to get to know them better." So then, inevitably, you find out they're going to a movie. What sense does that make?

Mibs says: That's a good point! I mean, you sit in a dark theater, can't see their reaction to what is happening on the screen, you can't talk...

Luke says: My point exactly.

Mibs says: I wish I'd never gone in the first place. When William brought it up, it made sense. It even sounded fun. It was NOT fun.

Luke says: Does William feel the same way?

Mibs says: *shrugs*

Mibs says: Confession time: I was horribly rude to William again when we got home. I mean, the dinner was nothing like last time. It was pleasant and everything.

Luke says: So, what makes you think you were rude to him?

Mibs says: Probably the way I informed him that I was determined to remain single. FOREVER. Emphasis in the original conversation…

Luke says: LOL. That'd probably do it.

Mibs says: I didn't like how the whole evening made me feel, so I just dumped my frustrations on him. I wasn't ugly, but it was rude.

Luke says: It sounds like an apology might be in order.

Mibs says: I'm making a hobby of it or something.

Luke says: That's one of the best things about you. You're not afraid to admit when you're wrong.

Mibs says: That's actually why I dinged…

Luke says: So, you need me there early tomorrow?

Mibs says: If you can.

Luke says: Sure, but where's Tina?

Mibs says: She left tonight for Yorktown. Her father really does have a dinner planned for her.

Luke says: I can't believe she left before you got home. I would have expected her to give a grilling that'd make William proud – if it wasn't his date she was interrogating you about.

Mibs says: I expect to get a call while I'm at Espresso Yourself begging for details.

Luke says: What time do you need me there?

Mibs says: Well, I told William's voice mail that I'd meet him at Espresso at eight, so…

Luke says: I'll be there at a quarter 'til.

Mibs says: Thanks.

Mibs says: Luke, I have this awful feeling. I know feelings are not always reality but…

Luke says: No, but sometimes feelings are that prompting we get when the Holy Spirit reminds us of something we've learned. What does the feeling tell you?

Mibs says: Well, it seems to me like William is TRYING to be "interested" in me. Like it is some kind of duty he has to perform or something. I mean, if that was what God wanted for our lives, wouldn't it happen naturally without having to work so hard?

Luke says: Well, you'd think so, wouldn't you? He's a good man; you shouldn't carelessly toss aside a good man who loves the Lord.

Mibs says: Ugh. I was so sure, but you're going to put doubts in my mind, aren't you?

Luke says: Well, I was also going to say that just because he's a good man doesn't mean he's the right one for you.

Mibs says: *sigh* Honestly, Luke, I am still struggling to learn the basics of housekeeping, parenting, and all the joys and trials that come with those. I don't think I have time for this.

Mibs says: Maybe that should tell me something. I mean, if William was "the one," don't you think I'd think differently? Don't you think I'd be willing to make time for the right guy?

Luke says: Maybe. It may be that you won't be looking when he comes. He may have to work a little to show you what could be there, and that's ok. Any guy who really cares about building a life with you won't mind that challenge.

Mibs says: Can I ask you something?

Luke says: Of course.

Mibs says: Is it even right to think about this stuff? Don't I have enough to do without spreading myself that much thinner?

Luke says: The right man will understand what he's getting into, Mibs. He's not going to mind sharing you with the children.

Mibs says: It just seems wrong to take more time away from the kids

Mibs says: Well, actually, since I'm not dating anymore, the only way I can see me getting married is if someone arranges it for me, so I think I'm probably worrying about nothing.

Luke says: Most worries are.

Mibs says: Are what?

Luke says: About nothing. It's late. I need to do a few things next door before I mosey on over there, so I think I'll have to sign off now.

Mibs says: Thanks for the chat, Luke. I feel a little better now.

Luke says: Get some sleep. You're going to need it.

Mibs says: Thanks again. I really appreciate it. Goodnight.

Luke says: Good night, Mibs.

Sugar & Spice

Chapter Seven

Monday, August 11ᵗʰ

Aggie's hands fidgeted as she tried to find the right words to explain to William why the date that he saw nothing wrong with was so disappointing to her. She didn't want to hurt him; he'd been so considerate, but she needed to ensure that he took her decision seriously. At last, William's hand closed over hers. "What's wrong, Aggie? What did I do wrong? I tried —"

"I know you did, William. I know, and I'm sorry, but that's actually the problem." She returned the gentle squeeze he gave her and tried to smile. "I don't want to have to 'try' at any relationship. I don't want that artificiality. It's not me."

"Every relationship takes work, Aggie. There's no such thing as a perfect couple who never had to work things through."

Her eyes closed as she prayed again for the ability to explain herself without being any ruder than she'd already been. "William, I understand that. What I am not so keen on is having to start a relationship with so much work. Can't we just keep being the friends I know we are, and if we change and become more to each other than we are now, that's ok?" She waited for him to meet her gaze. "Can you honestly say that your heart will break if we don't go out to dinner every other week?"

"Well no, but—"

"Then what's the problem? You can come over, or we can take the kids to the park, we can talk, laugh, play games… all the stuff we do now, but there's no pressure to make it into some big romantic thing." She swallowed. "If I really thought you were falling for me in some way, I wouldn't be saying this. I'd be reexamining my own heart. I'd be more willing to see if I could learn to care for you in a more intimate way…" Her voice trailed off as she tried to find a non-insulting way to tell a man she wasn't salivating to have more time alone with him. "Since neither of us is there yet, why do we have to work to get there? It's a lot of pressure, William—for both of us."

"Yeah. That's true." He seemed lost in thought for a while. "I guess, I just assumed that if you're friends with a woman, a mother in particular, you need to be willing to commit to that no matter where it goes."

Aggie's smile crinkled the corners of her eyes in that delightful way that gave her added attractiveness. "It means so much to me that you said that. I really appreciate that you were willing to invest *all* of yourself to be my friend—that you *are* willing to do it still." Her eyes twinkled as she added, "Let's make a deal. If either of us changes how we feel about the other, we'll just say so. No awkwardness, or as little as we can manage, no expectations, just open honesty so the other can know what to expect."

"That I can get into." His hand gave hers one last squeeze before he stood and gathered their trash. He accompanied her out the door and to her van. Before William opened the door, he brushed her cheek with the back of his hand in a way that sent waves of dread over her. "I wish my little sister was like you."

"What do you mean?"

"You're understanding; you'll talk out a problem. You give people second chances." He knew that several store merchants had their eyes on the scene before them, all speculating about the deeply romantic moment they thought they saw, but for once in William's highly regulated life, he didn't care. "Is it silly to say I hope I fall in love with you or someone like you?"

"No, I think that's flattering. I could say the same thing about you—most of the time."

His laughter rang out sending more glances their way. He shut the door behind her and leaned his arms on the window as it lowered. "Tell Sullivan I said to get your room done. You look tired, Aggie. You need your own space."

"He's probably working on it now."

William shook his head. "We both know that he's goofing off with the kids. He'd never leave them alone without someone watching them."

He was right, and she knew it. "Yep. I'd better get home so we can get it done."

"Let Luke do it, Aggie. Your ankle is still on the stiff side. Don't risk it."

Tuesday, August 12th

A door slammed, waking Aggie from her impromptu catnap on the sofa. She bolted upright, and glanced around her, blinking. "Um, wha—" The room was empty. Shouts filtered downstairs, but she still wasn't certain who was shouting or why. Dragging herself off the couch, Aggie glanced around the room, wondering where Ian was. This wasn't good.

At the top of the stairs, she overheard Vannie sob, "I always have to watch him! You never do! I just want to finish my book!" Guilty eyes met Aggie's as Vannie realized she had an audience. She shifted a whimpering Ian from one hip to the other, embarrassed.

Before Aggie could speak, Laird's door flung open, and he snapped, "Fine. Just give him to me. Why do you always have to wait until I'm in the middle of something he can't be around—"

"Why didn't you bring Ian to me?"

"Tavish would, if she'd just ask him—"

"Tavish watches him more than all of us put together." A flush covered Vannie's face. "Well, except for Aunt Aggie."

"Gaggie!" Ian's delighted little voice brought smiles to all faces. He reached for her, and Aggie took him.

"Listen; all you had to do was bring him to me."

"But you were resting. Laird was just—"

The boy's voice interrupted without apology. "What Laird does doesn't matter. It's unimportant because Laird does it. Now, if Vannie does it, it must be of vital importance and must not be halted for any reason."

"Stop." Her voice, quiet but firm, showed that she had little patience left for their nonsense.

"But—"

Aggie glared at her niece. She wasn't proud of the anger rising in her and showing on her face, but frustration won over conscience and before she knew what she'd said, Aggie snapped, "Listen to me, young lady. When I say stop, I mean *stop!*"

Defiance, something she'd never seen in the girl, welled in Vannie's eyes. "No. I won't stop. You act like this is all my fault, and it's not. Laird is being lazy and getting away with it—again. I hate this! I want Mommy back. She'd make him do what was right."

With a flounce worthy of any overly dramatic teen movie, Vannie stalked to her door, flung it open, and slammed it shut again. Unsure what to do, Aggie turned to Laird and pointed inside his room. "Just go in and stay there until I come talk to you."

"I'm sorry, Aunt Aggie. I should have just taken him."

"No, Laird. You should have asked me what you should do. Ian isn't your responsibility." She pinched the bridge of her nose. "Just go do whatever you were doing. I'll be back."

Shoulders slumped and tears in her eyes, Aggie started to climb the stairs to talk to Luke, but retraced her steps and went downstairs singing, "*Guide me o Thou great Jehovah pilgrim through this barren land. I am weak but Thou art mighty. Hold me with Thy pow'rful hand...*"[5]

On the couch, she squeezed a wriggling Ian and whispered, "Oh little man, what am I going to do?"

Tavish entered from the kitchen, and Ian ran to him squealing. "Can I take him outside to make mud pies with the girls?"

Aggie nodded, not thinking of what mud pies would mean. She hung her head in her hands and rested her elbows on her knees. P-mails flew heavenward faster than she could recognize them as hers. Her heart, burdened by the uncharacteristic outburst Vannie had displayed, felt as if it was breaking all over again. If she lost control of the older children now, she'd have no hope of keeping the little ones in line.

Two feet appeared on the floor in front of her. The shoes were now as familiar to her as her own. "You heard?"

"You ok, Mibs?"

"Frankly, no. I'm not. Once again, I've proven that I cannot do this job."

"Don't do it. Don't let your mind go there." Luke sank down onto his heels and tilted his head to see into Aggie's pained eyes. "If you let yourself convince yourself that it's too hard, pretty soon every little bump will be overwhelming."

"Maybe that's because it *is* overwhelming. I just hate this."

"Hate what?"

"Not knowing what to do. I am so unprepared for everything. Did I make a big mistake when I agreed to do this? I can't go back on it now, but was I selfish? Over optimistic? Was I just arrogant enough to want to prove something to my sister?"

Luke took her hands in his and was silent for so long, she nearly jerked them back and used them to shake whatever he wanted to say out of him. Sometimes she allowed herself the illusion of believing she'd grown accustomed to his long thoughtful silences, but then, inevitably, something happened to snap her back to reality. Just as she started to demand to know his thoughts, she realized he was praying. Her heart swelled with gratitude even as her anger deflated.

When he finally met her eyes again, Luke's own eyes were concerned—pained even. "Mibs, I think the only bad thing about your situation is that you have no one to encourage you. You jumped into something that few mothers ever experience, and when they do, they slowly add to their job, one child at a time." He sighed. "They also usually have someone that comes home at the end of the day, holds them close, and tells them how much it means that they do all that they do. You don't have that. Everyone needs encouragement, but I've seen it; all you get is incredulous and rude comments from people who cannot see how painful their words are."

"Not from you or your mother. Sometimes William—" She stopped. Most of William's comments had been reminders of her failures and that she needed help. "Should I consider hiring help? It'd be a lot of money, but surely living with family and having help to do things like laundry and floor mopping and stuff would be better than having to get used to a new guardian when I crack."

"What makes you think you'll crack?"

"I thought you heard."

The man's lips twisted as he shook his head. "Heard what?"

"Vannie's outburst; Laird's guilt when she lost it. Everyone thinking that they carry more responsibility than they should?"

"I heard," he said after a minute or two, "a young teenaged girl become overly dramatic because her brother didn't do what she expected him to do. Laird usually acquiesces to anything Vannie wants. She didn't get her way this time, so she did what most teenaged girls do when they think they can get away with it: she created a scene."

"But she lashed out at me too."

"I think she has begun to see herself as on par with you. You're not an authority figure anymore; you're Aunt Aggie, the girlfriend who shares late night confidences and ice cream." He hesitated again before he continued, "Mibs, I've heard you. You act as if you're afraid to tell her what to do. She's picking up on that, and it's too much for her."

"So, I need to step back and stay the mom-type rather than the comrade aunt-type?"

"I think you need to balance them. She needs you to exercise your authority when it's appropriate so that she learns where that line is." He sank back on the floor and wrapped his arms around his shins. "I bet when you first moved in with them, Vannie was hesitant to give you advice."

Aggie groaned. "Yes. I remember when Cari cut her hair, Vannie was so apologetic about saying anything, but she told me what she thought Cari needed."

"You need to get back to that spot and somehow blend it with Sunday night."

She stood, smiled her thanks, and glanced at the back door. "Will you make sure Ian isn't drowning in mud? I have a teenaged girl to upset."

Luke waited until she reached the steps before he answered. "Mibs?"

"Hmm?"

"She needs to apologize. No matter what lines have been blurred, she knows what she did was wrong."

"But what she said was probably true too. She does want her mother back."

"And she used that fact as a weapon when she realized that she'd stepped out of line."

She didn't know how to respond to him, particularly since she disagreed, so Aggie said the first thing that came to mind. "Thanks, Luke."

Outside Vannie's door, Aggie sent a fresh string of P-mails heavenward and knocked. No answer came. She knocked again, and again, no answer. Frustrated, she turned the knob, ready to call out a warning, and found the door locked. Stunned, she stood there staring at the knob, unsure of what to do. The temptation to pound on the door and demand the girl open it was nearly overpowering, but Aggie controlled herself just in time. Instead, she turned on her heel and went in search of Luke. She found him starting up the stairs.

"I need the smallest screwdriver you've got."

"Locked the door?"

"Yep," frustrated, Aggie almost ground the word between her teeth.

"Not good." He reached into a pocket of his tool belt and found a skinny screwdriver. "I'll be praying for you."

"Thanks. Oh, I'll need a regular sized Philip's head screwdriver too." With tools in hand, Aggie retraced her steps and began fumbling with the door. A muffled protest, followed by a screech when the door opened, prepared Aggie for the girl's mental attitude.

"Aunt Aggie!"

"Vannie!" Aggie echoed with a little more sarcasm than she'd intended.

"You can't just barge in here!"

"I can, and I did. You've just lost the privilege of a lock."

"I wish Mommy had chosen someone who knew what they are doing. You don't know anything."

"I know," Aggie said calmly as she unscrewed the door knob, "that your mother would never let you talk to her like this, and I won't either. I also know," she continued before Vannie could interrupt, "that you know better than this. There's a right way to issue a complaint in this family, and you know how to do it. You chose to—"

Tears exploded from Vannie who flounced to her bed and flung herself across it in a display that was freakishly familiar. Aggie remembered making a similar gesture when she was upset with

Allie, and her mother didn't show sufficient sympathy. She also remembered her mother's very effective response.

"Get up off that bed and blow your nose."

"No."

"You can do it yourself, or I can do it for you."

Vannie's head shot up, stunned. "You—"

"Will treat you as you act. If you want to act like you're Cari's age, I'll treat you like Cari. Let's go."

"I can't believe this," Vannie muttered as she shuffled out of her room, into the bathroom, and blew her nose on a tissue. She followed Aggie downstairs and into the kitchen. "Laird gets away with murder—"

"You can focus on what you think Laird did wrong and end up in trouble for hours or days, or you can own up to your own faults and leave Laird's between him, me, and the Lord. Which will it be?"

"I—"

"Think carefully before you answer."

"This isn't fair!"

"In the corner." Aggie swallowed hard and prayed that Vannie didn't see.

"What!"

"Nose in the corner." That lazy, almost bored, expression that Aggie had been practicing came in handy. She schooled her features into perfect lazy ranks and raised one eyebrow as if using it to point to the corner.

"This is ridiculous! You're treating me like I'm five!"

"You're acting five. Every second you argue results in that many more minutes in there. Go."

Though still obviously inwardly defiant, Vannie marched to the corner, looking like a giant version of a livid Cari, and crossed her arms as she faced the corner. She muttered a few more times, but when Aggie didn't respond, she gave up. Aggie, working to control her emotions, began unloading the dishwasher as if nothing had happened.

The seconds ticked into minutes and then into the better part of an hour. Each time Aggie began to suggest Vannie could come out and they could talk like mature people, the girl began a fresh whine fest worthy of any preschooler. At last, Aggie spoke. "When you're ready to come talk to me on the couch with some self-control and respect, you can come out. But," she continued with an authoritative tone she rarely assumed, "if you come out with the kind of display you've been showing this morning, you'll go right back in there, so be sure you're ready."

Vannie whirled in place, fury on her face, and at Aggie's shake of the head, spun back into the corner. Her fists were clenched, her body stiff and rigid. Aggie began to despair of the girl ever softening her heart. With a sigh, she grabbed a dust cloth and the polish and went to work on the living room furniture.

The three littlest girls raced into the kitchen begging for snacks, and then stopped, frozen in shock, at the sight of Vannie in the corner. Cari's awed voice whispered in a near shout, "Vannie does bad stuff too!"

Loyal to a fault, Lorna shook her head. "Maybe not."

"She's in the corner!" Cari protested with a tone in her voice that seemed to scream, "duh" at the end of the sentence.

"Maybe Aunt Aggie was wrong." Kenzie seemed confused — worried even.

Cari raced into the living room. "What did Vannie do? Why is she in the cownew? Did she get swats?"

As she knelt to Cari's eye level, Aggie dashed another P-mail off to the Lord for wisdom. "I think that is for Vannie to tell you if she ever wants to." The child whirled to go ask, but Aggie stopped her. "You can't bother her right now. Right now, I think you guys need to go get apples and then play outside with your mud pies." Aggie tried to ignore the dirt crusted fingernails and shoes.

To her absolute amazement, Cari smiled, hugged her, and dashed off to the kitchen shouting that they could all have apples. At the back door, the child let the others go ahead of her and crept back to where Vannie stood. "You should make that mad go away. It feels nicew when it's all gone." Then, as if nothing had interrupted her play, she skipped outside again, calling for dibs on a mud hole near the fence.

Humming to herself, Aggie resumed her dusting, expecting a long wait for Vannie. She wasn't aware of the song she hummed or even that she was humming at all. However, the young girl in the corner heard her and the softening in the girl's face would have been visible had she not been staring at a corner. The living room and library were both dusted and the rag just put away when Aggie heard a sniffle. Her heart leapt at the thought that this could be over, but after puttering around the room for a few minutes, she gave up and pulled out the vacuum. With all the hardwood floors in the house, she hadn't expected to need it anymore, but once the area rugs were down, it had become essential.

The peppy hymns of praise that usually seemed to try to drown out the noise of the vacuum were noticeably absent. She hummed a few bars of different hymns, but the joy that generally radiated from her as she worked was gone. Section by section, she vacuumed, lifted the rug, sucked up any dirt that had beaten its way beneath it, and then vacuumed over the surface again. So intent was she to get one corner straight, she didn't see Vannie appear at the library door.

"Aunt Aggie?"

Aggie glanced up and saw her eldest niece standing in the doorway, tears pouring down her face. "I am so sorry."

All doubt disappeared at the visible repentance in Vannie. She hurried to hug the girl and pulled her to one of the loveseats in the library. "I forgive you."

They talked for nearly an hour, and when Vannie finally climbed the stairs to make things right with Laird, Aggie had a better understanding of what was on the girl's heart. All day, she mulled their conversation in her mind, anxious to talk it out with Libby when the children were in bed. Just knowing that someone was there to help her think through things filled her with a sense of gratitude. Vannie spent most of the rest of the day close by— as if needing reassurance that all was well between them. That day, another facet of their relationship was chiseled to reflect a brighter light.

Mibs says: Libby? Ohhhh Liiiibbbyyyy....

Libby says: I see you've embraced your nickname.

Mibs says: Well, I was saving that to tease Luke with; I just forgot to change it.

Aggie says: There.

Libby says: Well, I think he'll be crushed if he gets online tonight and sees you've changed it. ;)

Aggie says: It's good for him to experience a few crushes now and

94

then.

Aggie says: Well, that didn't come out right.

Libby says: It was a little amusing. I wasn't going to say anything, but I did chuckle.

Aggie says: Oh well, you know what I meant.

Libby says: That I did.

Aggie says: Did Luke tell you about our drama-fest today?

Libby says: A little. He said that Vannie has been putting too much responsibility on herself.

Aggie says: After we talked for a while, I found out that she has been trying to shoulder everything she can so Geraldine can't find just cause to have them taken away. She'd pushed herself to the breaking point, and then snapped when Laird wasn't ready to give her the break she needed at that precise moment.

Libby says: Then it's a good thing he didn't.

Aggie says: I was trying to think that way, but I failed. I just want them to have as normal a childhood as possible.

Libby says: Aaah, but Vannie is at that lovely but terrifying age where she doesn't feel like a child anymore, she knows she's not an adult, and the alternative is terrifying.

Aggie says: What alternative?

Libby says: A TEENAGER.

Aggie says: She will be thirteen in a couple of months...

Libby says: So, did you work out a solution for her?

Aggie says: I showed her the court papers, the restraining order, and her father's letter to me. I had her speak to Mr. Moss, and I think she's not so afraid of being taken away anymore.

Libby says: I think that was a very good decision.

Aggie says: On a brighter note, Luke said he would move my furniture back into my room tomorrow. He didn't have to sand down my floors or anything, so I guess the room is done!

Libby says: I can't wait to see it.

Aggie says: It's going to be strange without him around as much for the next two weeks.

Libby says: Don't be surprised if he finds excuses to stop by on his way home a few dozen times. I'm not sure my Luke can survive for two whole weeks without his Stuart-Milliken infusion.

Aggie says: I'm going to use that time to try to help Vannie finish up her clothes, get the kids enrolled in school here, and buy all the millions of school supplies that we will need. Three out of five backpacks were worthless at the end of last year, and the other two won't make it the whole year this year.

Libby says: Buy all new ones then. They will inevitably fail on a rainy day when they bring home their most expensive books.

Aggie says: Aaah. Good point.

Libby says: Oh, there's the phone. My Luke is calling to say goodnight. I'd better go.

Aggie says: Thanks, Libby. I hope to see you soon.

Libby says: You will. We have more clothes to make. I just need to help Melanie while her little guy gets over the chicken pox.

Aggie says: Thanks! Night to both of you!

Libby says: Luke says goodnight too. Goodnight, Aggie.

Snips & Snails

Chapter Eight

Monday, August 18th

With Tina on kid patrol, Aggie grabbed her purse, guardianship papers, the children's birth certificates, and school records. Waving gaily at Mrs. Dyke as she passed, she drove serenely through town, onto the highway, and into Brunswick. Brant's Corners only had a small private school, which she'd considered for Cari and Lorna when their year for Kindergarten came, but for now the school-aged children would ride to Brant's Corners on the same big yellow school buses that the rest of the children in town rode.

The elementary school was first. She found the school office and from there strolled to the cafeteria where several teachers and the principal gathered to help parents transition students into school. Only a few women, two with their children in tow, and a man stood in line ahead of her. The cafeteria was bustling with activity. Papers rustled, pens scratched, records were checked, and it seemed like a mountain of paperwork grew beside each smiling face. Aggie couldn't help but wonder if those faces would look just as fresh and cheerful in May as they did that morning.

One of the women tried to strike up a conversation, but her daughter, dancing from foot to foot, needed a trip to the restrooms. Aggie moved up in line, determined to offer to let the woman back in her place if she returned in time. The man now ahead of her gave her a small grimace and shrugged. "I've never done this before. I hope I have everything."

"I don't know. I've never done it either."

"You looked too young to be experienced at the wonders of kindergarten enrollment." Flashbacks of a rude single father from Kenzie's graduation made her uncomfortable for a moment, but then she felt silly. Just because a man was friendly at a school did not make him a creep.

"I am, but I'm not enrolling kindergarten. This year it's first, and fourth. Oh, and I forgot to ask if this school has sixth or if they lump it in the middle school."

"Babysitter? They won't let you enroll someone else's child."

She smiled. "Legal guardian of my nieces and nephews." His eyes asked the question he was polite enough not to ask. "My sister died in February."

"I'm sorry to hear it. Her husband…"

"Died the same night." She hated these questions, but the man seemed genuinely sorry and interested.

"Oh, those poor children. I really admire you and your husband for taking on three children. So many kids would end up in foster care these days."

For a moment, Aggie was tempted not to correct him, but her innate open personality and the feeling of dishonesty that washed over her for not correcting his misconception, sent her explaining again. "Actually, she left eight children, and I am not married."

The man didn't respond. His eyes widened, his jaw slackened just a little, and she saw him blink a couple of times, before he gave himself just the slightest hint of a shake. "I'm sorry, how rude of me. I just keep prying, but I can't help but ask how you do it."

The question was an awkward one. She didn't like when people treated her like a super woman just for doing what Allie had done for years. She tried to formulate an intelligent response that gave credit to the Lord without sounding too pompously pious and then shrugged. "I don't know. One day at a time, I guess. Oh, and a *lot* of prayer."

"Do you have a good church?"

Aggie nodded. "Brant's Corners has a wonderful church."

"Well," the man fished a business card out of his pocket, "with a good church, you're probably set for help without needing a stranger, but if you ever need anything—toilet overflows, sprinkler head breaks, tire goes flat, anything—just call. My work hours are very flexible, so I can come if you need me." He rolled his eyes. "That sounds freaky, doesn't it? You can call The Assembly here in Brunswick for a reference."

"Nate Christman. You live up to your name, don't you?"

"I've never thought of it that way." The surprise in his eyes showed that he hadn't. "Thanks—"

The woman returned just then, trying to quiet her whining daughter, and Aggie stepped aside for her. "I saved your place for you."

"Oh, thanks! I thought there'd be fifty people behind you, and I'd never get out of here."

Before the woman's chatter could prevent it, Aggie smiled around her at Nate. "Thanks again. I can't promise I'll call, but this card will encourage me even if I don't."

A fresh stream of whines and a few stomps of the feet echoed around the cafeteria. Aggie watched the ineffectual attempts to control the child's display of displeasure and thanked the Lord for women like Iris and Libby. Cari and Kenzie, probably Lorna as well, would all be just as demanding without the lessons provided by Aggie's mentors. Nate offered the mother his place in line and stepped back next to Aggie. "Do you mind?"

"Of course not!" She pointed to his file folder. "What grade is your child in this year?"

"Kindergarten. Abby turns five next week."

"Aw, that's such a fun age. Kenzie is just six, and always amazes me with her observations."

"Just a year either way and they might have shared a classroom." Nate sounded more relieved than disappointed as was Aggie. The man wasn't going to hound her. That was nice.

Before they could talk any further, Nate was beckoned to the third table. Aggie watched as each parent pulled out their paperwork, waited for it to be verified, signed documents of some kind, and then received several packets of paperwork. One woman couldn't find her driver's license and hurried out to see if it was in her car, while others complained about lunch program rules and school supply lists, insisting that they should not be required to purchase Kleenex for the entire classroom. Aggie frowned.

At last, her turn came and she sat at the table next to Nate and shook hands with the principal. "I'm Aggie Milliken. I'm here to register my two nieces and a nephew — or two."

"Or two?"

"I forgot to ask when I called if sixth grade is here or in the middle school."

The principal's features took on that familiar authoritative look. "Sixth is at the middle school, but I'm afraid students must be registered by a parent or legal guardian."

"I am their legal guardian." She flipped open her folder and flipped through pages until she found the letter she sought. "Here's a letter from the vice principal at Washington Elementary in Rockland. He explains everything."

Nate sent her an encouraging look while she waited for the principal to read the letter. "Well, Ms. Milliken—"

"Miss is fine."

"Miss then. You have quite the responsibility here. Let's get started on your paperwork."

Aggie filled out enrollment forms, liability waivers, insurance forms, school lunch program waivers, and initialed a dozen school rule, guideline, and requirements forms. While she worked on Ellie's, the principal John Beaudine, checked through Kenzie's school records, ready to tick off each box on the checklist.

"Why has a six year old had general science? Computer lab? What—" The man frowned. "Who is Vanora Cheyenne Stuart?"

"How did Vannie's—" Aggie opened Vannie's folder and found Tavish's report card, Vannie's vaccination records, and Kenzie's birth certificate. "What—" She stopped herself short. "I think I need to let you help someone else and go sort this. I've apparently had 'help' with my paperwork. Everything is all mixed up."

"Since we have to go through everything anyway, just keep filling out the papers, and I'll find what I need." A twitch around Principal Beaudine's mustache was lost on Aggie, but Nate grinned at the teacher helping him. School wasn't going to be dull with Aggie and her clan there.

After several long minutes, Aggie pushed her forms across the table. "Ok. I think I got them all."

The principal passed several packets to her, and with his pen, pointed to the sheet clipped to the front of each one. "I put Elspeth and Tavish in separate fourth grade classrooms." Aggie nodded. "MacKenzie, I put in Mrs. Liszak's room. She's one of our most beloved teachers, and her class is small, so MacKenzie will get the kind of individualized attention that she likely misses in such a large family. Just follow the directions to each classroom to meet their teachers. Tavish's teacher won't be in his room until after noon. He's over there at table five."

Still stunned by the assumption that Kenzie was craving personal attention, Aggie nodded, fought back angry tears, and thanked the principal for his time and help. As she walked away, she heard him mutter to the teacher helping at Nate's recently vacated table, "That is going to be a problem household; we'll have to keep an eye on them."

For just a moment, she had the wild temptation to storm back to the table, grab the enrollment forms, and run from the building. Into what kind of hostile environment had she just enrolled the children? It seemed as if the principal was predisposed to dislike her and her children simply because of their numbers. Similar thoughts troubled her all the way to Kenzie's and Ellie's classrooms.

Exhausted, Aggie collapsed on the couch, a stack of folders, packets, envelopes, and her own files sliding every which way. "Enrolling children is a fulltime job. I am so glad I won't have to do *that* again."

Tina dropped Ian in her lap and then began stacking paperwork. "No, but you'll get to do class assignments for high school for the next thirteen or fourteen years. Yay for you."

That thought nearly sent Aggie over the edge. After the day she'd had, nothing sounded worse than trying to juggle biology and driver's ed. in the same year. "Well, at least we're good until next year on that, eh? Laird and Vannie are at the middle school, but they ride the same bus as the others. I thought that was good. No worries about bullying with your older siblings there, right?"

"Speaking of older siblings, I think Vannie needs help with the skirt she's working on. She ripped out a zipper three times this afternoon."

"Where is she now?"

"I took her and Laird to a movie. We just got in before you did."

"What movie?"

"The dollar theater was still playing the adaptation of *The Lost Princess*, so they went there. They said they hadn't seen it…"

"That sounds good. I should have thought about taking them to a movie." She grunted as Ian used her stomach for a trampoline. "Or bowling, or putt-putt golf, or the zoo…"

"You've been busy, girl!"

"I'm a mother. I don't get these days back just because the back porch needs the rail fixed or the toilet overflows."

"I think," Tina began carefully, "it might be smart if you spent more time concentrating on whatever God puts in your way next, rather than whining about your perceived failures." At Aggie's attempted protest, she added, "For example, how often did Allie take them to the movies, the bowling alley, swimming at the public pool, or the zoo?"

"I don't know. Isn't that what moms do?"

"Your mom never did."

Aggie sighed. "I know, and I understood, I did. I just never wanted to be that mom."

"What if you had a heart condition like your mom? Would you still feel like a failure for not being able to do everything Polly Perfect does?"

"But I don't—"

Before Tina could argue further, Tavish burst into the house staggering under the bulk and weight of a large box. "Look what I found! This truck just drove by, and this box fell off. The guy saw it, slowed down, and then took off!"

A suspicious yelp and whimper seemed to echo from the diaper box the boy held. "Did I just hear—"

"Puppies!" Tavish agreed, excitedly. "They're so cute! Black with little white spots…"

Heedless of the look of dismay on his aunt's face, Tavish set the box on the floor and pulled out a pup. "Isn't he—" the boy examined the underside for a moment. "Yeah, he cute?"

As much as she resisted, Aggie felt herself being pulled into the vortex of puppy breath, bitty teeth, and yaps that would grow into loud and obnoxious barks. "Oh, he is cute, isn't he!" She reached for the animal.

Tina snorted. "Sucker!"

"Just feel that fur…" Lost in the sensations of puppiness, Aggie asked, "So how many are there?"

"Six." The record playing that moment of her life screeched to a halt.

"Six! We cannot keep six puppies! I'll have to call the pound."

"No! Please, Aunt Aggie. I'll find homes for them. The minute you call the pound, their days are numbered. Let me do it; I know I can!"

Closing her eyes and ignoring Tina's shaking head, and much against her better judgment, Aggie nodded. "If you don't show progress in a week, I'm calling, though."

In a display of affection and excitement she hadn't seen from him, Tavish grabbed her, hugged her, took the puppy, and almost ran through the house with the wobbling box in his arms, shouting to the children to come see. Tina shook her head. "Do you have any idea what you just got suckered into?"

"I have a feeling you do."

"Eight kids weren't enough? You needed a half a dozen puppies to make your life really interesting?"

Wednesday, August 20th

Sluggish from another night of serenades from crying puppies, Aggie stumbled down the stairs, anxious for a cup of coffee. A glance at the clock told her she could have stayed in bed another half-hour at least, but Aggie had given up. The puppies had to go; she just didn't know how to tell Tavish. Laird and Vannie had plastered the town with signs, Tina put an advertisement in the local sales sheet, and Tavish had plans to take the wagon and drag the puppies door

103

to door to find them homes. If they weren't successful by the end of the day, she was calling the pound.

One look at Tavish's hopeful face weakened her resolve. After breakfast, he gave each puppy a bath and towel-dried them, leaving water and a laundry load of dirty towels strewn from the bathroom, through the mudroom, and outside, and then loaded the wagon into the van. She'd expected him to walk up and down the streets of Brant's Corners, but when she climbed into the van after him, he announced that Brunswick had more houses and therefore a better chance at finding homes.

Aggie spent most of the time trying to keep the puppies in the wagon while Tavish wheedled men and women alike. He sounded like a spokesperson for the SPCA as he railed at the cruelty of someone abandoning puppies in the middle of the highway and the responsibility of humans to care for God's creatures.

After several streets of consistent rejection, Aggie loaded them up and drove to Wal-Mart. There she purchased six small bags of dog food, six puppy collars and leashes, and a bag of chew toys. Surely, people would be less resistant if the initial needs were provided. Back they drove to the same neighborhood and started on the next street. Now Tavish sounded like a combination snake-oil hawker and missionary to lost puppies.

The mission became a comedy of errors at one home. It looked innocent enough. Yellow house, white shutters, white picket fence — it didn't get much more all-American than that house. The door opened, and chaos erupted. Five cats streamed out of the house, one after the other, and the last was skittish. It took one look at the puppy in Tavish's arms and jumped into Tavish's arms, sinking its claws into the poor puppy's back. Tavish yelped, the puppy screeched, and the woman who opened the door screamed.

"Get that filthy animal off my porch! Oh, poor Penelope! Here, baby, I'll protect you from the bad dog." She glared at Tavish as she pulled her cat from the writhing puppy's back. "Shame on you! How dare you bring your flea-bag dog to my house. Get out of here! Shoo!"

Stunned, Tavish couldn't move. As if on auto-pilot, he began his rehearsed speech about the wonders of puppies and the responsibility for people to care for unfortunate animals. Aggie rushed up to the porch and dragged him away, apologizing

104

profusely. Her heart wanted to lash out at the woman who berated her child, but she knew it was wrong. A few children gathered around the gate, some whispering loudly, but Aggie didn't pay any attention to them.

"In the van, Tavish. Let's find another neighborhood."

Their next house was almost a success. After finding rows of tree-canopied streets, she pulled up the van to one corner, and helped him put a bag of pet supplies in the wagon. This time, she suggested putting two puppies there. It couldn't hurt, and maybe seeing more to need homes would elicit sympathy in the hearts of the people behind the door.

At the first house, a man opened the door, took one look at the puppy, and asked how much they wanted for it. Tavish handed him the bag of food, asked if he wanted a boy or a girl, and raced to the van to retrieve a boy, but by the time he returned, a woman stood there. "Sorry, but we can't have a dog. Greg always forgets how allergic I am to them. I'm sorry. I hope you find homes for your puppies soon." The door shut firmly behind her.

Undaunted, Tavish pulled the wagon up and down the streets, stopping at every house, always polite, ever patient, certain that he'd find homes. Aggie, on the other hand, wasn't so sure. The sight of a cat strolling down the sidewalk sent the injured puppy running back down the street, his tail between his legs and howling with fear. Aggie tried to chase him, but the dog raced into the street, narrowly missed by a passing car. The driver pulled over and helped take up the chase. With no one watching the van doors, the other puppies tumbled from their rolling prison and wandered through the neighborhood, sniffing fences, marking territory they'd never see again, and making friends with the children who found them.

As it happened, two of those children were allowed to keep their new canine friends, and at that news, Aggie called it a day. "Come on, Tavish. I'm hungry, I'm tired, and I need a bath.

Luke says: Hey, I heard you adopted a few more orphans.
Aggie says: Six, to be exact. However, two have been placed in homes. Four to go.

Luke says: Well, I'm glad to hear that. How is everything else?

Aggie says: So-so.

Luke says: Want me to ask around and see if anyone wants one?"

Aggie says: Sure! Don't you think Meggie's pups exhausted your list of canine fanciers?

Luke says: Nah. She's purebred as were her pups. They were sold before I bred her.

Mibs says: Well, then. Find me homes, Sherlock.

Luke says: Mibs again, eh?

Mibs says: Only when I talk to you. It gets confusing for other people.

Luke says: Well, you don't HAVE to…

Mibs says: Are you complaining?

Luke says: No…

Mibs says: Then find me owners, and you'll add another hero star to your list.

Luke says: What kind of dogs are they?

Mibs says: Well, definitely black lab and then something that has white in it.

Luke says: Standard mixed pups. Great. People love those dogs. I was afraid you'd say Chow or Pit or something.

Mibs says: I'm not up on my dog breeds, but I'm pretty sure neither of those are in these poochies.

Luke says: Have they had their shots?

Mibs says: I doubt it. The kind of people who would let a box of puppies fall off a truck and just leave them don't seem to be the kind of people who get shots first.

Luke says: I've got some parvo and rabies here. I'll bring it over on Saturday and whatever you have left will get them. It might be easier to give them away if you can say they've had their shots.

Mibs says: Thanks.

Luke says: Are you keeping one?

Mibs says: I keep trying to convince myself to say no.

Luke says: Tavish loves animals, Mibs. If you can stand it, I'd consider it.

Mibs says: But we've already got the kitten.

Luke says: Well, for the boys I knew growing up, a kitten just isn't the same as a dog.

Mibs says: I'll think about it. Maybe if we have one we can't get rid of or something. I want to try at least. I think.

Luke says: Softy.

Mibs says: Tina would say sucker.

Luke says: I call 'em like I see 'em.

Mibs says: So, how are your projects?

Luke says: I have the roof on, the new cabinets in, and the countertops come tomorrow. All I have to do then is paint the outside, add a few plants, and get 'er on the market.

Mibs says: Will you finish this week?

Luke says: Most of it. Planting will be done early next week, and then I have that deck to build over in Brunswick.

Mibs says: Oh.

Luke says: Now that's a very curious word. Oh. What does "oh" mean?

Mibs says: Sorry, I forgot about the deck.

Luke says: Anxious to get that guest room done?

Mibs says: And the basement, and the kids miss you. They've asked every day when you'll be back. I think Laird misses having a project to do, but everything he asks to try, I don't know if it's a good idea or not.

Luke says: Let him call me, and I'll tell him.

Luke says: Or, if you like, let me pick him up a couple of times. He can help me paint the outside of the house, plant those flowers, and work on that deck.

Mibs says: Really?

Luke says: I'd love to have him. He's a good worker. I'll pay him.

Mibs says: You don't have to do that, but I bet he'd love coming.

Luke says: Actually, if you like, I'll come get him tomorrow morning and he can help me clear away the overgrown weeds and plants in the front yard while we wait for counter guys.

Mibs says: Why wait?

Luke says: I had a choice between counters sometime tomorrow between jobs, or in two weeks at a specific time. I picked tomorrow.

Mibs says: I'll have him ready at eight; is that all right?

Luke says: Perfect. Thanks.

Mibs says: LOL. You thank me for letting you babysit my kid. That makes sense.

Luke says: No, I thank you for trusting me with your son and for allowing him to help me.

Mibs says: Ok, ok. So I'm just a paragon of unselfish virtue.

Luke says: LOL. Or something like that.

Mibs says: Oh, did you hear? I figured out what Vannie was doing wrong on her zipper!

Luke says: That's great. What have you sewn?

Mibs says: Did you hear? I figured out what Vannie was doing wrong on her zipper!

Luke says: Not much yet, eh?

Mibs says: Did you hear...

Luke says: Great job, Mibs.

Mibs says: Thanks. So, are you ready to tell me what Mibs means?

Luke says: Nope.

Mibs says: Am I going to be insulted?

Luke says: Nope, well, I hope not!

Mibs says: Is it a good thing?

Luke says: It's just an appropriate one.

Mibs says: Ah well, I tried. I keep yawning, so I think I'll go to sleep now. Thanks for everything, Luke. Sometimes I don't know what we'd do without you.

Mibs says: And your mom.

Luke says: And we can't imagine life without you and your kids, so it's even.

Mibs says: Well, this mutual admiration society must adjourn for the evening.

Luke says: M'kay. G'night, Mibs.

Mibs says: Nighters, Luke.

CHANGES

Chapter Nine

Saturday August 23rd

After two days of working with Luke, Laird showed a new confidence in his interactions with people. Aggie immediately noticed a similarity to the way Luke deferred to her, was ready to help, and sometimes anticipated her needs before she could identify them herself. It was as if, overnight, he left the little boy years behind and entered a new phase of young adulthood—about two years too soon in her opinion. However, when she asked Libby about it, the older woman had been firm.

"Don't discourage him, Aggie. The boy is testing new ground. He's been watching, he's had a chance to have his efforts validated in the past couple of days, and now he needs to be given the chance to find the balance on his own. If, in say a month or two, he has an unhealthy predisposition to 'act grown up,' then we can plan a way to balance him, but give him the chance to figure it out. I think we emasculate our boys when we jump in too quickly, trying to protect them from themselves."

With the younger children, Laird developed a different kind of patience. For most of his life, the laid-back boy had simply ignored or tolerated his siblings' immaturity and annoyances out of laziness. Even Vannie had noticed a change in his interaction. When Kenzie did something foolish and almost destroyed Ellie's latest watercolor, he took the girl for a walk and talked to her. The scene was so similar to something her father would have done, that she'd gone upstairs, closed her door, curled up in a ball, and wept. Aggie found her there a while later and was surprised at Vannie's simple tears.

"I missed you downstairs. Are you ok?"

A sniffle reached her before Vannie's head peeked out from beneath her arm. "I'm good."

"You look upset. Are you sure?"

"I am upset. Isn't that silly?" The girl brushed her hair from her face and sat up. "I— I don't know how to explain it, but it feels good to cry this time."

Aggie climbed up onto her niece's daybed, the one on which she'd shared confidences with Allie at Vannie's age, and tried to pry a more coherent answer from the girl. "Why does it feel good? Why tears?"

"I saw Laird with Kenzie. Usually, he'd just let Kenzie be foolish and careless, and Ellie would be the one hurt when her painting was ruined, but he didn't."

"What did he do?"

"He took Kenzie's hand and walked with her to the far field at the edge of the property." Fresh tears pooled in Vannie's eyes. "Oh, Aunt Aggie. It looked just like Daddy. Daddy used to do that when one of us was being reckless. He'd take our hand, walk us up and down the street, and talk to us. He showed us how to think of other people." She swallowed hard. "This looked just like that— well, except that Laird is shorter."

"So, it felt good to cry about missing your father?" None of Vannie's words made sense, but what made less sense was that she agreed with the girl.

"It felt good to cry about a good memory instead of because he was gone."

As insane as the words sounded, Aggie understood. She started to respond, but a squeal from the front sent her flying to the window. "Oh, it's just Luke. I thought someone was going to start wailing."

"Aunt Aggie?"

She stopped at the door, and at the sight of Vannie's face, retraced her steps. "Hmm?"

"Are you sorry Mommy and Daddy left you in charge of us?"

"Of course not!" No one would doubt the sincerity of Aggie's protest. "Why would you ask that?"

"Remember when Laird and I rode to the library last week?"

"Yeah..."

"Well, there were two women in there. They didn't see me come back for my library card, and they were talking about us."

A frown began to grow on Aggie's forehead. "What did they say?"

"Just stuff about how it's a lot to ask of someone your age and how no one would want to marry someone saddled with eight kids."

Stunned, Aggie sat beside her niece, wrapped her arms around the girl, and whispered, "I am so sorry you had to hear something so thoughtless and untrue."

"But it is true, Aunt Aggie. Not that they won't want to marry someone so great, but they won't get to know how great you are because they'll see all us kids and go running."

"Did it occur to you, Miss-Vannie-with-the-care-of-the-world-on-my-shoulders, that the kind of man I'd want to marry is the kind of man who wouldn't let that stop him? If I have to pick between you kids and marriage, it's a no brainer for me. I pick you every time."

"But—"

"Do you think I haven't thought of this?"

The question was obviously unexpected. Vannie's eyes widened, she frowned, and then shrugged. "I guess I thought you hadn't."

"Well, I have. And besides, William has taken me out twice and would go again if I told him I wanted to. Every man on the planet isn't afraid to be my friend."

"Luke is your friend too, but he hasn't asked you out."

The obsession with her love life was getting a little annoying, but Aggie managed to keep her tone strictly matter-of-fact. "Well, not every guy who is a friend thinks he has to declare his undying love. Some guys can be friends without all that." Remembering something her father once said, she added, "Unfortunately, there are a lot of men who can't. I think that's why William keeps trying to make

111

things into something romantic. He doesn't know how to be a friend with a girl."

"But Luke can?"

"Well, it seems like it, doesn't it? He's about as close to an older brother as I've ever had, and he hasn't gotten all goofy or anything."

Vannie must have heard something in Aggie's tone that hinted at dissatisfaction. "Would you though?"

"Would I what?"

"Would you want to go out with Luke if he asked?"

Tired of the discussion and ready to get the pups inoculated and ready for new homes, Aggie stood, smiled at her niece, and shook her head. "Oh, I don't think so, Vannie. I like things how they are. Going out with men seems to make nice things all complicated, and I'm just not interested in that."

Luke's voice called out softly before she could reach the door. "Aggie? Are you up here? Mom sent some popsicles." His face appeared in the doorway. "Can I let the kids have them?"

"Sure." She slipped past and hurried downstairs to cut one apart for Cari and Lorna before someone gave them each a whole sugar infusion.

Luke waited for Vannie before following them downstairs. The young girl gave a quick glance over her shoulder and saw something in his face she wasn't meant to see. Dejection.

Vaccinating the four remaining puppies was not the easy task that Aggie had pictured. She'd imagined they'd grab a puppy, Luke would stab the shot into the pup's rump, and it'd be over. She didn't take into account activity, readying the needle, or the little ones. Although Ian ignored the proceedings, obsessed with his spoon and a dirt patch in the yard, Lorna and Cari had very decided opinions on the use of shots in any form. At the sight of the needle, Lorna screeched, Cari wailed, and Luke jumped, dropping the syringe.

"What!"

"You won't do that to ow puppies! You won't huwt them wike that!" Cari pushed him, as if to forcibly eject Luke from the property.

Aggie turned the pup over to Tavish and led Cari onto the porch to administer a sound scolding. Before she could open her mouth, Cari kicked her shin and ran. Lorna, seeing reinforcements on the way, pushed Tavish and grabbed the puppy. Unfortunately, she was only able to grab his tail, and a bite was the thanks she got for rescuing him from the evil Dr. Luke.

The ensuing chaos resulted in a row of children sitting sullenly on the front steps, a call to the police for a domestic disturbance, and a visit from Murphy. The woman took one look at the line up, the traveling vet show on the back of Luke's pickup bed, and Aggie's harried expression, and retreated to her home, reserving her snickers for her own yard. Tavish winced each time Luke grabbed a leg, but his determination to keep the pups from the pound was stronger than his trembling stomach.

The ordeal took ten times longer than either Luke or Aggie had expected. By the time he was done, Luke was stifling guffaws, and Aggie was ready to send the kids back to bed— for a month! While he packed up the syringes and the bottles of vaccine, Aggie stood, hands on hips, Megan looking on with her own amusement barely hidden behind her hand, and addressed her troops.

"What on earth do you think you are doing?"

"'tecting the puppies! You said that we have to 'tect the puppies. Wuke was huwting them!" Of course, Cari spoke first.

"And you think I'd let Luke do something mean to the puppies I told you to protect?"

"Well…" Confusion flooded Cari's face.

"The shots hurt! You don't know, 'cause you don't have to have them." Little Lorna spoke with complete confidence.

"I got one just a few weeks ago, remember?"

"You did?" Lorna's brain searched her recent memory banks for something that resembled an instrument of prickly torture and came up short. "When?"

"When I got poked by the nail in the attic. I slept a lot, remember?"

"See!" Cari's sense of logic went into overdrive. "The shots made you sweepy, and Wuke had to wake you up all the time. I wemembew! Shots are bad!" Her little arms crossed as if she'd delivered the final verdict—guilty.

"The shot made me very sleepy, but it also stopped a very bad disease that could have made me very sick, or even—" She hesitated. Mentioning death at a highly emotionally charged moment was a recipe for disaster that could result in histrionics. "Worse."

"But the puppies didn't step on nails, Aunt Aggie!" Kenzie's literal translation of Aggie's words nearly sent the frazzled young woman into a tirade she'd regret for days.

Luke stepped in, his supplies locked in the cab of his truck. "May I?"

"They're all yours. When you're done with them, Cari owes me an apology for kicking me."

Happy to get away, Aggie scooped up Ian and carried him into the house. While she loaded the dishwasher for the third time that morning, Aggie opened a lower cabinet full of plastic containers for Ian to stack, dump, and slide across the floor. As she worked, she sang. *"Take time to be holy; be calm in thy soul. Each thought and each motive, beneath his control. Thus…"*[6]

She didn't even realize she'd started at the last verse. She just sang until her whole being was lost in her prayerful hymn. So engrossed was she in her song and the eradication of dirty dishes from her kitchen, she didn't notice that Ian disappeared from the room. In fact, only Ian's screech of protest and Vannie's sharp, "No, Ian! Bad boy!" brought her out of her reverie and into the harshness of reality.

Stepping into the living room, she saw Vannie dive for the toddler. "Vannie! What—"

A calm stole over her that even she didn't recognize. A part of her, that part of all people that wants to deceive ourselves into believing that we're a better person than we are, was happy to see how unflapped she was by the Sharpie-induced artwork on her living room wall. Her real self, the one she desperately wanted to pretend wasn't there, knew it was that deadly calm before the storm.

"I'll take that, little man."

"Gaggie!" His one word was usually a source of joy for her, but this time she heard it with no emotion whatsoever.

"Vannie, would you take him outside, up to bed, to the moon, something?"

"Um, sure." The confused girl picked up her brother and scurried outside.

The wall had a row of scribbles three-feet hight scattered across it and its chair rail. Aggie wanted to cry. She took a deep breath, but it did no good. The frustrated tears hovered at the back of her eyes but she willed herself to keep them under control.

"Mibs?"

"Know how to get Sharpie off the wall?" The quaver in her voice irritated her. She needed to learn not to care.

"Are you ok?"

"I will be when I get Sharpie off that wall," she ground out the words between clenched teeth.

Luke turned her away from the scene of the crime and pushed her toward the kitchen. "What's the matter, Mibs?"

"I just decided that I won't care anymore. Caring will leave you disappointed. I have to resign myself to a house full of dings, scrapes, dirty corners, and marker on the wall."

"First, no you don't. You teach them how to care for things and fix it when accidents happen. This isn't irreversible. If a 'magic eraser' won't take it off, we'll just paint over it." Luke shook his head as she reached into the broom cupboard and pulled out one of the scrubbing erasers. Taking it from her, he continued, "But apathy won't fix it. "

"I don't care, Luke. I can't. Life is going to be one series of disappointments if I let myself care about things like the state of the house or —"

In an uncharacteristic move, Luke interrupted her. "Just a couple of minutes ago, you were singing your heart out to the Lord. Those kids went from stubborn know-it-all-ness to eager listeners almost immediately after you started singing." He wandered into the living room, still talking, and began to scrub the sharpie from the wall. Even Aggie could see that it was destroying the sheen of the paint, but the marker did fade quickly. "I see two problems with your plan."

"What plan?"

"Not caring about what happens to your home."

"Ok, shoot." Why she even asked, Aggie didn't know.

"First, you're lying to yourself. Even if you pretend not to care, act like you don't, and even learn not to notice, you do."

"Second thing?" She didn't like the uneasy feeling that he was right.

"Second," he began, standing and frowning at the obvious streaks of scrubbed area, "is that your children will never learn to take proper care of things. You can't do that to them."

"I hate it when you're right."

Luke laughed. "And I need to get the paint out and fix that."

"I can't paint the walls every time a child —"

"Sure you can. It's a tiny section, not an entire room."

With hands raised in surrender, Aggie took a few steps back. "Ok, ok. Just wait until he's down for his nap, will you?"

She knew she sounded ungrateful, but Aggie didn't know how to respond anymore. She was weary— over-weary actually. It seemed as if every day was a huge lesson in coping skills, and everyone else had the answers while she floundered in an abyss of confusion. "It's just not fair," she whispered.

"What, Cari?"

Aggie glanced around to see what her little charge needed, but didn't see anyone. "Huh?"

"You sounded like Cari. 'It's not faiw, Wuke!'"

Laughter at herself seemed to crumble the walls of discouragement and dissatisfaction. "I guess I did." She forced a smile that slowly became genuine and said, "You know, someone, probably your mom, told me not to let myself wish away their days, but I've been doing that."

"Wish their days away?" Luke rinsed his hands and stowed the 'eraser' on the back of the sink. "I don't get it."

"Well, I've been counting the days until school starts, so I get a break." She glanced around to make sure none of the children were in earshot. "Six hours of just the younger three sounds like a vacation right now."

"Mom's probably right, but I can see how fewer people in the house would mean less work and less mess. That has to be appealing on a hard day."

Tears, accompanied by indignant wails, interrupted their conversation. Laird brought Lorna, covered with scratches and scrapes, to Aggie and then disappeared out the back door, assuring them that he'd make sure the puppy corral was fixed. His words made no sense, but Aggie called thanks and started cleaning off Lorna's injuries. "What'd you do?"

"The puppies got out. I catched them. Then I fell." The child gave her injuries an angry scowl. "They's bad puppies."

Luke glanced out the window, and then beckoned for Aggie to come see. "That's some good thinking. I'm impressed."

As she dabbed Lorna's arms and legs dry, Aggie watched Laird dig a trench around the outside of the makeshift puppy enclosure and drop it below ground a foot. The chances of the puppies climbing a three-foot fence were much lower than them digging down a foot. Just as she started to comment, Laird enlisted the help of Ellie, Tavish, and Kenzie. The children began a search for something, but Aggie couldn't imagine what.

"What do you think they're looking for?"

A huge grin split Luke's face. "He is having them find rocks."

"Why?"

He started to answer, but Ellie brought back the first good-sized stone. "Watch, see?"

She did see. Laird took the stone, and then another rock from Kenzie, and laid them along the edge of the fence. Even if the dogs did try to dig under the chicken wire, they'd find a rock on the other side. "That's pretty impressive. Seems like a lot of work for a temporary situation, though."

"Well, it shows he's thinking. It won't hurt them at all, and who knows, now you'll have a nice little chicken yard."

"Oh, no. No chickens for me. Nuh uh." One last glance at the project in progress made Aggie shake her head. "I wouldn't have been surprised to see Tavish do that, but Laird..." She frowned. "Then again, he did make my shoe holder."

"That thing is ingenious. Corinne has put in an order for one as soon as she can find a chest big enough for me to convert."

Aggie frowned and began pulling leftover hot dogs from the fridge. "With your woodworking skills, why not just build it?"

"I am. She just doesn't know that. It didn't occur to her to have me do that, so I get the fun of surprising her."

"Laird is so funny. Half the time he's oblivious to the world around him, lost in whatever it is he does when he's not goofing off with the kids, and the other times, he really gets into a project and does a great job."

"He thrives on praise. It doesn't take much either. Just a few words telling him that he thought something out well or did a good thorough job, and he'll happily work for hours."

"I think working with you has been good for him." Aggie popped the plate of grilled dogs in the microwave and dragged out a bag of buns. "He seems more mature. I thought maybe it was too much, but your mom says he'll balance himself." Another glance out the window brought a fresh smile to her face. "I hope she's right. I like this side of him, but I'd miss the goofy kid that dusts ceiling fans with socks if he disappeared."

"Mom's probably right." Luke scrounged through the pantry. "Do you have a can of pork and beans?"

"A can. That's funny. Yes, there are a few cans in there. It'll take at least two, maybe three. I like to start with two though. Fewer leftovers is a plus. I'm no good at using up leftovers."

Luke grew quiet. He found the beans, opened them, dumped them in a pan, and set it on the stove. While she assembled hot dogs with condiments, he chopped a few stalks of celery into sticks and slathered most of them with cream cheese. Aggie noticed the plate with plain sticks and smiled. He knew how her children liked their food. There was something comforting in that.

"Mibs?"

"Hmm?"

"I have a confession."

A glance at his face told her he was upset by something. "Well, I hear it's good for the soul." Her joke fell flat, and she knew it.

"I just hope it's good for the friendship." He glanced at her before continuing. "I overheard your conversation with Vannie this morning."

At first, his words meant nothing to her. He watched her face as she tried to remember what conversation and what they'd discussed. At last, she shrugged. "Ok, enlighten me. I don't remember."

"She's very concerned with getting you paired off with someone, isn't she?"

Understanding sent a flush of embarrassment to her face. "I hope I didn't offend you. I wasn't trying to imply there's anything wrong with you. I was just trying to get her to see that men around didn't have to mean romance."

"I understood that, Aggie." The familiar working of his jaw, the silence, and the deliberate movements he made stirring the beans and replacing the celery in the fridge brought a new smile to her face. She could almost anticipate his conversational delays these days. "I just felt bad that I'd listened to a private conversation, and I think you told her something that may not be accurate."

"No worries on the conversation. If I'd wanted it truly private, I would have shut the door."

"That won't do much good in there without a door knob."

"Yeah, I need to put that back on. She's earned it, I think."

"I'll do it after lunch." He leaned his palms on the island and waited for Aggie to meet his gaze. "I want you to know, Mibs, not every man can only be either a friend or something more. Some men are willing to maintain a good friendship until the time is right for something more."

Mibs says: Mom?

Martha says: Mibs? What is Mibs?

Aggie says: Sorry, I change it to that for Luke.

Martha says: And why—oh! Cute. That's clever.

Aggie says: Well tell me, because I'm totally lost on it. I mean, seriously!

Martha says: You don't know why he calls you Mibs?

Aggie says: No, and he won't tell me.

Martha says: It's a perfect nickname.

Aggie says: Aggie is a nickname for Pete's sake!

Martha says: Well, Pete must not have told Luke that. Besides, I think it's charming that he nicknamed you at all. I'd gotten the impression he wasn't one of your local admirers yet.

Aggie says: Well, yesterday I would have agreed, but now I'm not so sure.

Martha says: What do you mean?

Aggie says: Well, he's always been friendly—like a big brother, you know?

Martha says: Yes, that's how he seemed to me. I respected him for it. He didn't ask you out did he? That'd ruin everything.

Aggie says: No, he didn't. I don't think he will either, but…

Martha says: Come on, Aggie. What's wrong?

Aggie says: Well, Vannie was on one of her, "How will you ever get married with all these kids," kicks. Honestly, that girl seems to think that marriage is the end-all of life or something.

Martha says: Well, it is a very important part of most women's lives. You always were a little more pragmatic about it than Allie or Tina. Most girls want to grow up, get married, and be a mommy at some part of their childhood at least. You always were happy at the thought—or not. Didn't matter to you.

Aggie says: I don't think that's totally accurate. I've been thinking about it, and I'm afraid that I never wanted to be disappointed, so I chose to think in terms of maybe rather than hopefully.

Martha says: That sounds like you. Even when you were a toddler, you'd rather I said no than maybe. "No maybe. Yes or no, mommy!"

Aggie says: *Groans* That sounds so much like Cari it isn't even funny.

Martha says: I've always seen a great deal of you in that child.

Aggie says: Oh, Mom. We both know I was the quiet and retiring Ellie!

Martha says: I did not laugh. I did NOT laugh! I am also a liar.

Aggie says: *giggles*

Martha says: So what happened to make you think Luke might have changed his focus on your friendship.

Aggie says: Well, it's not that exactly. I don't think he'll be any different tomorrow than he was today, yesterday, or last month but…

Martha says: I don't get it then.

Aggie says: Well, I tried to explain to Vannie that friendships with men don't have to be romantic, and she used Luke as an example of a man who was my friend but didn't want to go out with me.

Martha says: I would have made the same comparison.

Aggie says: I know, right? So, then she asked if I'd go out with Luke if he asked, and I said no. I told her that going out with guys who were friends seemed to mess up the friendship and he wouldn't want to anyway so it was good. Or something like that.

Martha says: So what's the problem?

Aggie says: Luke overheard us.

Martha says: Oh, no. He didn't come in and ask you out. Tell me he did not ask you out. I thought that boy had more sense.

Aggie says: He didn't. He just told me that I was wrong. He said that maybe some men could only be either a friend or a boyfriend, but not all men. He said some men can be just a friend while waiting for something more.

Martha says: So you think he was saying he's waiting?

Aggie says: Well at first, no. At first, I thought he was pointing out that William was willing to be a friend for now until I was ready to move into a different direction. That William was just giving me space until the right time.

Martha says: That makes sense. He seems to have a good pulse on what's going on around there. I've been tempted to add him to the messenger just to get his take on things sometimes.

Aggie says: Go ahead. He'd probably love it. Well, it may be that. I'm probably being overly sensitive to things right now, but after he left today, I was thinking about some of the things he's said and done, and I wondered if maybe I misread them at the time.

Martha says: Like what?

Aggie says: Well, mostly compliments and such. There was that time he caught me goofing off and

Aggie says: Oh, I'm being stupid.

Martha says: Just tell me, and I'll decide that.

Aggie says: I was singing that old Pippi Longstocking song, but I changed it to "Aggie-Millie-Mommy." Yeah, it was stupid, but I was happy and it was fun. He saw me, and looking back, some people might think he flirted with me.

Martha says: What did he say, Aggie?

Aggie says: Well, I was disgusted with my appearance at first, and I think he must have seen that because he said something like, "You look nice but then you always do." I was kind of taken aback.

Martha says: Doesn't sound too flirty to me. It sounds like something he'd say to anyone.

Aggie says: Well, that's not what got me. I walked away and said something like, "What got into him?" kind of under my breath, you know?

Martha says: Yeah, I can see that.

Aggie says: And then he was right there behind me. I tell you, that guy can sneak up on you even when you know he could! Anyway, he said, "I can't imagine."

Martha says: And that seems flirtatious to you?

Aggie says: Not alone, but considering who it is and similar things...

Martha says: Like what?

Aggie says: Ok, remember that movie, Funny Face with Fred Astaire? Now, I feel stupid. I bet you're right. It's probably nothing.

Martha says: Yeah, go on.

Aggie says: Well, we were watching it one night, and you know how much I love that scene where Fred Astaire knows she's at the chapel.

Martha says: Right.

Aggie says: Well, I must have sighed or made some sappy-eyed movement, because he asked if I was a romantic. I told him I thought the whole thing of knowing where she'd be was enchanting.

Martha says: Yes, it is, isn't it? Hollywood used to be good at that.

Aggie says: I wish they'd regain it. Anyway, we were talking about what enchanting really is, and Luke said that if my definition of enchanting was right, then I was enchanting because I know what people like and do it for them.

Martha says: Well, that's a little more personal. I can see maybe...

Aggie says: Then he said what made me wonder. I didn't think anything of it at the time, but now...

Martha says: Is it too personal, Aggie? You seem awfully reluctant to tell me about this. I thought maybe you were just feeling foolish, but if you just don't want to share...

Aggie says: Oh, no. You're right; I do feel foolish. And, I'm a little scared that maybe I'll mess things up.

Martha says: Well then, do tell. What'd he say?

Aggie says: I'll never forget it. I was lying on the couch, and he was in his chair. So, I just rolled my head back to see what he was trying to say, you know how he does that. Anyway, he just looked down at me and said, "Then again, you've enchanted me for a long time."

Martha says: But at the time, you didn't think anything of it?

Aggie says: No, not really. It just seemed like Luke's way. I hadn't really added his little comments together until today, but after him telling me that some men wait, I wondered.

Martha says: Well, I don't know. He's probably giving you a gentle hint to be careful of William's feelings. You know, don't lead him on and stuff, but that's a pretty personal comment. The only reason I don't assume that he meant more is that you didn't think anything of it at the time. I know you don't see a potential boyfriend behind every face, but you're not obtuse either.

Aggie says: What do I do?

Martha says: Why do you have to do anything?

Aggie says: I guess.

Martha says: Look, Aggie, if he wanted to turn this into something more, he'd have said so. As it was, he gave you a bigger picture of what you'd told Vannie. I just think if you think about this too much and get too worked up, you're going to make things miserable when he comes back to finish my room and the basement.

Aggie says: Your room, huh?

Martha says: That's right. My room. I intend to use it a lot.

Aggie says: I miss you, Mom.

Martha says: Isn't this technology stuff wonderful? We'd never get to converse this much a hundred years ago.

Aggie says: Uh oh, I think Kenzie is having another nightmare. I better go.

Martha says: Well, you sleep well, and don't worry about the Luke thing. If he wanted you to know he had feelings for you, he'd have told you. Luke doesn't seem like the kind of man who would be evasive about stuff like that.

Aggie says: No, you're right. He wouldn't. If he wants me to know something, he'll tell me. I think what he wanted me to know was that I only saw half the picture. Thanks, Mom.

Martha says: Night, Aggie.

Aggie says: Night.

WARDROBE WORKSHOP

Chapter Ten

Tuesday, August 26th

It felt like a sweatshop was in full production in the Milliken-Stuart household. While Aggie ran interference between the younger children, kept Ian from destroying half the house, and tried to catch up on laundry, Luke worked on the guest room. Libby and Vannie, with occasional stints by Aggie during naptime, cranked out skirt after dress after nightgown. Libby made shorts for Kenzie to wear under her dresses from the same fabric as the skirt of the dress, and Aggie questioned her.

"Why matching shorts? Why not just a couple of generic colors?"

"Well, two reasons. One, if you get behind on laundry, she'll be without them. Two, if you have shorts out of the same fabric as the skirt, then when the skirt comes up, you still see 'skirt' so to speak."

"Well, that's something I'd never have thought of!"

"You didn't raise three daughters!"

Vannie's eyes twinkled. "Well, she'll have raised at least five by the time we're all grown!"

The stunned look on Aggie's face sent Vannie and Libby into titters. "Oh, Aggie," Libby gasped. "Your face!"

"I just never thought about the fact that I have five daughters. Five! That's five weddings!"

"And five graduations, and five sweet sixteen parties, and then five proms—"

"Oh, will I get to go to prom, Aunt Aggie?" Vannie's eyes were wide with amazement.

"I don't know. What would your mother have said?"

"Mommy thought that they'd disintegrated into very inappropriate dancing and immodest clothes."

"Well, I'd say that was true at mine. We left early."

"Who did you go with?" Once again, Vannie latched onto anything that smelled like romance.

"Tina."

"As in Aunt Tina?" The girl's face couldn't have been more disappointed.

"Yep. We got dresses, corsages, had our hair done, went out to dinner, and then went to the prom. We lasted about an hour before we decided it was the dumbest thing we'd ever done."

"Why?" Libby and Vannie grinned as they spoke in unison.

"Well," Aggie almost felt cheapened knowing that her sister had probably disapproved of her evening. "I guess because the room was full of people dancing in ways we wouldn't, talking in ways we wouldn't, and behaving in ways they'd never behave if their parents could see them. It was revolting. Not everyone, mind you," she hastened to add. "Just so many that it ruined the atmosphere. We had more fun getting ready, taking pictures, and eating ice cream and watching a movie when we got home, than we did there."

"So, probably no prom." It was hard to tell if Vannie was disappointed or relieved.

"I can probably promise to go check out the prom the year before your turn and see what I think of it. If it looks like the clean fun it should be, you can probably go. After all, you'll be going to Brunswick High, not Rockland or Yorktown. It's a smaller town and those places tend to be a little more conservative."

"No one will probably ask me anyway." The dejection was unmistakable.

"Vannie?"

126

The girl glanced up at her aunt. "Hmm?"

"First, that's not true. I think it's unlikely that you won't get an invitation. Second, you're too concerned with what will happen years from now. You have at least four years. Don't worry about it yet." She grinned, "And last, even if you don't like the guys that ask you, you'll probably have friends to go with. It's more common for girls to go in groups now."

"I guess." The girl held up her finished skirt. "I'm going to go try it on with that shirt Aunt Tina found."

Once Vannie was upstairs, Libby turned to Aggie. "I know you feel insecure in your job. It's hard to know if you're doing the right thing, saying the right thing…"

"You're telling me."

"But Aggie, you're a natural at it when you're not concentrating so hard on doing everything perfectly. That was a brilliant conversation."

"Really? I thought I botched it."

Libby made an exaggerated roll of her eyes and threw up her hands as if to say, "What do I do with her, Lord?" She hugged Aggie briefly and said, "You gave her hope but made no promises. You showed her that you'd be reasonable but wouldn't compromise standards. You also didn't let her dwell on things that were untrue about herself—a lesson you could learn."

Before she could continue, Vannie called for her from her room. "Can you come see this, Mrs. Sullivan?"

"I think she's discovered that she used a zipper too long. I mentioned it once, but she thought she knew best."

"Ugh. The story of my life."

While Vannie and Libby sorted out the issue of the zipper, Aggie went to check on Luke's progress. It seemed odd that he was working on things without her, but she'd decided to focus on clothes until he went to work on the basement. It seemed as if things were going much slower without her—a fact that was gratifying.

"So, how is it going?"

"Well, the floor is sanded, and I have primer on the walls anyway. It's taking forever to get everything smooth."

"See, and you thought I was no help. Ha!"

Luke's eyes smiled before it reached his lips. "Aggie, we got what we got done as fast as we did because you never quit. You're like the Energizer bunny. You kept going, and going, and going..."

The happiness his words brought was evident immediately. "I wondered if I didn't slow you down. It's not like I know much."

For a moment, it looked as if Luke was going to say something, but he turned and opened a new tack cloth. Starting at the far corner, he began wiping, and as he did, he spoke. "Aggie, I overheard some of your conversation with Mom and Vannie."

"That's becoming a habit of yours, isn't it?" Her hand flew to her mouth. What had been meant as a joke sounded like a rebuke. "Oh, Luke. I'm sorry. I was teasing but—"

"Well, it's true, isn't it? It isn't intentional, but still..."

"But, I know you weren't being nosey. You know that anything that goes on in this house is open to your knowledge, right?"

He glanced back at her. "That is quite a trust you've given me. Thanks." Several more swipes of the cloth came before he spoke again. "Mom's right, you know. You're good with her. You're good with all of them. I think your sister was a blessed woman to have someone like you to trust her children with."

Thursday, August 28th

Late Thursday afternoon, Tina and Luke admired the row of outfits hanging on the doorjamb to the library. How they'd accomplished so much in so little time, Aggie couldn't tell. She'd finished two skirts and two t-shirt dresses in three weeks. During that time, Vannie had completed three dresses and four skirts. Libby, on the other hand, had created six outfits for Kenzie, three each for the twins, and a couple of church dresses for Vannie. Somewhere in that mess of things, each girl managed to acquire three nightgowns. Aggie was both discouraged and impressed.

"How did you get so much done when you weren't here for a week!"

Libby looked a little embarrassed at Aggie's effusive praise. "Well, if you want the truth, I sew faster at home and alone. Most of this I did while helping Corinne." She glanced over their work.

128

"This'll only get them to the first cold part of winter. They'll need warmer things by then. We have more sewing to do."

Aggie's gulp was clearly visible. "Oh, help. I don't think I can do it again!"

"You're learning," Libby insisted charitably.

"At the rate of a snail across a porch, maybe."

Tina interjected an opinion before Aggie could disparage her work further. "Well, considering that you created something wearable, cute, and that won't fall apart without repeated applications of glue, I'd say you've come a long way, baby." She elbowed Libby as she continued. "I've a mind to take pictures and email them to Ms. Slade."

"You do that. Meanwhile, I fully intend to collapse on the couch until one of the kids demands my attention." She sighed. "Tina, remember my idea for moving into a tiny house so the kids would have to stay in eyeshot or earshot?"

"Yeah?"

"I think I should have done that. This getting up every few minutes is for the birds."

The other two women exchanged glances, and before Aggie knew what happened, the children were changed into swimsuits and packed into the van. "We'll bring them home in time for bed and not a minute before. Take my car, go see a movie, go out to dinner, or go take a long, hot bath."

"Oh, you don't—"

"We want to, Aggie. Goodbye!" Libby's cheerful voice rang out on her way to the van. Squeals of excitement faded as they drove down the driveway and off to town.

Luke glanced at her. "Ok, what's it going to be?"

"What's what going to be?"

"What do you want to do? Movie, dinner, bath—" He frowned. "That did not come out right."

Laughing, Aggie dragged herself back off the couch and pointed to the basement. "Let's see if we can get that drywall finished."

"Oh, no. I am *not* going to risk a tongue-lashing from mom. No siree."

"Coward." Her eyes challenged him to recant.

129

"I do not deny it. If you'd lived with my mom for twenty-eight years, you'd never consider crossing her. It isn't allowed."

"But I want to get it done. I want this house project finished. I'm tired of all the upheaval."

"Yeah, it'd probably be nice to have your family back to yourself more often, wouldn't it?"

She'd forgotten that with the house finished, Luke wouldn't be there every day. "I—"

"It's ok, Aggie. I understand. Anyone—"

"No, Luke. I just forget that finishing meant you wouldn't be around anymore." She sighed. "We'll miss you."

"I'll have to bribe the kids to unplug appliances and unscrew door knobs so you'll call and ask me to come help."

"You don't need an invitation, silly man." Aggie grabbed an armful of the hanging clothes and started for the stairs. "I have a bad feeling that we've taken terrible advantage of you. I hope you'll come back and just be here because we like having you around, not because we need something from you."

Obviously amused by her inability to ignore work, Luke grabbed the rest of the garments and followed her upstairs. "You should be reading a book, taking a bath, or ordering food that you never get to have anymore. You should not be doing laundry."

"This isn't laundry! I'm putting away the fruits of our labors. First stop, Cari and Lorna's room."

Each garment was hung in its proper room, the nightgowns removed from their hangers and folded into proper drawers. She carried the empty hangers back down to the laundry room and turned to find Luke watching her with an unreadable expression in his face. Assuming he was ready to scold again, she feigned defeat. "Ok, ok. How about this? You go get us Chinese food, and I'll take a shower and find those movies Mom got me for my birthday."

"Deal. Do you like it spicy or mild?"

Aggie shrugged. "I'm good with either. Just make sure there's crab and cheese fried wontons."

"Rangoons?"

"Yeah. Those."

Grinning, Luke stuffed his hand into his pocket, retrieved his phone and keys, and dialed a number before he made it to his truck. Eager to be dressed and downstairs before he returned, Aggie rushed up to the top floor, panting after two flights of stairs, and threw open her dream of a closet. The mostly empty shelves and sparsely filled rods looked a little forlorn, particularly when most of the clothes on them looked so ratty. She started to reach for her most comfortable skirt and then paused. It was stained with paint, ripped in two places, and had a bleach spot the size of a coffee cup on the back. What was the point of having time to herself if she had to look tatty to do it?

Most of her clothing fit in two categories—dilapidated and dressy. She flipped through piece after piece until she found a skirt that she'd forgotten she owned. It was a perfect compromise. Once the basement was done, she'd wear things like it every day. Her favorite white blouse wasn't too wrinkled after hanging for a few days. "I need to rediscover the joys of ironing," she muttered.

She was downstairs, the movie zipped past the thousand and one previews, plates and utensils waiting on the coffee table, and drinks on coasters before Luke returned carrying a huge brown paper bag of food. "You're fast," he teased, pulling a placemat from the drawer in the kitchen and grabbing a couple of serving spoons.

"We probably won't finish before the kids get home, but I thought we could try."

"What are we watching?" Luke pulled out two containers. "Sesame Chicken or Beef Broccoli?" He smiled as she reached for the container closest to her. "That's a pretty skirt, Mibs."

"Both, of course." Aggie was not about to let the topic drift to anything personal. She was still just a little jittery after his last discussion.

"Is it new?"

"Is what new?" She dug through the bag looking for her wontons.

"The skirt? I've never seen it before."

"Well, I can hardly wear it painting, or I'd ruin it, wouldn't I?"

He shrugged. "So, it's not new then."

"Who cares?" With a wonton in each hand, she offered one to him. "Want one?"

"Sure." His grin told her he was enjoying her discomfiture. "I know how much it's frustrated you to have to wear the same worn things all the time. I just thought it must be nice to wear something different and wondered if it was new."

Aggie felt terrible. "Sorry. I think I'm a bit sensitive about my wardrobe these days. I keep expecting Geraldine to show up any minute and tell the world that my clothes are proof that I can't afford to take care of these kids."

"Well, Geraldine can't show up without going to jail, so I think I wouldn't care what she thought."

"True." She took a bite of broccoli and sighed. "Oh, this is so good."

"I overheard someone last week say that Wong's was the best beef broccoli they'd ever had, so I tried it."

She gave him a sidelong glance. Was he really going to let her avoid the question? "Luke?"

"Hmm?"

"It's not new. Well, that is I haven't purchased it recently. I bought it just before Allie—" she swallowed hard. "Well, I just haven't had much chance to wear it. I think I had it on when I went van shopping. Maybe that's why Jeff the Jerk was so insufferable."

"Jeff the Jerk?"

With her legs curled beneath her, Aggie sank into the couch cushions and allowed herself to relax. "Well, I had to have a new van. All I had was the little Beetle convertible I'd driven since high school— doesn't really hold everyone."

"I imagine not."

"Well, I got out at this one place and this guy, Jeff, came up to me. He kept trying to sell me whatever they must have been pushing that week. First a Miata, then an SUV. When I told him I wanted a van for my eight kids, I think he asked if I knew what caused 'that.'"

"You have to be kidding me."

"Nope. Then, when he found out they weren't my biological kids, he asked why my sister was so selfish as not to leave their van to me for the kids. It was just horrible."

"Oh, Mibs, I'm so sorry." He sounded angry rather than sorry.

"It's so common now, the kids and I make fun of it, but that was the first time I had to hear how excessively prolific I seemed to people."

"You sure his name wasn't Chuck?"

"Sure. Why?"

Luke grinned. "There's a guy named Chuck. I think he works for a car dealer too. Let's just say that that sounds exactly like

132

something he'd say." Luke pointed to the remote. "So, what are we watching?"

"*For Me and My Gal.*"

"What's it about?"

"Gene Kelly is a vaudeville—"

Luke pretended to groan. "Gene Kelly and vaudeville. Let me guess. It's a musical."

"It won't work, mister. You voluntarily stuck Fred Astaire in while I was gone one night."

With a fresh pile of fried rice on his plate, Luke leaned back in 'his' chair, put his feet up, and nodded. "A guy has to try. I'd be kicked out of the man-cave club if I didn't at least pretend to hate musicals once in a while."

"Well, that'll last you for a week or three."

"I bet William truly does despise them, doesn't he?" There was an indefinably odd sound to Luke's voice.

"I don't know, but if I had to bet, I'd say he couldn't stand them. I really have a hard time imagining tough-guy William watching Gene Kelly dressed as a clown and dancing."

The opening music began, and Aggie sighed. "I have a feeling he's the one missing out on things."

When war broke out in Europe, Luke reached for the remote, brushing her hand away, and paused it. "Thanks."

"What for?"

"For picking one that has a little action beyond guy meets girl and singing and dancing his way into her heart."

"There's a side of you that abandons the prose, isn't there?"

Luke laughed. "Look who is talking. 'Abandons the prose.' Are you sure you were a history major?"

"Definitely. Grammar is not my forte."

Without any contradiction, Luke punched the pause button again and set his plate on the table. The movie continued for the next half hour in absolute silence. Gene Kelly had just stopped the convoy when the lights of the van pulled into the driveway.

"Drat." Aggie's hand flew to her mouth. "Oh, that was bad."

"There's nothing evil about wanting to finish a movie, Mibs. Don't be so hard on yourself."

"It just seems rude— irresponsible even."

Luke's response was drowned out by the shrieks and greetings of weary but hyped-up children. The movie paused while children clamored for hugs, kisses, and goodnight prayers. Luke and Libby, rookies to Lorna, Cari, and Kenzie's unorthodox prayer style, found themselves covering their mouths, trying not to laugh.

Cari started with thanks for ice cream, swimming at the pool, and puppies before her prayers took a unique turn. "Thank you fow puppies. Don't let them die fwom bad shots. Fowgive Aunt Aggie fow huwting puppies. I's sowwy I kicked hew. She was bad, but I's sowwy anyway." She leaned close to Lorna and whispered, "Did I sound sowwy enough?"

Her twin, with a glance at Aggie's face whispered back, "You should say really sorry. That means it's true."

The child's face frowned, and her fingers clasped tighter as she held her hands folded in Aggie's lap. "I— I—" Cari whispered to Lorna once more. "I bettew not say it then, cause I weally don't feel sowwy. I just want the puppies to be ok."

A strangled cough nearly upset Aggie's composure. Her eyes slid sideways at Luke as if to say, "Don't you dare make me laugh, buster."

"Ok, Jesus. That's all. Goodnight. Amen." Bright but sleepy eyes smiled up to Aggie, confirming to all that confession is indeed good for the soul.

With another round of hugs for anyone willing to accept them, Cari followed Tina upstairs to change into a new nightgown and brush her teeth. Lorna, next on the prayer agenda, seemed fixated on her sister's unrepentant kick. "Jesus, forgive Cari. She's not sorry, but I am. Can I be sorry for her? Thank you. Thank you, Jesus. Goodnight. Amen."

As if in a reality show designed to compete for most bizarre children's prayers, Kenzie hardly let Lorna move from her spot before she dropped to her knees and began an imitation of one of the elderly men at *The Church*. "Oh, Jesus. Oh, my Jesus. Thank you Jesus for Jesus. You are my hard place in the rock. You are my soul's satisfaction. Thank you for your intense blessings. Forgive us our tresses and deliver us from thy kingdom forever amen."

Pleased as punch at the impressive sounding prayer she thought she'd delivered, Kenzie very primly bade everyone goodnight, and with mincing steps, made her way to the stairs. The room erupted in unfortunate laughter when, looking back over her shoulder to see the effect she had on her audience, she tripped and landed on her posterior. Tears of mortification combined with wails of misery until Tina hurried down the stairs, scooped her up, and tried, unsuccessfully, to carry her up the stairs.

"Sorry, kiddo, you're just too much of a big girl to carry."

"They laughed at me!"

"Kenzie, you were putting on quite a show. Of course, they did. If you don't want people to think you're goofing off, then you have to be sincere about serious things like prayer..." Tina's voice faded as she led the embarrassed girl up the stairs and into her room.

"Well, that was original," Libby commented with a last chuckle at the memory of the unusual heavenly petitions.

Aggie scooted over closer to Luke's chair and patted the couch. "Come watch with us."

The woman began to demur, but something in her son's face changed her mind. "What are we watching?"

"For Me and My Gal. It's almost over. I'd suggest starting over, but I think Luke would kill me."

Luke snatched up the remote again, and punched the menu button. He found the option for the beginning and clicked. "Never say that I hate musicals, Aggie. This is one of the best I've ever seen."

With a girlish sigh, Libby pulled a throw pillow from the corner of the couch, bunched it under her arm, and curled into the opposite corner from Aggie. "I haven't seen this in so many years..."

Aggie says: I know you're probably not home yet, but I wanted to thank you for taking the kids to the pool and out to dinner. Having a few hours to myself really refreshed me.

Libby says: Well, I knew I was a nobody, but I didn't realize just how much.

Aggie says: Huh?

Luke says: Just dropped mom off, and she had me come in and help put a few things away. I saw your ding and had to tease you.

Aggie says: Well, you're right. That was really ungracious of me. I'm tired and not thinking very clearly.

Luke says: Mibs, don't. I was just joking. It wasn't a rebuke. I knew what you meant.

Aggie says: You're right. I seem to be a little out of sorts tonight.

Luke says: I should have gone with them so you could have peace and quiet.

Aggie says: Nah, watching movies with you is fun.

Luke says: Uh, oh. Mom's ready for me. She'll be here after she tells me what to do. She's good at that, you know. She's had my lifetime to perfect it.

Aggie says: Oh, you're going to be so busted when she sees that...

Luke says: Sees what?

Luke says: I am not Luke. Hmph.

Aggie says: He closed out, didn't he?

Libby says: What is my Luke up to now?

Aggie says: He was saying something about how you had a lifetime to perfect how to tell him what to do.

Libby says: Oh, he did, did he?

Libby says: Traitor

Libby says: My Luke is being very naughty.

Aggie says: He's hanging around with bad influences.

Libby says: You're hardly a bad influence, Aggie.

Aggie says: Who says I meant me? I was thinking of Cari and her unrepentant kicking.

Libby says: Please tell me you wrote that down somewhere.

Aggie says: My journal is upstairs, but I'll try to remember.

Libby says: I've taken to keeping a computer document open to type out the funny things the kids say when they're at my house. I print them out and send them home with their mothers so they can have a record of it.

Aggie says: That'd work. My laptop is usually open on the counter for recipe reference, email, chatting with my mom, or music playing.

Libby says: I hadn't thought about music on mine. I'm still in the dark ages of CD players in a stereo system.

Aggie says: Tina considers me "dark ages." I don't have an iPod or any other "i" product.

Libby says: I'll have Luke show me how to put some of my favorites on the laptop. That'd be better than blasting music from one end of the house to the other.

Aggie says: True. Anyway, I know it's really late. I didn't mean to keep you. I just wanted to thank you for taking the kids tonight. I really appreciate it. It was nice to relax, watch a movie with a friend, and not have to fear the silence from the rest of the house.

Libby says: Oh, yes. The silence. That is one of the most terrifying "sounds" to a mother's heart. Well, I am glad you and my Luke got to rest. I was half-afraid you'd con him into working, and you both need the time off.

Aggie says: Libby, do I expect too much out of him? He'd tell me, wouldn't he?

Libby says: Mom showed me your question. I'd tell you, Mibs. As you've seen, when I need to be gone, I am whether it's more work or a day with Rodney or fishing with Chad. I've done them all this summer, so we're good.

Aggie says: Thanks. Well, goodnight. I'm going to bed before it's too late to bother.

Libby says: Night, Aggie.

Losing Her Marbles

Chapter Eleven

Friday, August 29th

Lost in what seemed to be a recurring bad dream, Aggie heard the cries of children and groaned. "Why don't people keep an eye on their children?" she muttered as she rolled over. "If I ever have children—" That thought dragged her, mentally kicking and screaming, from that wonderful world of somnolence into the world of consciousness.

"Cari! Lorna! Where are you?" She threw back the covers, her eyes gritty enough to make it impossible to see clearly, and stumbled from her room and to the stairs.

Two little girls, looking absolutely adorable in their new nightclothes, regardless of, or perhaps because of, the grumpy looks and tears streaming down their faces. "Aunt Aggie, we's feels awful." Cari, as usual, spoke for both girls.

"Well, come curl up with me in my bed, and we'll all feel better in no time." Aggie hoped to settle them enough to doze for another half an hour or so.

The moment they hit the sheets, each girl curled up against her as if they'd feel better the closer they were. The extra body heat was stifling. Summer was the wrong time for early morning snuggles under the covers. Just as she decided to get up and get them some breakfast, she realized that it wasn't just their proximity. The girls were over-warm.

"Aunt Aggie, I scratch."

"You scratched yourself?"

"No," Lorna shook her head a little gingerly. "I scratch. My tummy scratches."

"Oh, it itches?"

The girl's forehead furrowed. "Well, I itched it some, but it doesn't help."

Laughing, Aggie corrected the child's terminology. "No, sweetie, your tummy itches and you scratched it. Itching is when it's irritating and feels funny. Scratching is what you do to try to stop it."

"Ok, then I itches and scratches isn't helping."

"Well, let me see it." Aggie prayed they hadn't found poison ivy or something equally contagious. The last thing the kids needed before starting school on Tuesday was a nice case of poison ivy.

Sure enough, a rash covered their little bellies, the upper parts of their arms, and the upper parts of their legs. "Oh, no! What have you guys been into?

Indignation darkened Cari's face. "We's hasn't been into anyfing! We's been asweep!"

"But yesterday. What did you do yesterday?" Aggie examined them closer, trying to see what they could possibly have.

"We played wif the puppies, went swimming, and had ice cweam." The child's recent ability to pronounce the "th" sound appeared to have evaporated overnight.

"Well, I don't know what this is. It could be a heat rash, I guess. It didn't cool off much last night..." Frustrated, she crawled from the bed again. "You two stay right here. I'm going to go get Tina. Maybe she knows."

Tina took one look and reached for Aggie's phone. "Call the expert. Libby will probably know just from a description or something. She seems to know everything."

Feeling like a needy nuisance, Aggie punched the number for Libby and waited for the woman to answer. "Good morning, Libby. I'm sorry for calling so early, but we have a situation here."

"What's up?"

Hearing the woman's voice made Aggie disgusted. It was her opinion that no human should be anywhere near that chipper on that particular morning. "The twins have some kind of rash. I don't even know what to call it to Google it. Can I beg you to come over and see? It's either you or the clinic, and you know how they already think I'm an idiot."

"Now, silly, I'll be over in a bit."

"Just as I suspected. Chicken pox." She smiled reassuringly. "So, who has had it and who hasn't?"

With a shrug, Aggie picked up her phone to ask her mother, but Vannie answered. "None of us have had it yet. Mommy wouldn't let us get the vaccine—something about overloading the body and effectiveness. Anyway, the doctor said that it's harder to catch now than it used to be."

The girl's words sank into Aggie's heart, weighting it down with new cares. "So, does that mean it's more dangerous to get now if you don't have the vaccine? Should I get the other kids shots right away to prevent them from getting it? School starts on Tuesday!"

Libby put her arm around Aggie's shoulder and led her to the kitchen. "Why don't you start on breakfast? I'll send Tina for some Caladryl and the girls will be comfortable in no time." At the look of protest on Aggie's face when she glanced at the confused and miserable little girls huddled on the couch, Libby added, "Don't worry. They're going to be fine. Getting the chicken pox when you're still young is usually harmless. Uncomfortable, but harmless.

"Ok... is it really contagious? Should we separate them?"

"Well, we can try, but it's probably not very effective. You're contagious for a day or two before the rash appears. All the children were in the car with them yesterday."

Those words didn't help Aggie's confidence. "And how long before the next person breaks out if they were exposed yesterday?"

"Aggie," Libby's voice was deliberately patient, and Aggie knew it. "They could have been exposed anytime in the last two weeks! Whoever exposed Cari and Lorna, probably Corinne's children," Libby sounded as apologetic as she looked, "most likely exposed the others too." Smiling, she added, "On the bright side, if Vannie and Laird haven't gotten them by now, they might have acquired an immunity somehow. Maybe a nurse gave them the vaccine without knowing she wasn't supposed to or something."

While Aggie pulled out boxes of cereal, milk, and the leftover honeydew melon from the previous day's snack, Libby took charge in the living room. "Well, now. I think we'll turn the library into sort of a sick room. There's no reason not to try to isolate the little ones on the off chance that they haven't already spread it.

"Oh," she continued, hardly pausing, "does the clinic have their medical records? You might consider having them sent, just in case someone gets really sick and you have to take them in."

Nothing, not even Libby's chipper attitude, could wipe the feeling of dread in Aggie's heart. As the children munched on their cereal, she read about chicken pox online, staring at the pictures of rashes as if they were the cause of her latest trial. She mentally calculated how long the disease could take if each child got them one at a time, and, a little over-dramatically, prayed that everyone was healthy by Christmas.

Luke arrived a while later with a bag full of items designed to soothe the children and make their ordeal more bearable. As he unloaded the items on the desk in the library, he glanced toward the living room and frowned. Aggie sat, head in her hands, the picture of dejection. Libby gave him an understanding smile and took a box of oatmeal bath powder. "Come on, girls. Let's get you a nice comfortable bath, and then I'll put pink lotion on all of your spots."

The other children had disappeared outside to play with the puppies. They all seemed quite determined to avoid getting what Kenzie persisted in calling, "the chicken *box*." Occasionally, someone peeked in the window to watch the spot-covering procedure, but the Milliken-Stuart household, sans Ian, had never been so free of ever-present children. The difference was so marked that Aggie said in disgust, "Now Murphy will come over to accuse me of stifling them. I can hear it now, 'It was too quiet, your honor.'"

As promised, the bath seemed to soothe the girls, and while Aggie made calls requesting medical records, Libby covered each individual pock that she could find with a drop of calamine infused with antihistamine. Tina took guard duty over Ian and Kenzie while Luke settled the little ones in the library with a stack of books, promising to read every single one. Between two Dr. Seuss silly tales, Libby gave them each a dose of Tylenol and brought them fruit and juice to enjoy.

As Luke finished yet another story, he glanced at the girls and quietly closed the book. Each girl lay curled in her own beanbag chair, sleeping. He glanced up at his mother as she cut out flannel nightgowns for winter and said, "This isn't exactly getting the basement done, is it?"

"I'm sure Aggie appreciates the help. She's going to need it. I tried to downplay her fears of weeks or even over a month of pox, but I think it's likely."

"How many of us got them together, Mom? I only have a vague recollection of it at all. It itched."

Libby's eyebrows drew together in a concentrated effort to remember. "I'm not sure, but I think it was two at a time. I know it was several years apart." She glanced in the living room where Aggie clicked her way through page after page of information on her laptop. "Go talk to her, son. I think this is overwhelming her, and I should finish folding these clothes and keep an eye on the girls."

He crossed the room and wrapped his arms around his mother. "You're the greatest; did you know that?"

"Oh, Luke—"

"No, really. Remember that song that Dad used to sing about wanting a girl like his dad married? That's exactly what I want—a girl just like Dad's best girl." A discernable sadness filled his eyes. "Dad would be so proud of you. He loved knowing you had a heart for young mothers."

With pink-tinged cheeks, Libby pushed her son away saying, "You certainly learned your father's gift for flattery. Go whisper sweet nothings to someone else; I'm not listening."

Aggie, once again, sat with her head in her hands, looking like the picture of dejection and despair. He looked back to the library and saw his mother watching. Her encouraging nod gave Luke the confidence to try to comfort her. At first he patted her back, trying to think of something encouraging to say, but then realized she was praying. Relief washed over him as Luke tugged her hand out from under her chin. Prayer was something he could handle.

Minutes passed before Aggie raised her head and smiled at him. Without a word, she rose, dragged herself into the kitchen, and he heard her pulling things from the freezer. The familiar clink of her whisk against the glass pitcher she liked to use for lemonade gave him hope that she'd come to terms with the children's illness.

As she handed him a drink, Luke noticed that the rueful expression she'd developed as his mother pronounced her diagnosis wasn't gone. Instead, she looked even more distressed than ever. "Hey, Mibs, are you ok?"

Aggie shook her head. "Actually, no. I called Mom to tell her about the latest drama in this house and see what she knows about school and chicken pox and stuff." Frustration was etched in her features. "Luke, Mom says I never had chicken pox either. I just never got it." If her distress hadn't been so genuine, she would have looked comical in her fresh waves of despair. "I was all over those little girls this morning, trying to figure out what the rash was. I scrubbed my hands and arms and changed my clothes but—" Aggie hardly paused in her frantic monologue of the day's ills. "They all went swimming together, were cooped up in that van all the way there and home... If you're contagious before you break out, then can I let them go to school on Tuesday? I mean, that's just crazy, right? How much school will they miss?"

"Whoa, Mibs. That's a lot of maybes and what ifs. We can take it one day at a time. Mom already said she'd help; this kind of thing is her specialty. I can be here working on the basement half the time, and when I'm not, I'll just be three streets over working on my new house, so—"

"You got it? You didn't tell me! I'm so excited. Does that mean the other two sold then?" The awe in her voice was a familiar one. He bought and renovated homes in less time than most people managed to find a house, move in, and get unpacked.

Luke nodded. "I'd planned to see if you'd let Laird help me after school sometimes. He really seems to enjoy the work, and it'd be a nice way for him to earn a little extra money." He took a swig of the lemonade, grateful for the refreshment, and added, "I really do enjoy his company."

"I can't expect you guys—"

"You don't have to expect. We're offering." Luke pointed at the open page on her laptop. "Did you read about shingles? You want to avoid getting this if you can. It's not the end of the world, but if it developed into shingles, you'd really be a mess."

"Why does all this stuff happen to us? We get three or four times more accidents and problems than most people!"

"You have three to four times more people! Of course you have more incidents."

Aggie shook her head. "In six months we've had an ant infestation, grandma drama, a major move, complete house renovation, trips to the clinic for head injury, a lost baby, the haircut fiasco, not to mention my two sprained ankles, nail poke, and tetanus shot. I really didn't need this added to it."

"Don't forget that you're on a regular 9-1-1 house check list thanks to the baby."

She shook her head. "I'm convinced it's a glitch in the phone line or something. That child was sleeping the last two times it happened."

Aggie's review of the family's recent troubles seemed to overcome her. She sniffled about incubation times, exposure, and the futility of keeping isolated when she'd already spent the morning snuggling with her sick girlies before finding out what was wrong. For what seemed like the millionth time, Aggie said looking despondent, "I still think my sister blew it when she named me guardian of these children."

A voice startled them from the doorway. So intent were they on their conversation, neither Aggie nor Luke noticed the quiet in the yard or the sound of Geraldine's trademarked pumps on the porch steps. "That is the most intelligent and honest thing I've ever heard you say. You're right; it was a mistake, and I fully intend to tell the judge I heard you say so."

In a move that seemed detached from herself, Aggie grabbed the phone on the coffee table and punched the speed dial for the sheriff's office. Then, while waiting to request assistance, she walked to the library and pulled the pocket doors closed, trying to prevent the woman from waking the sleeping girls. An amused smile twisted

145

the corner of her mouth. How ironic that the paragon of appearances would be caught eavesdropping!

When the dispatcher came on the line, Aggie stepped into the bathroom, and requested that a deputy come out to enforce a restraining order. "It's going to be ugly. I'm trying to be pleasant, but it's going to go south fast if you aren't here to prevent it."

Knowing she'd never be able to forcibly eject the woman from her home, Aggie chose to take the higher road, and upon her return to the living room, offered Geraldine a glass of lemonade. Of course, the woman refused, pulling a pile of papers from a briefcase-like tote. "I have an order from the judge. I have thirty-six hours of unsupervised visitation every other weekend. I am here to pick up the children."

The woman passed the papers to a stunned Aggie and narrowed her eyes, raking them over Luke in disgust. "At least in my care, the children won't be exposed to your philandering right in your *living room*!"

The ludicrous idea of what the woman imagined sent Aggie into nervous hysterical laughter. The library door slid open and then shut again behind her as Libby stepped into the room. Concern was written in her features. "Is something wrong, Aggie? You sound a little overwrought."

"I shouldn't wonder. People tend to become hysterical when caught in compromising positions."

Libby turned to see who had maligned her son and friend. With a voice as gracious as she could muster, she nodded to the unwelcome guest and introduced herself. "Why, hello. I don't believe we've met. I am Libby Sullivan, a friend of Aggie's. Have you met my Luke?" She gestured toward the man who now poured over the papers Aggie handed him. With the grace shown to the unwanted intruder, no one suspected the instant and pronounced dislike Libby felt for the overbearing woman.

"I am Geraldine Stuart." A tone in her voice seemed to expect that name to explain all. "I am here to collect my grandchildren. I have received visitation rights, as is explained in those documents, and I mean to take them away from this horrible place now."

Turning to Aggie, she added, "Since I seriously doubt you could have them ready in a reasonable amount of time, we will provide them with everything they will need. Douglas is picking up the van we purchased and will be here shortly. Please take me to the children so I can have them ready before he returns."

Libby started to object, but Luke interrupted. "Aggie, may I see you in the kitchen?"

Weary of the constant drama and almost ready to concede, Aggie followed him to the island where Luke spread out the paperwork Geraldine had given her. He leaned closely, making it look like an intimate conversation to anyone who could have seen, and whispered, "These don't look like final court documents, Mibs. Look at the date. Doesn't that mean she filed with the court just yesterday?"

Aggie looked closer. "It doesn't have any other date on them. Just yesterday's."

"There's no judge's signature anywhere, and wouldn't you have been notified or something?" He glanced around the corner, through the dining room, and into the living room. "She's looking more agitated. When will William be here?"

"I'm not sure. It's his day off, but they usually call him in since he's dealt with her." She covered her face with her hands. "How can she do this? I almost fell for it too." With fresh tears of frustration hovering in the corners of her eyes, Aggie looked up at Luke. "We're going to end up in court, aren't we?"

As if her words solidified her fears, Aggie began weeping in earnest. Luke leaned into the dining room to request his mother's help when he overheard Geraldine Stuart begin a rant about "emotional, incompetent, overgrown teenagers" that nearly caused him to lose his temper and eject her from the home. Before he could take a step toward them, Libby pursed her lips, shook her head, and then mouthed, "Comfort her."

Using every ounce of his inner strength, Luke turned away from the woman he wanted to throttle, returned to Aggie's side, gathered her into his arms, and held her as she sobbed out her anxieties and frustrations. "It's ok, Mibs. We've got this. No one is going to hurt you or those kids while Mom and I are here to stop it. It's going to be ok."

For the next minute or two, he awkwardly patted her back, stroked her hair, and murmured words of encouragement as Aggie sobbed out all the pent up angst of the morning. The sight of Geraldine frowning in the kitchen doorway irritated him, but when she let loose another slew of lewd accusations against Aggie, the limits of his patience snapped. With a glance at his mother that said, "Don't let her follow," he led Aggie to the swing in the backyard with instructions not to move until someone came to get her.

Luke intended to try to intimidate Geraldine into leaving the house, but when he returned to the living room where Libby and Geraldine sat in a silent duel of wills, he watched William's Corvette pull into the driveway and that diverted him. "I'll be right back, Mom."

As William exited his car, Megan arrived in her vehicle, in uniform and ready to take on the nightmare of arresting Geraldine Stuart. Luke jogged up to them and shook his head. "This is going to get ugly. She has 'papers' that she thinks gives her access to the children, but I think they've just been filed, not approved. The date on them is yesterday. I don't know if she just wants to see the kids so badly that she is willing to try to use them to gain access, if she really believes filing is all she needs to do, or if this is a way to do worse."

"We'll take care of her, Luke. Why don't you go get the papers you have?" William's face was grim.

Luke started back toward the house and then turned. "Lorna and Cari are sleeping. They woke up with the chicken pox today. They need their rest." He kicked a rock from the drive. "I have this horrible feeling. There is nothing to base it on aside from past history, but I think if Geraldine gets those kids in the van her husband is supposed to be bringing, we'll never see them again."

William's expression registered shock as he led Megan to the porch. Luke took his expression to mean that he'd been over-imaginative, but then the off-duty deputy said, "Man, Sullivan, I don't think I've heard you speak that many words voluntarily at once." The lighthearted joke brought a smile to Luke's face before William added, "She has a restraining order, right?"

"I thought so, but she didn't mention it..."

"Where's Aggie?"

"Out back. I told her not to come in again. The vile things that woman said—" Luke choked back the words. "Let's just say I restrained myself, but barely."

William did an about face and jogged back down the steps. "Wait there, Megan. I'll get the order, and then you can arrest her."

Aggie sat in the swing on the back corner of the house, tense, rigid, fuming. Her earlier despair had given way to anger. At the sight of William, she unleashed her wrath. "Who does that woman think she is! Did you hear what she said? Did Luke tell you what she did? I almost bought it! I want her off my property immediately."

Tear stains on her cheeks told William that things had been as bad as Luke described. He sat next to her, put an arm around her shoulder, and gave her a gentle squeeze. "We'll take care of it, Aggie. Where's the restraining order?"

His calm direct manner helped her regain control. "Ok, in the kitchen, there's that little desk over by the mudroom door? The bottom right drawer has files in it. It's in the file marked GIL." She blushed. "It's the only file that is marked — getting paperwork organized hasn't been a priority, but I thought that one was."

"You were right. We'll be back in a bit. Stay put."

"Everyone keeps telling me to stay out of the way. I can't decide whether to be relieved or insulted."

William took her chin and turned it toward him. "Ags, we wouldn't do it if we didn't care. Just think about your favorite coffee and the relief that comes next Tuesday."

"Tuesday?"

William grinned. "School! Every mother's favorite day of the year, isn't it?"

Without waiting for an answer, William opened the mudroom door, went to the desk in the kitchen, and found the restraining order exactly where Aggie had said it would be. Carrying it to the living room, he looked through the window, signaled for Megan to step inside, and then stood before the intruder. "Mrs. Stuart, I regret to inform you that you are in violation of this restraining order. The laws of this state require that I arrest you and take you in. You have a right to remain silent..." William droned on in his professional monotone as he read Geraldine her Miranda rights as the woman screamed threats to everyone present.

"You are in breach of a court order! You can't do this! I have the right to come! Look at the court papers!" the woman screeched as she tried to avoid being handcuffed. She fought, kicked, and eventually landed a solid kick to William's shin.

Turning to Luke with derision dripping from every word, he said, "Looks like she wants to add assault on an officer to the charges."

Megan, with his help, led the irate woman to her cruiser, shut the door behind her, and gave William a thumbs-up as a thank you. He walked around the side of the house to tell Aggie the coast was clear, and found Luke with her. Something in the scene before him seemed too personal to intrude, so he retraced his steps, knocked on the front door, reminded Libby to have Aggie come down to the station and sign a statement, and shuffled out to his car. Aggie saw the brake lights of his car at the edge of the driveway when she came into the living room, but didn't ask why he'd left.

"Where are the other children?" Dismay washed over her as she realized she hadn't seen them since the whole fracas began.

"I—" Libby shrugged. "I just don't know. They all went out after we said chicken pox…"

"Tina has Ian, but where is Tina?"

"Last I saw," Luke began, "She took him and Kenzie upstairs. Maybe…"

Aggie was already on her way up to see. Seconds later, she jogged back down the steps and went outside, calling for Vannie, Tavish, and the others. No answer came. Murphy peeked her head out the door and asked who was missing this time, and Aggie lost it. "How should I know? I'm incompetent, remember?"

"Mibs," Luke warned. "Don't get ugly. It's not her fault."

"It's not my fault either! Where did they go?"

Libby's voice called from the kitchen. "They're here. They're fine."

She rushed inside and found Vannie, Tavish, Laird, and Ellie all huddled around Libby. "Where were you?"

"We snuck in and hid in the basement when we saw Grandmother come. We didn't want her to see us. We thought—"

Whatever Vannie and the others had thought was muffled in Aggie's bear hug. "I'm just glad you're safe. Why don't you go wash up for lunch, and I'll find something to scrounge up."

"Aggie?" Libby's face was a study of repressed hilarity. "Breathe."

"Huh?"

"Now, sniff."

Aggie made an exaggerated sniff and rolled her eyes. "When did you put a casserole in?"

"While Luke was reading stories. Go tell Tina it's safe to come out, and let's eat!"

Mibs says: Luke? You there?

Luke says: I'm here. How are the girls?

Mibs says: Grouchy.

Luke says: Not much changed then, eh?

Mibs says: Nope. Your mom has them as comfortable as possible. She's sleeping in Lorna's bed and the girls are sharing Cari's.

Mibs says: Oh, and Tina loves what you did with the guest room. She says the bed is much more comfortable than the air mattress. I think she likes the chair too.

Luke says: Well, good. With all the help she's been, she should get a good night's rest.

Mibs says: Yep. I'm going to miss her when she goes back to the university.

Luke says: I bet. Hey, did you get your statement signed?

Mibs says: Yep. Oh, and Douglas Stuart never showed up here. Isn't that weird?

Luke says: I thought he'd show up long before I left. She talked like he was coming right then.

Mibs says: I have wondered if all her drama wasn't because she's going a little senile or something. You know, one of those dementia diseases making her unreasonable. If he didn't know he was supposed to pick her up...

Luke says: Did she come get her car?

Mibs says: Yep. When she posted bail, Megan drove her back and escorted her off the property. I think they kept her as long as possible.

Luke says: I don't blame them. That was brutal.

Mibs says: That's why I dinged. I wanted to thank you for being there for me. I really needed the support.

Luke says: Always, Mibs. Always.

Mibs says: Did I tell you that Mom knows what Mibs is?

Luke says : ☺ She does, eh? So did she tell you?

Mibs says: Nope. She thinks I should figure it out for myself.

Luke says: I like your mom.

Mibs says: Well, that's convenient. She likes you too. Anyway, I shouldn't keep you. I just wanted to say thanks.

Luke says: Hey, before you go…

Mibs says: Shoot.

Luke says: Nah, never mind. I'll talk to you about it some other time.

Mibs says: What? I'm not going to bed any time soon.

Luke says: No, I'm sorry. I need to think and pray a bit.

Luke says: It's just something that needs to wait. Sorry.

Mibs says: Ok, whatever. I did want to say that I hope you don't feel obligated to come while everyone's sick. You have things to do, and I understand that. You're getting paid so little for all you do as it is. Do it when you don't have other things to do. The important rooms are finished anyway.

Mibs says: Oh well, goodnight, Luke.

Luke says: Night. Sleep well, and leave your cares with Jesus. He can take it.

A Pox Upon You

Chapter Twelve

Sunday, August 31st

Lost in denial, Aggie spent Saturday jubilant that no more children broke out in the now-familiar rash. Libby tried to remind her that it took a few days for things to incubate and then an extra couple of days before the rash appeared, but it seemed as if Aggie needed to hold onto the hope of just Cari and Lorna having the disease. When not a single spot appeared by nightfall, Aggie slept soundly in the confidence that as soon as the little girls scabbed over, this addition to the family's experiences would be nothing more than a crazy memories.

Sunday morning shattered those dreams. When Aggie went to pull Ian from his crib, his little belly and shoulders were covered in more pox than both twins combined. Without Libby there, Aggie called for Tina and begged her to take Ian downstairs. "It's probably a waste of time, but I feel like I have to try to avoid getting it."

Tina shooed Aggie downstairs to make breakfast, and the moment she was gone, picked up the phone. "Libby, Ian has pox now. What are the odds that there won't be anymore?"

"Oh, no." The woman's sigh came through the phone clearly. "And the odds of Aggie avoiding them are also pretty slim. Tell her that Luke and I will be there to help right after church. She should try to stay away from the children as much as possible, but at this point, she's been exposed, and there's no getting around that."

Just as Libby and Luke stepped into the house, Kenzie stumbled downstairs with the most comical-looking face Libby had seen since Luke's bout with the pox when he was back in elementary school. "Oh, sweetie. Do you feel icky?"

Aggie heard the question from the kitchen and stepped into the dining room. One look at Kenzie's face and all hope that she'd avoid a household epidemic dissolved. The school problem would have to be resolved, but she found it too overwhelming to consider — yet. "Oh, Kenzie. I'm so sorry."

The child ran and threw herself into Aggie's arms before anyone could stop her. "I feel awful, Aunt Aggie. Just awful. Can you make them go away?"

Libby gently peeled the girl from her aunt's arms and led her to the stairs. "Let's get you a bath, and then I'll put the same lotion on your face that I put on Cari and Lorna. It'll help."

Luke hunkered down on his heels and pulled a package of washable markers from a Wal-Mart bag. "I bought markers. Once you're all cleaned up and have your spots covered, I'll help you connect the dots and make pictures."

"Thanks, Luke. That'd be like getting my face painted." Somewhat cheered, Kenzie disappeared up the stairs while the twins clamored for pictures on their arms and faces.

Aggie made sandwiches and sent the other children outside to enjoy them and a Popsicle, while Libby and Tina tended the afflicted children. As she worked, her mind whirled with ideas for how to handle school. Would they allow any of the exposed children to attend classes? What if they didn't? How many weeks of school would they have to miss? As it was, Kenzie would definitely miss the entire first week. She couldn't even go get the child's schoolwork without potentially exposing other children to the disease. Tina would have to go. The following week would be even worse. Tina would be gone, and it was too much to ask Libby or Luke to drive to Brunswick every day.

She wanted to sing. Every part of her soul craved the comfort of hymns, but she was beyond tired. The twins had been awake several times in the night, and Ian, whom she'd assumed awoke from the noise, had slept fitfully himself. While loading the dishwasher, she hummed a bit, fired off a dozen P-mails, and tried to remember every comforting scripture she'd ever memorized.

Unfortunately, her patience level was not refueled quickly enough. After the third time she snapped at a child, Luke put down his markers and went to talk to her. "Aggie? Do you feel all right?"

"I'm just tired."

"And a bit out of sorts. Laird was just trying to help."

She gripped the counter as if it'd anchor her enough not to lose her temper again. "He still managed to ignore my instructions to stay out of the kitchen."

"He wasn't in here when you gave those instructions. You sent him outside with the trash before you told the others to stay out."

Realizing Luke was right did little to improve Aggie's disposition. "He could have told me—"

"I think that's what the, 'I'm sorry, I didn't hear—' was all about."

"So I'm an evil aunt who is mean to her kids. I can take it. It's not like I've not heard it before."

Taken aback, Luke stared at Aggie in shock. That kind of sarcasm was out of character for her. "Come on, Mibs. Why don't you go upstairs and take a nap. You're not yourself."

At first, she resisted. That part of her that was determined not to let the latest crisis dictate her actions wanted to protest, but after a few gentle rebukes from Luke and his mother, Aggie climbed the stairs, her legs feeling like jelly, and crawled into her bed. Within minutes, she was sound asleep.

Downstairs, the children were fretful and listless. With the four youngest children covered in spots, the older children avoided the sickroom side of the house, choosing to go upstairs for the bathroom in hopes to avoid germs. Tavish and Vannie spent their time reading, while Ellie and Laird played with the puppies and tossed water balloons at each other from time to time. Whenever they got thirsty, they snuck in the back door, guzzled a drink, and raced back outside.

After an hour or so, Luke's patience was growing thin. The children's behavior had disintegrated into whines and demands for anything they thought they could finagle out of Libby. At last, he pulled his mother aside to work out a solution. "Mom, I know they're miserable, but honestly, I think they're getting away with murder." He glanced at Kenzie who sat with arms crossed, shaking her head at Cari's latest "suggestion." "I can't help but think that if we don't put a stop to it, Aggie is going to have even more work on her hands when they're well again."

Though a little amused at the forethought Luke had for Aggie's children, Libby nodded in agreement. "You're right. I'll put a pallet on the floor of Tina's room, and we'll let them know that anyone who is unpleasant will have to lay alone in there with nothing to entertain them."

"Be prepared. Cari will pitch a fit and be the first one incarcerated."

"I imagine so."

Within ten minutes, Luke's prediction came true. Cari, unimpressed by the latest video offering, demanded to watch something else. "I don't wike this one! I want to watch the wetters movie!"

"Sorry, Cari. It's Kenzie's turn to choose a movie, and she chose this one. You'll have to wait your turn."

Despite Libby's stern reminder, the girl increased her protest. Kicking and wailing, she pushed Kenzie who began crying as well.

"Stop your fussing, Cari, or I will put you in the other room. It's time to settle down."

"No! I want the wetters! Kenzie is selfish. Make her put on the wetters!"

"Ok, come on. It's off to the other room for you." Luke lifted the kicking, screaming girl into his arms and carried her from the library and into Tina's room.

"I don't wike you anymore, Wuke. You's mean!"

Any hope that the solitary confinement option would curtail Cari's fury dissipated as her defiance increased. The decibel level on her wails grew to the unbearable, and he had to stand guard to ensure the child didn't leave or damage anything in her fit of anger. Libby peeked her head in the door, ready to help, but Luke waved his hand behind his back as if to say, "I've got this. Please go."

As the drama increased, the noise made it to Aggie's room where she awakened from her nap. The weary young woman

156

dragged herself from her bed and shuffled down the stairs. With the noise as her guide, she arrived at the guest room door, and even the children in the library quit moving and fussing when they heard one loud word. "Stop."

Impressed by her effectiveness, Luke stepped from the room and closed the door. Minutes later, the wails and pounding returned. He glanced at his mother for direction, but Libby shook her head and beckoned him to join them in the library. As he turned to leave, the muffled sound of Aggie's voice as she spoke to Cari reached him. The screams and stomps soon gave way to soft cries and then silence.

Several minutes later, Aggie led a repentant Cari out of the guest room and into the library. The chagrined little girl dragged her feet across the floor until she stood before Luke, her spotty little face the picture of dejection. She tapped his knee and whispered, "Wuke, I's sorry. I was ugly, and I's 'posed to be pwetty. You fowgive me?" Luke's heart melted as the child threw her arms around him, sniffling. "I'll obey next time. I pwomise."

"Of course, I forgive you, Cari. Why don't you sit with me, and we'll find some more pictures on your arms?"

Luke glanced up at Aggie and gave her a thumbs up. The young woman nodded and then shuffled to the couch. Just as she laid down again, her cell phone rang. Luke watched as a frown appeared on her face and she shook her head. "He never came, William. We just thought maybe Geraldine called him from the station or something. Where could he be?"

Tuesday, September 2nd

The driveway looked empty without the imposing white van taking up most of the side section. As she waited for Libby to return, Aggie's stomach was in knots. She considered it a personal failure that her children might not be able to start school on time. Kenzie still had several miserable pox that had not yet scabbed, and the others were walking chicken pox bombs.

At last, just as Aggie was ready to go crazy and call Luke, the van pulled into the driveway and four children piled out of the vehicle and dragged up the steps. Laird burst through the doors, flung his backpack on the floor, and flexed his fingers. "A whole week! We get off at least one whole week!"

Vannie, looking as crestfallen as a child with coal in her stocking on Christmas, dragged herself up the steps and indoors. "I don't even have a fever, but they won't let me in. I'm going to be so behind!"

Her older elementary charges, chattering with Libby, entered the house with hardly a comment and went straight upstairs, changed, and dashed out the back door. Libby shook her head. "I could have predicted the reactions perfectly. Vannie was near tears, begged for her assignments—you need to go get them Thursday—Laird cheered and didn't think twice about the missed school, and Tavish and Ellie took it in stride."

"A whole week? Aren't they concerned about the kids getting behind? What if someone breaks out?"

"Both principals said that they could come back in a week if no more outbreaks happened. If anyone else breaks out, we have to call." Libby patted Aggie's shoulder. "He did ask me to thank you for not coming yourself. He thought that was very considerate since we don't know if you're contagious or not."

Before Aggie could answer, Tavish burst in through the kitchen, distraught. "The puppies are *gone*! Something bent the fence down and they're gone!" The words were hardly out of his mouth, before he continued into the library and demanded to know what the younger children had done with the puppies.

"Tavish!" Aggie followed him, grabbed his sleeve, and pulled him from the room. "What do you think you're doing?"

"The puppies didn't crush that fence by themselves. It could only happen if someone tried to climb it and bent the stakes over. They did it!"

"I don't see how, Tavish. I was right here in the living room watching for you guys to get home. I would have seen them."

"But—"

"Wouldn't it make more sense," Libby began calmly, "to spend your time finding the puppies than looking for someone to blame?"

A flush colored Tavish's ears and neck. "Yeah, I guess."

What started as a simple search and rescue turned into an area-wide pup hunt. After half an hour of searching, Aggie called for reinforcements. Luke and William arrived at nearly the same time, both looking a little perturbed to see the other on the case. They combed every inch of ground, under the house, and even across the nearby highway, but to no avail. Tavish was beside himself, Aggie was worn out, and the men were both determined to be the hero of the hour.

Libby, the only one detached enough from the situation, found the scene hilarious. After a few minutes of observing the battle of testosterone, she went to check on the girls, and moments later, peals of laughter sent everyone in hearing distance racing for the house. There, in the library, three guilty looking little girls each held a puppy in her lap, awaiting their sentencing.

"We just wanted to play. Puppies can't get chicken pox, can they?" Kenzie pleaded with her eyes for understanding.

The men exchanged glances, each feeling ridiculous for the unspoken competition and even more silly when they realized no one won. William shuffled off to the cruiser, Luke offered to take Laird and Tavish to his renovation job a few streets over, and Aggie collapsed in relief that the puppies were safe. Just as she gathered enough energy to scold the girls for their prank, the phone rang.

Tina jogged downstairs with Ian on one hip and the phone in her hand. "Someone calling about the puppies. They want one, and want to know when they can come by to see them."

As Aggie took the phone, she saw the disappointed look on Tavish's face as he took a puppy from Kenzie's arms and carried it outside to the enclosure. She'd planned to insist that all the animals found a home, but now she wasn't so certain. Perhaps the boy needed a more congenial pet. The kitten, as adorable as it was, already showed a preference for playing in the house, lounging in the sun, and gentle strokes by mature hands that didn't pull tales or legs at inopportune times.

Once she disconnected the phone, she glanced at Libby. "What do you think? Should I let him keep one?"

"Oh phooey!" Libby covered her mouth with her hand. "I almost won."

"Won what?"

"Luke and I had a bet going on how long it'd take you to decide to keep one or two."

"And you said?" The bet sounded like the kind of thing Luke and Libby would do. Their relationship reminded Aggie of her relationship with her father.

"I said soon after the third puppy left. I almost made it."

"What did Luke say?"

"He said before the third one was gone. I think he was sweating bullets when the puppies went missing. If they didn't find one, technically he'd lose."

"Well, that explains the intensity with which he looked anyway," Aggie remarked. "I couldn't believe how serious he took finding a few puppies!"

Libby gave Aggie an enigmatic look. "Couldn't you?"

"Miner. I think he looks like a coal miner—all black and dusty." Tavish cuddled the pup under his chin and beamed up at his aunt. "Thank you so much. I'll take good care of them; I promise."

Aggie glanced at her niece, as she encouraged the other puppy to wrestle with a stick. "What about that one?"

"I want to name her Sammie."

"That's a boy's name," Tavish protested.

"No it's not. Not if her real name would be Samantha if she was human. Sammie—with an I. E." Ellie giggled at the unintentional somersault the puppy made. "She's too much of a tomboy to have a more prissy name."

"Ok, then," Aggie agreed, rubbing her hands. "We have names." She glanced at the fence with the crumbled chicken wire. "We'll have to get a real fence put in soon. That won't hold the puppies much longer."

Still doubting her decision, Aggie strolled back to the house, entered the mudroom, and pulled the clean clothes from the dryer. The laundry, like most of the housework, had a tendency to get away from her, but she was determined to conquer the domestic beast. Of course, her plan had included fewer bodies at home to undo her hard work before she had a chance to finish. That idea would have to wait another week or two.

Wails from Ian calling for "Gaggie" invaded the lower floor long before Tina brought him downstairs. At last, she arrived with the bespotted baby, apologizing as she came. "I'm so sorry, Aggie, but he won't settle down. He wants you." She nearly stumbled as Ian made a lurch for Aggie's arms. "Vannie volunteered, but I thought it was best not to risk it."

With the miserable boy snuggled against her chest, contentedly sucking on his thumb, Aggie shrugged. "I can't avoid all of them all the time. I just can't. The chances of me not getting them is so slim already —"

"Well, I tried, but he just wants his mommy." Tina sank into the nearest chair. "I don't know how you do it. You're amazing."

"I have a little more on the job experience. I'm sure you saw the lost puppy fiasco."

"How did they get those animals in there without you seeing them?"

"They must have done it while I was in the bathroom getting them fresh washcloths. They were fast, though. Really fast. I still don't see how they pulled that one off..."

A little snort interrupted the conversation. Aggie stood and reluctantly carried Ian up to his bed. The room was hardly recognizable with all of Tina's things cluttering Tavish's half of the room. Tavish had been sent to sleep with Laird until one of them broke out in the pox in the hopes that by isolating them from Ian, neither would.

As she laid him down, Ian awoke and started to fuss, but a few pats on his back and he settled back down and returned to sleep. Relieved, Aggie continued up the stairs to her room, grabbed fresh clothes, and went for the shower. Every time she helped a child, held a child, or had any prolonged contact, she washed her hands thoroughly, but after a sleepy Ian drooled on her shirt, she decided a more thorough fumigation was in order.

By the time she returned downstairs, Tina had the little ones involved in a game of duck, duck, goose, and Luke drove up into the yard with a truck full of fencing supplies. At the sight of a roll of chain link on Luke's shoulder, she diverted her path to the library in favor of seeing what he was planning. "Hey, I don't remember ordering a fence!"

"But Mom did, and I never argue with Mom."

"Why," Aggie began, sounding like her old self for the first time in days, "do I have a feeling that this has not always been true?"

"Well..."

"Just as I suspected."

Luke nudged her with his free elbow and then spun in place. "So, where do you want this happy doggie home?"

A dog run hadn't been a consideration until that morning. Uninspired by the view of her yard, Aggie shrugged. "Got any suggestions for me?"

"Well, if you were ever going to have a garden, you'd want to avoid there," he pointed to the exact place Tavish had placed the makeshift enclosure, "that's a perfect spot for a garden. I'd probably put it over by the carport. That tree would give them shade in summer, then again, if you put it near the front of the house, they could go under the porch for coolness."

"Yeah, but I hate to ruin the look of the house with a dog run." She felt silly even as she said it. "Is that selfish?"

"Sounds reasonable to me. Why put all this work into a house to mar it with something like a kennel? Why don't we put it behind the tree house where the trees will help shade them?"

She agreed and helped him carry the rest of the supplies. When everything was ready for him to begin digging, Aggie, eyes full of uncertainty, tugged on his shirtsleeve to stop him. "Did I make the right decision? I have eight kids here! Two puppies is like adding more. Is that crazy?"

"Aw, Mibs. I think it was a great decision. A kid needs a dog — particularly an animal-loving kid like Tavish. It was a good move."

"M'kay. If you say so. Feels crazy right now."

"Your life is a bit crazy right now." He shook his head. "Only you could 'inherit' eight kids who have never had the chicken pox."

She smiled. "Oh, I think lots of people could do *that*. No, only *I*, the only girl my age in the greater Rockland area who has not had the chicken pox *or* the shot, could inherit eight kids who also haven't had it. That sounds more like an Aggieism."

Friday, September 5th

By lunchtime Friday, Aggie was feeling confident. It seemed as if the older children had acquired immunity while at school—or that's what she prayed was the case. P-mails had flooded heaven's inbox that week, and they only had to make it through three more days of no new patients for the school schedule to be back on track. Throughout the afternoon, she grew more and more assured that the worst was behind them.

Vannie, paranoid about getting behind on her schoolwork, spent half of her time reading and doing homework in her room. Laird, on the other hand, took the work that Libby brought home for him, stuffed it on his shelf, and declared he'd do it on Saturday and Sunday nights. Aggie chose to ignore it. Tavish and Ellie managed to fly through the assignments given them and then stuffed them back in their backpacks and enjoyed their extended vacation without another thought.

She stared at her pantry trying to find something interesting for dinner. "Hey, Libby, do you think enchiladas would be bad for the kids?"

"Not at all, why?"

"I think I have the ingredients. I wanted something different. I'm going to try it."

Aggie grabbed the tube of defrosted ground beef from the fridge and snipped it open, squeezing every bit she could into a pan. Humming a few bars of a hymn she barely remembered, she concentrated on reading each part of her recipe from greasing the baking pans to opening the can of tomato sauce.

Once the meat was drained, the onions, garlic, and taco seasoning added, and simmering on the stove, Aggie pulled out a saucepan and dumped the tomato sauce in it. Had she managed to continue uninterrupted, everything would have sailed along like clockwork. Unfortunately, Vannie stepped into the kitchen looking as miserable as any almost thirteen year old ever has.

"Aunt Aggie? I think—"

Aggie turned and at the sight of Vannie's face, dropped her spoon. "Oh, Vannie, no!"

"I'm sorry."

"Oh, it's not your fault. I just know how you were looking forward to starting school, and now…"

Libby entered the kitchen to learn what the problem was, and wrapped a comforting arm around Vannie's shoulder. "Why don't you go upstairs and take a nice long tepid bath. Use that box of oatmeal bath salts. You'll feel better. Then use a q-tip and dab a bit of the calamine on each spot. You'll feel better."

The instructions felt so repetitive to Aggie that the young woman wanted to scream. Nothing, not even the tantalizing scent of spiced beef and corn tortillas seemed able to soothe her. Frustration mounted as she dreamed of adding oatmeal and calamine lotion to her dinner as a preventative measure. She read the recipe, grabbed spices, shook them in the sauce, stirred, added some sauce to the meat mixture, and started filling steamed tortillas from the microwave with the meat and lots of cheese. After the first few cracked as they dried under the ceiling fan, Aggie began ladling a little enchilada sauce on each one to keep them moist.

"There. That should do it," she muttered to herself as she shoved the baking dishes into the oven. However, her self-confidence shattered as she put away ingredients. The cinnamon, not an ingredient in her recipe, stood proudly on the counter, the lid off and waiting to be replaced. She swallowed hard.

"Libby?"

Luke's mother came into the kitchen carrying Ian. "Smells wonderful."

"Do you think cinnamon in enchilada sauce would taste ok?"

The woman's forehead furrowed. "Well, I—I don't know! It could be wonderful or—" Libby dipped her finger in the leftover sauce. "Mmm. That is good. If that's any indication, I think it makes it yummy."

"But I missed the cumin."

"It tastes like… well, like Mexican. What's in it?"

"Taco seasoning, garlic, onion, and the cinnamon instead of extra cumin like the recipe said."

Libby took another swipe at the pan and savored every bit of it, trying to taste it with a critical palate. "Well, forget the cumin, this is delicious." She winked. "These'll be your 'famous' enchiladas someday. People will beg to know your secret."

164

Luke, finished at his house nearby, entered the kitchen with a box of laminate flooring in his arms. "What secret?"

Aggie dipped her finger in the sauce and held it up for him to taste. "What do you think?"

"Delicious. What is in there? It's... a little exotic, but it's good."

"That's the secret ingredient, son. I bet once they're baked, those enchiladas will be some of the best we've ever had."

"They'd be better with shredded beef, but I only had that ground beef."

With an exaggerated roll of his eyes, Luke shook his head and continued toward the basement. "Beef is beef. Give me beef, or give me chicken; I always say."

After dinner, Luke pulled Aggie aside and asked her to take a short walk down the road. As they strolled down the driveway, he seemed to struggle with finding the right words. At last, he stopped and waited for her to meet his gaze. "Mom is looking a little rundown. Do you think you and Tina can handle things if I insist she goes home?"

"Of course! She doesn't have to stay at all!"

"Well, I know she wants to, but I'm worried about her getting too worn out. If you get this, she's going to need to be here, and if she's already sleep-deprived..."

Unconsciously, Aggie checked her arms for spots. "I'm probably going to get it if Vannie did. They can't go to school on Monday. Not with Vannie broken out. It's a matter of days most likely. Maybe Kenzie later next week, but then why not wait until the following Monday? Oh, I don't know. No matter what happens, they're going to be behind, the new kid sticking out, and unfamiliar with everything."

"They'll pick up on your attitude, Mibs. If you see it as a horrible thing, they will too."

"I wish I had listened to Zeke," she moaned.

"What did Uncle Zeke say about it?" Luke sounded confused.

"Well, not for this, but when I didn't have a way to get them to school if they missed the bus. He said I should home-school them and save the hassle. I think he meant for the rest of the semester, but maybe I should consider it for this semester and then put them in after Christmas."

"Or not put them in at all." Luke's retort was surprisingly quick.

"At all?"

"Why not? They're going to spend the majority of their waking hours either on a bus or in class and definitely apart. Why not cut that down and give them more time together? They are such good friends as it is, why not capitalize on that?"

She'd never considered home-schooling fulltime, but Aggie had to admit, there was a part of her that found it very appealing. "Well, after all those years preparing to be a teacher, it would be nice to actually do some of that teaching stuff." She shook her head. "I don't know. Is this a good time to make these kinds of decisions?"

"Why don't you call your parents and see what they think? Maybe talk to Tina or William…"

"William would tell me it is a horrible idea and that I should let the professionals do their jobs."

"Forgetting, of course," Luke added with a smirk, "that you *are* one of those professionals."

Aggie giggled. "You're right. That's funny." She kicked a stick out of her way and slid her eyes sideways. "Luke?"

"Hmm?"

"Is it bad that I want to do it more now that I realize that William will disapprove?"

His laughter rang out into the darkening twilight around them. "Probably, but I think I'd feel the same way."

"It's not fair for me to say that," Aggie admitted. "He just forgets that he's not always on duty and every difference of opinion isn't a violation of a law."

"I suspect it's an occupational hazard. Kind of like I tend to see everyone's house in light of what I'd do to it instead of just enjoying their hospitality."

"So, should I ask your mom's opinion? I don't want to disregard the idea any more than I want to jump into it just because it seems like a solution to the current crisis."

He turned and steered her toward home. "Let's go talk to Mom and Tina." Several yards later, he added, "I don't want to pressure you to do anything you don't want to do. It was just the most logical idea in my mind. Corinne asked about it the other day, I haven't been able to get it out of my mind."

"She asked about me and home-schooling?"

"She said something about not knowing how you could handle getting them to two different schools — three next year — the lunches, the bus schedules, the different programs, the school drama coming home every day, and then, after all that, the homework." Luke sounded drained just thinking about it.

Aggie says: Mom?

Martha says: How are the polka-dotted darlings?

Aggie says: Vannie is our next victim.

Martha says: Oh, that poor girl. No school next week for her then, I suppose.

Aggie says: No. Oh, and that's why I dinged. Luke made a suggestion tonight.

Martha says: Tell me it isn't some romantic idea.

Aggie says: LOL. No. He suggested that I consider home-schooling.

Martha says: Allie always wanted to do that, but Geraldine made such a fuss when it was mentioned that they never pursued it.

Aggie says: Really? That would make me feel a lot better.

Martha says: What would? Doing what your sister always wanted or annoying her mother-in-law because it can't ruin relationships anymore than they already are?

Aggie says: Both?

Martha says: LOL. Well, I always hated how discouraged Allie became during those first weeks of school. The children's loyalties inevitably shifted, and that bothered her.

Aggie says: I guess that is only logical.

Martha says: Well, I saw it when you girls were young, but I just thought it was normal. Allie didn't think it should be normal. She considered private schools, but couldn't find one in a reasonable distance that had the kind of "one room schoolhouse" model she was

---

hoping for.

Aggie says: Why that model? Seems like a lot of work for one teacher.

Martha says: And yet, remember when you read "The Long Winter," and you were astounded at how well educated Laura was? She taught several terms of school without ever having graduated. All from just a few years of education at home with Ma or in little one-room schools.

Aggie says: Ok, but why couldn't a top-notch private school in Rockland do as well?

Martha says: Educationally speaking, sure. I think they could. But Allie thought the one room school idea helped encourage close sibling relationships by not segregating children from their siblings.

Aggie says: I think I remember her talking about that once. Somehow, I hadn't associated it with prairie schools or home-schooling. I just thought she thought modern schools encouraged the anti-sibling bias that seems to prevail out there.

Martha says: I think she gave it a little too much credence. After all, you and she weren't at odds all the time, and remember the Wainwrights? They had what, five children? I've never seen a closer set of siblings, even today, and they were involved in all kinds of stuff apart from each other.

Aggie says: So you think I shouldn't do it?

Martha says: I think you should consider it, but no, I don't think that it's an automatic "must do" just because Allie liked the idea.

Aggie says: I was kind of looking for a mom mandate. "Thus saith the ma" kind of thing.

Martha says: We'll support you no matter what you decide. You know that, right?

Aggie says: Yes, but the decisions become overwhelming. I have decisions every day. What to eat, what to buy, what to finish, how to handle this discipline issue, where to shop for that thing, should they have a pet, where to order food because I ruined lunch—again. It's exhausting!

Martha says: I know, hon. I'll talk to your dad, but since you have to be the one to do it, I don't think he's going to be willing to say you should or shouldn't. It's hard to help with decisions that you have to do and be responsible for. We can tell you what brand of vacuum we like, but it isn't far reaching like if you should take them on a mission trip or put in a pool.

Aggie says: No and no.

Martha says: LOL. I knew you'd say that. After that bout of giardia, I didn't think you'd ever try mission trips again.

Aggie says: Ugh. I don't think so.

Martha says: Just one thing. I think you should pray about why you're considering it. Is it because someone suggested it, because you like the idea, or because you're feeling guilty about them starting late? Not all of those are good reasons and none are necessarily bad ones by themselves. Maybe do some research online or something. Decide on Monday when you have to let the schools know that they won't be there quite yet.

Aggie says: That's a great idea. I'll research tomorrow and Sunday and decide then. Thanks, Mom.

Martha says: You're welcome. I had a few questions for you, but your father is giving me that "get to bed or I'll carry you there" look, and we both know he can't do it but he'd try.

Aggie says: Night, Mom.

Martha says: G'night, Aggie. Try to get some rest. You still could come down with this thing, you know.

LIKE DOMINOES

Chapter Thirteen

Sunday, September 7th

Trapped at home with a houseful of itchy, miserable children, Aggie spent her time starting baths for the next child in line, adding calamine lotion with a q-tip to avoid contact, and making gallons of juice. Vannie, her mouth full of pox, refused to drink anything but ice water and ate nothing but vanilla yogurt and beef broth. Tina dashed back and forth to the store bringing home anything she thought she could get the children to eat, while Tavish, Laird, and Ellie fended for themselves downstairs in the basement or out in the yard.

"Ok, so there is a whole website for legal aid for home educators, Tina. Should I take this as a positive thing or proof that William will show up to arrest me sooner than later?"

Tina shrugged. "I found this site that has everything you need to teach your children at home—free."

"Message me that one. I gotta see this!"

With the site pasted into the messenger, Tina clicked through several years' worth of lessons and studied the information. "Well, you'd get a standard basic education, but I can't say I'd want to teach it or learn it this way."

"I found another one like it, but a different approach. It seems as if the lesson plans are free and some worksheets and things, and the rest you buy curricula from other places."

"This site has a list of books they recommend you pick from if you're considering home-schooling. I could call and see if a bookstore in Brunswick or Rockland has any in stock." Tina's hand hovered over her cell phone waiting for instructions.

"Sure! That'd be great." A new website grabbed Aggie's attention just as Ian's wail announced that he'd awoken and was miserable again. "His majesty calls."

By the time Aggie returned downstairs with Ian attached at her hip, Tina was going through a list of books with someone at a bookstore. She saw book after book crossed off Tina's list, but by the time the call ended, the list still had several titles on it. "Ok, three stores have several books each, so I'm going to go grab 'em. I'll be back in a couple of hours. If you need help, call Libby."

"Ok, ok. Get out of here. We still have work to do."

"You're going to do it. I don't know why you keep convincing yourself that you haven't made up your mind."

Stunned, Aggie stared at her friend. "What makes you say that?"

"Because I know you. You'd have dumped this idea immediately if you weren't going to do it. When you are going to do something, you always take forever to plan it out and 'research' all the angles so you can justify your decision to yourself."

A protest welled up in her throat, but Aggie exhaled instead. "You're right. I do do that, don't I?"

"No, I just say things like that to sound deep and introspective."

"Sarcasm does not help, Miss Warden."

"Oooh," Tina began, impressed, "you sounded just like Professor Jovan. That was eerie!"

"Go buy the books. Then I can have the pleasure of beating myself up for wasting the money on something to justify this decision I apparently made."

Seconds after Tina's car disappeared around the corner, Kenzie skipped downstairs and announced that she was "all better." Aggie, clearly seeing unscabbed spots, tried to explain how the disease

172

progressed, but the little girl was stubborn. With every word that Aggie spoke, her face grew more determined. Her hands clenched into little fists, her arms crossed, and one foot stomped in protest.

"I prayed. Mrs. Sullivan read us from the Bible about praying, and it says if you believe you will receive. Well, I believe so I got. I'm well."

"That's not what that means. God isn't Santa Claus—"

"No, He's better 'cause He's real."

Several times, Aggie tried again, but each time, Kenzie refused to accept the idea that she hadn't been healed of the pox that was upon her. At last, Aggie tried a different approach. "Ok, you know what? It is possible that you are well—"

"Good. Then I'm going to go play with the puppies."

"Nope. That you aren't going to do."

"Why not! I'm well, so I should get to go outside like the other well kids."

Turning the girl toward the library, Aggie pointed to the room. "You will go color, do a puzzle, read a book, or watch a movie."

"Why!"

"Because I said so."

"But I'm well!"

"It doesn't matter if you're well or not. I said you'll stay in there for now, so you will."

"That's not fair!"

"I won't argue with you, Kenzie. It's in there, or bed. Take your choice."

"No! I never get to play with the puppies, and I'm well now, so I *am* going!" The child moved as if to go outside, but Aggie caught her arm.

She didn't move, she didn't argue, she didn't yield in any way, she just stood there as Kenzie fought, half-heartedly, to get free. "Let me go!"

"Kenzie, hush. You won't talk to me like that."

"You're not being fair!"

"I'm not going to argue about it. Go upstairs."

"But I don't want to," the child protested.

"You're acting like you want to. Little girls who disobey do not get what they want. You know the rules. Go to your room and lay down."

"I just got up!"

"Little girls who throw temper tantrums obviously need a nap. Go lay down."

With dramatic wails that gave Cari a run for her theatrical money, Kenzie marched up the steps, stomping on each one as hard as she could, and slammed her door shut. Aggie groaned. She could not let that display of temper go, even if the child *was* ill. Kenzie, in particular, took every minor victory as proof that she could win if she fought hard enough. With p-mails flying faster than she could count them, Aggie followed her niece up the stairs, opened the door, and beckoned the girl to follow. Elated that her protest worked, Kenzie skipped to her Aunt's side and followed her down the steps.

"Ok, now, walk back up those stairs the way you're supposed to, and do not close your door at all."

The child's stunned face was almost comical. "What? I—"

"Don't argue, Kenzie. Walk nicely up those stairs and go back to bed."

With an expression that implied the desire to do serious bodily harm, Kenzie walked quietly up the steps, entered her room, and sat on the bed with arms crossed. Aggie took a deep breath, and squared her shoulders, beckoning the girl to follow her again. Shock registered and then resignation. She followed Aggie back down the stairs and walked back up again, her face a study in apathy.

"Ok, that's better, but now do it without looking depressed. It's not that terrible, so I want you to try to look… nice." Even as she spoke, Aggie knew she sounded unsure of herself—the one thing certain to make Kenzie dig in her heels further. "What I mean is that right now you look like you ate something nasty. I want you to look like you are about to do something nice."

"I don't understand. I did it. I didn't stomp."

"But you were sulking and trying to look like you didn't care when both of us know you did." Aggie's hand cupped the child's chin. "That's lying, Kenzie. It's lying with your face and your attitude instead of words, but it's still lying."

"If I pretend I'm happy, I'll still be lying."

The child had a point, but Aggie knew something about it wasn't quite right. "Well, that's partly true. What I am telling you to do is practice having the right attitude even when you don't feel it. You're not lying; you're practicing."

For some reason that Aggie couldn't fathom, Kenzie took to that idea cheerfully. She skipped up and down the steps as if rehearsing a play until Aggie told her she could stay on her bed. "When the clock says eleven-thirty, then you can come down and play in the library if you like."

"Ok, Aunt Aggie. I want to draw a picture." Three steps back up the stairs and the child turned. "Can we bring the puppies inside for a little while after lunch maybe?"

Part of her felt duped, but Aggie realized it was a valid request. "I think that can be arranged. See you in a bit."

A trail of toilet paper showed Aggie where Ian had been while she'd been involved with Kenzie. She still had a dangerous habit of getting too focused on one task, and with most of the children sequestered in various parts of the house and yard, her usual spare pairs of eyes were absent. With children in school, she'd have to become more self-disciplined to keep at least one eye on him all the time.

That was another negative on the home-school front. If she was busy teaching several grade levels at once, how could she take care of the youngest twins and Ian? She knew there must be a way, according to what she'd seen, many larger families home-schooled, but she had no idea how to accomplish it. Maybe the idea would be better after Ian was potty trained and a little more accustomed to staying where she put him.

As those thoughts bombarded her brain, William's cruiser drove up the driveway and parked. For a moment, Aggie was tempted to meet him at the door to keep him from coming inside and seeing the mess that awaited him. "What's the use," she muttered to herself. "He already thinks I'm incompetent, why not prove him right?"

"Come in."

William entered to find Aggie following a trail of toilet paper, winding it around her hand until she reached the end near the kitchen trashcan. "Well, that's convenient."

She gave him a glance. "Ya think?"

"Has he been a handful while he's sick?"

"You could say that." She didn't feel like listening to her failures in alphabetical or chronological order, and knew that any encouragement at all would just reinforce the idea that her life was too much for anyone, much less someone as inexperienced as she.

"I thought Sullivan's mom was hanging around and helping."

"I was trying to give her a day off. She does too much already."

"Where's Tina? Should you really be here alone with all these sick kids?"

She'd been agitated before he arrived, but William's apparent lack of any confidence in her put Aggie on the defensive. "It's my job, William. I know that you think I'm completely incompetent, but the fact is, I can handle a lot more than you give me credit for. If you can't be supportive, just leave me alone."

"Whoa! I *was* being supportive. I think you're way overtired. Why—"

"Did you need something specific?"

"I just came to make sure you hadn't heard from Douglas Stuart."

"The phone works." Aggie knew she was being rude, but it seemed as if she was unable to help herself.

"Hey! What's eating you?"

For a moment, she almost unleashed a tirade of every critical comment and every perceived slight that she thought had ever crossed his mind. However, after one look at the hurt and confusion in his eyes, she couldn't do it. "I'm sorry, William. I know you don't mean to, but do you realize how often you tell me that I can't do what I *am* doing every day?"

The man's shoulders drooped, just for a second, before he straightened, erect, and met her gaze. "No, I didn't. I wonder if you hear what I say or what you expect me to say. I remember telling you what a good job you're doing with the kids. I remember acknowledging that you'd never hurt them. Did you remember *those* things too, or are you just fixated on me being the bad guy?"

He turned, ignoring her attempt to get him to stay and talk, and left the house. His shoes thudded on the steps and the crunch of the gravel had never sounded louder to her ears. "Oh, Lord, now what have I done?"

After staring down the drive for a few minutes, she turned, set Ian down, and began singing as she picked up stray articles of clothing, toys, and books that littered the living and dining rooms. Soon, she had a laundry basket full of things that needed to be put away and was singing to soothe her heart. "*... are lightly spoken, bitt'rest thoughts are rashly stirred. Brightest links of life are broken by a single angry word...*"[7]

Her eyes traveled heavenward. "Lord, I apologized. You'd think he'd understand at a time like this..."

Tuesday, September 9th

Luke had to wait for an inspection on his income property, so he chose to spend Tuesday working on the basement. The flooring was nearly ready to install now that the drywall had been completely painted. The bespotted children were all feeling the effects of cabin fever, so Aggie called the healthy children indoors to bake cookies in the kitchen, while the rest had an hour of sunshine and freedom to run. None of the children with the pox were quite as energetic as usual, but soon squeals and giggles erupted in the front yard.

Once the cookie sheets were covered in cookies, Aggie carried the bowl down to the basement. "Want some chocolate chip cookie dough before it's all gone?"

"Thanks. Just a second." He finished measuring a section of the floor and made a note of the measurement. As he turned to accept the bowl, a strange look came over his face. "Um, Mibs?"

"Hmm?"

"Better check a mirror."

Though she knew what his words meant, nothing could have prepared her for the sight she found in the little powder room mirror. "I look like I have acne!"

"It's just a few spots. They'll go away, and unlike acne, they don't come back." Luke's words were anything but helpful.

"Gee, thanks." She rubbed the back of her neck, finding more in that unconscious gesture. "No wonder I'm so tired."

Luke shooed her upstairs, dialing his mother as they went. "Go take one of Mom's prescribed baths, use the calamine, and then if you're still tired, take a nap. I'll send Tina up with something to drink and snacks."

"She's going to kill us, you know. We assured her we could handle things today."

177

Grinning, Luke pointed to the next flight of stairs. "Go. Besides, she won't kill us. She'll just scold. Mothers like to do that."

"Not all moms. I personally despise it."

A strange look hovered in Luke's eyes. "I know you do, Mibs. Honestly, no mom likes to scold or reprove her child, but good moms do it because it's best for the kid."

Halfway up the stairs, Aggie called back down, "Well, you'll have to do the switcheroo. I can't tell if they're getting overtired from up here."

"Oh, Aggie. Rest, woman!"

She did an about-face and took the steps back down two at a time. "Why? Why can you see something I'm doing right, and all William can see is how pathetic I am?"

"Oh, Mibs. I don't think he thinks you're pathetic. Inexperienced maybe, but you are. Maybe in his line of work it's hard to look past that inexperience and see the actual success or something."

"He's mad at me again."

A familiar twist to Luke's lips told her he found that highly amusing. "Well, it wouldn't be a normal week around here if he wasn't, now would it? What horrible thing have you done now?"

She sank to the third step, rested her chin in her hands, and sighed. "He was here wondering why your mom and Tina weren't here with me, saying that I probably shouldn't be alone with all these sick kids, and I got snippy. He's always telling me how everything is too much. I know he doesn't have a clue how often, but it's wearying."

"I can see that." In true Luke style, he said nothing else.

"Well, I snapped at him, he asked what my problem was, and I was ready to let him have it, but..."

"It's hard to blast a friend sometimes, isn't it?"

"Oh, no, it would have been easy if I hadn't seen his face. I hurt him. So, I apologized and tried to explain what the problem was."

"Well, that was good. This time you got to apologize when he was here. That's improvement." Luke sounded like he was grasping at straws.

"Yeah. I guess. He just reminded me of the two times he had something positive to say as if that should eradicate the dozens of other comments. It hurt more than the first words."

178

She saw something she'd rarely seen in Luke. Anger. The man nearly had steam coming from his flaring nostrils. "That's just wrong—manipulative, really. I hate that kind of thing."

"You don't think it was a little justified?"

Luke shook his head. "I do not. You don't whip a woman with the words you think she should want to hear—particularly when she's already struggling. I thought better of him." His jaw worked as Luke struggled to control his irritation. "I suppose he's probably really busy at work or something"

"I think he was looking for more information on Douglas Stuart. I don't think they know anything about him yet. Geraldine probably didn't bother to tell them when she found him."

She stood, shook off her skirt, and turned to go upstairs, but Luke reached out to take her arm and stopped her. "I know William is impressed with all you do and have accomplished. I think—" He swallowed hard. "I think maybe it's part of his 'fix it' mentality." Aggie tried not to shake him as she waited for his next words. "He wants to solve problems and make 'traffic flow smoothly' so to speak." It was easier to wait once his comforting words had a chance to soak into her soul. "He sees what would overwhelm him and projects that onto you."

"Should I try to apologize again?"

"No. You apologized. He was also in the wrong. Pushing him to accept yours will likely make things worse."

"Ugh. I need worse like I need more pox on my face."

Luke laughed and gave her a gentle shove back up the stairs. "Now that can probably be arranged."

A hand gently shook her from her dreams. "Aggie, c'mon, wake up. There's a guy here about the kids."

"A—what?"

"A guy. He says that Kenzie, Tavish, and Ellie are all truant."

Her head swam. "Ok, let me go to the bathroom, and I'll be right down."

179

Truant made no sense. She'd kept the children out of school at the decision of the principal. Unable to think clearly, she crept into the bathroom, shook two aspirin from the bottle in the open medicine cabinet, grabbed a handful of water from the tap to chase it down, and then stumbled downstairs without bothering to close the cabinet—again.

Tina gave her a funny look, but Aggie's attention was trained on the pleasant faced man sitting in "her" spot on the couch. "Hello, I'm Aggie Milliken, and you are…"

"Tim Rouse." The man stood to shake her hand. "Pleased to meet you, but I am sorry to wake you. I'm sure this is just some clerical mix up. It usually is."

"I don't understand. My friend spoke to Principal Beaudine on Tuesday of last week and Monday of this week. Both times he said not to bring the children to school."

Mr. Rouse was already dialing a phone number. "Sara, can I have Wes please. It's Tim." He listened for a minute. "Um, Stuart." Several seconds passed as he waited for something on the other end of the line. "That's why I need to speak to Wes. I have them down as having five consecutive unexcused absences, but the guardian says Wes told them to keep the kids out of the school due to—" he took a second glance at Aggie's face and choked, "Chicken pox."

Her eyes rolled before she could order them to behave in a mature fashion. Tim Rouse's attempts to control his amusement were strangled at best. "Hey, Wes. I'm out at the Stuart household in Brant's Corners. I'm speaking with…" his eyes begged for her name again.

"Aggie Milliken."

"—Aggie Milliken who says you told her to keep the children out of school while they recovered from the chicken pox, but she's on my list, obviously."

Tim's eyes mimicked Aggie's roll perfectly. "Wes, you gotta start giving Sara the memo on these things. She can't do her job if you don't do yours. All right. Bye."

"Sorry 'bout that. All the principals tend to get busy and forget to let their office managers in on little things like attendance excuses and such, but Wes is the worst. He said to tell you that if it'll be another week, you need a doctor's excuse."

"I have to take the kids to the doctor to prove they have chicken pox?"

The man shrugged, signed a paper, and stuffed it in his leather folder. "That's what he said."

"I have to take sick kids into a clinic and expose them to all kinds of other kids, just because some principal thinks he needs a signature from a guy with a boatload of student loans?" Aggie's voice rose with each word.

"If you'd rather decline, I suggest calling the office, but I'll probably end up back out here to tell you that you're going to have to tell it to a judge if you don't." He smiled. "Sorry. I agree it's ridiculous, but the principal is just doing his job. Two full weeks of unexcused absences really do need to be substantiated or parents could just keep their kids home whenever they didn't feel like getting up on time in the morning."

His words swam in her head as she escorted him to the door, shut it behind her, and sank to the floor, her back to it. "I can't believe they can do that."

"Well, they can't. Not once you turn in your 'notice of intent.' Then their involvement is gone." Tina stood, hands on hips, and shook her head at Aggie. "You know, that Tim was a nice enough guy, but this whole thing just bothers me."

"It's the kind of thing the GIL would use against me too."

Luke came up the stairs wiping his hands on a rag. "Did I hear William?"

"Nope. I just had my first run-in with a truancy officer."

"I think they're called 'attendance officers' now, Aggie," Tina added helpfully.

"Whatever."

"Well, I've got to scoot. Libby has a grocery list a mile long."

"Where is she?" Aggie struggled to her feet, accepting Luke's proffered hand gratefully.

"She has them all lounging in the kiddie pool. Tavish, Laird, and Ellie are forbidden to go near it now." Tina grabbed her purse, tugged at her hair, and dashed out the door.

"What's gotten into her?"

"Um, Mibs?" Luke hardly met her eyes.

"More spots?"

"Um no, but I think Tina was hinting that your hair is a bit—unconventional."

At the sight of matted hair, Aggie groaned. "I know better than to go to bed with it wet." She sighed. "I'm too tired to brush it out. Would it be a ridiculous waste of water to take another shower?" Her eyes grew wide. "No wonder Mr. Rouse kept staring at me oddly! AAAK."

Luke grinned. "Well, you gave him a great story to tell tonight around the dinner table."

Aggie says: Luke? You there?
Luke says: Yep. I thought you were sleeping.
Mibs says: I couldn't sleep.
Luke says: I'm sorry.
Mibs says: Were you going to bed?
Luke says: Not for a while yet. I have some things to do.
Mibs says: Oh, I shouldn't bother you then.
Luke says: Bother away. I can multitask just fine.
Mibs says: Ok, if you're sure. Just tell me to go away if you need to.
Luke says: Got it. Make Mibs go away if you need her to. Note written to self.
Mibs says: *giggles*
Luke says: What did you do tonight?
Mibs says: Tina and I narrowed some of the curriculum choices down.
Luke says: What did you pick?
Mibs says: I found a video course for Vannie that covers everything she was going to take except band. I'll have to find a private teacher for that, I guess.
Luke says: Is band a requirement?
Mibs says: Well, no...
Luke says: Why not wait until after Christmas then. Not so many

182

changes at once.

Mibs says: That's what Tina said, but I thought since I am keeping her out of school, I should try to replicate whatever I can.

Luke says: Look, if you go into this with that kind of mindset, the kids will think you are a pushover, and they'll push. You have to decide what is best for your school semester.

Mibs says: What makes you say that? I don't know…

Luke says: What did they teach you about lesson plans? Did they tell you to plan based upon what the kids wanted or what you and the general guidelines thought best with your materials?

Mibs says: Well. Just throw that up to me.

Luke says: I'll send my bill.

Mibs says: You do every week…

Luke says: Well, this week's bill will have an extra line item.

Mibs says: LOL.

Luke says: Is everything ok? You're usually not so quiet.

Mibs says: Are you saying I'm too talkative?

Luke says: No, I'm saying that you are being extra quiet. It's not like you.

Mibs says: Sorry. I think I'll go. Night, Luke.

Luke says: Aw, Mibs. What is wrong?

Mibs is offline. *Any messages you send will not be delivered until she is online.*

Aggie snapped the laptop shut. She knew she was being oversensitive and ridiculous, but she couldn't seem to help herself. From the first eruption of pox, through the visit with the attendance officer, and then the conversation with Luke, she felt agitated and unlike herself. Tears, of the frustrated variety, pricked her eyes, making her throat swell. For a moment she was tempted to open her laptop and try to catch Luke to apologize, but the effort seemed wasted. Either Luke would understand or he wouldn't. After her misunderstanding with William, Aggie had no desire to make an uncomfortable situation worse.

She grabbed her pillow and went out onto the front porch, felt the night breeze, and hurried to retrieve a throw blanket before she curled up on the wicker settee to "be still" before the Lord. Weary, she was too muddleheaded to pray, so she concentrated long enough to ask the Holy Spirit to make sense of the disquiet in her soul, and rested. Though she fully expected to fall asleep instantly, she didn't. Instead, she listened to the sounds of the frogs serenading the night creatures and the crickets chirping warnings to their friends of the location of their frog foes. As calm began to settle over her spirit, Aggie inhaled the comforting scent of damp earth and freshly cut grass. How had she not noticed that Luke had done that? She'd let it get extra long knowing that she could do it while the children were at school and the little ones were sleeping, but that hadn't happened.

After a time, headlights turned onto Last Street, and then pulled into her driveway. At first, it was difficult to see the vehicle for the lights, but abruptly, before the vehicle even came to a stop, they disappeared. "Luke?" she whispered.

He didn't leave his truck for several seconds. Their eyes met through the windows, but still they sat. Eventually, Luke opened the door and gently pushed it shut behind him. Hands in pockets, he strolled up the steps and paused near her. "You ok, Mibs?"

"I'm sorry, Luke. I know that was rude —"

"I didn't ask for an apology. I just wanted to see if you were ok."

"But I am sorry —"

"Ok, apology accepted." He lowered himself into the seat next to her. "Now, are you all right?"

Her smile, the first genuine one she'd had all day, flashed at him and was reflected in his eyes. "Frankly, no. Well, not until you arrived. I know leaving abruptly like that was an immature and snotty thing to do, but now I'm glad I did. Knowing someone cared enough to come see is exactly what the Doctor," she glanced heavenward with exaggerated dramatic effect, "ordered."

After several minutes, Luke spoke once more. "Mibs —"

"Luke, will you please tell me what Mibs is all about?"

"Will you regret me telling you when you're well?"

"Nah. I was about to Google it while we were talking, but then I got in a snit over something I didn't even understand at the time, and forgot."

"Well, Google would definitely give it away." Luke's chuckle warmed her heart, and she knew he saw it. "Aggie... what is an aggie?"

"Short for my real name?"

"Which is?" His tone told her he hadn't noticed it. Mail came to her, the court documents he'd read so carefully had her name all over them, but he'd never truly seen it.

"I'm not telling. This is your revelation, not mine."

"Oh, well then!" he joked. "Ok, other than short for your really ambiguous real name, what are aggies?" At her shrug, he shook his head. "I should have known a *girl* wouldn't even know the toy with her name on them."

"Aggies — marbles."

"Yep."

"So... what does that have to do with Mibs?"

Luke nudged her shoulder gently. "Mibs are marbles too. They're the targets in a game. They used to be made of clay. I always think of you as a marble that God fashioned exactly how He wants you to be."

"He's the Potter, after all." She scratched a pock on her arm absently until Luke moved her hand. "Or, are you just saying that I'm going to lose my marbles."

"It's just a private little reminder that you're exactly where God wants you, and He's making you into exactly *who* He wants you to be."

Her eyes dropped to her lap. "And here," she joked, "I thought it was something personal. I thought you were teasing me. Alas, you're just trying to keep me from picking up my marbles and going home."

"Oh, Mibs. If you only knew..."

Hours but very few words later, Aggie waved goodbye and went inside the house. She was drowsy, but an idea grew as she saw her laptop, so she flipped it open. Luke wouldn't be home, but that didn't matter. The messenger popped up and showed Luke online, but that wasn't possible. He'd left the minute she closed out their last conversation. That information was amazing to her.

185

Mibs says: Hey, just wanted to thank you again. I'll wear my moniker proudly.

Mibs says: Sleep in. The basement will wait. You want to be fresh for your inspection.

Mibs says: Luke… thanks. Really. Thanks.

Imaginationally Challenged

Chapter Fourteen

Thursday, September 11ᵗʰ

"Aggie?"

Tired, Aggie didn't even open her eyes. "Hmm?"

"Do you think you'll be feeling better by Sunday?"

"Probably, why?"

Tina played with a ring on her right pinkie finger. "I just thought maybe, well, with me having to be in class on Monday afternoon, we could invite William and Luke over for dinner on Sunday—kind of a 'back to school, new home-school, the pox are winding down' celebration. Is it rude to invite people over for dinner when you have chicken pox if both have been in the house of their own free will?"

"I don't think it's rude at all, but why invite them?" Ignoring her protesting itchy body, Aggie pushed herself up off the couch and tried to concentrate on her friend.

"I just thought it'd be nice…"

"Tina… that sounds deliberately ambiguous."

187

The petite blonde sat cross-legged and leaned against the coffee table. "Ok, fine. I wanted a chance to get to know William a bit better— see who he is. Every time he is here, there's a reason—an agenda. I want to know if he's really interested in you or if he just has overactive protective genes."

"I can tell you that. The latter. We've discussed it."

"You have? Really?" Tina seemed stunned by that revelation.

"Yep. I was telling Vannie that I thought William just didn't know how to be 'just friends' with a girl so he keeps trying to do the 'boyfriend thing.'"

"That makes sense—sort of. I've known guys like that."

A memory teased Aggie's mind. "But Luke warned me about him, I think."

"Really?"

"Luke overheard Vannie and me talking, and told me that I was wrong. He said that some guys could be just friends with girls while waiting for more. Mom and I thought he was trying to let us know that William really is interested or something, but now I disagree. We've talked. I don't think William knows how to lie or be deceitful like that."

Tina rested her chin on her knees. "So, I take it you don't want to do dinner."

"No, if you want to do a dinner, we can do that. Of course, with the kids around, who knows what it'll be like..."

"I thought we could feed them first, and then send them to the library for movies, and Ellie, Laird and Tavish could watch something on your laptop in his room or in my room, and we eat after that."

"Ok, then," it was hard for Aggie to show any enthusiasm, but she tried, "what do we want to have for dinner?"

"Guys like beef, right? Can we do a roast or something on the grill?"

"Roast works. The grill is too iffy. We don't want to be in a house with two hunger-crazed men."

Before Aggie could offer any other beef dishes, Mrs. Dyke knocked on the door. "I brought snicker doodles!"

Tina jumped up and went to help the woman carry a turkey platter loaded with the cinnamony sugar cookies. When she returned, Aggie was asleep on the couch. Mrs Dyke took one look at her and shook her head. "The poor little woman has so much on her plate, and now this. How long do you think she can continue to do this before she burns out?"

Anger flooded Tina's face until she realized the neighbor was truly concerned rather than issuing a condemnation of her friend. "She'll do it until the kids are grown or the Lord takes her home. That's just who Aggie is."

The gentle rap on her screen door was a familiar one. "William?"

"Can I come in?" Why he asked when he was half in before he finished asking the question, Aggie didn't know.

"Sure. I wouldn't have asked you to stop by if I didn't want you to come in, too." Her attempt at a light hearted joke fell flatter than a cake in a malfunctioning oven. "Have you heard anything about Douglas Stuart?"

"All I know is that he's home. I guess he has been since that day. Why Mrs. Stuart didn't call and tell us, I don't know. If I hadn't put out a call to the police in towns around the loop, I wouldn't have known." He peered closer. "I think you're getting a few new ones."

"Just what every girl wants to hear. Flatterer."

William laughed. "Even sick, you can make me laugh."

"I actually called you over to see if you wanted to come to dinner on Sunday. Tina has hatched a plan to keep the kids occupied in other rooms while we eat and talk."

"You and me?" He blanched. "I thought—are you saying—"

"I'm saying that Tina and I are inviting you and Luke to dinner on Sunday."

"Luke and Tina? Is this some kind of double date?"

"It's more like a couple of girls who want to have dinner with a couple of guys they know." She fidgeted with the throw pillow and then blurted, "I think she's nervous about going back to school without really getting to know you well."

"I thought we all got to know each other the night you and Luke were working on the library and the bathroom."

189

"Well, maybe I misunderstood, but that's the gist I got. She's looking out for me. I think she's afraid someone's going to break my heart or something." Aggie threw the pillow behind her head and flopped down. "As if I have time for that."

Before William could respond, Tina breezed into the room. "Hey, William. Has Aggie convinced you to have dinner with us yet?"

"Absolutely. Just tell me when to be here."

"Seven is good. The kids can watch a movie, go to bed, and we can all have a good chat." Tina thrust a notebook and sheaf of papers into Aggie's lap. "Look! This group is packed with information. I got you a letter of intent form for each child, although one woman says you just need one for both schools. There are co-ops and field trips and they even do school pictures!"

"What is she talking about?" William took the first paper off the stack and frowned as he read it. "Tell me you aren't actually considering this."

"I ordered curriculum for Vannie today. We just have to decide on the others. I don't think Laird will be so independently motivated, so I chose not to do the video course for him." Aggie chose to ignore the continued disapproval from William. "What did they say about choosing curriculum?"

Tina's face twisted in a mixture of disgust and frustration. "I asked almost every woman there and they all agree."

"So why do you look revolted by their choice."

"Ask me." Tina kicked off her shoes, sat cross-legged across from them, and leaned back on her hands. "I dare you to ask me what kind of curriculum you should use."

"Ok..." The whole thing seemed ridiculous to Aggie. "What kind of curriculum should I use?"

With a falsetto that made William and Aggie snicker before they even heard the answer, Tina said, "Oh, you have to find what works for *you*."

"What!"

"The good news is, I did figure out how to get a feel for what they'd suggest if they weren't so adamant about everyone blazing their own trail through the home educating wilderness."

William's face grew more disapproving with every word. "How?"

"I asked what they use. I went back to every woman and asked what curriculum they use and why."

"Genius!" Aggie's momentary push to the brink of a breakdown was halted by Tina's forethought.

"Yep. Here, I've got the final tally. I spoke to eight classic home educators who mostly used the same core curriculum, nine Charlotte Mason people, several of whom use that one website we found, remember?" Aggie nodded and gestured for her to continue. "I found four who use strictly textbooks from companies that supply Christian schools, and two that use those worktext type things we looked at."

"I liked those because it looked easy to implement for the first year."

"Oh, and then here are eleven..." Tina continued as she flipped the next page. "Eleven!"

"Eleven what?"

"Eleven mothers who call themselves 'eclectic.' They use whatever they like from whatever company and use them in various ways." She studied the page a bit more. "Oh, and there were three 'unschoolers.' Apparently, some people fill the home with educational materials and things and encourage their children to explore them as they like. It sounded fascinating, but..."

"Yeah, I'm not ready for that," Aggie agreed.

"Well, I'm glad to hear it." William interjected with exaggerated relief. "That sounds irresponsible at best. I wonder that the state doesn't get more involved to make sure these kids are learning what they're supposed to be."

Tina, passing the notebook to Aggie, shot him a dirty look. "Listen, until you are reasonably acquainted with responsible home education, I think you can just keep your uneducated opinions to yourself. I was so amazed and impressed tonight by how thorough these women are. They had ideas and plans for things that I heard mentor teachers only dream of when we were doing our student teaching."

"Like what?" Aggie ignored the stormy look on William's face as she listened to Tina's story.

"Ok, the best example was this gal from California. You know how they have all those cool missions and amazing state history?"

"Yeah?"

"Her family started in San Diego and drove and camped all up along the coast to see every mission. They created notebooks—oh, man you should have seen those notebooks. It was just incredible. The whole thing was on display along with a few other things. One family did their own version of Colonial House but tried to live as Native Americans for a month. The dad is a teacher, so he had July off work. They said it was amazing trying to survive."

"Wow."

"How does that help a child learn math?" Skepticism dripped from every word.

"It doesn't. It helps a child learn geography, history, and an appreciation for technology and modern science. It was a great experience that the family had on their month *off* school." Tina's eyes narrowed. "You know, I thought I liked you, but I'm beginning to wonder."

Aggie laughed. She knew William would miss the sarcasm Tina tried to employ to remind William that he was being rude again. "Tina doesn't appreciate uneducated opinions, remember?"

"Whatever. I just think Aggie has enough work without adding more."

"That's an opinion I can get behind. She does. But," Tina leaned forward excitedly, "that's something I really learned a lot about tonight. Yes, it's hard work, but it's exchanging one kind of hard work for another. One of the moms put her kids in school last year because she needed a break. She said it was just as much work, just different. She had to run around more, help with homework, volunteer in classrooms… it was a lot of work."

"But was it that much work last year, Aggie?"

Before Aggie could answer, Tina piped up again, "Well, and then there's the rewarding factor. Aggie trained for five years to be a teacher. This way, she actually gets to use her training. That alone has got to feel good after a year of formula, diapers, and ant farm disasters."

Aggie decided to stay quiet and listen to the debate rage. It was hilarious to watch Tina shoot down every one of William's objections. Slowly, their words made no sense, as she grew groggy, until at last, only the faint drone of their voices entered her consciousness. Time became nebulous until she dreamed of bouncing over dirt roads from mission to mission and William complaining, "This isn't easy going up, you know."

Gentle dreams drifted from her, pushed away by the morning breeze through the window. Summer was definitely waning. Aggie stretched, as the last vestiges of sleep evaporated, and her first coherent thought of the morning forced her to a sitting position. "How did I get in bed?" She glanced down at the blouse and skirt. "I know I did not climb into bed in these clothes of—" A memory intruded. "Seriously, Lord? She thought it was a good idea to make that man carry me to bed? Seriously?"

Aggie flopped back on the pillows, wondering how much weaker she'd fallen in William's eyes. He could make their new educational adventure a nightmare if he chose. She stretched. "Hey, the soreness is gone!" She was hungry, and if the itching were any indication, she had more pox, but the queasiness and achy feeling seemed to have dissipated in the night. "Well, Lord, thanks for that!"

Her words gave her a snicker as she began singing, "*Thank you, Lord for saving my soul. Thank you, Lord for making me kindasortawhole. Thank you, Lord for giving to me…*"[8]

The silence of her house unnerved her, so Aggie rolled to check the clock and found a plush chicken holding a box of pansies and sitting on her trunk-turned-nightstand. "What—" A small "card" tucked beneath the chicken's wing diverted her questioning. She unfolded it and read the note inside. *Praying that you feel better today. May she inspire many smiles just as you inspire so many of mine. Luke.*

Before she could process the information, Libby entered carrying a glass of juice, a muffin, and a bottle of ibuprofen. "Morning, Aggie. Kenzie has been perched on the top step for the past half hour waiting to hear you moving around. She just came tearing down the steps seconds ago."

"I didn't hear her."

"She's wearing her skid-free socks 'to keep quiet for Aunt Aggie.'"

"Did you see what Luke brought me? Isn't she cute?"

"I did. That's why Kenzie has been waiting so patiently. I think she's hoping for some personal bonding time with the clucker."

Libby winked as she handed Aggie the juice. "Drink up. We have to keep you hydrated."

As she sipped her drink, Aggie leaned back against the headboard and rubbed her shoulder blade against it, scratching a pock. "How did he know I love pansies?"

Libby, with a thoughtful look on her face that made Aggie feel like she'd missed something, stood before her—silent. At last, after several long seconds, the smiling woman recited,

"Pansies are for thoughts.

So let it be:

Mine are for you.

Let yours be of me."

"I've never heard that before. How does it go again?"

Libby recited the little poem once more, and her voice held a reminiscent aura as she added, "I wonder if Luke remembers that little verse. I used to recite it each year as we planted them along the walk. Those are special memories for me."

"It sounds like your children had a delightful childhood. I never planted flowers with my mom."

Sympathy filled Libby's face. "I imagine that is a hard thing for your mother at times— remembering the things she wished she had the strength to do with you and your sister."

"Did Luke enjoy planting them? Did he help?"

After pushing the muffin plate into Aggie's hands, Libby settled herself on the end of the bed as if ready to share a wonderful story with a child at bedtime. "Oh, yes. They all helped. Corinne liked to create the layouts and boss everyone around, Luke did all the digging and clean up. Except the snapdragons. He always planted a corner of snapdragons that were just his. My Luke used to bring them to me whenever he'd gotten into trouble. Cassie planted the seeds and Melanie always transplanted the potted plants." She grinned remembering. "And if she dared hurt one of the pansies or if Corinne didn't plan enough of them, they were sure to hear about it."

"I suppose he just sent his favorites, eh? Well, I'll have to let him know that they're my favorites too."

Libby, with a gaze that held Aggie's hostage, continued with a soft voice, "Considering my Luke's feelings for you, I think he chose them for you rather than for him." She pointed at Aggie's half mangled muffin and mostly full juice glass. "Finish your breakfast, and take your time. I expect Laird to start spotting soon. He's looking a little tired, and he was complaining about being hot when Tavish suggested a hike through the fields."

Aggie stared at the empty doorway lost in thought. Had she heard what she thought she had? Her mind whirled over past and recent conversations, but each one seemed more contradictory than the last. Nothing made sense, and her head began to ache with the concentration. "Ok, Lord. Can we revisit this one later?" The p-mail flew from her lips before she realized she'd spoken.

The cool morning air sent shivers over her. She reached into her closet and found the box marked "winter clothes" and plowed through it, looking for her comfortable knit pants and her oversized t-shirt. "Perfect clothes for a lazy morning when you're sick," she muttered as she stumbled through to the bathroom, her feet still "asleep" from sitting on them in bed.

Grabbing a brush, she pulled it through her hair a few times, tied a hair tie around it, and washed her hands. Running her tongue around the inside of her mouth, she was relieved to discover no new pox. Vannie's mouth looked miserable, and Aggie was a little nervous about oral eruptions.

As she stepped from the bathroom, her bed mocked her. She hated leaving her room disheveled, but as often as she'd been napping lately, it seemed like a waste of time to make it. Forcing herself to ignore the guilt, Aggie hurried downstairs, the crummy plate in one hand and half-empty juice glass in the other. Libby, seeing the unfinished juice, gave Aggie a "look," but the girl promised to drink it.

"I got so used to watering down some for Ian that I prefer mine diluted now."

"Now if that isn't a mother's occupational hazard, I don't know what is."

"Waking up with a chicken's box full of pansies?"

"I wondered if you'd get the joke." Luke sounded pleased.

Aggie was startled at the sound of Luke's voice. She turned to see him on a ladder replacing a light bulb in the dining room, and shook her head. "Oy. Those are all new bulbs, even!"

Everyone seemed to disappear from the room as they spoke— well, everyone but Kenzie. "Aunt Aggie, can I go bring your chicken down so she's not up there all alone?"

Luke grinned down at the little girl. "Why don't you do that, and I'll help you plant the pansies later."

As Kenzie skipped out of the room, Aggie's eyes caught Luke's and held them. "Thank you. It was a nice thing to wake up to today."

"Mom used to recite a verse every year as she planted them, but there wasn't room on that dinky little card."

"Something about pansies and thoughts? She quoted it for me, but I can't remember it." Aggie's brow furrowed in concentration.

"Yep. I'll write it down for you later if you like." His ears burned, much to Aggie's amusement.

"That'd be nice."

Awkwardness hung between them until Luke whipped out a marker. "You and several others have new pox and bare arms and faces. I think it's time for pictures again. What do you think?"

"Lead on, artist dude."

Luke rolled his eyes. "Dude? Really?"

"It works!" she protested, scuttling to the library. "Luke is drawing pictures. Line up and see what he finds today!"

For the next hour or so, Luke drew pictures on arms, legs, and faces, they watched *Anchors Aweigh*, and put together puzzles in teams, races, and upside down. Luke, once finished drawing on everyone else, arrived at Aggie's side, took a fractious Ian from her, and gave the baby to his mother. "He needs a nap, and Aggie needs a decorated face."

He returned and wiggled his pen at her menacingly. "Ok, which arm gets a picture? You can't be the only one without war paint."

Aggie stuck out her arms. "Both!"

"Ok, close your eyes and see if you can figure out what I draw."

He drew each line in long slow movements, but Aggie immediately identified it as a daisy. The picture on her next arm wasn't as obvious. Two loops made her tempted to say daisy again, but the rest was all wrong. At last, she surrendered. "I don't know. What is it?" As she opened her eyes, she grinned. "That is the most lopsided rabbit I've ever seen, but I like him."

He began drawing on her cheek, but mid picture, Luke's face fell as his eyes noticed something. "Oh, no!" He glanced around the room and groaned. "Um, it's good that you like them... do you want me to finish this or not?"

"Why? What's wrong?"

Closing his eyes, he passed the marker over to her. "I thought I grabbed the washable one..."

"Sharpie. I swear; I should ban these things from the house." As severe as she tried to sound, Aggie's laugh betrayed her. Luke looked ready to fire back a witty retort, but William's knock interrupted them.

"Can I come in?"

Aggie beamed up at him from the floor. "Sure! How do you like my arms?"

Lips pursed, William held the door open. "Do you feel up to a chat on the porch?"

She rose, shrugged her shoulders at Libby and Luke, and followed William to the octagon that housed her furniture. With one leg tucked under her, she settled into the wicker chair and sighed, contented. "Isn't this weather just beautiful? If I didn't itch so badly, I'd want to take the kids apple picking or something. I wonder when apples are ripe, anyway." Aggie chattered as if unaware that William must have come for a reason. "Did I tell you that I found out Luke's sister home-schools? I'm going to call her this evening after her husband is home to watch the kids and talk about curriculum choices. Tina and I are making the final decisions tonight. They've already missed two weeks as it is. We'll be starting behind, but Libby says—" She stopped. "Sorry. Did you need something?"

"Well, apparently you needed some adult conversation, so we're good."

"Well, that's silly. Luke, Tina, and Libby are here. I get lots of adult conversation these days."

"Maybe you're just in need of male adult conversation then."

"What do you call Luke?"

William shrugged. "I don't know. Anyway, I found out what happened to Douglas Stuart."

"Is he all right?"

"Well, sort of. He drove all the way to Rockland, pulled into what he thought was his driveway, parked and locked the van, walked up the steps, let himself into the house, and made himself at home in the family's home office. He spent several minutes trying to get into their password protected computer, and then started ranting and screaming at it. A woman came in to see what was going on, and

197

he ordered her from 'his' house. So the terrified woman ran out, went next door, and called the police."

"Why would he do that? Is he ok? Is the *woman* ok?"

He leaned his forearms on his knees and clasped his hands together. "Yep. Once she heard what happened when they took him to the station, she dropped charges."

Aggie waited, but William didn't elaborate. After several seconds, she saw his lip twitch. "You're not Luke. You won't get away with it. What happened?"

"Well, apparently when he got to the station, they called Geraldine. She came down, and as soon as he saw her, his whole persona changed. It was as if he didn't remember how he got there or what he'd done. He was horrified when the arresting officer told him." William ran a frustrated hand along his jaw. "Mrs. Stuart promised to get him medical attention immediately. We're probably looking at some form of dementia—possibly Alzheimer's."

"Oh, I can't believe I'm saying it, but that poor woman!"

"Anyway, she asked me to tell you that she'll have to withdraw her petition for visitation pending the doctor's diagnosis and treatment options."

Aggie was thoughtful for a few seconds before she asked, "Do you think if I had the children make cards and send them it would be ok? It wouldn't jeopardize the restraining order or anything?"

"I think that's a very gracious idea." He stood and walked to the steps. "By the way, it's good to see you in pants, Aggie. I'd thought you were one of those self-righteous 'skirts are holy; pants are evil' types." With that remark hanging in the air like a bomb ready to explode, he jogged down the steps toward his vehicle.

"Oh, no you don't. Get back here. Who do you think you are insulting me and then just walking off like that!"

William turned on his heel, stunned. "I just paid you a compliment."

"Backhanded one at best. You just passed judgment on a whole slew of people who are guilty of nothing but having different preferences and convictions than you. Since when is it a sin to choose not to wear pants?"

Taken aback by her confrontational attitude, William forced himself not to become defensive. "It's definitely wrong to judge those who don't walk around in dresses all the time."

"That sounds suspiciously like judging people to me! You're assuming that if someone is wearing a skirt that they're automatically judging someone who isn't. That's just as bad as if they actually are." William tried to speak, but she continued in her tirade. "Do I act self-righteous when I'm in a skirt? Do I look down on Tina or Mrs. Dyke or anyone else wearing pants? Do I preach at them or judge them?"

"Well, no, but—"

"Then next time you see someone like my sweet Vannie wearing nothing but skirts, don't you dare judge her and assume she's judging everyone around her. That's just as bad as assuming that anyone from the South has to be racist. I thought better of you." With those words, Aggie stormed inside, allowing the screen door to slam behind her. William walked thoughtfully to his cruiser and drove down the road.

Everyone in the house all seemed on edge—almost walking on eggshells, unsure what to think. Libby spent much of the next hour giving Luke stern glances that were highly ineffective considering the smirk hovering around the corners of her mouth. Luke, on the other hand, seemed quite chipper. He whistled while he worked, while he played with the children, and while he tried to tease Aggie into better humor.

Just as they sat down for lunch, a florist's van arrived with a "get well" bouquet. Tavish brought it in and presented it to Aggie with a flourish announcing, "Look! An imaginationally challenged bouquet special!"

Vannie flushed, frantically waving her hands and trying to swallow her soup in order to stop her brother, but it was too late. The three adults stared at one another and at Tavish who was clearly confused as to why they looked at him as if he'd committed a terrible faux pas. "Tavish, that was daddy's private joke for us. You just—it's just that— Oh, Tavish!"

"What?"

Libby took the arrangement from Aggie's stunned hands and carried it to the sink. With kitchen scissors, she carefully snipped each stem of the flowers, inhaling their scent. "I love the spiciness of carnations, don't you? Oh, look. It's hard to see under that big bow, but the mug says, 'Rx: One bowl chicken soup, one funny movie, and lots of hugs from loved ones.'"

Aggie took the card and read it aloud. "'Hope you are feeling better. I am sorry I offended. William.'" Aggie pasted on a smile. "Well, that was thoughtful."

Vannie took a deep breath as if performing a dreaded task. "It's something daddy used to joke about, Aunt Aggie. Every time someone did something traditional like sending flowers, giving chocolate, using candles with dinner — anything like that. He always called it 'imaginationally challenged.' Anytime he brought Mommy flowers, he would say, 'Sorry, I was a little imaginationally challenged today.'"

A few snickers, followed by chuckles, eventually evolved into hysterical laughter that even the twins and Ian, although they didn't understand why, joined in enthusiastically. Not even ever-gracious Libby could suppress her amusement. Aggie and Luke, trying to control their mirth, failed miserably and spent the rest of the meal snickering and chuckling whenever someone muttered, "imaginationally challenged."

Determined not to be caught laughing while thanking him, Aggie called and left a thank you message on his voice mail. As she hung up the phone, she turned to Luke. "Do you think he's going to wonder why I sounded so strangled in thanking him?"

Before anyone could reply, Laird lifted his shirt to see what had bit him and groaned. "My turn, I guess."

Luke says: What are you doing up? You looked done for two hours ago!

Aggie says: I fell asleep for exactly an hour, and now I'm wide awake.

Mibs says: Oops. I think I forgot to change my name after talking to my dad the other day. Mibs was confusing him. He kept seeing the M and thinking he was talking to Mom.

Luke says: Well, I guess I won't get offended then.

Mibs says: You're so understanding.

Luke says: Is Laird still taking it hard?

Mibs says: Yeah. Poor kid really thought he wasn't going to get it. Apparently he did some boasting to Tavish too, so Tavish going last… the little brother thing…

Luke says: Yep. I never had a little brother, but I imagine a sister is about as mortifying… if not more so. On the bright side, a little humiliation is very character building.

Mibs says: You speak from experience, I assume.

Luke says: Guilty as charged.

Mibs says: Well, not to change the subject but…

Luke says: You have another subject.

Mibs says: Very astute of you Mr. Sullivan.

Luke says: It was, wasn't it?

Mibs says: So, are you up for dinner with William this weekend?

Luke says: If he wants to ask me out, why doesn't he do it himself? I would have thought after the Mrs. Dyke fiasco…

Mibs says: *giggles* That's a good one.

Luke says: Seriously, though, why would you want both of us there?

Mibs says: Well, at first I thought Tina wanted me to invite him so she could get to know him better. She seemed not to trust him. Now, I'm wondering if there isn't a little more personal interest there. She took great offense to his objections to home-schooling. I just don't want to be a third wheel.

Luke says: Oh.

Mibs says: Is it a problem for you? I'll understand if it is. Ick, it feels like I'm asking you out or something.

Luke says: I understand. I'll be there.

Mibs says: Thanks, Luke. Both for understanding and for coming.

Luke says: Mom is bugging me for the computer. I'll let you talk to her if you like. I'll be back in a bit. Her dryer isn't drying the clothes.

Luke says: Hello, Aggie! Has William asked about your message yet?

Mibs says: LOL. Nope. I think he's going to chalk it up to awkwardness with a machine or something. I invited Luke to have dinner with Tina, William, and me, but he didn't seem very enthusiastic.

Luke says: Oh.

Libby says: There. At least I don't feel so masculine now. As for Luke, I think he considers William to be some serious competition.

Mibs says: Competition for what?

Libby says: You, of course. My Luke is very fond of you.

Mibs says: Oh, I think you're mistaken.

Libby says: Well, I won't argue with you or try to make you uncomfortable, but I also won't pretend not to see what I see.

Mibs says: Thanks. You're a good woman, Libby. Have I told you that?

Libby says: Frequently. I am in danger of growing a bobble head from all your flattery. Ahh, Luke is shooing me off to bed. He seems to think I'm yawning too much. I'll close out though, so he doesn't see our conversation.

Mibs says: Thank you. I think it'd embarrass him. Thanks for everything. I always feel like I never show my appreciation.

Libby says: Well, you do. So goodnight and don't worry about it.

Mibs says: Night.

Luke says: Well, if you want to get rid of me...

Mibs says: Your name isn't Libby — the name I was typing to before you switched.

Luke says: Mibs, you really need to sleep. You hardly rested at all today, and I know you're exhausted.

Mibs says: I know. I just can't seem to settle.

Luke says: Take some Benadryl to stave off the itches. It'll knock you out in no time.

Mibs says: You're right! Itching is what woke me up too!

Luke says: Goodnight, Mibs. I'll be a couple of streets over tomorrow if you need me. Just send Tavish if I don't answer my phone.

Mibs says: Goodnight, Luke. Thanks.

GETTING AN EDUCATION

Chapter Fifteen

Sunday, September 14ᵗʰ

Dinner over, Tina and William sat on the porch "discussing" Aggie's new educational adventure, rehabilitation of prisoners, and other equally benign topics of conversation. Luke and Aggie, having spent an entire meal struggling not to laugh at the constant debate over everything from politics and religion to best vacation spots and stereotypes of the wealthy, had kicked the couple out of the kitchen with promises of dessert after the dishes were done and the kitchen cleaned. Once the counters shone and the sink sparkled, Luke presented Aggie with the week's tally of hours worked. The list included flooring, painting, and a line item at the bottom that read, ".02 for opinions on curriculum choices."

She batted him with the invoice on her way to her desk, pulled out her checkbook, and wrote a check for one hundred sixty-two dollars and two cents. "That was probably the first check that I've ever written for all this that didn't make my heart sink. Thank you."

"Mibs," pain filled Luke's eyes. "You know I'd do it without charge, right?"

She passed him the check and sank into a barstool. "Luke, if you saw the bank statements I get every month, you'd demand that I treble your salary."

"No, I wouldn't." He almost sounded hurt.

"It was a joke." Aggie covered her head with her hands while she struggled to regain her composure. "Luke, I could do it and I wouldn't even notice it in my accounts. Allie and Doug were well insured, well invested, and the Stuarts paid a mint for that huge house they owned, and you know what I paid for this."

"I don't understand."

She stood, pulled a cheesecake from the fridge, and began slicing. "It's a frozen one, but the gal at the store swears you can't tell the difference, or so Tina says." As she slid a piece on a plate, Aggie leaned against the counter, her knife sticking out at an awkward angle. "I keep picturing all the kids coming back for Thanksgiving some year after they're grown, looking around the house and saying, 'You spent our inheritance on this place just so you could have a nice house.'"

"Oh, Mibs, they wouldn't. The house is for them. They'll know that."

"The rational part of me knows that, but…" She wiped the knife blade on a paper towel and made another cut. "I don't know how to be frugal with the money and keep up the kind of lifestyle the kids had. I've never had private lessons for this and country club memberships and all that stuff that Allie had and hated."

"That's because you can't, Aggie. You aren't Allie Stuart, wife of Douglas and daughter-in-law to Douglas Sr. and Geraldine. You're Aggie Milliken. You have to live as Aggie would. Your sister knew that when she chose you."

Aggie handed him two plates and grabbed a few napkins before she took the other two. "I suppose." At the kitchen door, she turned. "Thanks, Luke. I know I get weird about this stuff. Mom says Allie wouldn't recognize me. The only time I've ever been able to save money was when I worked those summers to buy my car, and even then I had a few setbacks. A missionary came, we had a chance to go to Storyland in Rockland, and then I bought my senior ring. Dumb move that was too. I never wear it."

"But," he said, nudging her through the house, "that was your money. Right now you feel like you're spending the children's inheritance."

"I am."

"No, you're spending the money left to you for their care. The money was left to you, not to them in trust with you. The money was left so that you wouldn't have to worry about paying the bills or scrimping." He pushed open the screen door. "The money was left for living now, not for giving later."

"So, what do you think about general textbooks for Tavish, Ellie, and Laird for this year, and then seeing how you can involve them in whatever you do for Kenzie?"

"Charlotte Mason for Kenzie?" Aggie was drawn to how natural the learning process was designed to be, and Kenzie wouldn't have as many preconceived ideas about how school should work like the other children.

"Sure. When you do nature studies, bring the others along. Whatever you read aloud, they all listen to, even Vannie if she likes."

"Use that website to start with?" Aggie couldn't imagine anything else, but Tina had been a researching machine.

"Yep." Seeing Aggie yawn, Tina pulled the laptop from her. "Go to bed. I'll figure out what you need to order first, and you can do it tomorrow."

Wednesday September 17th

A restless night, thanks to itchy spots, left Aggie tired and miserable. Ellie, the latest victim, woke up with dozens of spots all over her arms, neck, chest, and face on Monday, and spent all morning recoating herself with calamine lotion. Tavish sat with her, refusing to leave unless she wanted something. At times, Aggie was certain she sent him for a book or a glass of juice just to get some breathing room.

It was the third day without Tina, and Aggie already felt the weight of sick children on her hands again. With Libby at the dentist for the morning and Luke working on his new house, she found herself chasing after Ian, settling squabbles between the twins and Kenzie, and then chasing after Ian again. By the time Libby arrived, she almost sobbed with relief.

"Would you mind if I went upstairs for just a few minutes? I haven't sat down all morning. I feel like I'm going to drop."

"Sure. Take a sandwich and your books up there, and don't come down until you feel like it. I can handle things here."

"Mrs. Dyke volunteered to come help if we need her, but try me first, ok? I really don't want to take advantage of her generosity." Hearing how thoughtless those words sounded, Aggie arranged her face into an exaggerated sheepish expression and added, "I'd rather take advantage of you."

"Get up there, silly girl."

Vannie heard her aunt climbing the stairs from her bed and followed. Just as Aggie arranged the bed comfortably, she heard a gentle knock and sighed. Certain Libby needed her after all, she called, "Come in," and began climbing from her bed. The sight of Vannie stopped her. "Are you ok?"

"I'm feeling a lot better, actually. I don't think I have any new pox today."

"Good! Maybe when your videos arrive, you'll feel up to doing them."

"I can't wait! I feel so behind already."

Aggie looked closely at her niece. "What's bothering you, Van? You look upset."

"I'm not really upset, but I've been thinking about something."

Scooting over, Aggie made room on the bed next to her. She made a mental note to find a loveseat for her room for just these kinds of aunt-niece/nephew chats. "Come sit with me, and tell me what has you looking so troubled."

The girl fidgeted for a few seconds, and then blurted out, "We all overheard your argument with Mr. Markenson."

"Yes. That wasn't one of my shining moments, was it?"

"Well, actually, I thought you made a lot of sense. I never knew people might think we thought badly of them for wearing different clothes."

"Well, I dare say William won't be making that assumption again anytime soon."

"Well, that's just it. I was surprised when you came down in those pants." Aggie watched as the girl struggled to articulate her thoughts, not unlike Luke's frequent pauses and restarts. "I mean, I thought you didn't wear pants — like us. Mommy never wore them, we weren't allowed to wear them — well, the boys were — and you haven't worn them before...." Vannie's eyes were wide and earnest as she asked the burning question in her curious mind. "So, you think it's ok for girls and women to wear pants?"

"Well, I've worn them most of my life, so I'd say so."

"Then why were you mad at Mr. Markenson for saying he was glad you were wearing them that day?"

"Because he made unjust assumptions about me based upon what I wear. Since he's always seen me in skirts, he just assumed that I was self-righteous about it, which, if you think about it, was awfully self-righteous of him."

"So," Vannie's tendency to examine every question from every angle was not lost on the conversation. "If you think pants are ok, why don't you wear them more often?"

With a deep breath, a p-mail shot heavenward for wisdom, and a forced smile, Aggie tried to explain something she'd never had to articulate to anyone. "Vannie, I'm not going to discount your mother's conviction on modesty standards, but I don't share them. I wear skirts or dresses most of the time because I like them; I'm comfortable in them. I want to look and feel feminine, and dresses do that for me." She paused, searching for the perfect words in her desire not to preach to and subsequently alienate her eldest niece.

At last, she thought she knew what to say. "You see, some people, your parents for instance, believe that the Bible requires women to wear only skirts or dresses — that because pants were originally worn by men in our culture, women are forbidden to wear them. That's fine for them, but I don't see that in scripture. I understand their argument, I have studied it, but I did not come to the same conclusion."

"Right. So you got mad because he thought you believed like Mommy?"

"I got mad because it's frustrating when people assume that if you do wear skirts or dresses all the time that you believe everyone must—that they're substandard Christians or something if they don't. It's, well, it's making a judgment of someone's motives—it's judging the heart."

"Jesus said not to judge, or you'll be judged in the same way."

"Right. I believe Jesus is telling us not to judge people's hearts and motives—that only God can see the heart and therefore judge it."

Vannie nodded slowly as if beginning to understand. "So the reason you told Aunt Tina not to buy us jeans was because Mommy didn't let us wear them?" The girl blushed. "Aunt Tina had me try some on anyway, but they looked weird and felt funny."

"Well," Aggie began, laughing, "with the kind of jeans she said you guys found, I don't doubt it. She told me about that. She thought I meant you had enough jeans, but when you didn't find any appropriate skirts or dresses, she thought she should get you *something* to wear."

"Does Mrs. Sullivan believe like Mommy? Does she think that girls should only wear skirts or dresses? I don't think I've seen her wear pants." The girl's struggle with some aspect of the topic was evident from the worry in her eyes to the wrinkled brow.

"I just don't know, Vannie. I've never asked." She thought for a moment. "I think you're right, though. I'm pretty sure I've only seen her in dresses—not even skirts I don't think. Then again, until today I'd never unpacked mine."

"Why not?"

"Well, as I said, I tend to prefer skirts anyway, but I think I probably subconsciously adopted a similar dress style. People tend to do that unless they have convictions against something or strong personal preferences. For example, skinny jeans make me feel claustrophobic, so I don't own any."

"So how do you know," the girl persisted, "if someone believes like Mommy or is like you? How can you tell?"

That question made Aggie nervous. Cautiously, and with each thought worded with Luke-like precision, she tried to handle the question as delicately as possible. "Vannie, why does it matter? Is it my business to know why someone wears anything? Why would you choose purple over brown or corduroy over denim? Why do some women wear a great variety of styles and articles and others have a more limited wardrobe?"

"But those aren't—"

"They are the point, Vannie. They are. Your responsibility before God is to please Him in everything that you do and leave God's convictions between Him and those He chooses to convict." Her eyes widened in surprise as she realized what she'd just said. "That's what I tried to explain to William. Instead, I got defensive and took up an offense for people who could probably care less what William thinks of their wardrobe choices."

Although Vannie seemed visibly relieved, Aggie could see lingering doubts in the girl's expression. "You know, while you all live with me, I want you to wear dresses. It honors your parents' wishes for you, but I want you to study this. Go to the Bible and read everything it says about clothing, modesty, femininity, masculinity. Everything. I'll find you articles by people who hold your parents' convictions and by those who don't. Examine what each side uses to back up their position. Are their arguments scriptural? See if they trying to excuse behavior with verses taken out of context. Make sure they are not trying to require behavior with verses taken out of context. Take it all to the Lord and see where He guides you through your study. Just base your own convictions on the Word. Don't base them on what I think or even on what your parents thought. Base them only on the Word."

"I don't understand something." Vannie's eyes were narrowed in that way that always made her look angry when she was actually concentrating.

"What is that?"

"Well, you say to study the Bible for myself, but you also say I have to follow Mommy and Daddy's convictions for us. Why do I have to follow one if I come to a different conclusion?"

Aggie had begun to think Vannie would make an excellent lawyer. "Well, it's like I asked William. Is it a sin to wear them even if you don't believe you must?"

"Well, no but—"

"Then, as I said," Aggie interrupted quickly before the girl could add any more arguments to the table. "We'll wear them in this house to honor the preferences your parents had for you. That is something that I believe is commendable. I can't do everything exactly how your parents would, but this one is so easy, I can't justify not doing it." She glanced toward her own closet, thinking of her favorite jeans, the long Bermuda shorts she'd never had a chance to wear that summer, and her favorite wool dress pants. Before she could change her mind, she added, "I think I'll toss my pants just so none of you feel like I'm setting a double standard."

"Oh, Aunt Aggie, no! You don't have to do that. The girl tried to apologize, visibly distraught that her questions had created such a 'terrible loss' for her aunt.

"Of course, I don't have to, but Vannie, they're just clothes. If I'm going to require this of you, I want to be an example to you and your sisters. Remember, it isn't a *sin* if I choose not to do what I believe I can."

She scrambled from the bed, found an old pillowcase in a stack of linens she hadn't been able to dispose of yet, and rifled through her closet finding the few pairs of pant-like garments that she owned. They stuffed them in the old pillowcase and tossed it in the corner. As she led Vannie from the room, Aggie whispered with a giggle, "Besides, William will be frustrated when he realizes that he has never seen me in pants again."

Later that afternoon, Libby pulled Aggie aside and gave her a warm hug. "Young lady, you are wise beyond your years. I overheard you with Vannie earlier. I heard voices from the window and went up to tell her to let you rest. When I heard what was bothering her, I was arrogant and just 'knew' you'd need my help, but I learned much from you. Thank you."

"Really? I felt like I bungled the whole thing. I didn't know how to get her off the fixation of why other people do what they do. I just wanted her to fix her eyes on Jesus instead of everyone around her." The young woman rolled her eyes. "Oh, honestly. Why couldn't I have said that!"

"Because, Aggie. Murphy's Law is alive and well and adapts itself to any occasion—particularly anything remotely related to parenting."

"Don't I know it," Aggie agreed dryly.

"Aggie? Aggie, wake up." Luke's voice jerked her from a dead sleep.

"Wha—what is it?"

"Mom and I just got here, and Vannie was doing everything she could to keep things quiet, but Ellie is running a raging fever. She's just coated with pox. Mom thinks you should take her to the clinic. She would have, but—"

"No," Aggie tried to drag herself from the bed. "They won't let her. "I need to do it."

"Sorry, Mibs. I didn't want to wake you."

"I know. Thanks. I'll be right down."

Minutes later, she whizzed down the road, trying to stay close to the speed limit, but with the sight of her niece in her rearview mirror, the needle crept higher and higher. "We'll be there in just a minute. They'll know how to make you feel better."

The doctor took one look at several of Ellie's pox and shook his head. "She's scratching in her sleep. Several of these are infected. That explains why her fever is still high."

He made a few notes, wrote out a prescription, and called for one of the nurses to call it into the pharmacy in Brunswick. Then, he wheeled an IV pole over to the table. "We're going to have a hard time finding a good place to do this, but she's a little dehydrated. We'll get an antibiotic started too."

Aggie frowned. "She's been drinking. Every glass we bring her is empty when she returns."

Ellie's already red face became even redder. "I didn't drink it," the child admitted in a whisper.

Aggie noticed the girl's cracked lips and sighed. "Where did it go?"

"Tavish drank..."

"Does it hurt your mouth?" Dr. Sanderson seemed to understand.

"Yes. I'm sorry."

"It's normal, sweetie. We'll send you home a special water bottle that'll squirt the water at the back of your throat. That way, you can drink without hurting so much." He patted the child's hand

211

as he spoke. "Just swish a bit around your mouth once in a while so you don't get too dry."

The morning dragged into afternoon as they watched "Miss Elspeth" as the doctor liked to call her, improve enough to leave. To help alleviate her pain, they gave her a swish of liquid lidocaine and explained to Aggie how to mix Mylanta and Benadryl for a similar effect at home. Before they left, the doctor made Ellie promise to squirt all liquids Aggie served her down her throat.

On the way home, Ellie sighed contentedly. "Dr. Sanderson is a very nice man. I love doctors."

Aggie shook her head, amused. Her children never failed to prove, at just the right times, that she would never be able to predict anything ever again. "The only thing predictable about children is their unpredictability," she muttered.

"What was that, Aunt Aggie?"

"I was just saying how unique each of you are."

Ellie beamed. "I love that word. Unique. It's a cool word — like angst. They both sound like the thing they are."

"My point exactly."

Once Tavish was the only child pox-free, Aggie quit trying to keep the children separated. Her most recent attempts were limited anyway, but at that point, it seemed silly. Just before dinner, she glanced in the mirror, saw a fresh outbreak of pox, and wondered if her body was going to erupt every few weeks for the rest of her life. Was she so contrary that she insisted on proving Luke wrong about the pox vs. acne thing?

Meanwhile, despite the fact that Vannie's videos were already en route, all hopes of beginning a minimal school week were gone with her new outbreak. She knew there was no way she'd be able to concentrate on making assignment sheets and with Ellie so sick and unable to start, everyone would end up on different schedules. It made sense to bump it back another week. She glanced at Libby as she made the decision, and sighed. "Remind me that they wouldn't be having much in the way of education even if I didn't send in that notice of intent."

"They wouldn't. Even with her books here, Vannie had a hard time concentrating. Illness and education don't mix will."

Luke carried boards through the mudroom and downstairs, making Aggie curious about what he was doing, but Ian wailed upstairs in his crib. "Ugh. He's being difficult about his nap today. I don't know what's gotten into him. I thought he was feeling better."

"I'll get him, Aggie. You rest. I think that's why you keep breaking out. You aren't resting."

As Libby climbed the stairs, Aggie glanced around the room. It was littered with Popsicle wrappers, pillows, childish drawings, and half-finished puzzles. There were socks, blankets, pillows, and calamine bottles everywhere. Relaxing wouldn't work. Until she had their home-school plan up and running, she wasn't comfortable with the idea of another visit from the "attendance officer" showing up and finding things chaotic as they were. So, ignoring Libby's prior admonitions to rest, Aggie stood, grabbed a trash bag from the kitchen, and began picking up the room—about five minutes too late.

"Knock, knock."

The sound of William's voice sank her spirits. It seemed as if he had internal radar for arriving at the worst possible time. "Come in." She shoved another handful of popsicle wrappers and used Kleenex in the bag before grabbing several glasses and carrying them to the kitchen.

"Are you feeling better?" Aggie turned and put her hands on her hips. One look at her face told him all he needed to know. "I guess not." His eyes roamed over the room. His discomfort with her home was much less than it had been only weeks earlier, but he still seemed to steel himself against the ghosts of his past before making himself at home. He grabbed the trash bag from where Aggie had left it and began gathering all the children's scattered pictures. Before she could stop him, he shoved them into the bag and set it next to the front door. "How was the first day of school go?"

"Ellie woke up miserable. I had to take her to the clinic, I broke out in more pox myself, as you can see, so I gave up on that idea. We'll just have to change the planned vacation days and maybe add in a few Saturdays or something." Aggie's mind tried to calculate a new idea to revamp the school schedule, but to no avail. Her brains were on sick leave.

Disapproval flooded his face. He grabbed several bottles of lotion, Benadryl, and Tylenol from the end table. "Where do these go? You shouldn't leave them laying around like that."

Protest rose in Aggie's heart, but she chose to ignore him. Becoming defensive wouldn't solve anything. "Here, I'll take them."

"They should be put up somewhere out of reach — locked would be best," he added helpfully.

Aggie returned with an empty laundry basket for discarded socks, towels, and other various things in need of washing. She tossed a couple of pillows on top and carried the whole thing to the mudroom. Upon returning, she glanced around. The room needed a vacuuming, desperately needed dusting, but at least it wasn't cluttered anymore, so she sank onto the couch — beat. That move set off a chain reaction that she could never have anticipated.

"You're tired." It was almost an accusation.

"I am. I can't believe how exhausting it is to be spotty. It's like my body gets worn out creating those stupid things."

"If you're this tired, if you're already weeks behind the school calendar, what makes you think you can actually *do* this home-school thing?" As plain as William's concern was, there was a slight air of patronization in his tone that rankled.

"I think you're forgetting that none of those kids would be in school before Monday regardless of where that school is. At least if I keep them home, we can start from any date and *do* all the work rather than missing it. They wouldn't have that opportunity in a regular classroom."

"That may be, but today's delay just makes me wonder, again, if you should even be doing all this. It's too much for one person."

From the corner of her eye, Aggie saw Luke carry something out of the basement and out through the mudroom. Curious as to what he was doing, she almost missed William's words. "Wait a minute. I shouldn't be doing what?"

"This — all of it." The stunned look on Aggie's face made William hasten to elaborate. "Not that I don't think you should be taking care of the children. I do. I admire you for it. I just think that enough has happened to demonstrate that it's too much work for one person alone — particularly someone so young."

"Happened? What are you talking about?" An inward groan punctuated her questions with exclamation marks. She sounded as defensive as she felt.

"Oh, come on, Aggie. You've been to the clinic too many times to count, you lost the baby—you know, the one with a knack for abusing the 9-1-1 system—you sprained your ankle goofing off, ended up with a reaction because you were messing around in that awful attic, you have a houseful of sick kids and need Sullivan and his mom just to get through the day—and now this home-schooling thing."

"What about it? I haven't started yet! You can't call me a failure for that until I actually have a chance to try it." Had William known her better, he'd have stopped before he felt the full impact of her anger.

"That's my point, Aggie. You had plans to start today—"

"I had plans for a dry run. Basic things like here's how things are going to go, let's do our Bible time, and acquaint them with assignment sheets. I had no intention of actually giving them any assignments."

"Because you're not even ready for that. You have no curriculum, no desks—"

"Well, I didn't intend to give them all desks, but that's beside the point." Aggie jerked the ponytail holder from her hair and reformed the up-do.

William glanced around the room. Aggie foolishly assumed it was another survey of her shortcomings, but she soon learned it was to ensure their privacy. "I've been thinking, Aggie."

"It's something most people do from time to time." The moment she heard her sarcasm, Aggie realized how close she was to exploding.

"You can't do this alone. I know we said we weren't going to worry about trying to forge a relationship or anything, but I think that was unrealistic." He jumped as he heard a board clatter down in the basement. "As admirable as your sacrifice for these kids is, you're just one person. You can't do this alone, no matter how much you think you can. You need support, and the kids need more stability. I can't imagine what a mess your finances must be in." She saw his attempts at humor, but the condescension in his tone was almost unbearable.

215

"You have no clue just how insulting that was, do you?"

"Insulting? I'm trying to be encouraging."

"Telling me how pathetic my 'attempts' at mothering are, assuming that you know what I 'need,' and telling me that I don't know a thing about finances is 'encouraging'?"

"Well, I didn't mean it like that. I was trying to show you how much you need help."

"I have help, William. I have Libby, Iris sometimes, Luke, and even you and Mrs. Dyke on occasion. I have help. If I needed it, I could call the Vaughns, and a man from a church in Brunswick offered to help anytime. I'm not unsupported here. If necessary, I can call my parents, or even hire out what I can't do. I have the Lord!"

"It's not the same. I've been thinking about this and praying like crazy, and I think we should just get married."

For one wild moment, Aggie had the inexplicable urge to laugh. Did he not know how ridiculous he sounded? "William, if I thought you were serious—"

"I'm perfectly serious. You need the kind of help and support that a husband and father gives. It's not something that you can hire out, either." He leaned forward, oblivious to the shock and fury simmering beneath Aggie's façade of calm. "The kids need some semblance of a normal life." He swallowed hard as if to gain courage, and continued before she could formulate a coherent response. "I know you are upset with me right now. You probably feel like I'm being hard on you, but I don't mean to be. I'm trying to show you why we should just do this. I get tomorrow and Sunday off, so I'm going to fly to Seattle for a game, but I'll be back home Monday. We can talk about it then."

He stood, nodded, and left before Aggie recovered from the shock. Her lips twisted in wry disgust. "Oh, and you should marry me so I can save you from yourself, but don't tell me how wonderful my brilliant idea is until I get back from a last hurrah as a single guy. Then you can fall at my feet in grateful adoration," she mocked in a ridiculous sounding falsetto. The moment she heard herself, remorse filled her heart. "Oh, Lord. Forgive me, but that man…"

A sound by the basement caused her to turn. Something on Luke's face told her he'd heard her— possibly William too. "I suppose it's too much to hope that you didn't hear that disgusting display."

216

"I heard." He carried the scraps in his arms to the mudroom and returned, pulling his gloves off as he did.

It occurred to her that she didn't know whose words he meant. "Which one, mine or William's?"

"Both." As he sat across from her, his arms on his knees, barely meeting her gaze, she saw concern in his face and a trace of something that almost looked like pain.

"Do you think he's right? Am I really blowing it with the children? Am I harming them? If I thought for even a minute —"

"No, Mibs, no." The sincerity in Luke's voice couldn't be mistaken. "You're doing an excellent job. Mom is always bragging on you to everyone. Corinne was saying that she's been to the Clinic more than you have this summer, and she only has three children."

"I keep thinking that I heard him wrong, but he was serious, wasn't he?" A sense of shock grew in her as she realized that William truly expected her to agree to his strange proposal. "He really thinks that marrying me is really a solution to whatever problems he thinks I have."

"I think so, yes." She heard the strain in Luke's voice and wondered at it.

"What do you think? I can't believe I'm even asking, but I am. Do you think marrying him would provide some kind of stability or something that apparently the kids don't have and need?" Dread caused her voice to stumble and break as she choked out the question.

"Well…" Luke seemed to search for words even more so than usual. "He is confident and responsible. Those are good things to have around when you are dealing with children." By now, the pain in his voice was unmistakable.

"I sense a 'but' coming in right about now." She could see him struggle to answer. Luke clearly didn't like being in the position of advisor this time—didn't want to have this conversation. However, as always, she asked, and he answered.

"No, Mibs. I don't."

"Tell me why. Not that I disagree with you or anything. I just want to make sure my reasons are rational instead of emotional. We both know that he's not going to take no for an answer if I sound emotional." She rubbed her head, dreading the oncoming headache. "I think I'm in shock or something. The only reason I can come up with is, 'because I don't want to.' That's not going to cut it, so tell me. Why shouldn't I marry William?"

"Not wanting to is enough for me, but you're right. Probably not for him."

"So, tell me why."

"Mibs," Luke began gently, never taking his eyes from hers. "My reasons are selfish; they're not something he's going to accept any better." Her eyes insisted he explain himself. "I don't *think* you should because you don't care for him. I don't *want* you to because I *do* care for you."

Surprise flooded Aggie's face followed by thoughtfulness and finally comprehension. All the subtle hints and not-so-subtle ones that Libby had left, and all of Luke's personal compliments and gentle teasing swirled in her mind, but before she could find some way to respond to him, Luke stood and dug his keys out of his pockets. "Aggie, pray about it. Just—just pray. I hadn't planned to share my heart with you yet. I thought you needed time, but…" He fumbled for a particular key and then shrugged. "Well, William spoke, you asked, and…" With the rest of his thoughts unspoken, Luke slipped out the door and walked to his truck. She saw him lean against it, obviously shaken—possibly hurting, although she wasn't sure why. Did he think she'd actually agree to William's crazy idea? The truck started and drove away, but Aggie didn't hear.

Unable to process the afternoon's events with her mind so foggy from a returning fever, Aggie just sat there for some time. The mail came, bringing the set of history DVDs she'd purchased, but Aggie didn't join the children for their video. Instead, she sat, her mind lost in confusing memories of the day. Libby read the children stories, helped them finish picking up, and fixed dinner, and still Aggie sat. After a long walk down the road, they returned to find her asleep, tears still fresh on her lashes.

Aggie says: Mom? Are you on? I really need to talk to you.
Martha says: I'm here! I was hoping you'd get on. How is everyone doing with the pox today?
Aggie says: Terrible. I had to take Ellie into the clinic, and now I have

---

a fresh crop of pox of my own.

Martha says: I've never heard of so many eruptions! Did the doctor say anything about it?

Aggie says: Yep. He said be glad I don't have shingles yet.

Martha says: Well, maybe your body is fighting that so much that it can't kill the pox virus or something.

Aggie says: Don't know if that's possible, but it sounds logical anyway.

Martha says: I suppose that probably put the kibosh on your test day of school.

Aggie says: Yep. And that turned a bad day into an Alexander day.

Martha says: As in "no good" etc.?

Aggie says: That's the one. My day went from horrible to nightmarish in one visit from William.

Martha says: Another 9-1-1 from Ian?

Aggie says: No, worse. Remember that hysterical scene in "Pride and Prejudice" where Darcy proposes?

Martha says: Oh, dear. Tell me he didn't. I was starting to root for Luke.

Aggie says: That's another story all together, but um, for the record, what is funny on the screen is not so comical in real life.

Martha says: Oh, I'm sorry. What happened?

Aggie says: I didn't even get a chance to answer. He told me I couldn't handle life without help, so he decided this was how to solve that little problem, told me what we should do, and then left. I was informed that we'd continue the discussion on Monday after he returns from Seattle.

Martha says: Seattle?

Aggie says: Football game. Can you believe it? He's probably considering it his last bachelor trip or something equally ridiculous.

Martha says: That sounds a little high-handed, doesn't it? Even so, are you sure you want to say no?

Aggie says: Oh, mom. Even if I were in love with him, WHICH I AM NOT, I'd still say no.

Martha says: Why is that?

Aggie says: The guy has a Galahad complex. That whole bit about how I can't cope without his help was just too much. It was insulting, and the pathetic part is, he thought he was being encouraging!

Martha says: Well, it's not exactly the dream proposal, is it?

Aggie says: Not hardly. So, mother dear, how do I gently tell him to forget the idea. Indefinitely. I don't want to be rude or unkind, but it shouldn't be too hard to be blunt and tactful since I know he isn't doing this out of his undying love for me. I just want to make sure it doesn't come up again and that he doesn't decide it has to do with his past or anything.

Martha says: Oh, no. We wouldn't want that. I suppose it wouldn't work to tell him that the last you heard, you didn't request the services of Galahad.

Aggie says: *giggles* That's the truth. I wish I could do it without sounding snarky. I would.

Martha says: Just be honest. Once it's over, he'll probably be just as relieved as he was when you told him you didn't want to do the dating thing.

Aggie says: Yeah, what's with that? We were both relieved. Why do this when we were both happy not to "go there?"

Martha says: It's like you said. He's trying to save you from yourself.

Aggie says: Well, all he's doing is ruining a perfectly good friendship.

Martha says: He'll get over it.

Aggie says: Do you think he's right? Am I really blowing it with the kids?

Martha says: Absolutely not. Your father and I are so proud of you. I wondered how you'd cope with so many new things at once, but you've done an amazing job. Allie couldn't have hoped for a better outcome to their tragedy.

Aggie says: Thanks, Mom. I really needed to hear that tonight.

Martha says: I have a few more things to say sometime, but I'm getting that "Get to bed, woman" look from your father. I've been a little winded this week, and you know how he gets about that.

Aggie says: Go to bed. I'll bug you tomorrow.

Martha says: We'll be down for Vannie's birthday, and your father finally agreed to Thanksgiving at our house. Can you bring up the kids for that?

Aggie says: We'll be there. I'll bring air mattresses, and we'll all sleep in the basement, so don't go to any work or anything.

Martha says: Your dad will love that. No work for me makes him a very happy man. He forgets that I love to prepare for guests.

Aggie says: Mom?

Martha says: Hmm?

Aggie says: Go to bed. I love you!

Martha says: You're as bad as your father—maybe worse! Night, honey. I love you too.

Aggie says: Goodnight.

MUSHINESS

Chapter Sixteen

Monday, September 22nd

Tina called Aggie early Monday afternoon apologizing profusely for missed and unreturned calls. "Sorry I didn't get back to you. I dropped my stupid phone in class, and I couldn't get in to get it until today. My laptop battery died, no one in town has one, and now I know why it is stupid not to have a landline. How is everyone?"

"Ellie's finally better, I haven't had a new pox eruption since Friday, which I consider good, and William proposed."

"He what?" Tina sounded both stunned and a little disappointed.

"Yep. Apparently he thinks I'm completely incompetent, so he decided to be magnanimous and put me out of my misery by marrying me."

Silence hung in the air for a moment. "Do you mean to tell me that he said those things or something close?"

"So close that *feels* verbatim even though I know it isn't."

"I'll kill him."

"For you," Aggie teased, "that's the equivalent of, oh, you'll spit and claw like our kitten every time the puppies come near it. Completely ineffectual, by the way. I've discovered that puppies aren't very intelligent."

"I'll have to up my game to at least a verbal claw or two."

Aggie stepped out the door to see if the twins were still building rock houses in the driveway. "Something else happened after all that."

"Luke clobber him?"

"No, but he told me I shouldn't marry William."

Tina laughed. "Well, that wasn't surprising, considering he's been waiting for you to notice he's a man for the past two months."

Jaw slack, Aggie shook her head as if to clear it. "You—why didn't you say something?"

"Because he didn't. It's not my job to be his mouthpiece. You've forgotten that my name is Tina, not Aaron."

"Funny. Very funny. Libby tried to hint, but I think I tuned her out or something."

"You have a lot on your plate, Aggie. On top of everything, there's William and the worst dates in the history of—" Tina snickered. "Ok, so they weren't that bad."

"Bad enough. Anyway, he told me he cares about me, and now I'm just confused."

"About what?"

For several seconds, Aggie struggled to articulate her problem. At last, she sighed, flopped onto her back, and said, "Because none of this makes sense. I'm supposed to be teaching kids how to multiply and do fractions, not weeding out my relational prospects."

"Well, after I give William a piece of my mind, I'll take the big lug off your hands. Meanwhile, you'll have to decide what you think of Luke, but don't you hurt him."

"Gee," Aggie began dryly, "thanks for the support."

The sound of rock against house sent Aggie flying for the door. "I've got to go. They're firing on Fort Stuart."

"Cari and Lorna?"

"Yep. Bye." Aggie tossed the phone on the couch as she flew through the door.

Libby decided that a nice long drive would be a perfect way to give William and Aggie privacy for their "talk." Luke, finishing work on his house nearby, was on call if Ellie couldn't come, but even Ellie seemed well enough to take a nice drive to Fairbury, around Lake Danube, and back home again. Grateful for the opportunity to deal with the unpleasant task without an audience, Aggie spent the rest of the afternoon in prayer, begging the Lord for wisdom in showing a fine combination of firmness and gentleness.

Just as Aggie decided to go downstairs and throw together something for dinner, Libby knocked gently on the door. Stepping inside, she whispered, "Aggie? Zeke called. He was driving home from the feed and seed and saw William on his way here." She crossed the room and laid a tender hand on Aggie's cheek. "I'll feed the children from that deli in Fairbury or something. We'll be gone for quite a while. Zeke has a new foal he wanted to show them."

"Thanks, Libby." A rogue tear splashed on the woman's hand.

"Aggie? If you need him, Luke is only a call away, but..."

The young woman looked up to her mother-like friend, questioning. "But what?"

"He told me how he spoke of his feelings." Her thumb caressed Aggie's cheek. "My Luke cares deeply for you. Please remember that when you decide what to share with him."

Aggie stood at the window and watched the van drive away before turning and seeking out fresh clothes from the closet. If she was going to tell William she wouldn't marry him—the thought made her head shake with the ludicrousness of it—then she was going to look as decent as possible while she did it. One glance in the mirror at her face made Aggie's heart sink. There was no way to look mature and serious with a polka-dotted face.

She made it to the bottom of the stairs just as William rapped on the screen door. Her heart bottomed out when his eyes lit up at the sight of her. Maybe he did care more than she'd thought. Luke could have been warning her not to hurt William, but hadn't he as much as said that he was talking about himself when he mentioned that some men could be friends while they waited? Confusion swirled in her mind, but Aggie didn't have time to dwell on it.

"You're looking better! I saw the van gone and thought maybe you weren't home."

"Libby took the children for a van picnic and a drive. Everyone's feeling a bit cabin feverish."

"But you didn't go?"

Without a word, Aggie walked to the kitchen, grabbed the aspirin bottle, pried open the cap, shook out two, and replaced it all. She downed the pills with a glass of water and returned to the living room, collapsing in her favorite spot without even attempting to be graceful. "So much for my maturity," she thought to herself.

"So…" William's failed attempt to open the subject showed just enough vulnerability to buoy Aggie's spirits. She needed to do this for both of them.

"William?"

"Yeah…"

"You know that this won't work, right? I mean," she hastened to add before he could get her off track, "it is so amazingly self-sacrificing of you, but it won't work."

"Marriage is always a little work, but we'll —"

"No we won't, William. I'll admit; at first, I was pretty mad at you. I know you didn't mean to be, but you were quite insulting in your assessment of my 'job performance,' and that hurt. However, once I had time to think about it, I realized just what a beautiful thing you did. In once sense, it was a perfect picture of a husband. You were giving yourself and your own dreams of whatever you've always wanted family-wise up for me and my children. That's a beautiful thing." Aggie waited until his eyes were back on her before she continued. "But it's flawed."

"How?"

"You aren't Jesus. It's hard enough for a man who truly loves his wife and children to be so self-sacrificing. To start things off that way—you'd resent us. Eventually, you'd resent us."

"Aggie, no…"

"Yeah, you would, and no one could blame you. Really!" She leaned forward and beckoned him to come sit by her. Taking his hand, she squeezed it gently. "You have a need to fix things, William, but we're not something you can fix."

226

The man's face was unreadable. He sat, expressionless, staring at her as the seconds ticked by into minutes. "I think you're scared of the idea, and I don't blame you. But, Aggie—"

"Don't, William. Don't."

"But—"

"Look, can you honestly say that you love me as most men love the women they ask to marry them?"

"No, but—"

"That's a lot of buts, William. Do you realize that?" She sighed and removed her hand from his, pulling her legs up against her chest and wrapping her arms around them. "I told Tina that I was afraid I'd lose a dear friend today. Please prove to me that I'm wrong."

William shook his head with evident disgust. "I thought you were more mature than this, Aggie. I can't believe that you're going to let silly ideals—"

"If I thought your heart was hurting; I wouldn't say this, but you're being a jerk. Your pride is hurt that you got turned down, but you only want to marry me as a solution to the so-called problems in my life. It's no solution, and I won't do it. If your solution is more important to you than our friendship, well, I guess I didn't know you like I thought I did."

"That's an unjust accusation. I've often thought you were mature beyond your years, but right now, you're acting like a junior high girl who got asked out by the wrong guy."

She forced herself up from the couch, walked to the desk in the library, rifled though a drawer for paper and pencil, and scribbled something on it. Returning to the living room, she passed it to William. "Tina would like you to call her." Something in his expression told her his thoughts. "Oh, and if you toss that, she'll just call you without it."

"You can't go around giving my phone number to whomever you like. That's wrong, Aggie."

"I wouldn't need to. She'd never ask. She'd just call the station and leave messages until someone forced you to do something about it. Tina is very persistent." She paused for effect before continuing. "Oh, and don't hang up too soon. You'll make it worse. She has a few things she wants to say so you might as well just get it over with while you can."

She didn't wait for a response. Instead, Aggie started up the stairs. On the third step, she turned and added, "I really hope I don't have to wait a long time before I get my friend back. I value friendships; I need them. Until then, I'll miss you. Goodnight."

Upstairs, she waited until William's car tore out of the driveway before she allowed herself to give way to a few frustrated tears. When she realized how brief her little cry was, she smiled to herself. After months of feeling like she cried at the drop of a hat, it seemed that she was returning to her old self. "At least some things are going right," she murmured.

It was quite dark when Aggie stumbled down stairs an hour later. Still groggy from her impromptu nap, Aggie blinked at the darkening sky, the strains of one of her mother's favorite songs drifting through her mind. *"Out of the mist your voice is calling...mmmm... twilight time..."*[9]

She never could remember all the words, but Aggie could never forget the tune. Luke found her on the porch, so lost in her reverie that she didn't notice him drive up or walk across the crunchy gravel. "Mibs? You ok?"

Aggie jumped. "Oh! How did I not hear you drive up?"

"I don't know... I drove right past your line of vision. Mom called twice wondering if I'd seen you yet. She won't come home until she knows you're ready for them."

"Oh, she could have come back." An awkward feeling washed over her as he hesitated to sit. "Sit, Luke. I'm not going to freak out on you."

"I never thought you would." He sat in his favorite chair, running his hands over the arms, remembering heart to heart conversations he'd had with his grandmother in those very chairs. "Did William come?"

"Yeah." She knew the tears choking her voice confused him — possibly hurt.

"Well, I'm sorry you're hurting." His words were genuine if a bit... safe.

"You wanna know why it hurts? He's a twit. He doesn't care about me — not like — " She couldn't bring herself to say it.

"Not like me?"

"Well..." Aggie ducked her head.

"It's ok, Aggie. I chose to tell you."

228

"Anyway, if he actually cared, I'd be more sympathetic, but he doesn't. Like I told him, his pride is hurt not his heart."

"And," Luke asked, leaning forward to see her eyes. "What about your heart? It looks as if your heart is suffering, Mibs."

"It does hurt. It hurts a lot. Right now, William has taken his opinion of me from 'incompetent' to 'immature' simply because I am unwilling to submit to his Galahad complex." She shook her head impatiently. "I'm going to lose a good friend to pride. It makes me mad."

Before Luke could respond, his cell phone rang. "That'll be mom."

Aggie stood. "Tell her I'm ready for my children. I could use some snuggles right now."

"It's going to be ok, Mibs. It is." Luke turned away and flipped open his phone. "Mom? Aggie's ready." He waited until he saw her round the corner into the kitchen and added, "I think she could use a hug, Mom." His ears grew red as he listened to his mother's reply. "I don't think that's a good idea right now."

The door slammed shut behind him, but William didn't notice. His neighbor glanced out the door in stunned disbelief, never having seen the deputy show anything but deliberate self-control. Inside his townhome, William tossed his keys onto the counter along with his hat and the newspaper, before collapsing into his chair. He grabbed the remote and snapped on his stereo system, anticipating the familiar sounds of his favorite Jazz ensemble. Instead, the instrumental hymn CD that he'd purchased on his trip to Seattle played an annoying tinkling piano rendition of *Just as I Am*. His plan to familiarize himself with Aggie's constant hymn-speak had been precipitous.

He jumped from his chair, punched the open button on his CD player, and jerked the offensive disk from the tray. On his way to the garbage can, he snapped it in half, enjoying a sense of satisfaction as he did. Yes, it was a little immature, but considering his company that afternoon, it seemed fitting somehow. His hands gripped the edge of the counter as he leaned over the sink, trying to control his emotions. He wanted to call Aggie and blast her. The selfishness alone was inexcusable. Those children deserved better than a novice mother and no father.

Shoving himself away from the sink, William walked toward his bathroom, unbuttoning his shirt, unstrapping his belt and holster as he walked. He paused before the mirror, and stared at the reflection. Perhaps discussing marriage with a gun on his belt had been a bad idea. He shook his head. That was a ridiculous thought. Aggie knew his job, yet had never shown distaste for his job or the weapons that came with it.

He'd intended to take a shower, but his running clothes beckoned him. In minutes, his feet pounded against the asphalt as his mind whirled with all the things he should have said. She'd have to listen to reason. As he thought about it, he realized that maybe she just needed time to adjust to the idea. She was young. She probably had dreams of romance that she needed to relinquish before she could accept the necessary. If only Tina could —

His mind darted in a dozen directions. Tina. She wanted to talk to him, and that probably meant she was upset. Well, she could forget it. He wasn't about to call her and let her lash out at him for being the voice of reason in the situation. Perhaps he should talk to Libby Sullivan. Maybe she could talk sense into Aggie—or maybe Luke could.

As a car peeled around the corner, William paused, hands resting on his knees, breathing heavily. "Buddy, if I had my car, you'd be busted," he gasped.

Angrier than ever, he turned and jogged home, fighting the urge to call and demand that Aggie stop being so selfish. Once home, he strode through the house, peeling his clothes off on his way to the shower. Usually, the water felt comforting as if pounding away the stress and frustrations of the day, but that night, William felt every drop hit and each struck a new nerve as it did.

Frustrated, he snapped off the water, toweled dry, and pulled on his favorite sweats and t-shirt. All of his routines were out of whack. He hadn't checked the mail, paid the bills, fed the fish, emptied his pockets—none of it. His pants lay draped over the end of the bed, so he started there. Inside the pocket, Tina's number mocked him from the paper Aggie had given him. There was no way he'd call her and no way would he let her call and blast him for doing the right thing.

Seconds later, he fished the paper from the trash and smoothed the wrinkles from it on the counter. A glance at the clock told him it was after nine o'clock, but William didn't care. In his experience, college students never went to bed before midnight. If he called and controlled the conversation, perhaps he could show Tina where Aggie was wrong. No one could talk more sense into Aggie than Tina— except perhaps her parents. Maybe he'd get Tina to give him the Milliken's number.

William pulled an enchilada dinner from the freezer, popped it in the oven, and then dialed Tina's number. The woman sounded distracted as she answered. "Hmm?"

"Tina?"

"William?" Her voice squeaked, making him smile. Something about Tina was always a little refreshing.

"I need your help."

"With what?" Tina sounded wary.

"Well, Aggie is being a little difficult about something—"

"You have got to be kidding me."

"What?" Even as he asked, William mentally kicked himself. He couldn't give her an opening. He tried to steer it back to his agenda, but he'd underestimated Tina's determination and grit.

"Look, William. I talked to Aggie today. You really have some nerve—"

"Why am I the villain here? Don't you think that Aggie needs help? Can you honestly say that you think she should have to do this job alone?"

"No, but—"

"So, when I step in and say, 'Look, I'm ready to help you. Let me take some of the burden off your shoulders so you can look back on these years with fond memories instead of exhaustion, I'm somehow being a jerk. You girls make no sense."

"Did you say those words, William? When you asked— did you even ask? It sounds to me like you told her you guys were getting married. You didn't even ask!"

He started to object and insist he had, but his own words came back to mock him. He had told her. "It wasn't some romantic interlude, Tina. You know as well as I do that Aggie and I aren't like

231

that. We tried, but it didn't work. Making it into a big deal would have made her furious."

"But telling her what she has to do with her life is going to make her jump for joy? Seriously, William? I really had a lot of respect for you. I thought you were better than this."

"She's floundering, Tina. She's going to burn out. I can't stand to watch it. She needs help." He hated how vulnerable he sounded.

"William, do you love Aggie?"

"Well, not like you mean, no. I think I could, but..."

"Look, Aggie isn't like me. I've always wanted the full package. I want a guy who loves me, who will romance me, who will make me feel like I'm the only girl for him. Aggie has never been that way. She's probably one of the few women I know who could take a situation like hers and agree to a proposal such as you devised."

"I hardly believe that." William began to believe he'd chosen the wrong person to help him. Obviously, Tina didn't know her friend as well as she thought.

"But William, I don't know a woman on the planet who would take well to, 'You can't handle your responsibility so you're going to marry me so maybe you won't fall flat on your face.'"

"I never said anything like that! That's an absolute distortion of my words."

He ran his hand through his hair as he heard her deep breath. "William, think carefully. Did you say or imply that she has too much on her plate?"

"Um..." He thought carefully. "Yeah, I said that she needed the kind of help and support that only a husband can give."

"And why does she need help?"

"Because she can't do this alone. All those trips to the clinic, she lost the baby that time, the kids haven't started school..." William jumped as the timer went off on his meal. "You've lived there. You know how chaotic that house is! Can you imagine the state of her finances?" William seemed unaware that he was almost rehashing his original conversation.

"Ok, so if you were sheriff of Brant's Corners, doing your job, having the normal speeders, domestic disturbances, etc., and a man came in and said, 'I can see that you are having trouble in town, so I'm going to be your supervisor and help you get this mess whipped in shape,' you wouldn't mind? You'd consider that an offer of gracious help?"

"I—"

"That's how it sounds to me. What you just told me sounded exactly like that. Honestly, if you'd made the same kind of offer to me, I'd have slapped you. Aggie has better self-control than I do."

William stabbed his enchilada and found the sensation quite cathartic. "She's in over her head. I just want to help."

"So take the boys hiking or fishing or on a ride-along or something. Push the little ones on swings or show up and grill for her. If you're worried about school, offer to help rearrange the library or help Vannie with her math. Don't tell Aggie how incompetent she is and try to rescue her from herself."

"So, do you think she'd listen to reason if I apologized, showed her what advantages a man would bring to the family, and asked her to marry me?"

"No." Silence hung between them for a few seconds before Tina sighed. "William, I'll be blunt. Aggie isn't the romantic that I am, but she's a woman. She's not going to enter into a relationship like marriage without being ready for everything that comes with it. Have you not thought about what that kind of marriage would mean to her? She doesn't think of you that way, and she knows you don't think of her like that. No woman wants to give herself to a relationship like that— not even someone as practical as Aggie."

"I didn't think—" He cut off his sentence mid- thought. "Tina, we can't think in terms of ourselves. We need to think about the children."

"I'm thinking about the children. I'm thinking about what message this sends to them. I'm thinking about Vannie seeing her aunt sacrifice another piece of her for their family and the guilt it'll add to that little girl's heart. I'm thinking about what those boys will learn about marriage—it's just something a guy has to do. Their wives will be a duty instead of a delight. Do you really want to teach an entire family—a large one at that—that marriage is nothing more than a duty? Do you really want those kids who have already been through so much to become a dysfunctional mess?"

"I don't think—"

"Well," Tina interrupted, "you're wrong. I've studied enough about this kind of thing to know exactly what'd happen. You know what abnormal relationships do to children. You've seen it in your own life. From what you told me about your mother, you should understand this."

"My mom is why I'm doing this! Do you think I want to see someone as sweet and gentle as Aggie reduced to lashing out at children because life is too overwhelming and she's frazzled beyond endurance? I can't take it. That house seems almost cursed. Maybe we can break it if she just has the help she needs."

Soft sounds of crying reached him. "Tina?"

"I'm so sorry, William. I can't imagine the hurt you went through. It's criminal."

"This isn't about me, Tina."

"Oh, but William, it is. Don't you see? Your experiences skewed your perceptions, and you've applied that where it doesn't belong."

"I don't think so—"

"Listen to me. Think about the GIL."

"Who?"

"Geraldine Stuart. Aggie calls her the GIL. It stands for 'grandmother-in-law" or 'Geraldine is livid.'"

"Sounds like Aggie."

Tina giggled, but a suspicious choke escaped at the end. "Geraldine had everything a woman could hope for—house, money, one child, position in society, the works. However, she was probably one of the most dysfunctional mothers you'd ever meet. On the other hand, you have Aggie's parents. Martha Milliken has steadily grown worse over the years. She could never do things like other mothers, always had to take it easy, and yet, that woman never lets her weaknesses control her spirit."

"I can't imagine Martha Milliken ever losing her cool."

"Well, she does, but only briefly. My point is that Aggie and Mrs. Milliken have something that people like Geraldine and your mother didn't have."

"What's that?"

"Jesus."

William squirmed. He hated it when people used Jesus' name as if it was a talisman. In fact, he preferred that people not use the name Jesus at all. When speaking of the Lord, he preferred to say Christ. Something about people saying Jesus seemed very affected.

"William?"

"Hmm?"

"Why does that make you uncomfortable?"

"What?" He didn't understand how she could possibly know how he felt.

"The fact that Jesus is the difference between Aggie and your mother. You're a Christian." She hesitated. "Aren't you?"

"Sometimes I wonder, Tina." He shoved his half-eaten plate of food across the counter and stepped into the living room, collapsing on the couch. "I don't have the kind of relationship with the Lord that some people do, but I know He has washed me clean. I'm saved, but I don't have that confidence that I see in people like you or Aggie or Luke."

He heard her take a deep breath and steeled himself for a mini-sermon, but she surprised him. "William, I think this is more about your past than you think. You're trying to create the perfect little —" She laughed at his chuckle. "Ok, not-so-little family in the place that was so horrible for you. You're trying to redeem the past, but you can't. It's over. You can't fix it."

"I don't think —"

"Ok, then don't think. I don't care. I do care about my friend, though, and you won't do this to her. You won't put her through this anymore. It's cruel. She feels like she's lost one of her best friends."

"Well, it's not like I'd never speak to her again unless she saw things my way!" The idea made him sick. He may not be in love with Aggie, but he did care about their friendship.

"But as things are, she's uncomfortable. You put a wedge in the friendship by leaving her with the impression that you think so little of her. I know you didn't mean to do that, but you did. That was what she got from you, and we both know that Aggie doesn't go looking to be offended by things."

This was true, and he had to admit it to himself. "If I tried again and was more careful how I did it, what are the odds that she'd reconsider?"

"Are you sure you're not even a little in love with her? You're really fixated on this."

"I know it must seem like it, but no. I think I could be maybe... someday. I just can't let the idea go."

"Maybe you're just more ready to settle down than you thought."

The thought terrified him, but he didn't want to admit it to Tina. "I thought about seeing what Sullivan had to say about it. Maybe he can talk to her."

"William, don't. Don't do that to him."

"Do what?"

"Are you really that blind? Come on, William."

"What?" He felt dense, but he couldn't understand Tina's irritation.

"When Luke arrives, what's the first thing he does?"

"Gets to work?"

Exasperation fairly crackled across the connection. "He looks for Aggie. When she enters a room, what does he do?"

"I don't know. I haven't been watching him, you know."

"He looks up. No matter what he's doing, he looks up when she enters. The only other person he does that with is Cari."

"Probably to see what mischief the girl is in now."

Giggling, Tina agreed. "Yep. Think about it."

William felt like a fool. "He's in love with her, isn't he?"

"Yep. You'd have broken his heart if you convinced Aggie to marry you."

"Does she know?" William swallowed hard. He hadn't thought about someone else stepping in as husband and father. He'd decided Aggie's family needed both and tried to install himself pronto.

"She does now. You kind of forced Luke to tell her how he feels about her before he thought she was ready to hear it."

"He's good for her."

Tina agreed. "He understands her." She cleared her throat. "William, the things about Aggie that drive you crazy are the very things that endear her to him."

"Does she love him?" His voice was quiet — pensive.

"Not yet, but given half a chance, I think she will."

"Thank you, Tina. I'd better go."

"William?"

"Hmm?"

"Don't hesitate to call to talk — about anything." She swallowed audibly. "I'd like to be a friend, William."

"I just might. Thanks again. Goodnight." He slid his phone shut and stared at the fish tank, unseeing. Aggie and Luke. If he were honest with himself, he'd have to admit it was perfect, but a small part of him still rejected the idea. He just didn't know why. No matter how hard he tried to fabricate deep feelings for Aggie, they never materialized. She was a fun friend, but nothing more. Slowly, relief stole over him. He didn't have to do it. Luke would give Aggie and the children the stability they needed, and his life would remain relatively unchanged.

"Lord, it really is pride, isn't it?" he whispered raggedly. "I think I need some help with that."

Tina stared at the phone, unsure if she'd left the conversation on a good note or not. Her roommate's laptop lay unused on the desk while the girl slept. Thus far, she'd rejected offers to use it, but this seemed like a good time to chat with Aggie. She flipped open the lid, found the messenger program, and signed in with her user name. Her contacts list popped up, but Aggie was offline. Seeing Luke's name gave her an idea.

Tina says: Luke, are you there?

Luke says: Hey, did you get your laptop fixed? Aggie said it was broken, so she wasn't getting on tonight.

Tina says: I'm using my roommate's.

Luke says: She'll be disappointed that she missed you.

Tina says: I'll just have to call. I want to tell her about my conversation with William.

Luke says: I hope it went well.

Tina says: I think he understands now, but I did have to tell him what I've observed about you before he could see the situation clearly.

Luke says: Observed about me?

Tina says: Aggie is too busy with her family to see what is a little obvious to the rest of us, Luke.

Luke says: I see.

Tina says: I'm sorry. I probably shouldn't have said anything.

Luke says: No, that's fine. I didn't realize I was so obvious. I was trying to give Aggie plenty of time to adapt to her new role before I let myself be transparent.

Tina says: I think that's why William hasn't seen it. I lived there for all those weeks. It's easier to see when you're there all the time.

Luke says: Aggie didn't. It might have worked if things hadn't gotten complicated.

Tina says: So the Lord had different timing plans. Who cares?

Luke says: I hadn't thought of it that way, but you're right.

Tina says: You're good for her, Luke. She respects you. She likes William, but while she respects his position as a deputy, she doesn't actually respect him—and this latest thing hasn't helped.

Luke says: Respect is a good place to start.

Tina says: So is this number. 555-3255

Luke says: How did you know I was looking for it? Their number is unlisted.

Tina says: Luke, it's who you are.

Tina says: Man, now I know what Aggie was talking about. You really do start typing and backspace or think a lot, don't you?

Luke says: I never noticed, but I guess I do.

Tina says: Oh, man. It's late. I need to call Aggie before she goes to bed. She'll sleep better knowing that William will be back to normal soon enough.

Luke says: Are you sure he's not more important to her than she thinks?

Tina says: Absolutely certain. You have no competition there.

Luke says: So where IS my competition?

Tina says: You have eight people to compete with. Somehow, you'll have to convince her that you want to join the team rather than compete with it. Until she knows that, she won't even consider it..

Luke says: Thanks, Tina.

Tina says: Anytime. Night, Luke. Poofs.

Luke says: Poofs?

Tina says: Ask Aggie. Nighters.

Luke says: Night.

VISITS & CHEESECAKE

Chapter Seventeen

Wednesday, September 24th

Luke's truck sped along the highways out of the Rockland area and north to Yorktown. He'd called Aggie's parents the first thing Tuesday morning and received permission to visit the next day. Though he had no doubt they guessed his reason for his trip, he appreciated that they hadn't made an issue of it over the phone. Some things needed to be said in person.

By the time he pulled up in front of the craftsman-style bungalow, Luke was beginning to feel nervous. He gripped the steering wheel and rested his head on the backs of his hands. "Lord, I hope You know what I'm doing, because I sure don't," he murmured. He had hopes and some very important dreams riding on his visit with Aggie's parents, but now that he was there, he wasn't as confident of their approval as he had been while on the phone with them in Brant's Corners.

Martha met him at the door with a hug. "Come in, Luke. I convinced Ron to let me make an apple pie. Are you hungry?"

Luke nodded, smiling awkwardly. "That sounds wonderful. Thank you."

She led him to the kitchen table and pulled out plates. "Ron will be here in just a minute. He's working on something in his shop and you know how that goes. He just can't stop in the middle of his projects. Varnish isn't very forgiving, from what I've heard."

"This is very true."

Ron entered the kitchen wiping his hands on a paper towel. "Hey, Luke. I'll shake your hand once I've washed mine. I'm covered with all kinds of garbage."

"Oh, Ron. Go change. You smell like solvents of some horrible kind." As her husband left the room, Martha set a plate of pie in front of Luke. "Coffee or milk?"

"Coffee, please. Thank you. This smells wonderful."

"Thank you." Martha's slippers squeaked on the linoleum as she returned to the coffee pot to pour him a cup.

Ron returned before the silence in the room could grow awkward. "So, Luke. How are Aggie and the children?"

"They're doing better. Tavish still hasn't broken out, but everyone else seems to be on the mend." Luke set his fork back on his plate, half the pie uneaten, and clasped his hands together with boy-like earnestness. "Mr. and Mrs. Milliken—"

"Luke, please call us Ron and Martha. I have a feeling we are going to be too close for formal names."

"Certainly, Mr—I mean Ron." He swallowed and tried to reformulate his thoughts. "I can't imagine you don't know why I'm here. I…"

Ron and Martha made the terrible mistake of glancing at each other. The moment their eyes met, they both dissolved into laughter. It took a few moments, but at last, Martha regained some composure and apologized. "I'm so sorry, Luke. Aggie's descriptions of you are… well…"

"Aaah. I see she has exposed my deep secret to the world. I cannot formulate and articulate my thoughts very quickly, it is true."

Luke's words, spoken so bluntly, sent Martha apologizing profusely. "Oh, Luke, we—"

"Oh, no apologies are necessary. It's sort of a family joke. My mother always says that I used to take three times longer during

240

bedtime prayers than the other kids—combined. I could never just *say* what I wanted to say."

Ron covered his mouth with his hand for a moment and then took a swig of coffee. "Well, I know Aggie found it frustrating at first, but she said recently that when you do finally say what you want to say, it's usually very wise. Coming from Aggie, that's huge."

He felt his ears go red at the compliment, but Luke forced himself not to be distracted. His hands twisted together for a moment, and then he rubbed his palms on the fronts of his jeans. "This isn't easy for me." A wry smile twisted his lips at the irony of what he was trying to say. "I've never been good at talking about myself, but I'm here because of how I feel about Aggie." Luke sipped his coffee, unconsciously wincing at the lukewarm drink. Ron grabbed the cup and filled it with hot coffee for him. "Thanks."

"We don't bite, son."

They all erupted in nervous laughter until Luke, after another sip of the coffee, tried again. "I'm in love with your daughter, Mr. um, I mean Ron." He forced his eyes to meet those of Aggie's parents and was encouraged at the understanding he found in them. "I didn't want to tell her yet. She seemed to need time to adjust to her life without adding in the complication of a..." He struggled to find the right word.

"Besotted swain? Suitor? Boyfriend?" Martha's eyes twinkled as she slowly modernized the relational words.

"I guess I'm a little old fashioned. I prefer suitor to boyfriend. Boyfriend sounds so—so—dispensable."

The way Luke paused, thought, reformulated sentences, and tried again was unfamiliar to the Millikens. Ron and Martha were used to the lively and quick conversation that characterized their family, but Luke's earnest confession of love for their daughter, and his evident desire to treat her well endeared him to them. They smiled their encouragement, nodded at appropriate places, and tried to keep him as comfortable as possible when it was evident that the man just wanted the ordeal to end.

"I'm sure Aggie told you about William's visit and how he 'suggested' that he and Aggie marry."

Martha snickered. "She said it was just like Mr. Darcy's proposal in Pride and Prejudice. I think her words were, 'it was quite imperious and just as insulting.'"

Luke shook his head remembering. "That's about right. I overheard it all, and it wasn't exactly the model proposal out of Emily Post. Frankly, it was somewhat degrading." He swallowed hard and clenched his hands together. "I confess, my mother and I laughed at how it sounded, but I couldn't laugh if I thought his heart was involved. I think Aggie saw, as I did, that William was being chivalrous. He truly believes Aggie needs to be cared for, and I agree."

Ron's eyebrows drew together as if annoyed, and Martha's smile faded. Luke saw their disapproval and hastened to explain. "Please understand, I don't mean to imply that Aggie isn't doing a marvelous job. She's a very capable and loving mother to those children. She's accomplished so much in such a short time. My Uncle Zeke keeps saying that she's a natural with them." His struggles with words seemed to dissipate as he spoke of Aggie. "Even things I know are difficult for her, the cooking, shopping, and housework are kept going even when many mothers would be falling apart. Of course," he added with a smile, "having all those little workers does help."

The red stole up his neck to his ears once more as Luke tried to articulate what was on his heart. "But Aggie needs more. She needs someone to care for *her*—someone to talk to, cry on, and someone who can dream wonderful dreams with her." He swallowed hard and forced himself to meet the Milliken's gaze. "I want to be that man."

The difference between how cautiously Luke spoke of William and himself and the confidence he displayed when speaking of Aggie was remarkable. Ron and Martha exchanged curious glances as the already familiar pauses gave way to undaunted speech. Ron nodded slowly as if processing Luke's words and asked, "And Aggie? Do you think Aggie wants you to be that person?"

The doubt in Luke's eyes elicited visible compassion in Martha. "I don't know, sir. I am here to ask permission to see if she can be. I want to leave here, go home, and be able to tell Aggie that you've given me your approval to try to win her heart." A sheepish look settled on Luke's face. "See, I told you I was old fashioned. 'Win her heart.'" He made a silly face at his own words.

"Well, Luke, you didn't have to drive all the way up here to get our approval, but I'm glad you did. It'll mean a lot to Aggie that you went to the trouble for her." His hand rested on his wife's and squeezed it. "I don't mind saying between the three of us that I hope she does choose you."

"Yes! I confess," Martha interjected with a smile so like Aggie's, "I've been rooting for you for some time."

"I guess I wasn't very subtle."

"Well, I'd say it's more like a mother sees things that others might miss." Martha's smile was infectious. "After all, Aggie's been so focused on the house and learning to mother those children — but I bet Tina and your mother won't be surprised."

"No," he agreed.

"But Luke, I want you to do something for Aggie." Martha took his hand and waited for him to meet her eyes again. "Give my girl a memorable..." she struggled for the word she wanted. "I don't know, courtship seems hopelessly old fashioned, but it works. You guys will never have that special alone time that most couples have for a year or so after marriage. Make sure she has a few months of special times to look back on when she's older. She's given up so much already —"

"I will, Martha. I will. And if Aggie does —" He couldn't bring himself to say it.

"If the day comes that you want to ask Aggie to marry you, you already have our blessing." Ron spoke, but Martha stood and hugged Luke.

"I'll be very disappointed if she doesn't."

Luke's sigh was almost missed as he grinned and agreed. "I will too!"

Libby, helped by Luke's Uncle Zeke and Aunt Martha, kept the children occupied playing games with all the children so Aggie could "rest." Zeke crawled on the floor like a much younger man, with Cari, Lorna, and even little Ian riding his back like a horse. Martha Sullivan played Concentration with Kenzie, losing more rounds than she liked to admit, while Libby played Trouble with Laird, Vannie, and Ellie. Tavish, lost in his book, laid on the couch and ignored the moans, shouts of triumph, and the popping of the Trouble bubble.

When Aggie tried to do laundry, Libby ordered her out of the mudroom. The moment the kitchen sink faucet came on, Martha insisted on the dishes being left for her. At last, left with nothing she was "allowed" to do, Aggie grabbed her purse and slipped out the back door. She'd go get a coffee at Espresso Yourself and drink it on one of the couches in the corner— just her, a coffee, and maybe a slice of cheesecake. They had the best raspberry white chocolate cheesecake she'd ever tasted.

Just as she began turning the van around in the driveway, Luke's truck pulled in. She started to wave as she continued to drive away, but he held up a coffee tray and paper bag. For a moment, she was tempted to wave, feign misunderstanding, and keep going, but the disappointed look on Luke's face couldn't be missed even in the moonlight. She slammed on the brakes and pulled back into her accustomed parking spot.

"Hey! Thanks! I was just going to go get some coffee and cheesecake."

"Before you call, I will answer? Didn't Isaiah say something like that?" Luke passed the paper bag. "They even included forks. I told them it wasn't necessary, but it was too late."

"I've been ordered away from the family. So, I decided to go sit on their couches and have some peace and quiet."

"Will the back swing do instead?" Luke took a sip of his coffee. "Oops, this isn't mine. I think you have mine."

Aggie tested it and made a face. "Oh, yuck. Yep. Definitely yours." She strolled around the corner of the house, oblivious to the adult trio inside who were now distracted from their games. "You came just in time."

"Well, it's probably a good thing. The way you keep erupting in pox…"

Aggie's face drained of color. "Oh! I completely forgot. That antihistamine that your mom found—the stuff that doesn't make you sleepy—it works so well that I forget about those things." She grimaced. "Except for when I'm in front of the mirror. Then I feel like Heather Walker from fourth period in the ninth grade. That poor girl had the worst acne I've ever seen."

"You can't look like her then, because your face is not remotely covered like a bad acne case." Luke pulled a clear plastic container from the bag. "Eat up."

"Thanks, Luke." Aggie took the tiniest bite of cake and allowed it to melt in her mouth before taking another miniscule bite. "Mmm... this is *so* good."

"So, can you guess what I did today?" There was something enigmatic in Luke's tone.

Her eyes widened. "You bought that house! The big rambling one between here and New Cheltenham! I can't wait to see it."

"Well, actually, I did that yesterday. It's mine in thirty days."

"Um, you finished the one on Kent Street?"

"Bzzz. Wrong again. Last guess."

"You started building that shed your mom wants."

Luke shook his head. "'Fraid not, but I do need to get on that."

"Well, then, what did you do?"

She took another teeny bite while waiting for him to answer her. Luke swallowed hard, took a swig of coffee, choked, and then said, "I took a little trip up north."

It took several seconds of waiting for him to elaborate for Aggie to realize he thought she'd make sense of his ambiguous statement. "That's nice..."

"I went to Yorktown to visit your parents, Mibs."

Aggie's head snapped up. Understanding slowly dawned, but she fumbled for words to stall him while she absorbed the news. Luke was exactly the kind of man who would talk to her parents about his feelings for her, but she didn't quite know how *she* felt about it. "Why would you do that?"

"Do you have to ask that?" His cheesecake sat untouched in his lap, but Luke had nearly downed his coffee.

"Well, obviously I do, or I wouldn't have." Though she knew Luke could see through her, Aggie didn't care. She'd never expected him to do something like that so soon. The idea unnerved her.

"Well, after we sat and talked a bit, I explained about what I shared with you the other day. I told them that I had planned to give you a lot more time before putting you in the position of dealing with..." A smirk made his face look comical. "I think your mother's exact words were 'besotted swains.'"

"She didn't!" Aggie's shock was palpable.

"Well, I think the other suggestions offered were suitor and boyfriend. Do you have a preference?"

"So you went to tell them that you told me you care about me? What for?"

Aggie, having avoided Luke's eyes, since she'd heard of his trip, glanced at his face and drew back, startled by the intensity she found in his eyes. Luke just smiled — a weak but genuine smile. "Oh Mibs, I couldn't tell you that I love you without ensuring your parents were ok with that."

"Why not?"

"Because, now that you know," Luke dropped his eyes. "I was hoping we — I mean I —" She watched as he struggled to find the right words. "I hoped —"

Aggie swallowed her next bite whole. "And they said?"

"They gave their approval for me to speak to you about what is on my heart."

"I don't know what to say, Luke." She shoved her cheesecake back in the bag. "I just don't know what you expect from me."

"I don't expect anything from you until I ask the question I have for you." Luke struggled to hide the smile that strained to break free. The expression on Aggie's face was priceless. It was evident from her eyes alone that she expected him to ask her to marry him. Though he was tempted to go down on one knee and really make her squirm, his mother's caution to "go gently, son" helped him resist.

"Well, do you ever intend to ask your question?" He saw her straighten and don a bravado that he could see she didn't feel and decided he needed to come to the point.

"Well, my question is whether you're willing to grant me the same permission that your parents did. Are you willing to give me a chance to win your heart?" His mouth went dry, and he swallowed several times to keep from croaking out his next words. "Last Friday, I told you that I love you. I want to know if you are willing to explore a more intimate — um, that's not — I mean personal — closer relationship with me." His face flushed as he realized how his words could have sounded.

The minutes ticked by as Aggie sat in thoughtful silence. For the first time in his life, Luke understood how nerve-wracking it was to wait for someone to speak. Her face was a study in conflicting emotions, but at last she spoke. "Will I lose my best friend in Brant's Corners if I say no?"

A pit grew to the size of a bowling ball in Luke's stomach, but he forced himself to give her a truthful answer that wouldn't add more pressure. "Mibs, you'll always be my friend. Nothing is going to change that."

"Good, because the last time a friend tried to date me, I almost lost a good friend. I don't want that to happen again. I don't want to start dating you only to find out that it's not going to work, and then things get awkward —"

Luke interrupted her. "Mibs, I'm not interested in some casual dating thing." His face fell as he spoke. "I'm hoping that you can learn to care for me — that you might eventually see me as husband material. If you don't think you can do that, tell me now."

Aggie opened her mouth to speak and then clamped it shut. "Are you asking me to marry you?" Confusion filled her voice.

"Not yet, no. You don't love me and maybe you never will." The words caught in his throat, and Luke knew she heard it and understood why. "I just had to be up front about this. I can't be casual with my feelings. I want us to take the next few months to get to know each other better. I'm hoping you'll learn to love me and *want* to marry me." He shook his head and tried again. "Mibs, all I want to know today is if you are willing to see if we can develop a relationship that is conducive to marriage." Luke stuck out his tongue in disgust. "That was romantic, wasn't it?"

He watched as she tried not to laugh and failed. Her snickers turned into giggles and finally laughter. Every attempt he made to look hurt and serious failed until he too lost all composure and joined her. The joke seemed to release some of the tension that had grown between them, and Luke relaxed enough to finish what he had to say.

"Aggie, you should know that I would marry you tomorrow, but I know you're not ready for that, and I wouldn't want to cheat you out of the experience of falling in love. If you can't learn to love me, then we'll deal with that later. In the mean time, in case you can, I want to do my part to give you the special memories and moments that come with a relationship like that. I don't quite know how to do it..." He shrugged sheepishly. "I don't think I'm naturally very romantic."

With an exaggerated shake of her head, Aggie said, "What do you call a stuffed chicken and a box of pansies… *'for thoughts?'*"

"You have no idea how close I came to leaving off the pansies. I wanted so badly to try to do something special for you – to cheer you up – but I thought it was still too soon." He shrugged. "I remembered Mom's little verse and couldn't resist."

"Pansies are for thoughts. Now let it be: Mine are of you. Let yours be of me."

"You have an amazing memory! That's word perfect, and I don't remember writing it down like I said I would." Luke's grin lit up his entire face even in the darkness.

She ducked her head, embarrassed. "I cheated. I did a Google search, found it, and memorized it." A satisfied smile settled over Luke's features and grew even more content as Aggie's face showed her trying to read his expression – and failing. Her curiosity overcame her self-control, as she demanded, "Spit it out, Luke."

For a brief moment, Luke wondered if answering would hurt his chances. He still hadn't received Aggie's agreement to give a relationship a chance, but he couldn't resist teasing her. "Well, it's just that it's hard not to hope that you care a little for me if you deliberately searched for a poem and memorized it just because you received flowers from me."

Red flooded her face until it was hard to see the spots anymore. "I – " She swallowed and shrugged.

"Do you need time to think about it?"

"Think about what? Us?"

"Yeah." The hope he'd allowed himself slowly dissipated as he saw her chew her lower lip. Just as he decided to tell her not to worry about it – he wouldn't say anything about it for some time, she raised her eyes to meet his.

"I don't know what I'm agreeing to really, but I trust you. If you say you can still be friends with me even if I don't return your feelings after months or years of whatever it is this is about, then ok."

Relief flooded Luke's heart. "That's an amazing gift, Mibs. Thank you."

"Good. Then you can tell me what I just gave you, because I'm still quite lost."

A truck started up in the front yard. "Uncle Zeke is leaving. Have you watched him and Aunt Martha?"

"Some."

248

"Then you've seen how in love they still are after fifty-some-odd years."

Aggie nodded. "Yes. It's adorable."

"What I'm hoping you agreed to was for me to have a chance to have that with you someday."

She closed her eyes and sighed. "How could I not agree when you put it like that?"

Luke rose and offered his hand. Just inside the kitchen, he took the cheesecake from her and took it to the fridge. Once she walked into the dining room, he exhaled, relieved. Unaware she could still hear him, he looked heavenward and closed his eyes. "Thank you, Lord. Don't let me fail her."

Luke says: What are you doing up still?

Mibs says: Your mom ordered me to bed after you left. I laid there until a little while ago and then gave up. I'm under orders not to get up until I'm absolutely rested.

Mibs says: I think your mom is afraid I'll have a nervous breakdown after this past week.

Luke says: It has been intense. I should have waited to talk to you. It didn't need to be tonight. I'm sorry.

Mibs says: I'm not. I'm not as fragile as people seem to think.

Luke says: You're right. Mom and I have often remarked on how strong you really are. So, what have you been doing? We both know you haven't been resting.

Mibs says: Well, actually, I was thinking about you.

Luke says: That's a nice thing to hear. Or is it?

Mibs says: Well, I was wondering about something.

Luke says: And that is...

Luke says: You know, it's unusual for you to be the one having trouble with what you want to say.

Mibs says: I just wondered if you'd considered that I am a package deal.

Luke says: Do you mean the children?

Mibs says: Yes. If you want me, you get eight children too.

Luke says: We'll manage. It's about priorities. We may not be wealthy, but we'll be fine.

Mibs says: Financially, Allie left me more than enough. I'm not talking about money. I was thinking more about the months or years that couples have for just them. I can't give you that. For that matter, I can't give any man that. Ever. How do you feel about that?

Luke says: I understand that, Mibs, but I'm not interested in having an experience. I want a wife and not just any wife. I want you. I also want the children, the kitten, the dogs, and the three turtles that Tavish thinks he's hidden from us in the back yard. I want it all, and if the timing was right, I'd do it tomorrow.

Mibs says: You're a rare man, Luke Sullivan. Hey, what's your middle name?

Luke says: Actually, I have two. Mom wanted to name me after Dad and Dad wanted me named after Uncle Zeke.

Mibs says: Luke Stephen Ezekiel Sullivan?

Luke says: Nope. Ezekiel Lucas Stephen Sullivan. Alphabetical. Since Dad was Stephen, and there was already a Zeke, I became Luke.

Mibs says: Oooh. Lucas. I love Lucas. Someday, maybe I'll call you Lucas. It can be my version of your mother's "my Luke."

Luke says: Mom does that with all of us. She's always saying, "My Stephen says… My Olivia went…"

Mibs says: That sounds like her. I love that. Which sister is Olivia?

Luke says: Olivia is the oldest. She was named for mom.

Mibs says: I assumed your mom was an Elizabeth.

Luke says: Mom says her big brother was just a toddler when she was born. They were going to call her Livvy, but he couldn't say it, so she became Libby.

Mibs says: I can't imagine calling her Olivia.

Luke says: Yeah, she's too down to earth for a formal name like Olivia.

Mibs says: You sound like you value and admire "down to earth."

Luke says: Well, I think the more accurate way of putting it would be that most of the people I admire happen to be down to earth.

Mibs says: That's beautiful, Luke. *wonders if she's considered down to earth*

Luke says: I'd say you are… you're definitely among the people I admire.

Luke says: Now, it's your turn. Aggie isn't your full name, right? It's short for something. What?

Mibs says: If you haven't seen my full name, that's not my problem. I'm not sharing.

Luke says: What about a middle name?

Mibs says: Yep. Aggie Grace Milliken

Luke says. Grace. That fits you. I just might consider switching out Mibs for Gracie.

Mibs says: As in "goodnight, Gracie?" You wouldn't dare.

Luke says: If you call me Lucas, I think it's fair. Besides, I don't even know your real name. It's more than fair. I wonder if Tina or your parents can be bribed.

Mibs says: Won't work, Luke. No one will reveal my name. Everyone lives in terror of my wrath. Even Mom feels guilty for naming me.

Luke says: Now you really have me curious.

Mibs says: Good. I succeeded.

Luke says: Will you do something for me?

Mibs says: Depends on what it is.

Luke says: Will you try to sleep?

Mibs says: I'll try. Thanks, Luke.

Luke says: Night, Mibs.

Mibs says: Not Gracie?

Luke says: Not this time.

Mibs says: Night, Luke.

School Days

Chapter Eighteen

Monday, September 29th

After weeks of almost twenty-four-hour help, the first day of Aggie's home-schooling adventure was a solo flight— a Murphy day if ever there was one. The children protested when she entered each room at seven o'clock calling for them to "rise and shine."

"Aunt Aggie!" Laird's protest earned him a look that no child would mistake.

"Get up and get dressed. Breakfast is in twenty-minutes."

Groans answered her, but Aggie hoisted Ian from his crib, grabbed clothes and a diaper, and carried him downstairs to the dryer. The baby loved getting dressed on the warm tumbling appliance. She shooed him into the bathroom, set him on the counter, and rinsed a washcloth with one hand while the other kept the wiggling boy from taking a dive onto the floor.

The difference in her appearance was marked. The spots were fading from her face, her hair was neat, clothes bright and fresh, and she looked rested for the first time in weeks. "Ian, I think we're turning a corner today. I even have a few new toys for you to play with while the others get started on their assignments."

In the kitchen, she strapped the baby into his highchair, scooped oatmeal from the pan, dumped fresh blueberries on top, mashed them with the spoon, and sprinkled a little cinnamon and sugar over the top. "Ok, let's see how much you can finish before everyone gets down here."

As she fed him bites, making the silly mouth opening movements mothers always do, Aggie glanced around at her handiwork. Breakfast was ready and had been since seven o'clock. Small glasses of milk were placed at each child's plate, along with spoons and napkins. It was perfect. If the entire day went as smoothly as it began, home-schooling would be a breeze.

There was still no sign of the children even after Ian finished his breakfast and Aggie cleaned his hands and face. The upstairs was suspiciously quiet except for the occasional squeals of Cari and Lorna who clearly were not getting dressed. After swiping the wash cloth over the highchair tray, Aggie unbuckled the tot from his chair and carried him back upstairs. What she found nearly made her see red.

Vannie was curled up in bed reading a book, as was Tavish. Laird faced the wall, snoring again, and Ellie and Kenzie still sat in their beds blinking as if trying to remember if they were awake or asleep. Lorna and Cari bickered over what to wear, each insisting on matching the other but with differing outfits. Aggie glanced at her watch. Nearly seven-thirty and no one was up and ready. School would never start on time.

"I said to. get up and get dressed. No one is dressed." She popped her head in Vannie's room. "I'm very disappointed in you. Since when do you ignore me?"

"I just wanted to finish my book…" The girl at least had the grace to look ashamed of herself.

"You can finish after school. I want you downstairs in ten minutes. Not a minute more." She held out her hand. "I'll take the book. You can have it after you're done with your work."

Vannie's face fell, but she crawled from the bed and handed Aggie the book, an expression of betrayal on her face. "I thought you said school was going to be fun, and we were going to get to explore things that interest us, not just follow the teacher's manual."

"And you truly think," Aggie asked trying not to laugh, "that reading…" She glanced at the book title, " —Sherlock Holmes is what I meant by pursuing interests?" Without waiting for an answer,

254

Aggie left the room and entered Laird's. Using the book as a mock paddle, she whacked the boy gently on the rump.

"Get up."

"But—"

"I'll apply this more forcefully next time unless I see you on your feet in the next five seconds."

Grumbling, Laird dragged himself from his bed, stood at the foot, and saluted with a scowl on his face. "I might as well have to catch a bus!"

"You'll catch it from me if you don't arrive downstairs, dressed, and ready to eat in ten minutes. I'm ashamed of you!" Her words hardly seemed to make an impact.

Kenzie and Ellie were digging through drawers by the time Aggie arrived in their room, but their movements were sluggish. "Come on, girls. This isn't difficult. Make the bed, put on the clothes, wash your hands and faces, and show up at the table. This isn't rocket science."

It took several calls for Tavish to return from wherever his book had taken him. Aggie pulled it from his hand and frowned. "Louis L'Amour? Really? Isn't he a bit mature for you?"

"Daddy gave them to me. He said I'd like them." Tavish frowned as he watched her turn with book in hand. "Can I at least have it back to put with the others?"

"You can have it back after your schoolwork is done. I'll decide about reading it later."

Downstairs, Aggie pulled a basket of toys out of the closet and set it on the kitchen floor. She'd learned the hard way that it made the most sense to pull Ian from room to room with her rather than trying to run back to check on him every few minutes—usually too late to prevent whatever damage or mess he caused while unsupervised. She stirred the oats, turned them back on to rewarm them, and frowned at the milk. It'd be warm now, but they could just learn to get ready faster.

Cari and Lorna skipped into the kitchen, each wearing half of two separate and glaringly clashing outfits. Compromise was a good thing; the result was not. A glance at the clock told her to deal with good taste on another morning. She helped the girls get their oats, admonishing them not to overload on sugar and blueberries, and carried their bowls to their places. Cari took one sip of her milk and wrinkled her little nose. "That is gwoss."

"If you had been to breakfast on time, it would have been nice and cold. You can just drink it like that."

"I don't wike warm milk."

Prayers whizzed their way to heaven as Aggie begged the Lord not to have a big battle before the day even started. "I don't blame you. I don't either. It'll help you remember to get dressed faster tomorrow, won't it?"

Something in Aggie's tone reached Lorna's conflict radar. She grabbed her glass and chugged the entire thing in one long gulp. "I drank mine. Now may I have some cold?"

Laughing, Aggie nodded. "After a few bites of your cereal, you can certainly have more milk."

Ellie arrived minutes later followed by Vannie. The others, however, were still MIA by the time everyone finished their meal. For a moment, Aggie was tempted to put away the food, wipe down the counters, fill the dishwasher, and declare the kitchen closed until snack time. Her mother's admonitions about nutritious food before school mocked her, though. She couldn't expect the children to learn without a decent breakfast, could she?

"Ok, everyone in the library. Vannie, can you take Ian with you, and Ellie, can you grab his toys and basket and carry them in for me? I need to go light a fire under those guys."

Upstairs, the other children were dawdling. Laird had his clothes on, but just stood staring out the window instead of making his bed. Tavish's bed was made and his pants were on, but he stared into his drawer as if waiting for a shirt to jump out and slide over his arms. "Come on, boys. Get 'er done! I'm about to close the kitchen, and you can just wait for lunch."

That helped speed both boys through their paces and down the stairs. Kenzie, however, just stood in front of her closet, staring at her clothes, confused. "What's wrong, Kenzie?"

"I don't know what to wear."

"Well, pick a dress and put it on."

"But do I wear school clothes or play clothes? I'm not *going* to school, but I'm going to *do* school. I'm going to play too so I don't know what I'm supposed to wear."

"Anything is ok. Just don't wear your church clothes. If you decide to play in the mud, make sure you are wearing your play clothes."

The child reached into the closet and then jerked her hand back. "I don't *know!*" she wailed.

"Ok, you're making this overcomplicated." Aggie pulled out one of the simple little t-shirt dresses. "Wear this. Downstairs immediately. You can make your bed during your break."

Once she had everyone seated in the library, Aggie was sure things would go much smoother. She handed Kenzie, Cari, and Lorna pictures to color, and told the others to read Proverbs twenty-nine. Confident that everyone was occupied, Aggie went over Vannie's assignments with her. In the middle of the "meeting," Aggie's cell phone buzzed in her pocket, but she ignored it.

"Aunt Aggie, why don't you answer the phone?"

"We're discussing your lessons. I can't stop every time the phone rings."

"But what if it's Gramma Millie or Aunt Tina?"

"They'll leave a message." Aggie knew better than to let herself become sidetracked. "Ok, so take my laptop upstairs and if you have questions, come get me."

With Vannie dispatched, Aggie moved to help Laird, but found Kenzie done coloring the picture and Cari and Lorna building log houses out of the crayons. "Ok, Cari and Lorna. Why don't you go find your dolls or your Duplos or something?"

The girls dashed upstairs, making a racket sure to elicit a cry of protest from Vannie, but all was silent. For a moment, Aggie considered checking in on them, certain something must be wrong if Vannie wasn't demanding the girls hush, but Kenzie started doodling on her paper, obviously lost in her own world. Aggie pulled the math workbook she'd purchased from the shelf and a pencil from the holder on the desk. "Ok, so you have three pages of math to do. It should be easy enough, since it's review of the work you brought home last year. I checked to make sure."

A sense of satisfaction washed over her as she saw Laird, Ellie, and Tavish reading their Bibles and Kenzie bent over the workbook, a look of intense concentration on the child's face. Laird looked up first, closing his Bible as he did. "Is Bible part of our school work?"

"Well, for now, you'll be reading a chapter a day. I wanted to start small. Let's go over your math." As she explained the day's and week's lessons, Aggie had a surreal sense of realizing that this is what she would have been doing all along had she continued with her career in education. Everything seemed to flow together so beautifully that it seemed almost too good to be true.

Ellie and Tavish accepted their math books without much concern and opened them to the appropriate pages. She gave them assignments, and asked if they had any questions before realizing that Lorna and Cari hadn't returned. "Someone keep an eye on Ian. I'll be right back."

Aggie dashed upstairs, but didn't find the girls in their room. She popped her head in Vannie's room to ask if the girl had seen them and saw Vannie flush with embarrassment and move her hands over the touch pad on the laptop. "Vannie? Is something wrong?"

"No, I—"

It was obvious that she was trying to close something out, but being flustered, she had difficulty controlling the unfamiliar touch pad. Aggie took one glance at the screen, and her face fell. "I'm disappointed in you."

"I'm sorry, Aunt Aggie. It was open when I opened the laptop and I read the little bit that showed before I realized it." The girl hung her head. "I scrolled up to read the beginning and then realized what I was doing. I was going to close it out, honest, but then I saw wife and thought maybe you explained why you didn't want to marry Mr. Markenson."

"I didn't realize that I hadn't told you that, but regardless, it's wrong to read other people's messages. It's no different than opening someone's mail without permission."

"I know. I'm sorry." Vannie did look truly miserable.

"Don't let it happen again, Vannie. I need to be able to trust you." Eager to change the subject, Aggie pointed out the door. "Have you seen Cari and Lorna?"

"I heard them come up a little bit ago, but then they went away again." She hesitated and then added, "Did Luke ask you to marry him too?"

"No, Vannie, he didn't." She hadn't intended to elaborate, but the girl's disappointed face tugged at her conscience. "However, as soon as he thinks I care for him, I believe he will."

"But you don't love him?"

Aggie shook her head. "Not like he loves me, no."

"Two men in one week. I bet that doesn't happen often."

"Well," Aggie said, deciding to enlighten the girl just a little, "William suggested we marry so that you guys would have a father-type figure around here. He didn't want to marry me for me. It was chivalrous in a way, but it wasn't romantic in the least. I actually felt a little insulted."

"But Mr. Markenson is so handsome and he's an *officer*!"

"Well, obviously you like men in uniform, but I don't consider a job and a handsome face to be the best qualifiers for a man." Her eyes softened at the disappointed look on Vannie's face. "Besides, Luke isn't exactly unattractive!" She glanced at the door. "I need to find those girls. Are you doing ok in here?"

"Yeah." Vannie swallowed. "I really am sorry, Aunt Aggie."

"I understand. That must have been awfully difficult to ignore."

With a wave, Aggie went on a twin hunt, searching through all the rooms, the downstairs, and even out into the yard. A giggle from above sent her feet flying through the house and up to her room. There, in her bathroom, her nieces were painting each other with the calamine lotion. "Is this dolls or Duplos?"

Cari, in a rare moment of penitence, shook her head, tears springing to her eyes. "No. I's sowwy, Aunt Aggie."

"Into the tub. Do *not* turn on the water, but get undressed and get into the tub. I'll be right back with clothes."

Vannie stuck her head out the door when Aggie thundered down the stairs to retrieve clean clothes. "Do you need some help?"

"They just decided to finger paint with calamine lotion—all over themselves."

"I could give them a bath…"

For a moment, Aggie almost accepted the offer. Kenzie was probably already done with her work and waiting for her next assignment. Remembering the large amount of work Vannie had ahead of her, Aggie shook her head. "That's ok. I'm going to give them a quick rinse bath—won't even fill the tub. You get to work on your assignments."

Clothes in arms, Aggie hurried back up the stairs and then down again. "Actually, can you go make sure they're still watching Ian? Maybe bring him up to play on your floor until I get done? It'll just be a couple of minutes."

"Sure!"

Aggie hated herself for doing it, but she went back upstairs with her mind unconcerned knowing that Vannie was watching the little guy. She rinsed off the girls, soaped them up, rinsed again, and then examined their hair. It seemed as if it had managed to miss the infusion of calamine, so she shut off the water and wrapped the girls in towels. "Ok, let's get you dressed and downstairs."

She stopped on the second floor to grab Ian, thank Vannie, and supervise the procuring of toys before leading them all to the library. The moment she brought them in, pandemonium erupted. Kenzie dropped her pencil, Ian grabbed it and tried to run, making Aggie lunge to avoid a fall-induced pencil puncture. Cari and Lorna tried to set up their Duplos on the table next to Ellie and Tavish earning them a snarl of protest.

"Whoa! Ok. This isn't going to work. Why don't you guys go work at the dining room table, and I'll take the little guys into the kitchen?"

After a shift of possessions from one room to the next, Aggie was sure the work would run smoothly, but when she went to check Kenzie's progress, she found a blank page. "Why haven't you done your problems?"

"You didn't show me a sample problem. Mrs. Tompkins always showed us a sample problem. We weren't allowed to do anything until she showed us the sample problem. I was waiting for you and waiting for you."

"I told you to do the problems, Kenzie. That means no sample problem."

"How am I supposed to know that? All I know is that we're supposed to wait. That's what Mrs. Tompkins did!" The child's voice sounded angry, but Aggie recognized the frustration behind it.

"I'm sorry, Kenzie, but how am I supposed to know how one teacher in one school that I've never attended told you something like that? If you'd gone to the school in Brunswick, the teacher there might not have shown you a sample problem on review work either." Aggie worked one problem with the girl and said, "Now finish the page and next time if I say to do something, you do it how I say to do it, not how you did it before."

Ellie grabbed Aggie's sleeve as she passed and asked for help. Aggie took one look at the girl's book and nearly snapped at the child. "Ellie, why do you only have five problems done?"

"I can't remember how to do these. It says to simplify six plus twenty minus two."

"Do you know how to do the fractions on the next box?"

"Oh, sure! Those are easy." Ellie beamed. "I just can't remember if I do twenty six minus two is twenty four or if I do eighteen plus six is twenty-four."

"Since the answer is the same, on that problem it doesn't matter. But usually, you work from left to right. Start with six add the twenty, then subtract the two." As Ellie picked up her pencil, Aggie stopped her. "Next time, don't just wait for help. Go on and do what you do know, and when I'm available, I'll help you."

Laird's work was slow, but appeared to be steady. He'd worked through about eight problems in the half hour she'd been distracted which seemed reasonable considering Ian might have kept him occupied. Tavish was nearly done with his assignment making Aggie wonder if she'd assigned enough work. The number of missed problems might give her insight into the speed. If he missed too many, she'd have to slow him down. He was probably trying to hurry up so he could finish his book. That thought sent her digging through her pocket for her phone.

Two text messages greeted her. One was from Tina reminding her that the printouts from online were still in the printer unless Aggie had moved them. The other was from Luke letting her know he was praying for her and offering to bring a treat around three o'clock. She sent Tina a message of thanks and started to send one to Luke but stopped. She'd planned to call her father about the L'Amour books, but changed her mind and dialed Luke's number.

"Hey, got your message. That's really nice of you."

"I'd be happy to do it." Luke's voice soothed the frazzled nerves she'd developed during the events of the morning. "How's it going?"

"So far, Murphy has the upper hand."

"The lawmaker or the neighbor?"

"Lawmaker. Right now, the neighbor would be a welcome distraction." She rubbed her temple, wondering if it was too soon to

261

resort to aspirin. "I was wondering what you know about Louis L'Amour."

"Westerns by 'America's Storyteller?'"

"That's the one. Too mature for Tavish?"

"I doubt it. There might be a rogue word or two, but they're clean in the smutual sense."

Aggie giggled. "Smutual?"

"One of Mom's words. Is L'Amour on the list for Tavish's schoolwork? Seems a bit advanced for fourth grade."

"I found him reading it this morning," Aggie explained. "I just didn't know what was in it. Westerns seem like something that can be a little racy, so I wondered. I'll just tell him to bring it to me if he thinks there's anything inappropriate for him to read."

Luke laughed. "He'll probably be bringing you a few damnations without the 'ations.'"

"Ah, well, I can handle that." She glanced into the dining room and saw Ian trying to climb into a chair and Tavish waiting for her. "Looks like I'm needed. I'll see you later then."

"Chin up, Mibs."

Luke found her in the back yard playing Mother, May I? with the children. Ian, always trying to join in the children's fun, copied each of the older children's steps, clapping his little hands after they told him he did well. Lorna saw Luke first and ran to him squealing. The child threw her arms around his legs and cried, "I missed you, Luke!"

A lump filled his throat as he knelt down to meet the child's eyes. "I missed you too."

"You didn't come for days and days and days. It's been a month!"

"Not even a week, but thank you." Luke winked at Aggie from across the yard. "There are cupcakes on the counter! Winner picks first."

The players redoubled their efforts to eek out as much space in each "step" as possible. Vannie teased Luke from the swing, protesting that she couldn't possibly win if she wasn't playing. "I think you're playing favorites!"

Lorna refused to leave Luke's side. "I'll pick last."

He picked up the girl and brought her to the swing, smiling at Vannie as he sat down. "How'd your first day go?"

"I have homework. Isn't that weird? Homework when all the work is at home."

"How does that work?"

"I didn't get everything done, so Aunt Aggie said I could have until four o'clock, and then I had to go back and finish."

"That makes sense," he agreed. "So, why didn't you get it done? Was it too difficult?"

"I just had to get used to watching the DVD, taking notes, stopping, reading the book. It's just different. I had a hard time concentrating. It's easy to get distracted when you don't have a teacher waiting to give you detention for not paying attention in class."

"Aaah. That sounds like a learning curve. Is the work difficult?"

Vannie shook her head. "Not really. I might even like it once I get used to it. Right now, I just miss what was familiar."

A squeal erupted from the yard as Kenzie dashed to Luke's side. "I won! Can I go pick?"

"Go ahead."

Aggie dragged herself up to them looking completely worn to a frazzle. "Vannie, why don't you go in and get your cupcake and then check and see if you'll need help on your grammar?"

The moment the girl rounded the corner, Aggie dropped her head in her hands, clearly willing herself not to cry. "I think William was right."

"Oh, Mibs no." Luke struggled with the desire to comfort her and knowing he didn't have that right—yet. The hope of a *yet* kept him from feeling utterly defeated. "It's the first day. I bet if you talk to most teachers in any school, they'll tell you their first day, or maybe even week, was frustrating."

"Is it horrible that I want to get in my little Beetle convertible, drive home, crawl up onto the couch next to mom, put my head in her lap, and let her stroke my hair and tell me everything will look better tomorrow?"

"What happened?"

263

"Well, no one wanted to get up. They seemed to think life is just one big summer vacation, and school was something they could do when they felt like it. Ian was always into everyone's stuff, Cari and Lorna decided to finger paint with the calamine lotion, Kenzie can't fathom school any way but the way 'Mrs. Tompkins' did it, and Laird is easily distracted. It took him two and a half hours to do about thirty review problems. Vannie over-thinks every instruction, relistens to each DVD half a dozen times, oh, and she read our conversation from the other night. I think we have some 'splainin to do Lukey."

"Lukey?" He wrinkled his nose in distaste.

"It's close to Lucy…"

He took a deep breath. "What's for dinner?"

"What?"

"What's for dinner?"

Aggie stared at him as if he'd lost the little sense he was born with and shrugged. "I don't know. I was so prepared for breakfast and lunch, but even though I spent most of the day in the kitchen—"

"Why the kitchen?"

"I had to move everyone to the dining room so I could put Ian, Cari, and Lorna in the kitchen and living room. Otherwise it was chaos."

Luke nodded. "Come with me."

He led her downstairs to the basement and glanced around the room. "Ok, what if we rethink the layout. I can shrink the storage room, but it'd add a lot of work for very little gain. I'm thinking that we move the swings inward a bit so we can add a half wall here as a visual boundary…" Luke outlined a study area between the family room and play area. "This way you have a comfortable spot to help the kids, the little ones have lots to do, and there's plenty of room to work." He settled his hands on his hips and waited for her verdict.

Aggie glanced around the room taking in his suggestions and then nodded. "How long? How long will this take?"

Luke glanced around him. The floors were done, the walls were done, and he'd have to build the half wall. The play equipment hadn't been purchased, and he was still working on the built-ins, but it was a lot closer to finished than he thought she expected. "If we get the play equipment tomorrow, I might get it done by the end of the week if I can come early and stay late."

"How does that affect your work schedule?" She shook her head. "What am I thinking? I can't do that to you. We'll make the dining room work."

"I'll do it, Mibs, but I'm confused."

"About what?"

"Why do you have to use the dining room? Why can't Laird work in his room where there are no distractions, Ellie and Tavish can work in the library, and you can move Kenzie with you wherever you need to go? If the little ones want to play outside, she can bring her work to the picnic table."

That idea had obviously never occurred to her. "Do you think it's ok to leave them on their own so much?"

"It's not like you're forbidding them from coming to you for help. But if Laird needs no distractions, then put him where there are none." When he saw Aggie's uncertain expression, he added, "You could always ask on the email loop Tina found."

She glanced around the room again as if assessing the proposed changes once more. "Well, I can also try it while you finish this. I wish I could help, but—"

"But you can't. Let me do this for you, Mibs. You have no idea how much it means when I have a chance to do something for you."

Aggie's eyes met his, and her smile made his mouth go dry. "You're always dong something for me, Luke. Always."

Luke says: Everyone in bed?

Mibs says: Yep. The house is finally quiet.

Luke says: Are you ready for tomorrow?

Mibs says: I still have Laird's math to correct. I never got done with it, and he can't go on until I do.

Luke says: I can let you go.

Mibs says: Oh. Are you busy?

Luke says: Are you kidding? I've been ignoring my dishes because I was afraid I'd miss you signing on.

Mibs says: Luke?

Luke says: Too personal?

Mibs says: Not at all. I was going to say that I really needed to hear that tonight.

Luke says: Do you have any idea how long I've done that? Even when you were talking to mom instead of me, I'd be chatting with her asking how you were doing.

Mibs says: How long, Luke? Either I'm really dense, or you're really good at keeping your feelings to yourself.

Luke says: Well, I was first intrigued by a sleeping woman with a sprained ankle and tear-stained face. I realized I had met a good friend when she dug a list of work out of her purse with "FIX THE WIRING" at the top.

Mibs says: LOL. I was so embarrassed that morning. But that doesn't tell me when...

Luke says: Well, I know something happened sometime while we were working on Vannie's room, because my heart sank the day I thought you were firing me, remember?

Mibs says: Firing you? When did I say that?

Luke says: You didn't. You got frustrated because you thought I could read your expression, but I couldn't. I thought you were going to fire me.

Mibs says: Oh right.

Luke says: And then there was the day we moved Vannie in. She said something like, "Aunt Aggie is one of a kind, isn't she?" and I agreed.

Mibs says: I think it's good that you're there and I'm here.

Luke says: Pink cheeks?

Mibs says: Brick red.

Luke says: Well, then maybe I shouldn't tell you that I just figured out when I knew I loved you.

Mibs says: That's cruel.

Luke says: You really want to hear it?

Mibs says: Who knew you were into torture?

Luke says: LOL. Mibs, I think I knew that I loved you when I heard you sigh at Fred Astaire searching the churchyard for Audrey Hepburn.

Mibs says: I think you asked me if I was a romantic at heart, but look who is the romantic!

Luke says: Guilty.

Mibs says: If William hadn't been such a twit, when do you think you'd have said something?

Luke says: I don't know. Probably not until next March or something. I'd have wanted to give you a full year to get used to your new life and know if you wanted to shake it up again. I'm really sorry, Mibs. Sometimes I think I was really selfish in saying anything.

Mibs says: Well, I'm glad you did. It's what I needed to hear at the time. You have no idea how cheap and useless I felt.

Luke says: I'm sure William didn't mean to make you feel like that.

Mibs says: Well, he did.

Luke says: Mind if I change the subject and put you on the spot?

Mibs says: Please do.

Mibs says: Well, change the subject. I'm not so sure about the spot thing.

Luke says: LOL. I was wondering if you think you CAN learn to love me. I'm a patient man, but if you really think it's not possible, I'd rather know now so I have time to prepare myself if the day comes when you say you don't want me to try anymore.

Mibs says: Wow. That's a hard one.

Luke says: Then leave it for another day or not at all. I don't want you to feel pressured.

Mibs says: No, it's not that. It's just that some things are hard to say. I do think I could learn to love you. What I don't know is if I will.

Luke says: Well, that is encouraging.

Mibs says: Sounds DIScouraging to me. Do you know how much I want to be able to say that I already do care?

Luke says: You haven't had time to think about your own life much less your heart these past months. You've had one single focus—the children.

Luke says: Speaking of children…

Mibs says: What? Who did what now and when?

Luke says: No one. I just wondered if you wanted to have children.

Mibs says: What do you call the many inhabitants of my house?

Luke says: LOL. I meant "your own" children.

Aggie says: You mean as in doctor visits, growing belly, food cravings, swollen feet, stretch marks, labor, delivery, morning sickness, nursing and late night feedings? Those kinds of children?

Luke says: So, that's a "Not on your life?"

Mibs says: A year ago, if you had told me about my life right now and asked that question, I would have been adamant that eight children was more than enough. Having been through part of that with Ian, I feel like I missed out with the others. I hardly held them as infants. I tended to admire from Allie's side and play with whoever came up to me. I was the aunt who showed up, brought bubbles, told stories, and then went home.

Mibs says: Is that bad?

Luke says: Is what bad?

Mibs says: That I want the whole experience too? God gave me eight wonderful children in varying ages, and I still want more.

Mibs says: I want to feel a baby kick from inside, the smell of a baby's head, the little chubby cheeks, the baby powder scent that follows them even if you don't use it, slobbery kisses, and most of all, that adoring look in a baby's eyes when it's nursing. I want it all. Boy that sounds greedy and selfish.

Luke says: I think it sounds quite normal.

Mibs says: What about you? How do you feel about children?

Luke says: I love them. Always have. Mom says I used to try to convince mothers in the store to let me take home their babies.

Mibs says: I believe it. Your love of children shows. Do you think it is irresponsible to consider having children when I'm already responsible for my sister's? People already think I'm overloaded.

Luke says: I think if you can provide their basic needs, food, shelter, and love, no one has any business putting in their unsolicited opinions.

Mibs says: So, what made you ask that question?

Luke says: I've been wondering if all the work had soured you on the idea of having children. It's something I've looked forward to for years.

Mibs says: You want your "own."

Luke says: I'll always love your children, Mibs. They already have their own special corners of my heart, but I also want to share pregnancy with my wife.

Mibs says: May I ask a very personal question?

Luke says: You can ask anything you like. I can't think of a thing I wouldn't answer, but I can't promise you'll like all my answers.

Mibs says: Well, this is awkward. I'm glad I'm asking here instead of in person. Does your business adequately provide for you?

Luke says: Yes. I'm quite financially stable. I can take risks now that I don't think I would with a family, but my father left us all a small inheritance, and I've used it well flipping houses.

Mibs says: That was a wonderful thing to do. He left plenty for your mother, didn't he? She doesn't have to work, so I just assumed...

Luke says: Between life insurance and Social Security, she's modestly provided for for the rest of her life. Dad was a great provider that way.

Mibs says: That sounds like Allie. She made sure that everything was in my name, they had a huge life insurance policy, the kids all receive Social Security benefits, and, of course the house was worth quite a bit.

Mibs says: So how did you get started flipping houses?

Luke says: Mom doesn't watch much TV, but she likes one of those shows on home renovations. She and Dad watched it every week, so I got in the habit of watching it too. I started trying some of the ideas around our house while working for a landscaping company. Then a house went on the market in an upcoming area of town. It was right after I deposited my money, so I talked to Mom, the girls, and our minister, Joe. They all recommended that I try it.

Mibs says: And did you make a profit? I've heard that first houses often don't.

Luke says: I did make a small profit on the first one. I could have done better if I hadn't been so chintzy with the fixtures. I kept trying to cut corners, but I cut them off too much sometimes. The second house though, I tripled my money. By the third one, I realized that I had to choose between going to college and doing what I loved. I chose houses.

Mibs says: Well, you did a great job with mine. I'm still amazed at how fast it got done.

Luke says: I was really slow with that first house. I didn't know what I was doing, so every step took forever while I read about it, tried it, redid it, etc. However, I've learned where to take shortcuts, where not to, and you and the kids did so much of the tedious work like peeling off wallpaper and scrubbing walls. I was able to work consistently without having to shift gears as often.

Mibs says: Ok, another topic change.

Luke says: Shoot.

Mibs says: What does this relationship thing mean? What's going to change?

Luke says: I don't know. I don't know how to do this. Why do you ask?

Mibs says: Well, I just wondered because everything seems the same as it's always been.

Luke says: Is that a problem?

Mibs says: No, it's good, actually. I just didn't know what to expect.

Luke says: I plan to find a way to romance you, Mibs. I just don't quite know how to do it. I'm new at this too. But, I think the biggest change is that you're aware of the possibilities now. That's the difference.

Mibs says: I can see that. There were things you said at times that I know made me do a double take, but life was so busy, I forgot about them immediately.

Luke says: Like what?

Mibs says: I enchant you. I always look nice to you. You can't imagine what has gotten into you. The last one was when you told me that some men can be just friends while waiting for something more. I was sure you were hinting that I should be careful not to lead William on, but a part of me wondered for a bit. Mom and I decided that it was definitely a warning about William.

Luke says: I kicked myself all the way home for that one. I was sure I'd given myself away, and you'd be telling me to stay away from now on.

Mibs says: I don't think I would have. I might have been a little freaked out at first. You can thank William for your "confession" being a relief instead of a burden.

Luke says: I thought I'd messed everything up. No worries, though. I'm sure to blow it eventually. Promise to love me anyway?

Mibs says: Ha! You aren't going to trip me up that easily.

Luke says: Well, I had to try.

Mibs says: I think I am going to like this.

Luke says: This what?

Mibs says: Oh boy. I've done it now. How's the weather over there?

Luke says: Mibs...

Mibs says: Ok, ok. It's not easy being transparent, but I have to admit that I like knowing that someone so special to me cares so much about me. It's a nice feeling.

Luke says: And since we're on a happy note, it's late. I think I should let you go to bed. I didn't realize how long we've been chatting.

Mibs says: You gave me an out. That is really sweet of you.

Luke says: Say goodnight, Gracie...

Mibs says: Goodnight, Gracie.

Luke says: LOL. I do love you, you know.

Mibs says: Yeah, I think I do know.

Luke says: Is it uncomfortable for you for me to keep telling you?

Mibs says: No.

Mibs says: Um, I want you to know, I won't say it myself unless I mean it.

Luke says: I'm glad to hear it. Goodnight, Mibs.

Mibs says: Nighters, Lucas.

LANGUAGE LESSONS

Chapter Nineteen

Friday, October 3rd

No one would ever claim that the Milliken-Stuart home-school had an easy beginning. By Wednesday, Aggie realized that the children simply didn't take it seriously. Even Vannie considered her lessons optional in relation to the rest of life. Kenzie fought every single direction that Aggie gave her. It didn't matter if it was putting away a pencil or reading a story, every single directive was met with, "But Mrs. Tompkins said" or "But Mrs. Tompkins didn't..." In desperation, Aggie began ending her instructions with, "And I don't care what Mrs. Tompkins said. I am your teacher. You need to say 'yes ma'am,' and just do it."

She'd seen Luke smirk at those words, but she didn't care. After Tuesday afternoon, he'd forbidden her to enter the basement. At night, when all the children were sleeping, she'd been tempted to tiptoe down there and see how it was coming, but the thought of his disappointment at her ruined surprise always kept her from doing it. Instead, she spent her nights into the wee hours of the morning chatting with Tina and Luke and correcting the children's work.

The housework suffered. Spending all day keeping her students on track and the little ones out of trouble left little time for things like laundry, meals, dishes, and dusting. Each night she tucked Ian into his crib with grandiose ideas of going downstairs and tackling the work waiting for her, but she never did. The minute she set foot downstairs, the schoolwork called to her for correction. She'd open her laptop and chat with Tina, Libby, or Luke while correcting spelling tests and math problems.

Friday afternoon, after standing over each of the children with threats of more work on Saturday, each of the children were finally finished by two-thirty. Aggie collapsed on the couch, grateful that the three littlest were still asleep. Within seconds, she was snoozing herself.

The clock chimed at three o'clock, startling Aggie out of a sound sleep. The house was quiet — too quiet. She dragged herself up off the couch and climbed the stairs. A peek into Tavish and Ian's room showed the baby still snoring, arms thrown back and one foot sticking out of the crib bars. Cari and Lorna were also still asleep cuddled together on Cari's bed.

Downstairs, she ignored the mess in the kitchen and went outside to see what the other children might be doing. As she rounded the corner, she overheard Luke talking earnestly with the children. " — thought I could trust you to do your work. Your aunt has enough on her plate without standing over you like she has been. You wouldn't have done that last year at school."

"But this isn't school. This is just — "

"No buts. If you got up on time, ate your breakfast, did the few jobs that Aggie asks of you, and then got to work on your schoolwork without dawdling, you'd be done before two o'clock every day. If you actually concentrated on that work, you might be done even earlier. My sister says that aside from some high school students, most home-schoolers she knows get their work done in less than three hours a day. That's nine to noon, guys." Vannie started to speak, but Luke interrupted her. "I see her up until two o'clock sometimes. She can't keep doing that. She'll wear out."

"Did she ask you to talk to us?" Laird sounded defensive.

"No, but if you don't make some changes, I'll be talking to her about raising her expectations. You can do it on your own because it's right, or you can do it because she makes you. Those are your options."

"Aunt Aggie doesn't like it when people tell her what to do. She won't like that you are trying to take over."

Aggie was stunned at the defiant tone in Vannie's voice and decided it was time to step in and back up Luke. "Aunt Aggie does like it when her children are respectful to the adults in their lives. You owe Luke an apology, Vannie."

"Sorry."

"No you're not. You might be sorry you got caught, but that's no apology. Try again."

Resigned, Vannie rephrased in nearly a monotone. "I was disrespectful. Please forgive me."

"You're forgiven, Vannie."

"Ok, everyone has work to do. If it's downstairs work, it gets done now. Go, go, go!"

Once everyone scattered to do the small chores they were responsible for, Aggie smiled at Luke. "Thanks for trying."

"They're walking all over you. I gave them four days, but it's just getting worse every day. You're right. They don't take this seriously."

"Should I put them back in school?" Defeat nearly overwhelmed her.

"No. That would teach them that you can be manipulated. You need to expect them to do what they should do and hold them to those expectations." He slipped his hand into hers and tugged her toward the house. "Come on. I have something to show you." At the top of the basement stairs, Luke flipped on the light and said, "Close your eyes."

She followed him, step by very slow step, down the stairs and waited for the ok to look. "This is torture!"

"Ok, open them."

The room was amazing. Much brighter than she'd expected, the space was everything she could have hoped for and more. They'd have a great place to work and play without anyone getting lost in the shuffle. "Luke..." She swallowed, a lump growing in her throat. Her first impulse was to hug him, but an unfamiliar shyness stole over her. Seconds passed as she tried to articulate just how wonderful she thought the space was. At last, she shrugged and wrapped grateful arms around him. "Thank you."

For a moment, he stood, unmoving, as if uncomfortable by her actions, but then he grinned and squeezed her until she lost her breath. "Is it really ok? The swings work there for you? The counters are ok?"

"It's perfect. How did you find one of those big couches so quickly?"

"Mom has been searching all over Rockland. One of those scratch and dent places was putting this on the floor as she walked in. She asked the price and told them to load it back up and deliver it to my place."

Aggie's hand trailed along the countertops he'd put at desk height as he spoke. "Do you really think they can do all their school work in so little time?"

"Corinne and Olivia both say it's common for elementary kids to get their work done in two to two and a half hours. I'm not saying you can't do more, but I think they should at least try to work faster."

"Well, maybe next week will be better. Meanwhile, what do we want for dinner? I've already called for pizza twice this week."

Tina arrived just after eleven while Aggie chatted on the messenger with Libby. Within minutes, the young women sat on opposite ends of the couch, a huge bowl of ice cream in their hands, and talking over the recent changes in Aggie's life. "So, what's the worst part of home-schooling?"

"Kids who don't want to do the work."

"I thought Allie's kids liked school!"

Aggie shrugged. "They seemed to last year, but this year it's like pulling teeth. I think they have a lousy teacher or something."

"That's ridiculous, and you know it."

"Luke says they're taking advantage of me because I'm not confident."

After a few seconds thought, Tina nodded. "That makes sense."

"We're going to try having higher expectations next week and see how it goes."

"'We,' huh? Interesting." At Aggie's blush, Tina grinned. "He's getting to you, isn't he?"

"He's a good man, Tina. I don't want to hurt him, but I don't know how to do this."

"Let it happen. That's how. You're going to sabotage it with your over-analytical tendencies. Just let him..." Tina searched for the word she needed. "I don't know, woo you. Ugh, that sounds stupid."

"Yeah, but I know what you mean. He claims he's going to 'romance me,' whatever that means, but I don't think he knows any more about it than I do."

"That'll keep things interesting." Her friend carried their bowls into the kitchen and returned with cups of piping hot coffee. "Ok, so tell me something, Aggie."

"Hmm?" Aggie sipped her coffee, burning her tongue slightly.

"If you had to decide today if you were going to marry Luke, what would you decide?"

Immediately, Aggie shook her head. "Oh, Tina. I couldn't do it. I have a lot of respect for him, I am fond of him, and I might even love him in my own way, but I don't really think it'd be right to marry him when I don't know how I really feel."

"Do you think he knows that?"

"He knows I'm not ready, yes."

"No, Ags. Do you think he knows that you might have some affection for him?"

With a slight shake of her head, Aggie sighed. "I don't think so." Tina's disapproving face elicited a protest. "I can't just say, 'Oh, and I thought you should know, I do have some kind of feelings for you, but I don't' know what they are. Just thought you oughtta know.'"

"Can't you find a way to show him instead of tell him?" At Aggie's stunned expression, Tina shook her head. "Not like that. I'm not talking about throwing yourself at him. I just meant that there had to be some way— compliment him or seek him out in some way so he notices you are making an effort."

"I suppose. I don't know, Tina, this is all so crazy."

"See, if you had accepted William's proposal, this would be a moot point. You'd probably be married by now."

Aggie shuddered visibly. "Oh, Tina. Wouldn't that be awful?"

"Maybe for you. Not every woman is going to see him as repugnant as you do."

"I don't think he's repugnant. I just think he's all wrong for me and that gives me the willies. He's a good man—handsome if you ask Vannie. She was quite disappointed that I didn't accept the man in uniform. I think she considers Luke a poor gal's William."

"Well," Tina began with an enigmatic smile that became clear as she spoke, "not every woman is as immune to him as you seem to be."

"You can have him."

Tina shrugged. "I think we have to let him decide that, and I'm not so sure he'll agree." The young woman stood, grabbed her duffel bag and backpack, and started toward the guest room. "I know it was crazy to come down like this, but I kind of missed your crew."

"G'night, Tina."

"Goodnight, Aggie. We'll figure out your love life tomorrow."

As Aggie climbed the stairs to her room, she replayed Tina's words in her mind. Her friend's lightheartedness was exactly the medicine her analytical heart needed, but the seriousness of the situation also tugged at her conscience. She brushed her teeth, washed her face, and coated her hands and feet in lotion as she considered the changes in her life.

Climbing beneath the covers, she snapped off the lamp. Once comfortable on her pillow, Aggie's heart reached out to the Lord in prayer. "Lord, I think I am ready for this. I'm a little excited about it, and I'm looking forward to seeing what it means in all of our lives, but Lord, please don't let me make a mistake. It'll hurt both of us and the children. I need to know that this is Your will for our lives. Help me make the right decisions so that I never ever regret it."

Saturday, October 4th

The bed shook as if an earthquake rocked the house. Aggie, groggy from sleep, pried her eyes open and saw Vannie and Kenzie bouncing on her bed as they tried to rouse her from sleep. Kenzie's voice pierced her eardrums as she screeched, "Wake up! Luke sent a really weird bouquet of flowers in a funny vase. There's a note and everything! Wake up!"

With her fists working the sleep from her eyes, Aggie tried to focus on the shifting blurs on her bed. "Can you go get it?" She hoped the few seconds of silence would help her wake up less painfully.

The girls flew from the room, their nightgowns billowing from behind like dresses in a period movie. Whoever spoke of the pitter-patter of children's feet had never experienced life in Aggie's house. With footfalls loud enough to wake the dead, or at least Tina, the girls thundered downstairs and then back up again, carrying the flowers as carefully as swiftly moving feet can— Ellie now following close behind them.

Vannie's sigh was comical in its predictability. "Isn't it pretty! It's so unusual. There's a little present, too— Kenzie, where is the present?"

Kenzie handed over a small book-like parcel tied in jute. The juxtaposition of the rough twine and satiny paper was lovely. Aggie wondered if Luke had excellent packaging taste or if Libby had helped him. Vannie's excited voice broke through her thoughts again. "What do you think is in the package?"

"Why don't you open it for me and see?" Aggie, her face buried in the bowl of flowers, was too distracted by the heady scents to realized that later she might be disappointed not to have opened it by herself.

Kenzie pulled the envelope from the floral pick in the bowl. "Can I read the note?"

"Sure." She hardly heard the question, being occupied with fingering the petals of a jonquil.

"Aunt Aggie," Kenzie's voice sounded as confused as her face looked, "why did Luke send a note that says, 'I hope that you can de—de—"

Vannie peeked at the note. "Decipher."

"Decipher all I want to say?'" Kenzie flipped the card over to see if the back held an explanation.

Thus far, aside from her brief confidence in Vannie, Aggie had hoped to keep Luke's feelings and intentions private, but she now realized it wasn't possible. Things would be too complicated if she didn't just explain now. "Well, it's kind of a long story, but a couple

279

of weeks ago when William was here, he told me he wanted me to marry him—"

Before she could continue, Kenzie bounced excitedly on the bed and squealed with delight. "Oh, Aunt *Aggie*! How exciting! Can we come?"

"I told him no, Kenzie," Aggie confessed, almost feeling as if she'd squashed the little girl's hopes deliberately.

Kenzie's face fell, but Ellie looked curiously at her. "Then why did Luke send you flowers?"

Aggie settled back against the headboard, stacking pillows behind her back for comfort, and crossed her legs yoga-style. "Before I told William no, I asked Luke what he thought. He's a good friend, and I value his opinion." Aggie's eyes met each girl's before she continued. "Luke told me that if I don't love William, and I don't, then I shouldn't marry him. Then he told me that he…" She grabbed her water glass and took a sip, trying to find a way to share the story without being careless with Luke's words.

"Aunt Aggie has *two* men who want to marry her! Isn't it exciting!" Vannie's eyes sparkled and her face glowed at the thought.

"Ok, girls I want you to listen to me for a minute. I know it all sounds very exciting and romantic, but things aren't always as they seem. Yes, William told me he wants to get married, but he doesn't. He wants to help me, and this was how he thought he could do that best. It was very noble of him, but it was wrong. I cannot agree to marry someone who doesn't want to marry me for *me*. Does that make sense?"

Three heads nodded, but Kenzie's face pouted. "But I love Mr. Markenson. He could be like a daddy."

"No one could be like Daddy." Vannie's voice showed that she felt Kenzie had betrayed their father by even suggesting it.

"I didn't say he could *be* daddy, I said *like* a daddy. Mr. Markenson likes me."

"Yes he does, Kenzie, but he doesn't love me."

"But Luke does, doesn't he, Aunt Aggie?" Ellie's voice was confident. Aggie often thought that little escaped the girl's notice.

"Yes, Luke loves me."

"And he wants to marry you too?" It was evident from her tone that Kenzie considered Luke second best but acceptable.

280

"Yes. Luke said he loves me and wants to spend more time with me. He wants to see if I can learn to love him too. How do you girls feel about that?"

Silence hovered in the air for several seconds until Kenzie shrugged. "I like it. I'd like Mr. Markenson more, but I like it. Maybe he can marry Aunt Tina. That'd be almost as good."

Anxious to change the subject, Aggie reached for the book Vannie had unwrapped and read the title aloud. "*Floriography: The Victorian Language of Flowers*. What a mouthful." She grinned at the eager faces waiting to know what it all meant. "So, who wants to help me figure out what these flowers mean?"

Ellie nodded, Kenzie squealed, and Vannie bounced just enough to remind Aggie that her eldest niece was still a little girl in many ways. "Ok, then. Ellie, you go grab me a pen and paper, Vannie, you find the flowers in the book." She stared at the bouquet, her face a picture of confusion. It became readily apparent that her knowledge of horticulture was sorely lacking. The illustrations in the tiny book were not much help, but after a time, they had compiled a respectable list.

"Well, I'll have to ask Luke if we have this right, but so far we have a red carnation. What is that?"

Vannie flipped to the R's and found nothing. Under carnation, she found several colors including red. "Ok, it says 'Alas for my poor heart.' What does that mean?"

"I think it means he's trying to garner sympathy. What about red chrysanthemum?"

Pages shuffled as she flipped a few. "I love." A group of collective sighs followed the pronouncement. Aggie couldn't help but wonder what a house full of incurable romantics would do to the testosterone levels of the boys.

"Ok, columbine. It's purple if that matters."

"They're all in the C's, aren't they?" Vannie muttered as she flipped through the little book on the quest for columbines. "Here it is, 'Resolved to win.'"

A small smile played around Aggie's lips. Luke had certainly been thorough. Tina stood in the door watching. After a nod and a smile, Aggie returned to their project. "Ok, daisies."

"I found that one easily enough. 'Innocence.'"

281

"Forget-me-not." Aggie frowned. "At least, I think that's what they are."

"True love. Forget-me-not." Vannie's nose wrinkled. "I always thought that was such a silly name for a flower."

"I suppose you prefer ranunculus?"

The girls all giggled. Ellie shook her head as Vannie turned the pages, trying to find the flower. "It sounds like ridiculous."

"I found it. Ranunculus. 'You are radiant in charms."

"Wow. Luke must really like you!" Kenzie's voice sounded awe-struck.

"How about honeysuckle?" Aggie pulled one of the blossoms from the flower and showed Kenzie and Ellie how to suck the nectar from it.

"'Generous and devoted affection.'"

With each floral declaration, Aggie's face grew redder. When Luke said he planned to romance her, he hadn't understated things. "Ok, jonquil or daffodil."

"Well, jonquil is 'I desire a return of affection.'" The girl fanned the pages searching for the daffodil. "Here it is; daffodil, 'uncertainty, chivalry, respect, or unrequited love.'" Vannie shook her head. "I think it's supposed to be a jonquil."

"Let's hope so. The lilac is purple if that matters. I think most lilacs are, but I've heard of white ones."

"Well, it says the purple lilac is 'First emotions of love.'" Vannie had begun to sound embarrassed.

"Lily of the valley?" Aggie ignored the snicker from Tina's side of the room.

"Um... 'Return of happiness.' What does that mean?"

"I have no idea," Aggie confessed. "Well, this one is easy though. Violet."

"Ok, hold on." Vannie's forehead furrowed as she concentrated on finding the right page. "'Violet—faithfulness; sweet modesty.'" The girl frowned as she realized that was all of the flowers. "There aren't any roses! Shouldn't there be roses? Even I know red rose means love and yellow means friendship."

"Maybe after hearing Laird describe 'imaginationally challenged' bouquets, he decided not to risk it." Tina's joke sent the whole room into snickers.

Before she could catch herself, Aggie sighed contentedly. Ellie frowned. "Aren't you happy, Aunt Aggie? I thought the bouquet and the flower messages were nice."

"I am happy, Ellie. It was a wonderful thing to wake up to this morning." Though she was embarrassed to admit it, Aggie forced herself to share the reason for her sigh. She wanted the girls to get a glimpse of what romance looked like when removed from the pink glow of Hollywood's lights. "I just got that funny feeling in my stomach you hear about and got a little emotional, I guess."

Kenzie's hand felt Aggie's forehead. "Does Luke make your stomach feel funny?"

"I guess you can say that. I've felt that same lurch before, but I never really gave it a second thought."

"You might be allergic to him. Maybe you need allergy medicine for when he comes over like Murphy takes because of the cat."

Amid giggles, Aggie tried to explain to Kenzie that sometimes a funny feeling in your stomach was a good thing, but the child was adamant that Aggie needed medication. At last, the young woman said, "Let's just say that I think Luke will be happy to hear that I felt a little odd when I got his flowers, ok?"

The young mother sent out a plea with her eyes for Tina to pull the girls away and give her a minute alone. As her friend led the trio of giggling girls down the steps, Aggie heard Kenzie say, "Aunt Aggie says she's not allergic to Luke, but I still think she is if he makes her stomach feel bad."

Knowing Tina was downstairs keeping an eye on her charges, Aggie sank back against the pillow again, turning the pages of the *Floriography* and occasionally sniffing a flower from the bowl-like vase. The deep red vase would look beautiful on her island, making Aggie wonder if it was purchased for that purpose. So intent was she in her reading, that she didn't notice one of her youngest nieces creep into the room until she felt a light tap on her arm.

"Hello, Lorna," she whispered. "Do you want to see my flowers?"

The child's wide eyes were solemn as Lorna shook her head. "Unh uh." The little girl's face was comical as differing expressions whizzed across the surface, but at last, in a conspiratorial whisper, she leaned close to Aggie and confessed, "I broke the picture of Mommy and Daddy that goes in our room."

As quietly as Aggie could muster, she replied, "Oh, you did?"

Lorna nodded solemnly. Her face, the picture of seriousness looked pixieish and endearing as she added in the same quiet whisper, "I hid it under Vannie's bed so you wouldn't find it, ok?"

Aggie snickered as she picked up the little girl. "Sweetie, I have a better idea for next time."

The child's eyes grew wide. "Am I in trouble, Aunt Aggie?"

Smiling at the girl's earnestness, Aggie shook her head. "Not this time, Lorna. Next time something breaks, just come and tell me, and I'll take care of it for you."

"M'kay."

"You didn't cut yourself on the glass, did you?" Lorna held out her hands for inspection, shaking her head as she did. "Good. It's never a good thing to try to cover up your mistakes. It's always better to confess to an adult in charge. Ok?"

"Yeth, Aunt Aggie. When I break something else, I'll tell you before I move anything."

Although not comforted by the assurance that Lorna expected to break more items, Aggie couldn't help but be charmed by the little lisp that always emerged when she was troubled. It never lasted long, but it did help Aggie differentiate between the girls at times. She sent the little one on her way, made her bed, and pulled fresh clothes from the closet.

Getting dressed hadn't been so fun in years. Now that she was no longer forced to exist in stained, worn, dingy clothing, the variety alone was a treat. In addition, knowing that seeing her dressed nicely made Luke happy helped keep the interest in her appearance from getting lost in the shuffle of life as a home-school "mom." She brushed her hair until it shone, left it down now that she had no worries about becoming a rogue paintbrush, and smiled at her reflection in the mirror. She'd never be the kind of beauty Tina was, but she looked nice.

On her way down the second floor hall to Vannie's room to retrieve the broken frame, Aggie stepped on something that sent a sharp pain through her foot. She reached down to pick it up, carrying it with her on her errand. How she would later wish that she had tossed it in the bathroom wastebasket just a few feet from where she stepped on it.

Mibs says: Libby? Are you there?

Libby says: Hello, home-school aunt of the week!

Aggie says: There, I changed my name. I think home-school flop of the week is more like it.

Libby says: You're too hard on yourself. My Luke says you're doing a wonderful job.

Aggie says: I think he's a bit biased, but right now, I can take all the support I'm offered.

Libby says: I understand you and he had quite the conversation the other night. My Luke saved it.

Aggie says: Oh, I wish I had thought of that. It might be nice to read them again later. Especially if… well, you know.

Libby says: I think that was his thought as well.

Aggie says: I dinged him and asked for a copy, but it says he's offline. At least now, he'll get it when he's on. It's odd though, he's always on at this time.

Libby says: That's because he's here fixing my garbage disposal. One of Olivia's girls dropped a quarter in it and now it's all seized up.

Aggie says: Well then, maybe I can ask him about the conversation when he's done.

Aggie says: Did he tell you what he did today?

Libby says: Oh, tell me all about that!

Aggie says: Well, I woke up to excited girls, a beautifully wrapped package, and an unusual bowl-vase of flowers from him.

Libby says: Not to brag on my boy or to give away secrets, but I know my Luke went to a lot of trouble with those flowers. He called every florist and gardener we know to get just the right colors and species. Some were very difficult to find, and I think one of them is actually silk.

Aggie says: I'll bet it's the mignonette. That's probably why it didn't look quite like the book.

Libby says: You're probably right. So how did he deliver them? He didn't tell me, but it seemed like he had something up his sleeve.

Aggie says: I don't know. Let me run see if Vannie is still awake. BRB.

Libby says: All right.

Aggie says: Back. I think HE delivered them. Incognito.

Libby says: Why do you say that?

Aggie says: Vannie says that a man with a gray mustache and gray hair, wearing a t-shirt that read, "ELSS DELIVERY SERVICE" on it. She said she remembers the letters because she wondered what an "elss" was. Those are his initials, right?

Libby says: Oh, you're right. That must have been him! He can be so clever about these things. He has a sense of humor that most people tend not to expect, but when he's among friends, he loves his practical jokes.

Aggie says: I'm learning that about him.

Libby says: May I put on my over-protective mother hat?

Aggie says: Of course!

Libby says: I know you're in a bit of an awkward position, and I don't want to be insensitive to that, but I'm watching my son and am concerned for him.

Aggie says: Concerned?

Aggie says: Libby, you don't approve?

Libby says: Of course, I do! I love you and your family very dearly. I hope you know that.

Aggie says: I do. I just wasn't sure if that translated to you being ok with Luke and me as something more than we are now.

Aggie says: That was an awkward sentence to write.

Libby says: It was actually very well worded. No, I am concerned for my Luke because of how he's reacting to this whole situation. He loves you—more than you know, I think. I've never seen him so happy and so sorrowful. He concerns himself so much with your feelings that I worry he'll forget to guard his heart adequately.

Aggie says: That's perfectly understandable. Any mother would be concerned.

Libby says: Please just remember he has put his heart on the line for you if you decide he isn't the man for you.

Libby says: Now, if that isn't an awkwardly worded sentence!

Aggie says: I understood it, though. Do you want me to let you in on a "secret?"

Libby says: Absolutely. If you really want to share, that is.

Aggie says: I don't see that happening — the deciding he's not for me thing. I just don't see it happening. He's already endeared himself to me in so many ways.

Libby says: I'd hoped I wasn't wrong in what I saw in you.

Aggie says: Well, I didn't know it until that awful day when William messed things up. Since then, I've noticed that I'm not exactly immune.

Aggie says: Is it silly that I refuse to give him less than my whole heart?

Libby says: I think that's wise. You wouldn't want to wonder if you "settled" for him.

Aggie says: Well, that and he only asked me to CONSIDER it. He never asked if any of it was his. He just assumed…

Libby says: That is so like a man — that combination of over confidence and insecurity is too funny sometimes.

Libby says: Now, what else happened around your household today? I miss being there with you all.

Aggie says: Well first, the girls woke me up with the flowers, so we looked them all up in the book he sent to find the meanings of each flower.

Libby says: All? Who all was there?

Aggie says: Vannie and Kenzie who woke me up, and then Ellie followed them back in with the flowers, and Tina arrived about the time we started looking them up.

Libby says: Oh my! That could be a bit… awkward.

Aggie says: Oh, it was, let me tell you. If I'd been awake, I think I would have saved the research for when they were otherwise occupied, but I'm kind of glad I wasn't. It's probably good for them to see what "real" romance looks like. Thus far they only have a few memories of their parents and Hollywood for examples.

Libby says: That's very insightful of you. So, what did they think of the flower language?

Aggie says: I have starry-eyed girls who are going to upset the very delicate testosterone levels of this house.

Aggie says: Oh, and then Kenzie said the funniest thing.

Libby says: And are you going to share?

Aggie says: Sorry, I dashed to refill my lemonade. See, when I read the list of all those very personal things, my stomach did that flip-flop thing you read about in books or hear about in movies, and I mentioned it.

Libby says: Uh, oh. I think no one warned you that anything you say can and will be used against you by your children.

Aggie says: LOL. Well, that's about right. Kenzie piped up and asked if I wasn't allergic to Luke. She strongly suggests allergy medicine.

Libby says: Oh, now that is too precious. You need to put that in her scrapbook. May I show Luke?

Aggie says: Sure. While you read, I'll type out what happened with Lorna. Just tell me when to send it.

Libby says: Excellent. BRB.

Libby says: Ok, we're ready for Lorna's story. I should tell you, my Luke is sporting a lopsided grin. I think he is very pleased to hear you felt "funny" about him.

Aggie says: Well, Lorna came to me after the whole flower thing and confessed that she broke something and hid it under Vannie's bed so I wouldn't find it. Can you imagine?

Aggie says: I told the girls he would be pleased to hear that, but Kenzie didn't believe me. Tell him not to get a big head.

Libby says: I'm afraid he already has one.

Libby says: That is one of the most adorable things I've heard in a long time. It needs to go in a scrapbook too. Print this conversation for reference so you don't have to worry about trying to remember.

Aggie says: That's a good idea! Thanks.

Libby says: Luke scrolled up to reread about your funny stomach again. I think he's enjoying this.

Aggie says: Well, this'll take his mind off the sappiness. William came by today.

Libby says: Oh, how the face falls.

Aggie says: *giggles* Anyway, I expected it to be a bit awkward. I haven't seen him since I told him I wouldn't marry him, and he didn't leave in a very good mood.

Libby says: Luke said that any man, even William, would be upset to find out they couldn't marry Aggie.

Aggie says: Mush by proxy. Only Luke…

Libby says: Good one. He's red.

Aggie says: He deserves it. Anyway, he — William that is — showed up, and I went outside to talk to him. I thought it'd be easier not to have an audience. The minute I saw his face, I knew it was going to be as bad as or worse than I'd expected. It was hard not to get irritated.

Libby says: I would have had trouble too.

Aggie says: He just stood there looking all troubled and confused — awkward, you know? I mean, he looked at me like I had two heads, and I don't think he said anything more coherent than "I…uh…er…um…"

Libby says: That seems extreme.

Aggie says: I know, right? Then a bug flew by my head, and I swatted at it. I hit my head instead. Um… yeah.

Libby says: We're lost over here.

Aggie says: This morning when I was going down to get the broken glass cleaned up, I stepped on this gaudy glittery hair thing that Kenzie loves. I just picked it up and took it with me, but my hair got in the way while I was working under the bed, so I scooped it out of my face and held it together with that thing.

Libby says: Oh, no. I bet that looked comical.

Aggie says: Ya think? I just stood there thinking, "I am trying to get William to take me seriously, and I have a green glittery dragonfly perched on top of my messy hair!

Libby says: Oh, no! LOL. What did you do?

Aggie says: I tried the silly approach. I struck a modeling pose and asked how he liked the latest fashion among home-schoolers.

Libby says: Mibs, this is Luke. I want to see you in that hair thing. It sounds quite adorable.

Libby says: Sorry, Aggie. He took over while I was getting some ice water. Naughty boy. ;)

Aggie says: Tell him to beware. I will have my revenge.

Libby says: So how did the rest of the conversation go?

Aggie says: Actually, I think we understand each other now. He thinks I'm nuts, of course, but then he always has.

Libby says: That's good. I'd hate to see a good friendship harmed over something, as misguided as it was, that was meant to be a good thing.

Libby says: I think I need to turn in. I worked hard getting the garden ready for winter today. I'm worn out.

Aggie says: Goodnight, Libby.

Libby says: Luke wants to get on, so I'll leave this open for him.

Aggie says: Ok. Hi, Luke.

Libby's Luke says: There. At least it's not Mom talking now.

Aggie says: Very cute.

Libby's Luke says: Aw, gee, I didn't know you cared.

Aggie says: Goodnight, Luke.

Libby's Luke says: Goodnight, Mibs. Dream of lilacs and ranunculus.

CELEBRATIONS

Chapter Twenty

Friday, October 10th

The house bustled with excitement. The dining room table was loaded with gifts, the island had a large bakery cake as the focal point, and children ran around the backyard searching for hidden prizes. Two small rolling suitcases and an overnight case sat in the little entryway, waiting for them to be whisked away to the Rockland Towers for a night of fun.

Martha Milliken sat on the couch in the living room chatting with Libby Sullivan about the children's progress in school, the completed house renovations, and the budding romance between Aggie and Luke. Ron, with an ear to the conversation, was charged with protecting the cake from little marauding fingers. Aggie and Luke had disappeared into the basement over an hour earlier and still hadn't reemerged to join the festivities.

"Here come the troops. I think they've found the last prize! Where are Aggie and Luke, anyway?" Ron sounded impatient. "The dinner reservations are for six-thirty!" The man hurried outside to stop the invasion from entering the kitchen.

"They'll be up when they're ready. Be patient, Ronnie!" Martha rolled her eyes at Libby. "He's a typical man. Needs to keep the ball rolling."

Libby stood and moved toward the door. "Zeke and Martha are here. This'll be interesting having two Martha's in the house."

Aggie and Luke arrived upstairs looking very pleased with themselves and carrying a beautifully wrapped package. Martha frowned. "I know you didn't wrap that, Aggie."

"Nope. I had Vannie wrap the box and lid separately so it was all ready to go the minute we needed it."

"Making her wrap her own birthday gift box. How cruel!"

Zeke's voice boomed as he entered the room. "That girl couldn't be cruel if she tried. She's just extending the anticipation."

"That girl could hang puppies from airplane propellers and you'd find a reason that it was a blessing for the pups," Martha Sullivan teased. "Zeke is just a bit too fond of Aggie."

Aggie handed Luke the box and gestured for him to add it to the table while she hugged her favorite farmer. "I love him too."

"I'd be jealous if he wasn't already married." Luke sounded wounded, but the grin on his face proved he was teasing.

"And if I was fifty years younger and didn't already have the love of my life, I'd give you a run for your money, son."

Shaking her head, Aggie rolled her eyes. "You're both silly." A glance out the window brought a new smile to her face—one that Luke visibly did not like. "William is here!" She hurried outside to greet him, leaving a room of bemused spectators in her wake. Luke went to call the children back in so that Vannie could open her presents, ignoring the sympathetic glances from everyone else.

William greeted each of the other guests cordially, but with the natural reserve that characterized the officer. Luke nodded as he returned with Ian in one arm and Lorna in the other. "Hey, William. Can I get you something to drink?"

The awkwardness that had tried to develop dissipated with a simple offer of refreshment. The room erupted in spontaneous conversation as Aggie led Vannie to the dining room table. "You can open your gifts here, or on the floor in the living room."

"I'll take them in so Grandma Millie doesn't have to get up."

For quite a while, Vannie opened gift after gift, many sent by Geraldine Stuart. The girl seemed pleased with everything but also a bit overwhelmed. The last gift made her smile. "I've never wrapped my own present before, and I still don't know what it is!" She lifted the lid of the box and flushed. "Oh, Aunt Aggie!"

"Well, show us what has you in a dither!" Zeke's excitement was infectious.

"I don't deserve it! Not after —"

"I think I know what you're ready to have and what you aren't."

Vannie shoved the laptop into her brother's hands and scrambled across her siblings, flinging herself into Aggie's arms. "I felt so bad. I was sure you couldn't trust me anymore! Thank you!"

"Luke set it up..."

The girl dodged a few more feet and wrapped her arms around the man she expected to call Uncle before another year passed. "Luke, you're the best. Thanks."

"Let's eat cake. The girls need to get on the road!" Ron was back in schedule mode.

Aggie lit the candles, waited for Vannie to blow them out, and then cut a generous piece of cake, sliding it into a plastic container. "Ok, we have our cake, the gifts are unwrapped, so I guess it's time to go. Laird and Tavish," Aggie waited for the boys to meet her gaze. "Please take all the gifts up to Vannie's room and put them on her bed. Lock the door behind you. We'll be home tomorrow night."

Luke grabbed the bags and carried them to the Milliken's sedan. After stowing them in the trunk, he opened the door for Vannie with a flourish. "Have a wonderful time, Vannie. Make delightful memories."

The girl squeezed him in a bear hug. "I love you, Luke," she whispered.

With a secretive smile on his face, he winked at Aggie and murmured into Vannie's ear, "Now see what you can do to influence your aunt to feel the same way, ok?" He waited for her to pull her legs into the car before he pushed the door shut behind her.

Aggie, lost in the scene before her, snapped out of her reverie and hurried to climb into the car, but Luke's voice stopped her. "Wait." She spun in place, nearly causing Luke to slam into her. "Let a guy be a gentleman, wouldja?" He grabbed her arms to steady her. "Have fun, Mibs."

"Why do I feel like I'm leaving for months?"

"I could say some sappy thing about how every second we're apart seems like an hour, but I think—" He winced exaggeratedly as she gave him a mock head slap. "—you might slap me for that," he finished.

"Say goodnight, Luke. I'll get on the messenger if I can't sleep."

"I'll be waiting."

Saturday, October 11ᵗʰ

After a night of dinner at The Oaks, a romantic comedy at the cinema, and late night confidences until Vannie fell asleep mid-sentence, the girls woke up ready to take on the city. "How about room service for breakfast?"

Vannie giggled, bouncing on her bed. "Oh, that'll be fun. Mommy always said we'd do that, but we never had a chance." The words that would have sparked a sob fest just a few short months earlier brought tears but without the overwhelming grief that once accompanied them.

"I know that if Allie said she was going to do it, she had every intention of it. Allie never made a promise that she wouldn't keep."

"Aunt Aggie?" Vannie's voice was so quiet that Aggie almost didn't hear her as she dug through the drawer for the menu.

"Hmm?"

"Is it selfish that I'm glad I get to spend today with just you?"

Aggie scrambled across her bed, menu in hand, and onto Vannie's. She wrapped her arms around the girl and squeezed. "Not at all. Maybe if you expected to spend every day only with me... that'd be flattering, but selfish. I'm just glad we have people who love us and are willing to help us so I can do things like this. I'd always planned to have girl nights with you when you got old enough, but with your grandmother, we had to be careful or she'd expect to do things too. You wouldn't believe the hilarious lengths Allie and I planned to make it happen when you were old enough to be trusted not to tell."

"Really?"

"Yep." After a quick consultation with the menu, Aggie passed it to Vannie. "Crepes and fruit for me. What do you want?"

"I'll take the same." Vannie didn't even glance at the choices. "Aunt Aggie?"

"Hmm?" Fumbling for the remote to watch one of those "fashion disaster" shows, Aggie wasn't paying much attention to her niece and missed the timidity behind the forthcoming question.

"Do you think Ellie, Kenzie, and the twins will get a chance to do things like this?"

"Like what?"

Vannie's arm swept the room. "Coming to the city and having dinner and a sleepover — stuff like this. If you marry Luke, will you still be able to do stuff like this?"

"Oh, Vannie. Of course, I can. This is what being a mom is, sweetie. It's spending time with your kids because you just love being with them. Luke or whoever I married would probably do similar things with the boys — take them fishing, hunting, and camping — things like that."

Relief washed over the girl's features. "I thought maybe a husband wouldn't like it if you went away."

"Not every day, no, but Luke understands my responsibilities and priorities. He would want me to take time to make special memories with each one of you."

"Are you going to marry him? I thought you weren't sure."

"I'm not sure, no, but it's hard to imagine my life without him, so..." Aggie shrugged. "Ok, let's get this breakfast ordered. We have spa appointments, shopping to do, and obscene amounts of money to spend."

"You never spend money unless you have to!" Vannie looked stunned.

"Well, we are today. Go get your shower, and I'll order breakfast."

Vannie grabbed her clothes and scuttled to the bathroom. Just before she shut the door, the girl peeked her head back out the door. "Um, Aunt Aggie?"

"Yeah?"

"Can I have Belgian waffles instead? I really don't like crepes very much."

"Tina's here! What is she doing here?" Aggie pulled into the drive behind her friend's car. She glanced at her niece. "So, are you ready to show everyone your new hairstyle and clothes?"

Vannie popped the sun visor down and peeked at the mirror one last time. "I feel like I look so different. Do I?"

"Well, the hairstyle really shapes your face. You look young, but a little more mature. I don't think we could have picked a better style, and your nails are awesome! I'm so glad you were able to grow them a little longer than usual. It really gave them something to work with."

Squealing children burst from the house and swarmed the car. Aggie watched as the children surrounded Vannie, all exclaiming over her "makeover." Luke came out onto the step and set Ian on the gravel. The tiny unsteady steps of her little "son" as he stumbled across the uneven ground of the drive tugged at her heart. She hurried around the front of the car, her purse abandoned on the hood, and rushed across the short distance to scoop up the giggling baby. "Gaggie!"

She snuggled the baby whispering, "I love you, little man."

Luke stepped closer, ready to welcome her home but his uncertainty was visible. Unaware of the audience watching through the dining room window, Aggie met Luke at the base of the steps and gave him a quick hug. "We talked about you."

"Oh, you did?" Though he tried to feign nonchalance, Luke looked pleased.

"You'll have to get any details you want out of Vannie. I'm not going there."

As she reached the top of the steps, Luke's quiet voice stopped her. "You were missed, Mibs. Not just by me— by everyone."

Aggie's eyes narrowed. "What's that supposed to mean?"

"It's supposed to mean that I thought you'd want to know you are loved and missed when you aren't around." The hint of hurt in his eyes told her he'd meant to encourage rather than reprove.

"Sorry, I think I've gotten too used to hearing criticism for my decisions and actions."

Luke jerked his head toward the house. "There's a room full of people in there just waiting to tell you how much they approve of you and your decisions. Listen to them for a while, and tune out the naysayers."

Embarrassed both by Luke's words and by her ungracious response, Aggie gave him a weak smile and carried Ian into the house. Libby worked in the kitchen preparing dinner, Tina was stuffing floor puzzle pieces in the appropriate box, and Ron Milliken dozed in a chair. "Where's Mom?" Her whisper was loud enough to be heard outside, but Ron didn't stir.

"It became a little hectic after your dad fell asleep, so I sent her to their room with earbuds and my iPod. She requested The Beach Boys, so I found the ones we downloaded for the Surf Party last fall."

"I'll go see her." Tina reached to take Ian, but the little boy clung to Aggie, burying his head in her shoulder. "I'll take him with me. I missed this guy."

"Looks like he's not the only guy you missed."

An involuntary glance out the screen door verified Tina's assertions, but Aggie wasn't aware that she was so transparent. She whispered silly nothings into Ian's ear, tickling it with her breath and slipped into her guest room, grateful for Luke's speed in finishing it. "Mom?"

Martha tried to "unscrew" the earbuds from her ears. "I just got these things to stay in too!"

"Sorry. We're back." Stating the obvious was a brilliant way to ensure she felt as foolish as possible.

"Did you have a good time?"

"We did. That girl really opens up when there's no one else around. She's a walking question!"

A knowing look covered Martha's face. "I know what you mean. Last summer they went camping for two weeks just outside of town, and Dad and I took a few days with each of the older kids at our house. I don't think that girl stopped talking the entire time. 'What was Mommy like when she was my age?' 'Did Mommy like to read books or watch movies more?' 'Did Mommy have lots of friends?' 'Did Mommy always want a large family?' 'Did lots of guys like her when she was in school?'"

"Of course— the guys. I'm terrified that we're going to have a boy-crazy dynamo on our hands."

297

"Well," the older woman began, watching her youngest grandchild cling to her youngest child in a way that visibly moved her, "I think this home-schooling thing might help with that. She'll have more time to come to terms with it all before she's flung into a world where it's expected — and so young these days!"

"That's true. She sure seems obsessed by who likes me and why. Who I like and why. When will I marry someone? Why won't I marry William? Why don't I love Luke as much as he loves me? When will she know she found the right guy if I'm having so much trouble?"

"You're having trouble?"

"Apparently." Aggie giggled. "You know, Vannie seems to have a very black and white approach to things. If someone loves you, you should love them back unless they're unlovable. When I asked why, she said because we shouldn't 'prefer' one another like that. So, I guess it's a first come-first served situation at the smorgasbord of love. Luke is out of luck. William got there first, after all."

A knock interrupted the mother-daughter conversation a few minutes later. "Aggie, can I talk to you?" Luke's face looked confused.

"Sure! Mom, do you think—" Aggie shook her head. "Nope. This boy isn't letting me go anywhere tonight." Stepping into the hallway, she closed the door behind her. "Is everything ok?"

Luke shrugged. "I don't know. Mom seems upset. She just asked if I'd take her home, apologized for not bringing the car—she never does that if we're both coming—and said she'd go wait out there for me."

"That seems strange. I hope she's feeling ok. So, what can I do for you?"

"I was wondering if you were too tired for me to come back later. I think Tina is staying, so I don't want to interfere, but…"

"She'll probably have to turn in early so she can get up early and be back at school." She smiled up at him, unaware that her expression made him swallow awkwardly. "I brought back a few westerns to watch. They're apparently adapted from Louis L'Amour's books. I thought it'd be fun for Tavish, but I want to preview them first. We could make popcorn…"

"That almost sounds like an invitation."

Aggie looked at the little boy snuggled in her arms. "You'd think a man would know an invitation when he heard one, wouldn't you?"

Ian's face never left hers, but he nodded and said, "Gaggie."

"There you have it. The little man has spoken."

Luke's hand rested on Ian's head for a moment. She saw reflected in his eyes the desire to touch her in some affectionate way. Just as she saw his hand move past Ian's head toward her face, he dropped it with a smile. "I'll be back then — as long as you're sure."

"Luke, I made an invitation. I'm not going to beg." What was meant as teasing sounded all wrong. "Oh, Luke, I'm sorry. That didn't come out right."

"See you after awhile, Mibs."

A sense of disappointment washed over her as he left. As much as she tried to discount it, Aggie knew she'd hoped he'd make that gesture. "Thanks, Luke."

He turned, halfway down the hallway, and paused. "What for?"

"Everything! You just do... everything for me — us. It's unreal how much you do for us. Thank you."

He retraced his steps, hands settled on his hips as if preparing for a battle instead of an acceptance of gratitude. His forearms flexed as if he forced them to stay in place. "You make it so easy, Mibs. You make it so easy."

"I don't know, Aggie. We were in here working on something, she went to check the dryer, came back, packed up her stuff, and took it to Luke's truck. I have no idea what got into her, but she was weird." Tina kicked off her shoes and shut the window almost all the way. "It's getting a little cool."

Aggie sighed. It'd been too much for Libby. For weeks, she'd given so much of herself, her time, and her self to Aggie's family, and now Aggie felt terrible. "You know that verse that says to leave your friend's house or he'll get sick of you and hate you? I think it works with help too. Aggie's paraphrased version goes something like this, 'Don't let dear friends help you too often or you'll become a burden and they'll want to stay far away from you.'"

"That doesn't sound scriptural, Aggie. What about the verses about bearing one another's burdens and such?"

"Dunno. So, what time do you have to be at school tomorrow?"

"I'm not going back."

"What!"

Tina shook her head. "Nope, I decided I need a trimester off — well, almost off. My Ed Psych class has an online version that my professor said I could transfer to — he's fixing that up for me — but I dropped the rest of them and told my advisor that I'd be back next trimester, but I needed a break."

"Why!"

"You're not going to like this…" Tina warned.

"Oh no. If you are getting back together with Rick — "

"Not that bad. Nope, I'm staying here and helping you for the trimester."

As usual, Aggie's thoughts flooded her face before her words could formulate in her throat. "You can't do that!"

"I can, and I did. It's not a purely selfless act of peace and goodwill."

"I've got to hear the rationale on this one. Do tell."

Tina's eyes sparkled. "How can I get to know William better if I'm halfway across the state?"

"Wow! That was fast."

"Nuh, uh! I've been waiting to make sure you were decided against him, took a week to pray about it, and then decided. You need help, and I want to know if he's the man I hope he is."

"Wow," Aggie knew her friend had shown interest, but this sounded more serious than she'd ever imagined, "I had no idea you were so… attached?"

"I'm not — yet — but I think I could be." Tina's eyes sparkled as she spoke and then clouded as a new thought came to mind. "Are you sure, Aggie? He's a really great guy. Yeah, I know, he has some issues, but — "

"I'm not interested." The finality in Aggie's tone surprised even her. "I — I'm just not, but I do agree he's a wonderful man — when he doesn't let his job take over his personality."

The crunch of tires on the driveway followed a sweep of headlights through the living room. "I think I'll go to my room now."

"You don't have to, Tina. We're not going to run you off."

300

"Do you really think I'm going to watch a movie with a name like that?" One eyebrow rose. "With you and your non-boyfriend boyfriend? I don't think so."

Luke entered just as Tina headed down the hallway, but Tina kept walking as she called, "G'night, Luke," over her shoulder.

"Don't you want to—"

"Nope. You'll see why when you hear the title."

His eyes traveled to Aggie's. "Should I be concerned?"

Aggie passed him the movie. "I thought I should preview it."

"*Heller in Pink Tights?*" He stared at her, stunned. "This is a western— for your son?"

"I thought it was odd, but do you know how hard it is to find Louis L'Amour movies?"

Shaking his head and muttering, "In pink tights..." Luke ambled into the kitchen. "I'll make popcorn; you get the—" he choked, "movie going."

As she unwrapped the box and put the movie in the tray, Aggie heard him muttering in the kitchen and smiled. This was going to be good. "Hey, don't forget the Parmesan!"

When Luke returned, he handed her a bowl and hesitated. "Oh, I forgot napkins. Do you want something to drink?"

"I think I saw root beer in there. That'd be great." As she waited, Aggie thought. When he returned, she gestured at the opposite corner of the couch. "Make yourself comfortable. This could be a long movie."

The man's face visibly relaxed. He settled into the couch, gave Aggie one more look that said, "I think you're nuts," and then uncapped the bottle. "Let 'er rip."

"I think that's illegal."

Luke frowned, confused. "Illegal?"

"Ripping DVDs. Isn't that illegal? Piracy and all that stuff?"

He reached across the couch and took the remote from her hand. Punching it, he tossed it back to her and waited for the credits to roll. Seconds later, he glanced her way again. "Ok, Grecian looking gals on a western movie board?"

"I don't know!"

The leading lady's high jinks were bad enough, but when she unknowingly separated a sketch of an unclothed woman as she opened a sliding window, Aggie and Luke both gasped. "I thought you said L'Amour was clean!"

"I've never read anything that described something like that! My guess is Hollywood license. What year was this made?"

Aggie grabbed the case from the table and searched for a year on it. When that failed, she reached under the couch for her laptop and pulled it out. Thanks to Google, she had answers in seconds. "Well, it's 'adapted' from the book *Heller with a Gun*. That's probably a big part of it. The year is nineteen sixty. I don't quite get that. Mom always said nineteen sixty-three was kind of the cut-off. Before sixty-three, Mom says most movies are pretty safe."

"Well this one sure isn't." Luke frowned looking uncomfortable.

Aggie started to offer to turn it off when the theater owner spoke a line that brought cheers from both of them. *No sir! You can't get away with makin' fun out of marriage in Cheyenne!*[10] "Ok, maybe it got the cheap thrills out of it at the beginning," Aggie conceded.

"We can hope."

Her suggestion proved correct. Aside from a few carefully worded propositions, the rest of the movie was not only free from undressed pictures but actually developed a plot. However, as soon as it ended, Aggie ejected it, returned the disk to its case, and tossed it in the kitchen garbage can. "Tavish isn't watching that, and I've seen enough for a lifetime."

From Luke's perspective, Tina's words as she disappeared behind her bedroom door made him nervous, but the sight of the movie box was worse. *Pink tights?* Luke forced himself not to give an honest opinion of any "western" that included pink or tights in the title. It sounded like a revisionist, politically correct, "alternative lifestyle" version of Robin Hood and his "merry band of men" — something he'd rather avoid wherever possible. To help keep his remarks internal, he volunteered to tackle popcorn duty.

As he plugged in the air popper, measured out a generous number of kernels, and popped a stick of butter in the microwave for melting, Luke's mind whirled. He needed to try to treat her as someone special to him— not quite as a fiancée, but more than a buddy. Deciding how to do that was harder than he'd anticipated. It was easier to make gestures like leaving a note— His mind froze. Notes. He could do that. Luke forced himself back to the topic up for debate in his exhausted gray matter.

Did he sit next to her? What would the point be? Any physical contact would be awkward at best. If he sat in his usual spot, it might look like he was distancing himself— not the impression he hoped to make When she gestured for him to sit near, but not right next to her, a tidal wave of relief washed over him. *You're making this too complicated,* **Lucas***!*

The cheesy credit boards, combined with Grecian ladies in a western movie nearly sent him over the edge. Sophia Loren had always been a favorite of his Aunt Martha's, but Luke didn't care for her. An hour and a half of Sophia Loren was almost torture, but Aggie was worth it. He smiled to himself as the thought danced across his mind. Yes, Aggie was definitely worth it— particularly considering that he wasn't going to be able to concentrate on the movie anyway.

Long before Aggie could have seen it had she looked, he felt the heat of embarrassment creep up his neck and burn his ears. As if transfixed by the scratched knuckles, he stared at his right hand until Aggie threw his previous words back at him— taunting him, almost accusing him, of misleading her about the safety of L'Amour's works. "I've never read anything that described something like that!" He knew he sounded defensive; he was, but Luke couldn't stand the idea that she thought he'd read something so risqué.

After the marriage comment, Luke lost track of the movie for a while, his mind wondering what would happen to the country if more people took such a strong stand in favor of marriage. Aggie's laugh at something captured his attention once more. Slowly, his interest returned. "I can't decide if she's that fickle or if she's playing Mabry."

"She's playing him. No woman would see him as a better choice than Tom."

That comment intrigued him. "Why? He's younger, better looking, more exciting... Why would she want a man who is so... so... boring?"

303

"The guy is a killer! Who wants to trust their heart and life to a man who gets paid to murder?"

"But," Luke continued, almost needing to hear her reassurances, "wasn't that something people were accustomed to?"

"I don't think she was, anyway. She recoils at the idea."

Luke shook his head. "But Tom comes off as weak— almost effeminate."

"No, Tom comes off as a man strong enough to stand behind his code of values and ethics—as warped as they are in some ways—and won't violate that code. Mabry has no code but to save himself." She shrugged. "I just think she's like most women. She wants a little security instead of a lot of uncertainty."

Her words soothed him. Though not insecure, Luke had wondered if a more assertive man might not be more attractive than his quieter nature. Hearing that she valued security buoyed his spirits immensely. "I can see that. I think I've seen too many 'girl goes for the bad boy' old movies where she thinks she'll reform him or something."

"Yeah," she agreed, unaware of how comforting her words were, "this was the era for those bad boy/good girl movies, wasn't it?" Aggie shook her head. "I never got that. I mean, *Guys and Dolls* is like that. Sky Masterson makes a big deal about how no guy wants to feel like he's got to become someone else to get the girl, and then turns around and marries a girl who definitely wants to change him!"

Luke waited until the movie was over and resting in the garbage before he decided to ask the question that she'd prompted with her observation of Sky Masterson's character. After removing their empty bottles and replacing them with cold new ones, he gathered his courage and asked. "So, do you think that that tendency has changed?"

Aggie blinked. "What tendency? What are you talking about?"

"Sorry," Luke felt like an idiot, "I was thinking about what you said about movies where the girl wants the bad boy but expects him to change. You're right; they were popular in that era, but what about now?"

"I don't know." The young woman shook her head. "I've really never thought about it, but really, isn't that what most teen movies are about?" She shook her head. "I never got that. I'd be afraid that changing someone like that would make you find out that you didn't really know the person at all."

"I can see that."

"You know," Aggie mused, "I think that's part of my problem with William. I always feel like I didn't give him a fair chance, but there's just so much drama surrounding him. It's exhausting. I think I like a guy more like my father. Dad spoiled me."

"What is your father like? I mean, I've gotten to know him a little now, but I wonder what you see in him that appeals to *you*."

"You can count on him. He's always what you expect. He's fun, and he's able to be spontaneous at the right times, but most of the time he's fairly predictable."

"That's not boring?" He knew he was pushing it a bit much, but Luke felt compelled to ask.

Aggie stared at him for several seconds until Luke squirmed inside. "Luke, is this about you?"

"Well..." He swallowed. "Ok, yeah. I was wondering..."

"Why not just ask? If you were someone I knew wasn't right for me, don't you think I'd have told you?"

"I wasn't thinking of it like that per se..."

She shook her head in amused disbelief. "For someone so confident, you sure do have an insecure side, don't you?"

"When it comes to you, yeah. I do."

He could see his confession touched her, but he didn't know if it was a good thing or not. He didn't want affection returned based upon pity. His mother had warned him repeatedly that a young woman like Aggie, especially in the vulnerable position she was, could easily be manipulated into assuming feelings she didn't truly have. The thought revolted him and contributed highly to the self-doubt he endured.

After one long swig of root beer, Aggie set the bottle on the coffee table, turned to face him, and reached awkwardly for his hand. "Look, Luke. You said you love me, right?"

Nodding, Luke smiled. "That much is indisputable."

"And you want us to come to a place where we both want marriage, right?"

"That's a great way of putting it. That's what I was trying to say the other night and couldn't."

305

"Well," Aggie continued, "I guess my question for you is how do we do that?"

"I have no clue." Luke felt as if he'd failed her. "I don't know. I know how to interact with Aggie the friend only, and I think I know how to treat Aggie the beloved—"

"That sounds like a sappy Amish romance novel. *Aggie, My Beloved.*"

"Well," he agreed laughing, "I do get your point, but it's true. I don't know what to do to try to get you to return my feelings. I don't know how to do this."

"Well, I don't either! I should talk to your mom. It's probably something I'm doing wrong. It usually is."

"Mibs…"

"No, really. I'm not fishing for disagreement and compliments. I'm serious. I'm clueless in this department, and with all the new stuff I've had to learn over the past year, it's no wonder I'm not catching on very quickly. I'm burned out in the learning center. Dead. Kaput."

"And on that note, I think it's time for me to go home."

"I didn't mean to run you off." Her voice, disappointment in every word, did much to soothe his heart.

"I know." He took a risk that surprised even him, and reached out to brush his fingers across her cheek. "I'm glad you're not eager to get rid of me—even this late."

"I've never been in a hurry to see you go." Clearly trying to bolster his spirits, she added with a teasing glint in her eye, "And I certainly can't say the same about William."

She followed him onto the porch and watched as he dragged his feet down the steps and across the drive. At his truck, he glanced back at the steps and paused, watching the breeze flick at her hair and send cold shivers over her. For a moment, the impulse to run back and kiss her goodnight nearly overtook him. He reached for the door handle and made up his mind.

Her smile as he retraced his steps encouraged him. "I forgot something."

"What's that?"

Indecision, as uncomfortable to him as indigestion sounded, sent a flush of heat over him before he gathered his courage and wrapped gentle arms around her, burying his face in her hair. "Goodnight, Mibs. I love you."

He was halfway to his truck before he heard her quiet reply. "Goodnight, Luke."

Aggie says: Libby, are you there?

Aggie says: Hmmm wonder if you're off doing something or if you just didn't turn off the messenger.

Aggie says: Well, when you get a minute, if you'd ding or call me, I'd appreciate it. I was sorry not to get to thank you for helping out with the children so I could take Vannie. I know it meant a lot to her too.

Aggie says: Hmm, you must be asleep. I hope you're resting well.

Aggie says: I really do need to talk to you about Luke, though. I'm so confused about some things.

Aggie says: But, I guess that's best saved for tomorrow.

Aggie says: Goodnight, my involuntary mentor. You have no idea how blessed I feel to have you in my life.

Findin' a Groove

Chapter Twenty-one

Tuesday, October 14th

"We've already made up one of the missed days of school by not taking Columbus Day off," Aggie announced to no one in particular. She closed her notebook with the attendance sheets in it with a self-satisfied snap. One day down, fourteen to go. She'd find ways to make them up if it killed her.

A glance at the clock told her it was almost time to call the children in for a snack. Tina had the little girls and Ian outside playing with puppies and dirt—a mother's nightmare and a child's dream—but the rest of the children were scattered about the house doing their work. Tavish and Ellie had awakened at six-thirty, gotten dressed, finished most of their chores before breakfast, and completed what was left half an hour before they were expected to start their schoolwork so Aggie did expect them to finish a little early, but was stunned when they both arrived downstairs with their books and assignments, declaring them complete.

"What did you do— pick a subject and fill in the answers for both of you?"

Tavish's eyes lit up. "That's a great idea! We could get done in an hour or less if we did that!"

"That's a terrible idea. You'd learn nothing."

"Besides," Ellie added, "you get lazy with your math problems and make silly mistakes. I'd rather do my own work."

"Are you sure it's all done?" Aggie couldn't imagine that they'd gotten a whole day's work done in just two hours.

"Yep. Ellie and I realized that if we worked fast, we could have most of the day to do whatever we wanted!"

Laird, stepping into the room with a question, heard the last part of Tavish's sentence and frowned. "Why do they get the day off?"

"They don't."

"But he said they could have most of the day to do what they want." The injustice of the idea clearly did not set well with Laird.

"And you came into the middle of a conversation without hearing the beginning," Aggie corrected. "Tavish and Ellie have finished their work, so of course they have more free time." She turned to the expectant twins. "I'll correct this now, but why don't you go wash some apples and use the slicer to cut them up for everyone?"

All ideas of sharing work went out the window as Aggie corrected the papers. Tavish, just as Ellie predicted, made several simple and unnecessary math errors, while she missed none. Her answers to comprehension questions included possible motives and thoughts of the characters while Tavish's answers were strictly focused on the facts that the story presented rather than the ideals. However, in science and history, Tavish's work included details that made his answers interesting to read, while Ellie's answers included only exactly what was required.

The work needed to have mistakes corrected, but she didn't find any more errors than usual. She'd expected, at the least, to find dozens of sloppily written answers, but instead, it was clear they'd done the work, done it right, and well. It seemed as if two of her students might have hit a groove for their new educational program.

Laird's voice reached her from the kitchen, and Aggie frowned. He needed to be finishing his work as instructed. She'd helped him find the answer to his history question, but he was supposed to go back to his room and finish the lesson before he came down for a snack. Just as she entered the dining room, Aggie froze.

"But how? How can you get so much done. Come on, did you take the answer keys? What?"

"No. We just realized that avoiding the work was wasting a lot of time. If we got it over with, kind of like taking out the trash and wiping down the cupboards, we'd have more time for what we want to do." Ellie always sounded so much more mature than her age.

"But if we do that, she'll never send us back to school. We'll be stuck at home forever."

Tavish's voice stunned her. "Good! Why would we want to go back if we can do the same stuff here in half the time? Who wants to sit on the bus for an hour, sit in school for several more, go back on the bus... This is better. I'm thinking about doing the rest of the week tomorrow. Then I don't have to do anything until Monday."

"You think she'll let us?" Even Aggie could hear the gears grinding in Laird's mind.

"Sure. We're supposed to do the work and learn the stuff. She keeps saying how it's ok that we're behind because all that matters is we learn it. Well, we'll learn it—just faster!"

The boy's words sent her heart racing. What would she do if she couldn't keep them occupied all day? The fact that she hadn't had a problem with them remaining occupied a month earlier didn't cross her mind until much later. Though tempted to march into the kitchen and inform her students that they would not get a day off if they worked ahead, Aggie returned to the library and dug through the home-school group's co-op list. The six-week classes all started that coming Friday, and suddenly, Aggie's prior decision to consider co-op classes for the next semester seemed like a very foolish idea. With a calendar in hand, she picked up the phone and called the coordinator. It was time to get serious about this schooling thing.

Tina stared as Aggie dumped container after container of leftovers into the garbage, muttering the whole time. After the third attempt to find out what the problem was, she turned, dug her cell phone from her pocket, and searched for Luke's number in her phone list. Luke, sounding slightly panicked, answered on the second ring. "Is something wrong?"

"Hello to you too."

"Sorry," he sounded like it too. "I'm not used to seeing your name on my phone. I was sure someone was half-dead."

"Well, Aggie's gonna be unless you get over here and stop her."

"What's she doing?"

"Well," Tina began, peeking around the corner before she hurried back toward her bedroom. "Right now, she's throwing everything in the fridge away. I asked what the deal was, but she either can't hear or is ignoring me. I think she needs an infusion of Luke mellowy goodness."

"That sounds like the insides of a s'more. Ew." His laughter assured her that Luke wasn't offended.

"Whatever it is, you calm her when she's agitated, and man is she agitated!"

"I'm coming. Should I bring coffee?"

"Is that place open this late?" Tina glanced at her phone. "Don't they close at like seven?"

"Usually, but I saw something about being open on Tuesday nights until nine for study groups. I think I can barely make it if I leave now."

"Then what are you waiting for," Tina shook her head at the phone as if it'd tell him something he needed to hear. "Get going. Get her a brownie too. Maybe this is PMS."

"Oh, ugh. I forgot about that. I've been away from daily living with my sisters for too long. Brownies it is."

Luke snapped his phone shut and grabbed his keys. His note, abandoned at the table as he answered the phone, looked a little forlorn and unfinished, but he'd finish it some other time. Aggie was more important. "Ok, Lord. Here we go!"

It took him longer than he expected to get the coffee in the packed little café. The brownies were hot out of the oven and couldn't be wrapped or iced, but Luke wheedled three out of the barista anyway. With brownies stuffed in clear containers, he watched impatiently as she stacked them in a brown paper bag and added napkins for good measure. Once his arms were full of coffee and brownies, he tackled the task of extricating himself from the crowds of non-studious teenagers using the special opening as an excuse for an outing on a school night. After all, what parent would forbid a "study group"?

Driving with one hand steadying three very hot cups of coffee wasn't as easy as with two, and trying to keep the brownies from sliding all over the seat nearly caused him to sideswipe a car. By the time he pulled into Aggie's drive, Tina was on the steps with feet and hands tapping exaggeratedly. She jogged to his truck, and opened the door before he could turn off the engine.

"Took you long enough! Do you hear that?"

Aggie was singing—that much he could tell. He strained to hear the words but they were indiscernible. "She's singing."

"Take the cof—" She stared at the three cups in the holder he carried. "You got me one?"

"Well, sure! I wasn't going to leave you out!"

"You have my permission to marry her."

Luke gave her a mock disgusted look. "Get her to agree with you and that'll mean something to me."

Tina shoved him toward the door and demanded he resolve her friend's angst fest. "I'm going to my room." She grabbed her coffee and turned, but Luke tapped her shoulder.

"Brownie?"

"Man, do me a favor."

"What?"

She winked as she took the plastic container from him. "Train my boyfriend whenever I get one."

"I don't think I could train a boyfriend. I don't even know how to be one!" Luke opened the front door for her.

"Could have fooled me."

Her words were lost on him. The moment Luke stepped into the house, he heard Aggie singing and frowned. It was after nine o'clock and she was in the kitchen singing about work? "What the..."

"Toiling on... toiling on... toiling on... toiling on... Let us hope and trust..."[11]

"Aggie?"

The frenzied young woman whirled at the sound of his voice, flinging a bowl full of unset Jell-O across the kitchen. He watched as she closed her eyes, took a deep breath, and continued the chorus she'd been singing. "... and labor 'til the Master comes."

It didn't work. Despite her attempt to reign in her emotions, Aggie burst into frazzled tears. Somehow, Luke managed to find the self-control not to laugh as he set the coffee and brownies on the counter and attempted to circumvent the piles of dishes and puddles of Jell-O. "Mibs, come here."

Aggie didn't seem to hear him. Instead, she sank to the floor, covered her face with her hands, and allowed herself to dissolve into unexplained hysterics. He paused, assessed the situation, and then pulled Aggie up from the floor, leading her through the mess and out the back door. At the porch swing, he pulled her down next to her and held her, letting her cry out her frustrations without trying to staunch the flow of tears.

When her sniffles became pronounced, he untangled himself, hurried into the kitchen, and grabbed a handful of napkins from the basket on the island. Aggie, blowing her nose and trying hard to regain some self-control, murmured apologies, but Luke resumed his position of chief Aggie comforter and again pulled her into his arms. "It's ok, Mibs. Just let it out."

"I feel so stupid. Crying over spilled Jell-O. How idiotic can you get?" She struggled to get up, but Luke refused to budge.

"Nuh, uh. You're going to sit right here and relax for a minute."

"Luke, I could sit here all night, but that's not going to get that job finished and that mess cleaned up."

"I'll take care of that. Right now, you're more important." Her sniffles started up again. "Uh, oh. What did I say?" The concern in his voice was evident, even to him.

"I just didn't realize how much I needed to hear that I matter to someone."

"Oh, Mibs. You matter so much to so many people. The children, your parents, your sister, my mother, Tina, William, me —"

"I know. Deep down in my heart, I know, Luke, but sometimes I need to hear it." She started to push away to look at him and then relaxed again, allowing herself to cling to his shirt and rest comfortably with his arms around her.

"Well, then, I'll have to make a point of mentioning that a bit more often."

"I had a feeling you'd be mushy given half a chance."

Luke's laughter sent the puppies into a yap fest that lasted for several seconds until he called for them to hush. "I come from an extended family of very mushy people. You should know this before you risk letting me —" He stopped mid-sentence. "You should know that."

"Before letting you what?"

"I just get ahead of myself sometimes. It's nothing."

"It is if you said it." She looked up, her eyes shining with the remnants of tears in them.

"I keep forgetting how pressured things must sound if I'm always telling you what's on my heart."

"You also forget," she added with a slightly lighter tone to her voice, "that I might just like hearing it so there'd be no pressure at all then, would there?"

"Will you tell me?"

"Tell you what?" Aggie made herself comfortable again.

"If it gets too awkward for you? It'd be a lot easier to try to do this if I wasn't always second-guessing myself."

"I can do that." She sighed. "But as wonderful as your offer was, I really need to get that kitchen done. The kids will be up sooner than later." Aggie glanced at her watch. "And, I think all hopes of talking to your mom are gone. By the time I'm done, she'll be in bed."

Luke stood and took her hand, pulling her up beside him. "Come on. You go talk to Mom; I'll take care of the kitchen."

"I can't let you do that!"

"You definitely can." Luke bent close, so close the temptation to kiss her was almost overwhelming. "Let me do things for you, Mibs. Let me show you how much you mean to me. It's the only way I know how to tell you." Once inside, he winked and added, "And besides, I may not be done by the time you and Mom are finished with your chat. I'll take all the help you want to give me then."

Her quick hug and grateful smile warmed his heart as he grabbed a dishcloth and filled a bowl with soapy water. As he worked, Luke unconsciously hummed the same hymn that Aggie had forced herself to sing when he arrived, but this time, the tune seemed joyful. Aggie heard him, and wondered how he could sound so happy singing something that had seemed so burdensome just a short while earlier.

Aggie says: Libby? Are you on?

Aggie says: Hmm... I wonder if Luke will believe me if I tell him you're not on.

Aggie says: He's not letting me help him with MY mess in MY kitchen. A little high handed, isn't he?

Aggie says: I'm disappointed. I've missed you twice now. I hope you're all right. I miss you.

Libby says: I'll be right back, Aggie.

Aggie says: Libby! YAY!

Libby says: Did you say my Luke was at your house?

Aggie says: Yep. He arrived just in time to save me from myself. I wonder how he knew I was falling apart...

Libby says: He's intuitive, but not prescient. Perhaps Tina called him.

Aggie says: Probably. Speaking of Luke...

Libby says: Yes. I have a question for you.

Aggie says: And I probably have an answer.

Libby says: What are your feelings regarding William?

Aggie says: I thought I told you. I'm not interested in changing our friendship in any way or at any time. Like I told Luke; he comes with too much drama.

Libby says: And Luke? What are your thoughts concerning him?

Aggie says: Well, that's partly what I want to talk to you about. We were wondering how to go about growing closer. I mean, when you say it like that, it sounds forced. Luke deserves better than me convincing myself that I feel what I really don't.

Libby says: Yes, he does.

Aggie says: I hate messenger sometimes.

Libby says: Why is that?

Aggie says: Because sometimes it seems like you're reading into other people's tone. It's hard to tell if something is meant to be as it seems or if it's just how the internet is sometimes.

Libby says: For example?

Aggie says: Well, when you said that Luke does deserve better than that, it sounded like it was a rebuke, but I know I haven't said or done anything to imply that I'd ever do that, so...

Libby says: Are you sure of that?

Aggie says: Um…

Aggie says: Libby, are you upset with me for something?

Libby says: Actually, I am. I've been praying about it since Saturday.

Aggie says: Would you mind telling me what I've done wrong?

Libby says: I don't know if you have now. I'm confused, to be frank.

Aggie says: If you thought something was wrong between us, why didn't you come to me?

Libby says: Because, to be honest, I've been waiting until I thought I could control my temper.

Aggie says: Wow.

Libby says: Wow what?

Aggie says: I had no idea. What on earth do you think I've done?

"Luke?"

"Hmm?"

Aggie swallowed hard. "Can you come here? I have upset your mother somehow."

"I hardly think so. She thinks you're as close to perfect as anyone who isn't her daughter—" he entered the living room wiping his hands on a towel and winked, "yet—can be."

"I like that yet, but I don't know if she does. Look."

As Luke read the conversation, a frown growing more pronounced with each second, the screen informed them that "Libby is typing a message."

"It's taking her as long as it takes you sometimes."

Luke gave her a sidelong glance, curious. "Is that annoying?"

"Not usually."

He shrugged. "Well, this is."

"Well, I suppose if I knew you were typing bad news, it might be annoying," she confessed. "Oh, there it is. I'm afraid to read." Despite her admission, Aggie read the message, her face flushing with both anger and embarrassment.

Libby says: Saturday I went into the mudroom to take clothes out of the dryer and couldn't help but overhear that my Luke was "out of luck." I distinctly heard you say that and that William was "there first." It was a kick to the stomach, Aggie. Now you're telling me that William is not an option.

Libby says: I have a hard time imagining you as disingenuous, but those conflicting statements do bother me.

Aggie says: You should know, Luke is reading this. I have to admit; I'm hurt.

Libby says: Then I am sure you can empathize with how I felt to hear something so opposite of what I thought I knew to be true.

Aggie says: Mom, this is Luke. You know Aggie better than that.

Libby says: I thought I did, yes. I don't want to think poorly of her; I love her. However, I can't ignore what I heard, and I was too upset to discuss it before now. I've been fasting and praying for three days about this.

Aggie says: Libby, you only heard the tail end of a story I was telling my mother. Vannie has a very black and white picture of relationships and in her mind, William asked first so he gets first dibs. Therefore, Luke is out of luck.

Libby says: Oh.

Aggie glanced at Luke, confused. Libby's short response seemed out of character. "I don't understand."

"It's not like Mom, and then it is. She's protective of her 'cubs,' but she's usually not unjust like this. I don't know what to think."

"Do I say something else, wait for her, what?"

"Give her a minute. She might be getting the kettle, answering the phone— things like that always seem to happen at the worst times."

They waited, Aggie's hands hovering over the keys, wanting to type so many things but waiting for some kind of response from Libby. Luke absently rubbed her back and urged her to relax. At last, they saw the message that Libby was typing once again.

318

Libby says: I'm sorry. I had to do something. I'm very sorry that I didn't ask you at the time. I know you better than to think you'd give Luke any encouragement if your heart was settled on someone else.

Libby says: I keep wanting to justify myself, but what I did and thought was wrong. Please forgive me.

Aggie says: Of course, I forgive you!

Aggie says: Isn't she the best, Mom?

Aggie says: He's incorrigible!

Libby says: I never could scold him for things like that. It's all my fault, I'm afraid.

Aggie says: I have a feeling I'd be the same way. He can be quite charming.

Libby says: He knows how to endear himself to those he loves.

Aggie says: Good.

Libby says: That is an odd response. Why do you say that?

Aggie says: Yes, Mibs, why do you say that?

Libby says: Luke!

Aggie says: Because, he loves me. If he knows how to endear himself to those he loves, then we don't have to worry about how to do this relationship thing. It'll just happen.

Aggie says: You should know, his ears are red.

Libby says: That sounds like my boy.

Aggie says: Traitor.

Libby says: Let me guess, Luke?

Aggie says: We're fighting over the laptop!

Libby says: Record the date. Your first fight.

Aggie says: Does that mean we get to kiss and make up?

Aggie says: That was Luke!

Libby says: I believe that. No, Luke. You do not get to kiss and make up.

Aggie says: Aw, ma!

Aggie says: *Giggles* He looks crestfallen.

Libby says: Thank you, Aggie.

Aggie says: What for?

Libby says: For being so understanding and forgiving. I broke trust with you.

Aggie says: We had a misunderstanding. It happens. So, if you'll just help me figure out how to convince my heart that Luke is the only man for me, we'll be set.

Libby says: Just let him love you. It'll work itself out. Don't try so hard. You'll only confuse yourself.

Aggie says: I think we embarrassed him. He went to clean my kitchen again.

Libby says: I meant to get to your fridge over the weekend, but we stayed busier than I expected.

Aggie says: You have no idea how encouraging that is to me.

Libby says: Encouraging?

Aggie says: If an experienced mom like you can't get to it, then it's not JUST because I'm incompetent. It might be part of it, but it means it might not be all of it. I really should go help him.

Libby says: He probably wants to do this for you.

Aggie says: He does, and as much as I love talking to you, I just thought it'd be nice to be able to work together again— even if it is just cleaning up Jell-O from all over my new cabinets.

Libby says: I'm not even going to ask. Go work with my Luke. Have a wonderful time. Just don't let him kiss you.

Aggie says: Why ever not?

Libby says: He needs to have to work for that.

Aggie says: Well, this kitchen might qualify, but I didn't have any plans for that anyway. He's probably going to decide I'm so not worth it when that subject comes up.

Libby says: Aggie, my Luke has already decided that you're definitely worth it. Now get off this thing.

Aggie says: G'night, Libby.

Libby says: Goodnight.

The kitchen looked exponentially better. Luke still rinsed and loaded empty containers into the dishwasher, but the floor and shelves were clean and the Jell-O no longer dripped down the island and all over the floor. The overflowing trash can needed to be emptied, the stench of sour food nearly overpowering her, so she grabbed a new trash liner and went to work on it.

"I'll get that."

"You're elbow-deep in furry plasticware."

Luke shut off the water and dried his hands. "And that is one heavy and disgusting sack." He pointed to the island stools. "Sit."

"Bossy."

"Flirting will get you everywhere but to the trash can. A guy has his limits."

When he returned, Aggie stopped him, her hand on his arm. "I miss working with you."

"Come out with me tomorrow when I take measurements on the new house," he invited impulsively. At the happy smile in her eyes, Luke shook his head. "Don't look at me like that. I'm liable to do something I'll regret."

"Such as?"

"Mibs..." The warning tone in his voice enlightened her to his meaning.

"Oh! Um, not a good idea. I'm under orders not to let that happen."

"Mom?" The disappointment she'd expected to see—hoped really—wasn't there. Instead, an amused smirk played about the corners of his mouth.

"How'd you know?"

"Mom has always encouraged us to reserve kisses for engagement. Actually, I think she'd be happiest with rehearsal dinners or weddings. She'd be very upset with me if she found out I'd, well..."

Aggie nodded. "Well, I'm not risking the wrath that would be sure to follow if Libby found out I'd sullied 'her Luke.'"

"Sullied. That's an interesting choice of words for a guy. Isn't that reserved for men trifling with young girls' reputations?"

She shrugged and tried to grab the liner, but Luke pushed her back in her seat. "I like working with you too, but let me try to make myself indispensible in your life, ok? What happened today?"

So, while he finished the kitchen clean up, Aggie described her day, the children's sudden obsession with working ahead in their schoolwork, and the classes they'd start on Friday. "Vannie has a writing and lab science class, Laird has some kind of invention class and something called "Grammar for Geeks." I don't know what it means, but since he seems to struggle with it, I went for it. Tavish and Ellie are doing geography and a book club, and all of them, including Kenzie, are in art and music."

"It might have been easier to send them to school."

"What do you mean?"

The familiar working of Luke's jaw and the passing seconds did something to Aggie's heart that she thought she'd have to examine later. Instead, she waited for him to answer, forgetting that he'd sounded disapproving. "Well, I thought part of the reason you'd chosen to keep them home was so you'd see them more? How is running them to all these classes going to accomplish that?"

"Well, I'll still be with them, and it's not every day all day. It's just a few days a week. It'll keep them with other kids their age and give them variety. The way they flew through their work this week..." She shook her head. "Luke, I'll never be able to give them enough to keep them busy."

"Why do you need to?" Luke dug through her drawers in search of more plasticware. "Why can't they just enjoy each other and their own little projects? As long as they're keeping up with their age group, what's the point of filling their days with more work just to do it?"

Frowning, Aggie asked, "What do you need all that for?" his question lost in her confusion as he pulled out the containers and lined them up on the counter.

"I had an idea for helping everyone know when to use what leftovers, but the containers are different sizes." He dug some more. "What lids go with what?"

"All the rectangles have the same lids, the squares, and most of the circles. I bought those when I got tired of digging for lids."

"Great. I'll label the lids. Got a Sharpie?"

Too tired to argue, Aggie dug through the desk drawer and pulled out the requested pen. "I don't even want to ask."

"It's simple. You stack by days in the cupboard." He rummaged through the cabinet next to the fridge and frowned. "Can the crockpot and toaster go anywhere else?"

"There is an empty shelf on the cabinet in the island on the left. I think they'll both fit."

Luke did a little rearranging and then dug through the lid drawer for a bread container that she never used. "This'll hold lids." He arranged the lids with Friday first and continuing from there.

322

"Why not start with Wednesday? Tomorrow is Wednesday."

"Well, the way I'm thinking it, you won't want to put the day that you put the food in here, but the day you want to eat it. Most people don't like to eat the same thing two days in a row, so I'm thinking that tomorrow you put your leftovers in 'Friday's' container. Then, Friday, you come in, pull out that container, and use it in some way for lunch. When lunch is over, anything left goes to the dogs."

"I see it now." Aggie looked excited. "This really works well because there's only two days worth of leftovers at any given time. No forgetting about them or not knowing how old they are so you leave it there forever... It's brilliant!" Her eyes thanked him from across the island.

"I'm just doing my bit to make myself indispensible to this family. Meanwhile, make sure you tell the dishwasher emptier that he or she has to put the days in order or it won't work."

"Days in order. Got it." A yawn punctuated her agreement.

"I'm going home. Goodnight, Mibs."

"Fine then, just clean and run. See if I care."

Luke laughed. "I guess I failed."

"At what?"

His hand covered hers for a second before he strolled from the room calling, "Making you care, of course," over his shoulder.

Aggie says: Hey there, just wanted to say thanks again.

Mibs says: Oops. Didn't change this back.

Mibs says: I didn't know how to tell you when you're here, but I want you to know how much it means to me that you tell me you care about me. It's probably hard when you know I don't yet feel the same, but it is the highlight of my day. Please don't stop.

Vows

Chapter Twenty-two

Thursday, October 9th

Before noon, all but Vannie had their work turned in, graded, and corrected. Vannie was sitting in the library, curled up on the loveseat, writing her report on the major themes of *Captains Courageous*. Tina arrived as Aggie was in the middle of a timed sandwich assembly and waited for her to finish before she pointed out the door and said, "Ok, bring 'em in, guys, bring 'em in. Meat in the mudroom, produce on the island, boxes on the counter. Hurry, hurry, hurry!

As the kids raced through the dining room into the living room and out the door, Tina slid the receipt and Aggie's debit card across the island. "I think I may have spent too much, but I got everything on the list."

In an unusual move, Aggie pocketed the card and tossed the receipt without looking at it. She just didn't want to know what the tally was anymore. Each month it seemed worse and worse, but there was no hope for it. The children had to eat. At least the repairs were done. She wouldn't be paying Luke every week. Perhaps it'd seem less extreme without those checks accumulating with the rest of the bills each month.

In what seemed like no time, the counters, island, and the floor of the mudroom were covered with plastic bags full of groceries. The cupboards were loaded amid squeals of delight for favorite foods. Cari and Lorna dodged between everyone's legs, peeking into bags and asking for nearly everything they found. Ian enjoyed rolling cans across the floor, until Aggie scooped him up and strapped him in his high chair with small pieces of banana fed to him between putting away bags of food.

"Ok, ok. I can't do this. Everyone get to the table and eat. Laird, grab those oranges and rinse them. You guys can peel them after you eat your sandwiches. I'll put this away."

Lost in the mudroom deep freeze, she didn't hear Luke come in until she felt hands close over her eyes. "Laird —" the moment her fingers found the hands, she laughed. "Luke."

"How'd you tell?"

"I can feel the difference. Laird's hands aren't rough like yours."

"How do you know how my hands feel?" He reached down to pick up a bag of chicken packages.

"Well, you're the only one around here who should have rough hands. I bet even William's are softer. He doesn't work with them like you do."

"Somehow, that isn't very reassuring."

Aggie rolled her eyes and took the chicken from him. "You sound like you assume I like soft hands in a man. What are you doing here?"

"I came to see if you were serious about seeing the house on Highway 37."

"I was, but —"

"She is, and she's going." Tina's voice startled both of them as she carried Ian past the room on her way to the stairs. "Don't argue with me; just get out of here."

With an exaggerated roll of her eyes, Aggie grabbed a bag of roasts. "Apparently I'm going."

They put the meat and frozen vegetables in the deep freeze and Luke gathered the plastic bags. "You ready?"

"I'm going to change. Be right back."

326

She bumped into Tina on her way upstairs, and Luke tried to protest, but Tina stopped him. "Let her go."

"We're just going to take measurements on a house and maybe check out some fixtures at Home Depot. She—"

"She wants to look nice for you. Let her."

"She does?" Luke's face was a study. Doubt clouded it briefly. "Nah..."

"If she comes down with her hair out of that infernal ponytail, you'll know I'm right. Aggie only leaves it down when she cares about how she looks."

"I don't think—"

Cari and Lorna raced past them, and Tina broke away to follow. "Girls, *stop!*" The twins froze on the stairs. She winked at Luke. "I am always stunned at how well that works." To the girls, she covered her lips with her finger. "Shh. Ian is sleeping. Let's go read a story before your naps. Let me get my book."

While the little girls impatiently shuffled their feet on the steps, Tina hustled back to her room to grab her book and a pillow. She gave Luke another glance as she made her way back to the stairs. "There's room up there at the end of the hall for two narrow bookshelves on each side of that window and a window seat. It'd be a whole lot more comfortable for me or Aggie, or anyone else for that matter, to sit on a nice cushioned seat and read while waiting for the troops to fall asleep. Just sayin'."

"I'll get right on that."

Luke started to follow them up the stairs to get a look at the spot Tina mentioned, but the sight of Aggie skipping down them stopped him. He watched as she paused, hugged her little girls, told them to dream happy dreams, and tossed her hair over her shoulders as she continued down the steps to meet him. A look from Tina above seemed to scream, "I told you so."

Aggie looked different—younger somehow—with her hair hanging down her back, and wearing a simple tiered skirt and sweater. Tina was right. She had changed her clothes and let down her hair, and when she reached the bottom of the stairs, he caught a faint whiff of the perfume that, in his opinion, could be renamed "Essence of Aggie."

"Nice sweater. You ready?"

The brightness in her smile and spring in her step seemed to fade a little, but she nodded. "Let's go."

All the way to the passenger door of his truck, Luke pondered her reaction to his compliment until he remembered something his sister once told him. "Compliment the woman, not the garment. You don't want us to feel like we wouldn't be anything special without that garment instead of us making the garment special. People before things. Don't forget."

He opened the door, his mind whirling through the different ways he could remedy his gaffe. Even as he pulled onto the highway, Luke ran dozens of retractions past his new filter, and failed to find any way to start over again. His laughter surprised both of them.

"Mind telling me what is so funny?" Aggie's voice sounded as strained as the silence that had hovered between them when he didn't respond to her attempts at conversation.

"I've been sitting here trying to figure out how to take back what I said."

"What did you say that you want to take back?" She obviously hadn't analyzed his comment as thoroughly as he had.

"Well, when you came down stairs, you were so—" he swallowed hard. "Pretty."

"If it's that hard to say it, maybe you shouldn't bother." Her words sounded hurt, but her face twitched with repressed laughter.

"It is hard to say it. That's why I made that inane comment about your sweater, as if I'd have even noticed it on anyone else." He chanced a glance her way and saw the twinkle back in her eyes.

"Why do guys have so much trouble complimenting girls? If I think a girl is beautiful, it's no big deal to say so, and I obviously am not shy about telling a total stranger that he's too good looking to be a lawyer."

"I don't know. Maybe—" Even as he spoke, Luke realized why and didn't want to admit it.

"Come on, why?"

The temptation to toss out a generalization that may or may not apply to him was acute. He glanced at her, marveling at how she personified the all-American "girl next door." Luke had overheard William say that she wasn't his idea of feminine beauty, but even William had admitted a certain charm and attractiveness. His mother said she was "fresh" and "appealing," and he now realized that those words were perfect.

Curiosity filled her eyes as she waited for him to work through what he wanted to say. "It's not easy to say. I think it's because, for me anyway, it's putting more of me on the line. It feels like I'm risking more rejection if I open myself up like that."

"More rejection?" Aggie frowned. "Since when did I reject you?"

"Ok, that came out wrong. It's an added risk of rejection."

"Have you considered that showing that kind of vulnerability might open doors rather than close them?"

"In other words, 'faint heart ne'er won fair lady?'"

"Yep. Exactly. Robert Burns was charming, wasn't he?"

"That was Cervantes."

"I know I've read it a poem by Burns. I remember because you can see his brogue even in the lines."

Luke shook his head. "You don't even like poetry. It was Cervantes. I remember seeing it on one of those signs people put in their houses. It listed it as Cervantes. That's kind of a hard name to ignore. Sounds like Scott, though, doesn't it?"

"I know Burns said—"

Luke's laughter interrupted her. "Perhaps Burns quoted Cervantes then? After all, wasn't the guy, Michael? Mario?"

"Miguel."

"Miguel, right. Didn't he live a long time before Burns?"

Aggie shook her head. "This is ridiculous. Neither one of us care about the guy. So someone said that. It's true. Some girls want a guy to jump through hoops for her. I think that's crazy. Guys aren't trained seals." She laughed as Luke wiped imaginary sweat from his brow. "But, even more reasonable females want to know they're worth a little effort!"

"Mibs—"

"Never mind. I know how you feel about me, and that's enough for now. What are we doing at your new place today?"

"We're measuring for flooring, cabinets, and planning new light fixtures." His hand slid across the seat to give hers a quick squeeze. "It's that 'for now' that keeps me awake at night."

"I think if you took that out of here, painted it white, and put it in the bathroom over the tub, you'd have one of those Paris-inspired-looking master baths."

"You think? I think it's horrible."

"I do too. It's not my style at all, but I've seen so many of those in magazines, that I have no doubt that it'd be a hit. You could always tell the agent that it could be changed out, but I bet it'd be a selling feature."

Luke pulled out his cell phone, snapped a picture, strolled upstairs to the master suite, snapped a picture of the tub area, and sent both to his real estate agent with a text asking if Aggie's idea was a good one. He knew it probably was, but it felt odd to do something so style specific in a house when he usually tended toward neutrals. "Well, we'll see what Amber says."

"She'll go for it. Ok, so what next?" Aggie felt her wrist for her ever-present ponytail holder and frowned. "I don't suppose you have a rubber band handy?"

"What for?"

"To get my hair out of the way."

Grinning, Luke dug into his pocket for a rubber band he knew wouldn't be there. "Tina was wrong. I can't wait to rub that one in."

"Wrong about what?"

"She said you changed because you wanted to look nice for me. I disagreed. She insisted that if you came downstairs with your hair down, it was because she was right. Now look at you."

"What's wrong with me?"

He held up empty hands. "Sorry, no bands. Nothing is wrong with you. You just forgot your hair tie after you brushed your hair. I win."

Aggie's face darkened. "You lost. Tina won." Without another word, Aggie left the room and hurried downstairs and into the kitchen.

Luke followed. He found her staring out the window. "Mibs?"

"What?"

"You're angry or at least irritated with me, why?"

"I'm more irritated with me."

Shaking his head, Luke contradicted her. "I don't think so. I think you're upset with me, and I don't know why."

"Because I did try to look nice, and it didn't do me any good. I always have to go back to practical Aggie mode. I can't work with my hair down, and I look like a twelve-year-old tomboy with it up."

With a gentle brush of his thumb across her cheek, Luke gave Aggie a tender smile. "Well, if that's true, then I guess I like women who look like twelve-year-old tomboys, because I think you look like the Aggie I love when you have your hair up like that. I love it down too, but up reminds me of hours of painting, scraping, sanding, and moving furniture. Do you know how often I wanted to tug it?"

She giggled. "You sound like a little boy in school. They used to tell us in the third grade that if a boy kicked you it was because he liked you."

"It's true. I kicked Melanie Carstairs to keep me from blurting out my undying love and affection. Of course, today I feel bad that I hurt a girl and am relieved that I did. The next day I saw her share her brownie with Jeff Garner. It broke my heart."

"You seem to have recovered." She shook her head. "I thought boys were supposed to think girls were cootie-riddled species from outer space."

"When you have the sappy family that I do, you learn early the advantages of a good woman— or girl." His eyes spoke volumes of what was on his heart. Aggie circled the island, retracing her steps and drawing her hand through the dust on the counters. Luke's forehead wrinkled, confused. "What are you doing?"

"I think you should move a few things."

"Like what?"

"The sink has to stay or it won't be near the window, but I think you should move the stove closer to it this way and the fridge should not be on the other side of the island. It'd be a bear to walk around all the time." She frowned again. "Actually, it'd be nice if the island could be bigger and have a cook top on it. Then a bank of ovens could go where the fridge was and the fridge where the stove was. Ovens over there wouldn't be so odd."

"Or," Luke gestured as he spoke, "I could put the ovens to the right of where the stove is now, and put the fridge here. That'd leave that whole wall over there for one huge bank of pantry cabinets."

"Then you could do glass doors and a few open-shelved cabinets in the uppers on this side."

"Or," Luke added again, "I could pull those cabinets there and there," he pointed to each side of the current window, "and double the window width. With that huge wall, you could lose four feet of upper cabinets without feeling the storage loss at all."

Excited at his description, Aggie's face lit up. "Are you going to do a big farmhouse sink?"

"Well, I'll probably do one in stainless. There's a place in Rockland where you can get hammered stainless steel sinks that are amazing. Since I can pick them up and can take seconds, I usually get a good deal. I just have them call when they have one that someone didn't like, and I take it."

"Why not porcelain? Aren't most farmhouse sinks porcelain?"

"Or hammered brass, but I'll want the sink to match the appliances." Luke shrugged at her accusing look. "I know, I know. It looks cold and sterile—too much like a restaurant and not enough like a home."

"You listen well."

"I do. However, I have to listen to what people buy, and thanks to those home improvement shows on TV, people want stainless and granite. I have to give them what they want."

Aggie walked around the room, taking in the planned changes and thinking. "Can you go with a dark brown stain then? You know, that brown-black color?" Even as she spoke, Aggie shook her head. "No, that won't work. This house is too traditional to go so contemporary. White. You need white. It'll work well with the stainless and it'll keep the room bright. Use a lot of molding and it'll be perfect."

"Architectural elements. I see where you're going."

"Yep. Get a granite in the black and gray tones." Aggie grinned. "And I have a few green bottles that'd look awesome on the window ledge for when you show the house."

He glanced around the house. "I don't even know if I have enough of my furniture to pull this off. It's so big."

"Furniture?"

"I keep style and color-neutral furniture in storage for when I'm showing a house. Some rooms can be left empty and people are fine, but others— not so much. I'll have to use both leaves of the table and

332

all of the chairs in that dining room. I'll need both sections of the sofa, and both chairs." He walked through the rooms pointing out what he'd put where. "But I don't have anything for those other two bedrooms, and I think the office might be better without anything than with too little. I'll have to see what Amber thinks."

"Does Amber sell all your houses?"

"And helps me find the new ones, yes. She's amazing."

Turning abruptly into the dining room, Aggie asked about the size of the necessary light fixture. "I think the other one was too small."

He noticed a faint catch in her throat and questioned her. "What's wrong, Mibs?"

"It's silly. Ok, so what about the broken porch and back lights?"

"What's silly?" She started for the door, but Luke caught her arm, allowing his hand to slide down and weave his fingers through hers. "I don't understand."

"I don't either! I told you; it's silly!"

"And I asked what was so silly."

"Me. Hearing about Amber and suddenly feeling very jealous that she knows something about you and your life that I don't know and don't have the courage to ask."

Luke knew the grin that grew on his face was as goofy as any that Mark Twain had described in his little friend Tom. "Dare you."

"Dare I what?"

"Dare you to ask whatever you want to know about me." He winked, "Or even about Amber."

"You're enjoying this, aren't you?"

"Enjoying hearing that you are feeling a little jealous? Oh, yeah!" He tugged her out the front door so she could get a feel for the necessary lights. He didn't need her input; they both knew he was perfectly capable of doing the entire renovation successfully and without any input from anyone. However, he wanted the time with her, he wanted her to feel included in his ventures, and have some measure of satisfaction when the house sold for the price he wanted.

"Luke?"

"Hmm?"

"How will you know?"

He chose not to show that he understood the question. "Know what?"

With each attempt to answer, Aggie grew more flustered until Luke took pity. "I don't know how I'll know, but I think you'll manage to tell me somehow. I can't see you walking up to me and proposing or anything, but you'll either give it away accidentally or you'll find a way to tell me— somehow."

"You make it sound certain. Are you really that sure?" Her eyes traveled to where their hands still hung intertwined between them, but she made no move to change that.

"Let's just say that after I told you about my trip to see your parents, I saw it as an if, but lately I've been thinking of it as a when."

She nodded. "Good. I wondered if it was just me."

"Just you what?"

The twinkle was back in Aggie's eyes as she said, "Just me that had started thinking of things as when instead of if."

Luke says: Mibs, are you there?

Luke says: Hmm… I thought you signed on, but maybe it's just Tina.

Luke says: Or, perhaps you're angry with me.

Luke says: Confused?

Luke says: Out with another man in a studied effort to break my heart?

Luke says: On a brighter note, maybe you're scrubbing toilets or something equally stimulating that doesn't involve other men. I like that better.

Mibs says: Aggie is settling Laird's hash over something. She'll be down in a minute.

Mibs says: Luke, do you not see the irony of you yakking away up there without hesitation when usually we have to pull conversation from you like a dentist pulls teeth?

Luke says: LOL. I was hoping she hadn't gone to bed with her laptop still online.

Mibs says: Uh, oh, I hear her coming. Bye.

Luke says: Bye, Tina.

Mibs says: Tina?

Luke says: I was having a nice chat with her.

Mibs says: I don't see anything.

334

Luke says: I think she must have closed it out then. I can copy and paste if you want.

Mibs says: Just give me the run down.

Luke says: I was making lots of little comments about where you were, who you were with, what you were doing, and Tina teased me and told me you'd be down soon. Did you get Laird all squared away?"

Mibs says: Yeah. He's mad at me.

Luke says: Why?

Mibs says: Well, I found him in his room tonight working on school work.

Luke says: Hooligan.

Mibs says: *giggles*

Luke says: So what was the conflict?

Mibs says: He was trying to do everything on his assignment sheet for next week. He was over half done!

Luke says: Are you sure you're giving them enough work?

Mibs says: I took everything they're supposed to do in a year, divided it by weeks and then days, and added a bit extra to make up for lost time and if they get sick. Everything I read says that until high school, most kids are done in under two and a half hours a day with our type of curriculum.

Luke says: So, then if you built in getting ahead, what's the problem with him doing it himself?

Mibs says: I don't think it's a good thing to have so much time between lessons. I think you need the reinforcement of frequent use to keep your mind sharp.

Luke says: That makes sense. So Laird didn't like it when you said he can't work that far ahead?

Mibs says: He acts like I've betrayed him or something. He took the ok to finish early in the day as an ok to finish whatever he wanted to WHENEVER he wanted to.

Luke says: So what did you say?

Mibs says: I told him that he had to do his work every day. He could get it done as fast as he liked as long as he did it right and showed that he knew the material, but he can't work days and days ahead.

Luke says: What does he do when he's not doing schoolwork?

Mibs says: Takes things apart, reads, works outside on different things, rides to the library, builds models, plays computer games, stuff like that.

Luke says: Well, since he's not vegging out in front of the TV, what if you came up with a compromise?

Mibs says: What kind of compromise?

Luke says: Well, what if he could finish the week up on Wednesday or Thursday and have one or two more days for that kind of stuff. Most of what you mentioned is very educational. If he was just laying around watching TV or playing on one of those video things, I'd be less inclined to suggest it, but building, taking things apart, working, reading— those things will help him just as much as taking longer to read history or do math problems.

Mibs says: You don't think that's too long between lessons?

Luke says: It's your decision, of course, but since what he's doing when he's not doing the lessons only increases his ability to learn and understand, no I don't.

Mibs says: I'll think about it.

Mibs says: I have something I need to talk to you about.

Luke says: What did I do wrong?

Mibs says: LOL. Nothing. I just realized that if I don't say something up front, things could get awkward in the right, or I guess that's wrong, situation.

Luke says: I'm lost.

Mibs says: Hee hee. Well, I'd be surprised if you weren't. So, since it's talk about it in person or on here, I'm going for it while it's on the table.

Luke says: Whatever "it" is…

Mibs says: It kind of has a back story to it.

Luke says: Should I call you Doofenschmertz?

Mibs says: Huh?

Luke says: Never mind. It's a cartoon that Rodney likes. I haven't mentioned it, because I have a feeling that half of your kids would get ideas…

Mibs says: Ideas like what?

Luke says: Building roller coasters in the back yard, robot tree houses, painting the unpainted desert…

Mibs says: The desert is painted. It's the painted desert— Arizona isn't it?

Luke says: Not in Phineas and Ferb. Anyway, there's an evil scientist, Dr. Doofenschmertz, who always has a back story. Ignore me and tell it all.

Mibs says: Ok, so in the seventh grade, I went to camp like I did every year. The story of the day for the girls was Hannah. I was captivated. The way my counselor told the story was almost like Hannah was the first saint or something. She'd prayed for years, fasted, wept, and finally promised to give her child back to God if she could just have him.

Luke says: One of my favorite stories. I love her husband.

Mibs says: Me too! Anyway, one of the girls asked why Hannah did it—why she gave up her son, so Candace told her about how serious vows are. How we only make vows to the Lord that we can make sure we keep.

Luke says: Candace. Too funny.

Mibs says: Anyway, I was caught up in the romance of the idea of a vow to the Lord.

Mibs says: Why funny?

Luke says: Phineas and Ferb's sister is Candace in the cartoon.

Mibs says: *rolls eyes* Anyway, I spent two days trying to figure out what vow I could make to the Lord.

Luke says: You're kidding me.

Mibs says: Nope. I wanted it to be something that was really big, but not too hard yet. I kept thinking about things like giving a tithe of everything I got— even Christmas and birthday presents. Then I realized I'd have to ask how much they were. I thought about promising to be a missionary— easy to do as a kid, but I was afraid I might not get accepted and that wouldn't be good.

Luke says: I like this glimpse into you as a kid. I think I would have liked you back then too.

Mibs says: I'm flattered, I'm sure. Anyway, then I caught two of the counselors making out behind the cafeteria. It was gross.

Luke says: I'll bet. *snickers*

Mibs says: So, I vowed that I'd never kiss anyone unless I was married. How I expected to get through dating and engagement without kissing, never occurred to me. I was very sincere about it.

Luke says: An understandable vow if I've ever heard one.

Mibs says: I told Tina about it, and she was livid. She thought I was ridiculous and asked if there was an out. That's actually how she became a Christian.

Luke says: By kissing?

Mibs says: *snort* No, by searching for some out for me in the Bible. She was sure I'd be able to get out of it. Once she started reading, she kept going, until one night she showed up at our house at bed time, in her pajamas, with her Bible, and demanding to know how to be a Christian. I'll never forget it. She said, "If Jesus can go through all that for me, I'm not going to waste it."

Luke says: Wow.

Mibs says: Then, after she was baptized, she turned to me and said, "Oh, and I found out how to get around that kissing vow —" right in front of the whole church!

Luke says: What I wouldn't give to see that.

Mibs says: Yeah. A riot. Anyway, Dad asked me what she meant, and got the whole story out of me. Tina insisted that according to Leviticus, Dad could, now that he heard of the vow, revoke it.

Mibs says: I should confess, at that point, I didn't care.

Luke says: Of course, you didn't. Tina was far thinking though, I'll have to thank her.

Mibs says: Um, Luke. Don't thank her yet. Dad refused.

Luke says: Still thanking her.

Mibs says: Why?

Luke says: Because she was thinking about the day you'd have a guy who wanted to kiss you. I'm not sure about how many of those there've been — probably more than you think — but still, it's a nice thought. Now, why did your dad refuse? This I gotta hear.

Mibs says: Dad said that he thought I needed to take responsibility for my actions. He knew I was old enough to know what I was doing, even if the consequences became a bit difficult as I got older.

Luke says: Have you ever regretted it?

Mibs says: Not until lately…

Luke says: How recently is lately?

Mibs says: The past month or so.

338

Luke says: That's good enough for me.

Mibs says: You're not disappointed?

Luke says: That you're a woman of your word? Not on your life.

Mibs says: Well, that's not what I meant, but...

Luke says: Not disappointed that when I get that first kiss it'll BE a first kiss? No way.

Mibs says: Well, for me anyway.

Luke says: For us.

Mibs says: Does that mean us as a couple or as individuals?

Luke says: Curious, aren't you?

Mibs says: Very.

Luke says: Both. It's going to be a trio of firsts, and I can't wait.

Mibs says: You're going to have to though, aren't you?

Mibs says: Wait, you said "going to be." That sounds pretty confident.

Luke says: You're the one who said you'd been thinking of things in terms of when, Mibs.

Mibs says: Luke?

Luke says: Hmm?

Mibs says: Goodnight.

Luke says: Goodnight, Mibs. I love you.

Mibs says: And that's a wonderful thought to fall asleep to.

Luke says: That's really nice to hear. Sleep well.

CoMMITMENTS

Chapter Twenty-three

Friday, October 24th

With Ian on one hip and Cari and Lorna in the double stroller, Aggie dragged herself through the crowd of playful children, trying to find her own in the sea of co-op participants. Mothers smiled encouragingly, but few took the time to seek her out, and no one offered to help. Aggie couldn't decide if it was because they were busy themselves, didn't want to be a bother, or if she, as a single mother of eight, was some kind of pariah. Disgusted with herself, she navigated through the obstacle course of children reminding herself that she'd grown too accustomed to a church and friends who were eager to lend a hand.

She found Kenzie first, and had several things thrust in her hands before the girl skipped away with another child. "Kenzie...aaandd... she's gone," Aggie groaned.

Vannie stood in a circle of girls laughing about something, and seeing her niece enjoying herself with girls similar in age added another pound of guilt to her already overloaded bucket. The girl needed more time to be just a girl and not the "oldest of eight children— the example." How to arrange that on top of an already overloaded schedule was something Aggie couldn't fathom, but it went on her mental "to-do" list nonetheless.

Seated on a bench outside the classroom door, Ellie looked so very alone, but at the sight of Aggie, a smile lit the little girl's face. "Aunt Aggie! Look what we did!" Ellie thrust a "stained glass" picture into her hands. "We drew our picture on wax paper, colored it, ironed it, cut it out, and put it back together. We have homework. We have to use this paint stuff to be like lead and bring it back next week. It was so fun."

The art teacher beckoned to Aggie. "You did great, Ellie. Can you stay with the girls while I talk to your teacher? Just call me if you need me." After admonishing the twins not to step from the stroller, Aggie carried Ian to the woman's side, still wrestling to keep the child from destroying the papers she held in her hand. "You're Evvie Berkshire, right?"

"Yes. Aggie Stuart?" The woman tried to consult her list, but a child dashed past, knocking the clipboard from her fingers.

"Milliken. The children's last names are Stuart."

"Their father's name?" The woman frowned.

"And their mother's."

"You're not their mother?"

The number of times she'd explained her situation seemed incalculable. "No. I am their aunt. My sister and her husband died last year. I 'inherited,' for lack of better word."

"Wow. That's a lot of work. How did your husband feel about that?"

"I'm not married." Aggie glanced at Ellie, making sure the twins were still seated in their stroller.

"Ok, that's it. First, I am sorry for your loss. Second, you are my hero. Third, your niece is beyond my capabilities. She needs a good art school. She's amazing. I've known professionals that don't have the eye and the passion that your little girl has." Evvie shook her head. "Fourth, if you ever need anything, you have my number. Call."

Relief flooded Aggie's heart. No matter where she went, she was out of place. She almost always had more children, she was the only unmarried person, and she never knew what she was doing. One thing that did encourage her was that, aside from occasional outbursts by Cari or Kenzie, she almost always had the most polite and well behaved children present. Though she couldn't take credit for it, Aggie considered that her nieces and nephews hadn't become unbearable little snots as proof that she wasn't a complete failure in her job.

"Thanks. You don't know how much it means that someone cares about Ellie's talents and doesn't condemn us for being different."

"Can I put you on the prayer chain? It's an innocuous way to let people know your situation. I'd love to think everyone would be encouraging and welcoming regardless of the circumstances, but unfortunately, this group is made up of sinners like every other group, and some people just judge."

"If you think it's best." Aggie hated the idea that people would pity her or treat the children differently, but she was tired of explaining the situation to everyone, and if there was any chance that someone might shun one or more of them because of her perceived "single mom" status, she'd suck it up and deal with it.

Before she could respond, Laird dashed up to her, thrust a box in her arms, and took off after two other boys to join an impromptu game of soccer. Seconds later, Tavish thrust the papers from his class in her overloaded hands and took off after Laird. Evvie shook her head. "Can I give you some unsolicited advice?"

"Sure." Aggie always thought that question an odd one. What was she supposed to say? No?

The woman pointed to Aggie's overloaded arms. "Don't be a slave to your children. Make a rule that they have to take their things straight to your van. You can't be a pack horse for all of them."

Even as the woman spoke, Aggie nearly dropped the box. "I take your point. Thanks for the suggestion regarding Ellie."

The crowd of children was smaller, but Aggie still had trouble rounding everyone up and getting them into the van. She still had to stop and pick up Ian's birthday cake, fill the van with gas, and get home before her parents arrived. She'd filled the van on Monday and already it was near empty. At this rate, their gasoline budget would be blown long before the month ended. It seemed as if every time she conquered one problem, another surfaced.

The van was a riot of voices all talking at once about their classes. Aggie rubbed her temple as she pulled into the gas station, climbed out, and almost forgot to turn off the engine. That thought terrified her. She was bushed. While the van filled with gas, she called the bakery to confirm the cake was finished, called Tina to make sure the decorations were procured, and called her parents to see how far they were from Brant's Corners. Ian's first birthday party was set to begin in an hour.

William watched the celebrations with a lump in his throat. The baby was happy playing with wrapping paper and boxes, Martha Milliken dragging fistfuls of the paper out of his mouth from time to time. The children played games, while the adults chattered and laughed at jokes, but at first, he was content to watch, a quiet listener to the festivities.

A cry from the yard, one he recognized immediately, sent him racing out the back door before the others could rise from their seats. Kenzie picked herself up from the ground, her knee scraped and bleeding, and wailed as the skin stretched and puckered. William was at her side in seconds. "Are you ok?"

"I fell. I always fall." Fresh tears fell as the pain intensified.

Unaware of the spectators watching from the kitchen, William lifted the child and carried her to the spigot. He rinsed the knee, trying to keep from soaking her dress and shoes, and then called for Tavish to bring him a kitchen towel. "It's too big for a band-aid, Kenzie."

The little girl nestled against his shoulder and listened as he told her of the scrapes, breaks, and scratches he'd endured as a child right in that very back yard. "I ripped open my leg on the fence over there. Had to get a shot for that one. I had two nails in my feet, and cracked my head open on the concrete." William left out the parts that included his mother, and focused on the injuries themselves. "It's part of being a kid, I guess."

"I guess."

William saw Tina creep around the corner of the house to listen to the conversation, but he didn't acknowledge her presence. He knew Aggie trusted him with the children, and either Tina was there to help if he needed it, or she'd learn he didn't need supervision in his interactions with the children. "Do you want to go play?"

"No." The child sounded pathetic as she clung to him. "Tell me more about how you lived here when you were a kid. Were you as small as me?"

"I moved into this house when I was just a little older than Cari and Lorna, so that would make me smaller."

Kenzie's eyes widened with amazement. "Wow. Now you're bigger than everyone."

"Gee, thanks."

"You're welcome!" Oblivious to the unfortunate way her words could be taken, Kenzie pointed to the swing and asked if they could sit there while William told her stories.

"How do you feel about Tina sitting with us?"

"Is Aunt Tina out here too?" Kenzie glanced around, spying Tina a few feet away. "Come sit with us! Mr. William is going to tell all about when he was little like me!"

"Wow, I wouldn't miss that for anything. Lead the way." As Kenzie pointed to the back porch swing, Tina winked at William.

Once settled on the swing, Kenzie crawled back in William's lap, wincing as her scraped knee dragged across his leg, and curled up against him. "Tell me about your favorite thing to do."

"Well," red crept up his neck as he felt Tina's intense gaze. Either she was very interested in the answer, or she didn't trust him to know what was and wasn't child-appropriate. "When I was your age, I liked to climb that tree. My father let me help build the tree house and it probably kept me from breaking my neck trying to climb it."

"You father built the tree house?"

"Yep. Luke has fixed some of the floor boards and a couple of places on the walls, but the rest is all Dad's work." The pride and hurt in William's voice was evident, even to Kenzie.

"What did your daddy do? Are your feelings hurt?"

"I just missed him, I guess. Then, when I was about Tavish's age, I liked to explore the fields, catch gophers—the farmer, Mr. Watson, used to pay me a dollar a piece for every gopher I caught— and I loved going to Mrs. Dyke's house."

"Mrs. Dyke? Really? She lived there then too?"

"Sure did."

Awestruck, Kenzie shook her head. "Wow. She's lived there *forever*!"

"Mrs. Dyke used to keep snickerdoodles in a big cookie jar on the kitchen counter. I'd walk to the street, look both ways and then look both ways again, just so I knew I'd really done it, and then run as fast as I could across and into the yard. Mr. Dyke liked to sit on the porch swing and whittle. I'd go into the house, get some cookies for us, and he'd tell me stories of when their boys were little or when he was away at war and things like that."

"War? What war?" Kenzie's forehead furrowed. "The War for Independence? Tavish is learning about that one."

Tina and William stifled snickers. "No, a later one — the Korean War. Their sons were all in the Vietnam war. They weren't drafted. All four of them signed up to go." He hugged the little girl, covering the child's ears as he did. "Only three came home," he whispered.

"What else did you do?"

"I learned how to fish and how to ride a bike, and they played games with me on Friday nights until I went off to boot camp."

"What's boot camp?"

Tina interjected before William could answer, "A place where they make you miserable in order to keep our country safe."

"They should have fun if they're going to make our country safe! I think we should write a letter to the President and tell him so."

Night fell, and still Kenzie plied William with questions about which room had been his, where he'd gone to school, and who had been his best friend. Tina got up a few times to help Luke and Libby with something, but returned quickly to hear the story and watch the tender way William had with Kenzie. Once the little girl fell asleep in her hero's arms, Tina smiled and nodded at him.

"You're good with her. You had a little sister, right?"

"Yes." William brushed hair out of Kenzie's face and shifted her to a more comfortable position for both of them. "I love this little girl. The first time I came here after they all moved in, she asked me if I was going to 'rest Aggie. I think I lost my heart to her that day."

"Not everyone sees this side of you, William. I noticed that right off — that and what a good conversationalist you are."

"Me?" He tried not to laugh, but failed. "I don't understand you sometimes, Tina."

346

"I think," she said quietly, "you underestimate yourself. Sometimes your need to control things takes over your common sense, but when you're relaxed and not in 'cop mode' you're a cool guy."

"Cop mode, huh… hmm."

Tina giggled. "Have you ever taped yourself when you're trying to convince someone how right you are? You lose all sense of proportion." William shifted uncomfortably, but Tina continued, "She's probably getting heavy. Do you think you could carry her to bed?" Even as she spoke, he realized she'd changed the subject for his benefit.

"She's filthy…"

"We'll give her a bath and change her sheets tomorrow. It's cruel to wake her up now. She's probably dreaming of bicycles, snickerdoodles, and writing letters to the president."

Gazing down at the child in his arms, William nodded. "You're right, of course. Let's get her to bed."

She followed him through the house and upstairs. In Kenzie's room, Tina turned down the bed, removed the child's shoes, and once William laid Kenzie down, tucked the blankets in around her. She tiptoed from the room, glancing back to see if William followed and saw him bend low and kiss the child's forehead before he backed away from the bed and turned to leave.

"As I said," she whispered, "you're a good man, William Markenson."

The sound of clanking dishes woke Aggie from a deep sleep. She glanced around her, confused as to why she was stretched out on the living room couch. The room was dark, the house seemingly empty, and only the occasional rush of water from the kitchen faucet or clink of silverware in the dishwasher marred the quiet stillness. A glance at the clock showed the time well after ten o'clock. Out front, her parents' car showed that they'd stayed as planned and that Luke was still there. Tina's car was gone. She'd already left for Yorktown. That left Luke as her kitchen elf.

Only the light over the sink illuminated his workspace as he loaded the dishwasher, cleaned the sink, and moved to the counters. Grateful, Aggie watched him for a minute before she crossed the room and wrapped her arms around his waist. "Thank you."

Luke glanced over his shoulder, smiling. "You better be careful. I could get used to that."

"Me too."

"What, the hug or the dishes done?"

An impish grin surfaced before she could prevent it. "Both."

"Deal." Luke twisted to be able to see her face and let his hands rest on her shoulders.

"Did I really just fall asleep in the middle of the party? I don't even remember being on the couch."

"You weren't. You were on the swing in the back yard with your mom. I brought you in when the kids went to bed." Luke stepped away, obviously disappointed to do it, and grabbed a piece of cake from the fridge. "We saved you some."

"Thanks."

"Mibs, go up to bed. I can finish this. You are obviously tired."

"I am, but I'm not sleepy anymore." Aggie grabbed a fork from the drawer and perched on one of the barstools with her cake. A glass of milk seemed to appear out of nowhere. "Thanks."

"You said that already."

"Well, thanks again then." She knew she'd snapped, but Aggie popped a forkful of cake in her mouth and concentrated on her plate.

Luke said nothing. He finished his cleanup, took her empty plate, glass, and fork, added them to the dishwasher, and with her hand in his, tugged her through the dining room to the coat closet in the living room. "Toss on a jacket. Let's walk."

"I say I'm worn out, and he wants to walk," Aggie remarked to the empty room.

"That's right."

Outdoors, the crisp autumn air filled her lungs. It was almost instantaneous invigoration. "Wow. This feels great."

Luke led her down the drive and up the street past Murphy's house onto a dirt road that separated the houses from the fields. "What's wrong, Mibs? You haven't been yourself all week."

"I'm just tired."

"Cold?"

"Nope, I'm good. This jacket is almost too warm."

"I meant," he clarified, "are you coming down with a cold?"

"No. It's just been such a busy week. We had classes every other day, shopping for the party, two field trips, and that interview with the Social Security people."

"Well, next week should be better, right?"

"Yep. No party and no Social Security thing. There's another field trip though. I'm hoping Tina is back in time to keep the three littlest home. That'd help a lot."

"Call Mom. She'll be happy to help if she can."

"I can't keep taking advantage of your mom, Luke. This is supposed to be my responsibility, but as it is, Tina is living here since she obviously thinks I can't handle things, you're not getting done what you need to get done because you're always here helping, and your mom practically lives here sometimes."

"You have a lot on your plate," Luke began.

"Yeah, and so do other moms. No, most don't have as many kids, but some do. There's a woman in the co-op with ten!"

Luke stopped mid-stride and wrapped his arms around her. "And those women have husbands and years of experience behind them. Give yourself a break."

Her sniffle cancelled her intentions of arguing. She couldn't do it. Fresh tears, ones that this time had nothing to do with the loss of her sister, overflowed as Aggie sobbed out her frustrations. "I don't have time for a break, Luke. Ian is already one. Christmas is coming, and I have no idea how to make a special holiday for these kids. They *need* it this year. They grow up too fast to just coast along while I get my mom legs under me. I—"

"I think it's a pretty good thing you made that vow, Mibs."

"Why?" She sounded like Cari when the child didn't get her way— right down to the pathetic little sob that punctuated the question.

"Because I'd be tempted to try one of those movie tricks and kiss you silent. Since I can't, you need to be quiet and listen."

"Bossy."

"When it's for your own good, sure." His hands brushed her hair from her face and then settled around her waist again. "Your family isn't going to look like anyone else's. It's going to change when it becomes my family too. It'll change when Vannie goes off to college or Laird gets an afternoon job. You can't be all things to all these kids all at once. You can't. Your sister didn't do that."

"Yes—"

"Hush, woman!" His voice growled, but Aggie heard the chuckle under it all. "She did not. Your sister had many hours a day with only a few little ones at home. For all you know, she hired out some of the housekeeping. She had a husband who was obviously a big help, and I bet she did not drag her children all over town for different activities."

"I don't know. I never asked."

"You have a lot of misplaced guilt, Mibs. You keep trying to make up for what you think those kids are missing, but they have everything they want or need. They have a 'mother' that loves them, a strong church behind them, and they have each other. That's more than a lot of people can say."

"Like who? Name someone who doesn't have that. That's just basic life, Luke." Aggie's frustration prompted her to try to push away, but Luke didn't let her.

"Nuh uh. You stay here and listen. William. There's one. He never had any of that. His mother showed him cruelty, he had no church at that time, and his siblings were stripped from him." He shook his head as she opened her mouth. "And, he's not a lone case. When those kids are fifty, they're going to remember those things. Sure, they'll have fond memories of other things, but the ones that matter most will be those."

"Wanna know something pathetic?"

"Sure." Reluctantly, Luke stepped back, turned, took her hand again, and started back towards her house.

"I keep waiting for Tavish to break out and start the infirmary all over again."

"I don't think he's going to. I think he got some kind of immunity somehow without getting them. Either that, or he'll get it some other year when he's exposed to someone else."

"That's encouraging… and not." Aggie's feet dragged.

"You getting sleepy finally?"

"Nope."

"You sure? You're slowing down."

She ducked her head and tried to pick up the pace. "I just didn't want to go back yet."

Luke pulled her back to him. "I'm good with that."

Their pace slowed to a lazy crawl as they made their way back to the house—neither speaking, both saying much. Luke stopped at his truck and pulled the door open. "I'd better go."

"You said something I really liked earlier."

His eyes smiled down at her. "And what was that?"

"You said, 'When it becomes my family too.' I liked that."

"I look forward to it, Mibs. It's the first and last prayer on my lips every day."

"Mine too."

"And you wondered why…" Luke's voice took on that tone that had an unsettling effect on her heart.

"Why what?"

"Why I love you."

Aggie's eyes widened. "How did you know that!"

"Your face, Mibs. It tells me everything."

"Not everything."

His chuckle morphed into full blown laughter. "Yes, Mibs. Everything."

As she digested the ramifications of Luke's words, he drove off toward home. It occurred to Aggie, as she climbed the stairs, that Luke would probably know the state of her heart before she was fully aware of it. That thought sent her rushing up the last few steps to see in her mirror what Luke might have seen in her face.

An envelope on her pillow diverted her. She kicked off her shoes, pulled the note from the envelope, and curled up on her bed to read it. A smile played around her lips as she read.

Aggie (A.K.A. Mibs),

Today as I listened to the inspector tell me what a good job I'd done on the house on Cygnet Street, I realized how rarely I remember to tell you how well you're doing. The children are healthy, happy, and growing spiritually and intellectually. I am sure your sister is very proud.

I also wanted to remind you that you are loved. Your parents, the children, Tina, my mother, and of course, I love you more than I know how to express. I think you need to hear it more than you do, so I'm telling you. I love you.

Yours,

Luke

Aggie reread the note, and then read it once more. Smiling to herself with a prayer of thanksgiving on her lips, she tucked it into her Bible, amused that the chapter heading was for Song of Solomon, and reached for her laptop. It wasn't there. Her feet pattered down the stairs and into the library. She retrieved her late night communication friend, and hurried back up to her room. While it booted, she changed into pajamas, brushed her teeth and hair, and washed her face.

The messenger showed Luke offline, but Aggie clicked on his name anyway.

Mibs says: Luke, I got your note. Thank you. I have a feeling I'll reread it so much that I wear it out.
Mibs says: Funny aside, I stuck it in my Bible and you'll never guess what book it landed in. Or maybe you will...
Mibs says: G'night, Lucas. You do not know how badly I want to be able to add "I love you" to that.

The messenger warning that Luke would receive her message once he got online made her smile. Before she could sign off, Tina's messenger box flashed on her screen with a message.

Tina says: Are you awake? Are you ok? I almost didn't go in case you were coming down with something, but Luke promised he'd call his mom if you needed help.
Mibs says: I'm fine. Just a very long day.
Aggie says: Week, actually.
Tina says: Was Luke still there when you woke up?
Aggie says: Yep. I ate cake, he cleaned the kitchen, and we went for a walk. For the record, he knows what I'm thinking.
Tina says: This is a surprise to you?
Aggie says: Not a surprise— just a terrifying reminder that I can't

---

keep my thoughts and feelings to myself.

Tina says: I don't think he wants you to keep them to yourself.

Aggie says: But I want to know them and be comfortable with them before I broadcast it to everyone!

Tina says: Then keep him away from the house?

Aggie says: Cruel. You are cruel.

Tina says: And you're half in love.

Aggie says: We've moved from if to when.

Tina says: If to when what?

Aggie says: We get married. At first, it was a definite, "if you ever care for me, this will happen." Now we both treat it as if it's a foregone conclusion.

Tina says: Well, duh. We all knew that.

Aggie says: I hoped, but I didn't know.

Tina says: You're always over thinking this stuff. Remember when Amy said that you liked Roger Cather? You spent a month analyzing every aspect of it while you tried to decide if she was right or not.

Aggie says: I decided I didn't.

Tina says: Well, it's possible that you did when you started, but man, you didn't once it was over.

Aggie says: I suppose. Whatever, I just want to enjoy this.

Tina says: You're not feeling pressured are you?

Aggie says: By Luke? Are you kidding? I have a feeling I'll be tapping my toes by the time he decides to... whatever.

Tina says: It's called proposing. Technically he's already done it. He's really just waiting for a yes signal so he can make it official.

Aggie says: I guess.

Tina says: You don't sound like yourself.

Aggie says: He thinks I'm doing too much.

Tina says: I already said that.

Aggie says: He thinks the kids need time to "explore their own interests."

Tina says: I said that too.

Aggie says: And the art teacher says that Ellie needs formal instruction.

Tina says: Didn't Iris say not yet?

Aggie says: What does Tina say?

Tina says: I think you should keep her supplied with books, different media, and inspiration. She has a lifetime to develop her talent more formally, but she needs the opportunity to keep growing on her own too.

Aggie says: What about the others? Do they have talents we're not exploring? Should I keep fabric around for Vannie? Let her play around with instruments in a music store? Sign her up for volleyball or basketball?

Tina says: Or just listen to her and see if she expresses an interest instead of trying to add more to your already cracking plate?

Aggie says: I think I need to go to bed. I'm worn out again.

Tina says: I can come back...

Aggie says: Enjoy your time with your dad. I'll be fine. Luke won't let me crash and burn. He is still angling for a wife.

Tina says: Preferably one with some spunk left.

Aggie says: Have I admitted how happy I think I'm going to be?

Tina says: Going to be? You're already over the moon. Go to sleep.

Aggie says: Nighters

Tina says: *poofs*

Tossing Cookies

Chapter Twenty-four

Wednesday, October 29th

"No never alo-ooh-oooh-ne, no, never alone. He promised never to lea-ea-ve me, never to leave me alone."12

William heard Aggie's song as he climbed the steps and shook his head. Now the girl was singing sappy country songs. Great. He should have known Aggie would get all girly over a guy. A slight pang hit his heart at the same time that a great wave of relief washed over him.

"The world's fierce winds are blo – oo – oowing, temptation shaa-arp and keen. I have a peace in kno-oo-owing my Savior sta-ands between..."

A hymn. He should have known — again. "Aggie?"

Her arm waved at him from the library. "In here."

Glancing around at the empty house, William strolled into the library with the unconscious swagger his gun belt created. "Hey, where is everyone?"

"I didn't get all the kids' work graded today. They always have so much more on Wednesdays now, so Tina took them to their classes for me."

"Couldn't she have graded them? I'd think you'd want to get out of the house now and then."

Aggie shook her head in amused disbelief. "Are you kidding? I'm never home. Haven't you noticed that the 9-1-1 calls have ceased? We're never here for Ian to commandeer the phone. That kid is going to think his car seat is an appendage to his backside."

"And you thought that school was such a bad idea?"

"William! They're 'schooling,' just not at the local elementary school. You act like they aren't being educated at all!"

He leaned his hands on the desk and locked eyes with her. "How do I know they are?"

"Why is it any of your business?"

Had William not been so certain of his superior opinion, he'd have heard the steel in her voice. "Didja ever notice the badge?" His attempt at a joke failed miserably.

"How could I not? You slap me upside the head with it every chance you get! Are you here on official business? Am I being charged with a crime?"

"Of course, not! What kind of question is that?"

"Then I think you should just leave."

Stunned, William started to protest, and then shook his head and stormed out of the room. At the door, Mrs. Dyke shoved a plate of cookies into his hand and pushed him back into the house. "Get in there, boy."

"Mrs—"

"You heard me. Move." The fierce look on the elderly woman's face would have frightened anyone.

In the library, Aggie looked up, ready to forcibly remove him to keep her sanity and saw Mrs. Dyke. "Hello!" She gave William a pointed look. "Thank you for helping Mrs. Dyke. I won't keep you."

"Yes you will. I heard the boy. He was rude and imperious— as usual."

"Wha—"

"Stuff it, William." The women, younger and elder, spoke in unison and then giggled.

"What did I do! I don't get it."

"William, son, remember the hand signal issue? From what I heard, this is that times ten." Mrs. Dyke took the cookies from

William and handed them to Aggie. "Have a cookie. They're sweeter than his disposition anyway."

"You can't do it all, Aggie. I know you think you're super –" A cookie sailed across the room and at William's head before even she knew she'd done it.

"That was mature," he remarked as he picked up the cookie. Another one whizzed its way across the room and hit him in the chest.

"Bullseye."

"Aggie! Grow up –" He couldn't finish his indignant protest before Mrs. Dyke lobbed one at him too. "What is this?"

Unlike Luke, who would have returned fire, William stood there, disapproval lined in every feature, while Aggie and Mrs. Dyke pelted him with every single cookie on the plate, gasping in laughter by the time the last ones left their fingers. "Do you feel better now?"

"Actually, I do. I need to hurry and pick them up before the ten minute rule ends," she joked as she grabbed the plate and started to clean up the cookie mess.

"Ten second rule."

"Do you *have* to do that? Do you *always* have to do that? I can't believe you." Shoving the plate into his hands, Aggie stormed upstairs, slamming her door behind her.

"I think this is too much for her. Did see that? And what was with you throwing too?"

Winnie Dyke pointed to the floor. "Pick them up, William. You were so out of line it isn't funny. I can't believe I got you a date with her."

"I –"

"That young woman," the furious neighbor began, "is doing the job of three women, alone, without the support of a loving husband, and better than most people ever do including myself and your mother."

"That was low."

"It was true. You like to preach about truth; well, here's a truth for you. Your words just stripped her of her self-respect. You don't know it all, William. Your pride was always your weakest point, and now you've used it to beat a woman emotionally. You're no better than your mother."

His arrogance fizzled as he stared dumbstruck at the woman before him. Pain filled his eyes as he choked, "Mama Dyke—"

"You know I love you, William. I've loved you since you were old enough to toddle across the street. I've spoiled you out of compassion for all you've been through, but I can't let you hurt that woman. It's hurting you too. You're going to hate yourself when you can see what you've done." On tiptoe, Mrs. Dyke gave "her boy" a kiss on the cheek, caressed it just as she had when he'd come to her broken over the latest attack from his mother, and shuffled back out of the house and home again.

Cookies littered the floor around his feet— two crushed by footsteps. He took a deep breath as he picked up the first, still wounded by Mrs. Dyke's words. *You're no better than your mother.* The accusation echoed in his mind until he thought he'd go crazy. Had Aggie said it, he would have gone through the roof, but how could he unleash the wrath building in him on the only person who had ever shown him a mother's love and care?

With each cookie replaced on the plate, William's self-righteous indignation returned—this time, directed toward Aggie. She'd done this. Once again, she'd played the helpless victim card rather than facing the fact that sometimes people need help. The irony of that thought contorted his face into further disgust until he was ready to storm up the stairs and unleash all the pent up fury on the one person who needed to hear it most. Yes, Aggie definitely needed to hear a little "faithful wounding" of her own.

By the time all cookies were nestled on the plate once more, William had, once again, resolved that Aggie needed to hear the hard truth—she couldn't handle the job alone. For the briefest of seconds, he was tempted to take his concerns to Ellene. She had the ability to make Aggie see sense. No, that wouldn't work. If Ellene wanted to, she could have the children removed for neglect, endangerment, and educational neglect. The clinic records—

His thoughts were arrested by Luke whistling up the steps and into the house. "Aggie? You here?"

"She's upstairs." Before William could say anymore, Aggie flew down the stairs, sobbing into Luke's arms.

An awkwardness filled the room as William tried not to watch Luke comfort Aggie. The tender way he had with the young woman was something William couldn't have imitated had he tried, and he knew it. Something akin to remorse pricked his heart as he saw how distraught she truly was. Had he been that unkind? He hadn't meant to be. He'd tried to show her that she needed to leave things to professionals and not expect so much of herself. Was that so wrong?

He couldn't leave. Luke and Aggie blocked his way. It'd be even more awkward to try to scoot past them. He waited for the comforting to morph into a make-out session, but thankfully it didn't. Luke managed to quiet Aggie and convince her to go back upstairs. William didn't know what she'd told him, but it looked like Luke intended to have words. Well, he could throw a few well chosen ones out himself.

"William—"

"Do you see how overwrought she is? You've got to protect her from herself." He expected Luke to interrupt or argue with him, but Luke Sullivan stood waiting for him to finish. "Well?"

"Are you through?"

"I— Well— For now."

"Then I have a few things to say." Luke's expression grew serious—almost stern. "Actually, I have a question. Can Aggie do anything right in your eyes?"

"Of course! She's a wonderful 'mother' to those kids. She obviously loves them and protects them as best she can. They're well fed, clothed... why?"

"Have you ever told her those things?"

William frowned. "You know I have."

"Let me rephrase. Do you leave her with the impression that you think well of her or that you think her incompetent?"

"She's not incompetent. She's just overworked. She's always asking for help, Luke. You've heard her when she's tired or frustrated. She'll admit she can't do it."

Luke shook his head as if unable to believe what he heard. "Anyone will say anything when weary. Sometimes Aggie just wants someone to acknowledge she's struggling without trying to teach her some great lesson or prove that the job is beyond her. She just needs to know that someone cares. She did this for months before she ever came here and without the help she has now. We offer this help because we love her and want to care for her, not because she's doomed to failure without us."

Unaccustomed to Luke speaking more than half a dozen words at a time, William actually listened. With Mrs. Dyke's reproof echoing in his mind, he nodded. "Can I go up?"

"Go for it. Just don't—"

"I won't."

William took the stairs slowly. For the first time that he could remember, he felt the impulse to pray outside his carefully scheduled prayer time. That impulse slammed into his chest making his heart feel burdened beyond anything he'd ever imagined. Step by step, he poured out his confusion, his concerns, and his desire to help rather than hurt. By the time he reached Aggie's room, he felt a peace steal over him so gently that he felt almost caressed by it.

"Aggie?"

"William, please—"

"Can I come in?" He didn't try to explain yet.

"I—" She took a deep breath. "Ok. Come in." Resignation was chiseled into every corner of her face.

With a tentativeness that he'd never felt before, much less displayed, William crossed the room to the loveseat near the window and sat next to her, taking one of her hands in his. "I am so sorry. I think I understand now— somewhat anyway. I see how I hurt you. That much I know for sure, and I am so sorry."

Without a word, Aggie curled against him, much as his little sister had so many years ago, and gripped his shirt in her hands. "I forgive you."

All his life, William James Markenson had been told that the most powerful words in the world were "I love you," but one fall afternoon he decided that equally powerful were their companions. "I forgive you."

Four pounds, three jabs to the doorbell, and finally a "Open this door, William Markenson," finally woke William from his impromptu nap. He stumbled from his chair, almost tripping over the ottoman, and unlocked the deadbolt, one hand on the holster he'd forgotten to remove. "Tina—"

"You have some nerve, buddy."

"I told her I was sorry. I didn't want or mean to hurt her."

Tina's clear blue eyes swam with unshed angry tears. Something, he couldn't identify what, swept over him as he watched her accuse him of cruelty, arrogance, and ignorance. By the time she sputtered her last accusation and turned to leave, he'd identified that feeling. Attraction. Oh, she'd kill him if he said anything now, but he had to try.

"Tina?"

"Yeah."

"I was wrong. Aggie forgave me. Can you forgive me?"

"I don't know."

Her choked back sob confused him. Why should she be so upset? Before he thought through the idea, William found himself sharing the "conversation" he'd had with Mrs. Dyke. "Mama Dyke said something today that scared me, Tina."

Instinctively, he knew that if he had used any other word but scared, she might not have listened, but the word wasn't chosen to manipulate. She turned, her eyes slowly raising to meet his, allowing him a breath of relief. "What?"

"She said that I'd become like my mother. She said I used untrue and cruel words to emotionally beat Aggie."

"You did."

"I didn't mean to. I really was trying to help, but I think I understand now. Luke said something that really struck home."

"You don't know how close you came to being decked." A sob caught on her last word.

"Tina?" His hand reached to brush the tears that finally fell from her lashes.

"I have to go."

"Why did you come?" As dense as William had been, he was starting to understand several things.

"Bye."

In a calculated risk, William reached out for her as she turned and pulled Tina into his arms. "I wish you'd forgive me."

"I'm afraid to."

His hands looked as though they could crush her as he wrapped them around her waist. Tina was so petite! "Afraid for Aggie or afraid for you?"

361

"Both?"

"Is that a question?" William fought the temptation to laugh. The last thing he wanted to do was add to the rift between them.

"You tell me." She refused to look at him as she whispered, "I like you, William. I think you have a lot of first-rate qualities, but this is the second time you have belittled and deeply hurt my friend. I'm afraid to let myself be vulnerable to you."

"You could play traffic cop."

"Huh?" Her eyes met his, but she didn't step out of his arms.

"If, or more likely when, I do that again, you could hold your hand up like a cop stopping traffic. I did that to Aggie once and she almost killed me for it."

"I would have." Her face lit up into a smile as he grinned down at her.

"I bet you would."

Friday, October 31st

"Want to watch another L'Amour with me?"

Luke's expression was priceless. "As long as there's nothing about pink tights…"

"This one is *The Quick and the Dead*. It's supposed to be about a family moving west from Pennsylvania."

"Sounds better than the last one already." Luke stood. "I'll make the popcorn."

"Nope." Aggie pulled him back to the couch and handed him the remote. "You man the machine. I bought junk food. If the kids are going to come home hyped up on sugar, I'm going to be ready for them."

A veritable smorgasbord of snack items appeared on the coffee table. Several brands of chips, salsa, bowls of ice cream, pumpkin-butterscotch cookies, and a huge basket of mixed candy were flanked by glasses of water and bottles of root beer. "If you expect me to eat all that…"

"Nope. Just whatever you want. I made sure I didn't leave anything out. I even have pizza on redial in case we get hungry."

"When will Tina and Mom be back with the kids?"

"They promised to have them in the door by nine o'clock, so I figure nine fifteen."

The opening scene of the movie sent a sigh of relief over Aggie. "That reminds me of *Little House on the Prairie*—even the music feels similar."

"It's a good start anyway."

Laughing, Aggie shoved a salsa-laden chip at him and pointed to the screen. "You're expecting a repeat of the last one, aren't you? *You're* the one who told me L'Amour was safe."

"The *books!*" Luke's eyes were full of laughter.

Their enjoyment and jocularity fizzled quickly. The men in the town were rough and coarse. Comments about dibs on the wife nearly sent Luke into cardiac arrest. Aggie blanched. "This isn't looking good, Luke."

His murmur of agreement dissolved into shocked protest when the so-called hero kissed the wife of the other main male character. "That's it. I can't take it. I don't care how they redeem it, I can't watch this. It makes me livid."

"So, I take it you won't go for me making out with other men?"

Luke's eyes answered for him. "Got any more movies of torture to weed through, or should we put on something we trust."

"I only have one more. *Shalako.* If it's no good, we can dig out *His Girl Friday* or *Christmas in Connecticut.* Those are safe enough."

"You like the oldies, don't you?"

She frowned. "Well, before this run of bad westerns, I used to say they were 'safe,' but this is anything but safe."

The movie swap was accomplished in seconds, and the next movie began. Almost instantly, there was a dual sigh of relief. They both sensed the difference immediately. For once, the heroine wasn't a married or attached woman who was immediately drawn away by the leading man. A plot, a genuine interesting plot, surfaced and as they relaxed, Luke found himself with his arm around Aggie curled beside him as if the most natural thing in the world.

"I could get used to this, Luke. I could so get used to it."

"You'd better. I plan to have a lifetime of nights like this— sans the junk food. I can't even look at it anymore."

"You're *supposed* to be watching the movie," she teased.

Remembering her mother's admonition to give her a cherished time of "courtship," Luke set aside his natural reticence and cleared

363

his throat. "I'd rather watch you watch it." Aggie's blush told him it was the right thing to say. "That's a lovely shade of pink you're wearing tonight, Mibs."

"Oh, be quiet and watch the movie."

"I told you..."

Aggie glanced up at him, ready to fire another comeback, but the look in his eyes stopped her. She swallowed hard. "Luke... you're making me wish I'd never made a certain vow."

"Good."

"Good! Why good?"

Luke's cheek pressed against her head for a moment. "It tells me that you're closer to caring for me than I thought you were."

"I cared about you before you ever—"

"Ok, loving me then." He shook his head and tried to focus on the TV screen. "It's hard for a guy to use words like love when you haven't, ok?"

"Luke, I—"

"Do you mind if we talk about it later? I don't want to be interrupted by the children and it's getting closer and closer to nine."

Frustrated, Aggie nodded. "M'kay."

His arm squeezed her shoulder once more. "You make me very happy, Mibs. I just want the chance to make you happy too."

"You assume that you don't."

Luke's reply was cut short by an intense scene springing at them from the Arizona desert. A coach fled from the Apaches who were determined to drive them from the reservation. Aggie buried her face in his side as the coach rolled and the Indians attacked. Just as they relaxed, the self-centered woman they'd despised from the beginning twitched. The following scene sent a shudder through Aggie. "I expected a different horror. I can't decide which is worse!"

"I—" Luke swallowed. "No, there's just no response."

As the movie came to a close, Aggie shook her head. "I can't decide whether it's ok for now or not. I mean, I think the unfaithful wife part would probably go over his head, but even if it didn't, they don't glorify it in any way. It might be good to show the pain something like that can cause. She earned her fate."

"Why not just put it away until you're confident?"

Aggie gave him a sly look. "Or, I'll just wait until it's your decision to make instead of mine — the books too. I don't want to deal with pre-reading the books, and now I'm nervous about them."

"I'll make a note to have Tavish start pestering you about that movie tomorrow."

Aggie says: Mom?

Martha says: How are you? Did the kids have fun at the church festival?

Aggie says: Yep. They're all loaded with enough sugar to last them a lifetime.

Martha says: Allie always scheduled dental visits in November for that reason. Geraldine loaded them with sugar on Halloween.

Aggie says: I thought they didn't "do" Halloween. We never did.

Martha says: They didn't. Allie didn't even do the festival at their church. Geraldine thought it was horrible and cruel, so she more than made up for it.

Aggie says: She didn't? I thought she must have. Laird said they did.

Martha says: Do you remember exactly what he said? From what I know of the boy, he won't lie, but he'll arrange the truth to his purposes.

Aggie says: Like restitution for the broken window. Yeah. Um... *Aggie thinks hard* Oh, yeah. You're right. He said, "Who is going to take us to the Harvest Festival?" as if it was just a foregone conclusion. I just assumed...

Martha says: As he wanted you to.

Aggie says: OY. I don't have time for these games. I had all kinds of fun stuff planned that I set aside for November 5 instead.

Martha says: Remember, remember?

Aggie says: I thought it'd be kind of a fun history lesson.

Martha says: It will! And vocabulary. They'll learn what effigy means.

Aggie says: *giggles*

Martha says: Is everything ok between you and William now?

Aggie says: I think so. When I'm not in the middle of it, I can see that he means well. He really does care about all of us. I just wish he

---

could see things through Luke's eyes.

Martha says: If he did, you might be married to him already.

Aggie says: I wouldn't have married him, Mom. I think I was already a little attached to Luke, even back then. I just hadn't had a moment to realize it.

Martha says: We love him already. William is a wonderful man, and we would have been happy for you, but Luke feels like family.

Aggie says: Tina is happy. She's finally made her presence known.

Martha says: She'd be good for him. She'd keep him in his place without stripping him of his masculinity. That's a delicate balance that most of us can't achieve.

Aggie says: That's a great way of putting it! I'll have to tell her.

Martha says: So how are things going with Luke? Do you feel pressured, or are you enjoying yourself?

Aggie says: I'm enjoying this so much, Mom. He really does love me. I don't know how anyone could resist that.

Martha says: Don't let you convince yourself that you feel what you don't. This is for life, Aggie. This is for the rest of your life. You have to trust him with the most intimate parts of your heart and soul. Don't pressure yourself.

Aggie says: I could marry him tomorrow and be truly happy for the rest of my life.

Martha says: Because you think he's a good man?

Aggie says: Because I know he's a good man, and I love him.

Martha says: Does he know that?

Aggie says: No. Every time I try to tell him, something messes it up.

Martha says: Wait a few weeks, sweetheart. Wait. Let him "work" for you. A man like Luke will enjoy the challenge.

Aggie says: I suppose. He's really very sweet about it. Tonight he brought me a huge sunflower. His mom had tied the stem with a bunch of raffia. I stuck it in that graniteware coffee pot that I keep up on the shelf over the sink. My kitchen looks sunshiny.

Martha says: He's a wise man.

Aggie says: Why do you say that?

Martha says: He's doing what he can continue with. He's not taking you on elaborate dates or bringing you expensive gifts when it doesn't fit with the lifestyle you'll have.

Aggie says: You're right. I hadn't thought of that, but it makes sense.

Martha says: I always prayed I'd live to see you married and with children. I just never expected it to happen on the same day.

Aggie says: Oh, mom. You'll get stronger, have the surgery, and live long enough to see great grandchildren.

Martha says: I don't know, Aggie. The doctor said that if my numbers go any lower, I'll have to go on portable oxygen.

Aggie says: Well, then, we just HAVE to get you stronger.

Martha says: You do that, and I'll keep fighting. They didn't think I'd live to see you go to kindergarten, then they said high school, and then they said I wouldn't see you graduate from college. I've already beat the odds three times.

Aggie says: I love you, Mom.

Martha says: I love you. Your father is glaring at me— again.

Aggie says: Goodnight, Mom.

Martha says: Night.

For Keeps

Chapter Twenty-five

Thursday, November 6th

Thursdays had become Aggie's favorite day of the week. Any other day, she might be scheduled or forced to leave the house for some appointment, class, or other obligation, but Thursdays had become sacred. Nothing but an emergency would induce her to pick up the van keys for any reason.

The children, all but Kenzie having finished their week's work the previous day, were busy with a game of hide and seek that rivaled any ever played in the history of the Stuart household. Ian slept in his crib, Tina relaxed on Vannie's bed, posting her opinions in her online class discussion. Aggie, on the other hand, enjoyed watching the game in process from her favorite spot on the front porch.

Children ran past, snuck by, and screamed as they raced to the tree house as "home base." The only thing missing was Luke. Even as she thought it, Aggie smiled. How much had changed in the past nine months!

Pat Jenson strolled up the drive, waving as she saw Aggie sitting on the porch. "Got a package for you from some library place. More curriculum?"

"Oh, those are probably the science videos I ordered. Great." Aggie accepted the small box and the stack of envelopes. Pointing to a plate on the little wicker table, she added, "Want a cookie?"

"No thanks.. Still working to lose those last five pounds. I'll probably gain it all back the first week from all the celebrating I plan to do, but hey."

"Keep walkin'!"

"You know it. I figure I'm helping to keep postal prices lower by walkin' it too." Pat waved and strolled back down the driveway.

Aggie tossed the box next to her and flipped through the usual stack of first of the month statements, bills, and junk mail, pausing at a large envelope from the Law Offices of Moss & Younger. Dread filled her heart as she unfastened the metal clasp on the back of the envelope. Surely, Geraldine Stuart was too busy dealing with Douglas' illness to start a new round of custody or visitation hassles.

Her eyes closed as she leaned against the back of the chair, willing herself to relax, trust, and pray. Just as a few quick p-mails left her mental inbox, she heard Luke's truck crunching on the driveway. As irrelevant as it seemed at the time, Aggie couldn't help but realize that she could recognize the sounds of several cars on the driveway without seeing who it was first.

Luke's face lit up when he saw her, making her heart swell. She'd never imagined how wonderful it felt to mean so much to someone. Yes, she'd seen a similar look in little Ian's eyes often, and several of the children made her feel indispensible to their happiness, but Luke's admiration and affection was different — more.

"Let me guess. Hide and seek?"

"Did Tavish reading on the other side of the fence give it away or what?"

Laughing, Luke lowered himself into the chair opposite her. "How was today?"

"Well, Tina explained how phones work to Tavish, and now he and Elspeth are trying to create some kind of working model. Tavish has read so much on telegraphs and telephones that I expect we'll have one rigged from upstairs to downstairs sometime next week."

370

She saw the concern in Luke's eyes, but Aggie couldn't help herself. The envelope in her hands sent such a fierce sense of foreboding over her, that Aggie couldn't shake it. "Come on," Luke urged, taking the pile of mail from her and setting it in the chair. "Let's go for a drive or something. I've hardly seen you all week."

"What are you talking about? You've been here nearly every day!"

With a boyish grin, Luke pulled her up and grabbed the mail to take inside. "But, you've been surrounded by children and friends. I want to have you to myself for a bit."

Aggie shrugged and grabbed the large envelope from his hands. "Well, I'm warning you. I don't feel very companionable. I just got this from Mr. Moss, and I suspect bad news." She tried to smile and show him some kind of encouragement. "But, I'll let you take me to get a French Crème at Espresso. Maybe it'll help me wash down whatever is in this thing."

Seated alone on the corner loveseat at Espresso Yourself, Aggie opened the manila envelope that she felt sure would destroy her happiness. Luke watched her, concern written in his expression, as he waited for their order. Inside the envelope was another, smaller, manila envelope and a business letter sized one. The larger one was addressed to her in Allie's handwriting, while the other was labeled with a computer generated label with Mr. Moss as the sender. A hand written admonition to open it first caused Aggie to shake down the contents and tear one end from the envelope.

Aggie sat in thoughtful contemplation as she read the letter enclosed and waited for Luke to return with their drinks. As he sat beside her, she passed him the letter. "Will you read this and tell me if I want to open the other envelope or not?" She passed the unopened manila envelope as well.

"From Allie?"

"Yeah." Aggie choked out the answer as Luke unfolded the lawyer's letter.

Dear Aggie,

According to the terms of your sister's will, I am instructed to forward the enclosed letter nine months after her death. While I have not read the contents of the letter, I am aware of what it entails and am prepared to take whatever course of action you choose as soon as you have made your decision.

I am sorry that you are put in this position, but as difficult as it is, I do think your sister made a wise provision.

Sincerely,

Robert Moss Attorney at Law

The trepidation Aggie felt was evident in her demeanor and even the rigid way she gripped the other envelope. He pried her hand from the source of her unease and began praying. That familiar gesture, always his first course of action in any unfamiliar, unpleasant, and even joyful situation, brought her more comfort than she could have expected. She loved the way Luke's heart was not only attuned to prayer but also how quick he was to include her in it.

Once finished asking for the Lord's strength and wisdom, Luke unclasped the envelope with Allie's letter and pulled the sheets of paper from it, handing them to her. Aggie smiled. "You knew that was the worst part for me, didn't you?"

"I knew you'd be less reluctant if it was already opened, yes."

Grateful for his insight, Aggie read the letter, reread sections, and tried to digest the contents. Her face was devoid of all emotion, something so unusual in Aggie that Luke grew visibly alarmed. When she passed him the letter, Luke gave her one more glance before reading the words that had clearly upset her even if it didn't show.

Dearest Aggie,

I promise I won't start with, "I guess I've gone to glory if you're reading this." Are you relieved? Somehow, I think you are. I can almost see your face as you're reading this.

First, I need to apologize. I know I never asked you if you'd be willing to take on such a huge responsibility. I know you never really understood what the paperwork was that we had you sign every now and then. You trusted me, and even as I write this, I feel like I'm abusing that trust, but it's for my children. You've lived with them for nearly a year. Have you learned what the love of one's children can do to a mother yet? Somehow, I think you have.

I deliberately chose not to tell you about our plans for their care, because I knew you'd fret over it. You'd make decisions for your life based on "what ifs" that might never happen. I look forward to burning these letters the day our older children are old enough to take over this responsibility for us.

It is unfair of me not to have given you a choice. For that, I am so very sorry. Leaving my children motherless is a horrible thought, but not providing for their welfare in that event is worse. I've rewritten this letter three times now. The day you turned eighteen, after Cari and Lorna were born, and then now as Ian is here. I had to have a plan in place that provided for their welfare immediately in order to prevent Mother Stuart from gaining access to them. While Doug and I have made sure it is clear that she is unfit to take them, she is capable of causing more grief on top of an already terrible time for the children, so we wanted some way to keep their lives steady during those first few months.

Losing their parents is going to be difficult enough without them losing their home, their church, their friends, and each other. We have named alternate guardians in a codicil to the will which is filed at Mr. Moss' office. These couples have willingly agreed to take the children and raise them for us in the event that this year has been too much for you, or you do not believe God wants you to continue. All I hoped for was a year of stability before changing up their lives further. They've always been so close. I hate the idea of splitting them up, but I realize that sometimes that can't be helped.

I did consider telling you up front about these other couples, but I confess, I was afraid you wouldn't allow yourself to embrace your role as their mother if you knew that you only had a year to invest in it. If that was too unkind of me, I beg your forgiveness. I'm not very good at this dying thing. Unfortunately, it's not something we get to practice.

If you choose to relinquish your guardianship of our children, all you need to do is go to Mr. Moss' office and sign papers he will have prepared for you. Please keep the children until after that first anniversary of our death, and then arrange for the transfer if that is what you decide to do. Remember, the other couples have been in a state of limbo for a year, wondering if you'll keep them or if they now have more responsibility, so please do make your decision quickly. The longer you take, the more likely something is to happen that will make one or more unable to do as they'd *planned and then the children would be at the mercy of the courts. I can't stand the thought of my children in foster care.*

Aggie, I love you. I have never been very good at telling you that, but you are always such a bright spot in my memories. If you can find it in your heart to continue to love and care for my children so that they can stay together, I know it would mean the world to them. But please, Aggie, please do not give up your life for this if you are not absolutely certain that it is what you and the Lord wants you to do.

Waiting with Jesus to welcome you,
Allie

Watching the emotions flicker over Luke's face unleashed Aggie's feelings, and tears began pouring down her face. Luke fluctuated between empathy for Aggie's loss and raw anger at Allie for not seeing the impossible situation her letter would create for Aggie. He couldn't imagine the turmoil in Aggie's heart as she'd read that letter.

"Come on, Mibs. Let's find somewhere a little more private. We can go to Mom's house, the church office, even the park—"

"Your mom's house. I think I'm going to need her advice."

All the way to his mother's house, Luke prayed. Hearing Aggie admit she needed advice worried him. Would she really consider giving up the children? He'd been certain she wouldn't, but now he wasn't sure.

The moment they entered Libby's living room, Aggie collapsed in tears in the woman's arms. Libby led her to the couch, patted her knee, passed her Kleenex, and then slipped from the room so Luke and Aggie could talk. Each wave of tears was less intense, until at last, she was able to speak. "What did Allie think I'd do? Did she really think I'd tear up their lives again?"

Relief washed over him, but Luke tried not to show it. "I think she had to at least try to give you an out for her own peace of mind. Deep down, she probably knew you'd never give them up."

"I don't know, Luke. Allie has never been the kind of person to play those kinds of games. She put this in here because some part of her thought that I might actually do it. I keep wondering why she thought it was possible when I can't imagine it. What am I missing?"

"I assume you'll talk it over with your parents before you decide?" Something in Luke's tone made her forget his question.

"What's wrong, Luke?"

Aggie heard the raw emotion in Luke's voice as he asked about her conferring with her parents, and her heart sank. Did he hope she'd turn the children over to the other families mentioned in the letters in order for her to be free to begin a fresh new life with him? As much as she didn't believe it possible, a niggling doubt created new tears that threatened to overtake her. She'd give up all hope of becoming Luke's wife before even considering handing over her children to strangers.

"I—" His characteristic trouble with expressing himself was oddly comforting. "I can't help but fear that someone will convince you that you need to release the children. I don't know what I'd do if you did that." Though Luke's conversational pauses were longer than usual, they did manage to give Aggie's heart time to heal from the beating she'd given it. "I love your kids, Aggie. I know it's still presumptive, but I have dreams of taking the boys camping, sitting on that wonderful porch with a shotgun, keeping away the droves of boys who will descend on us someday, seeing the little ones give their hearts to Jesus..." He sagged against the cushions. "I've been premature, haven't I?"

In the kitchen, Libby overheard snippets of the conversation, her heart growing heavier as each minute passed. Hearing her son's love and dreams for the children made her heart break for him, and she began praying in earnest. So lost was she in her prayers, that she jumped when Luke's voice spoke from her elbow. "Well, Mom, it appears that Aggie has the option of rescinding her guardianship of the children if she chooses."

Though she'd heard enough of the conversation to know about the codicil to the will, Libby was stunned at the matter-of-fact tone in her son's voice. "You won't do it, will you, Aggie?" Overcome by the thought of the loss of the children in her life, Libby excused herself and fled.

Luke glanced at the stove, making sure that nothing would ruin in his mother's absence saying, "Go to her, Mibs. Mom needs you right now." He wrapped his arms around her for a moment, swallowing her in a bear hug that left her breathless. "I love you. We'll get through this."

Libby sat in a rocking chair in her bedroom, struggling to staunch the flow of tears. Seeing Aggie in the doorway, she beckoned for her to enter. "I'm sorry, Aggie. I know this isn't about me and what I want, but I couldn't help myself."

"I know. It's exactly how I felt."

"What are you going to do? I assume you'll talk with your parents?"

The young woman shook her head. "I can't, Libby. It'd kill mom to think that I'd do it, and it'd kill her to see me 'give up so much.' It's best to take care of it, and then tell her about it when it's all settled."

"So you've decided?"

"It's so weird. I feel as if I'm supposed to feel like a prisoner who has been pardoned, but I didn't feel like a prisoner, and I don't want that pardon."

"You know the family will do anything to help you and Luke raise those children. If it gets to be too much at times, we'll take them for a week or three. That's what family does."

Aggie's heart swelled at the sound of her name coupled with Luke's. She didn't have to run the mothering race alone. "It's so strange. I've felt so often as if I was running a marathon all alone, but it's more like a relay race, isn't it?"

Libby's face showed that she didn't understand. "Why a relay?"

"Well, I just realized that sometimes I pass the baton to someone else while I rest. Is that what marriage is like? One person carrying the load while the other rests sometimes?"

"That's a good way of putting it. Sometimes you carry it together, others you take turns so the other can rest."

"If that's marriage," Aggie said smiling, "then I look forward to it. That's a beautiful picture."

"I recommend it, Aggie. I've never been happier than I was married to my Steven."

"I'd say I can't wait, but I guess I'll have to. Luke says he wants to join our little clan sometime, but he's so cautious about not pressuring me and 'letting things run their course,' that I don't know how to encourage him."

"You haven't told him that you love him yet, have you?"

Aggie's head shook slowly. "It's not something you just blurt out, and we're almost never alone. I don't want him to hear it from me over the computer or in a room full of noisy nosey children, so I keep waiting and assuming God has a reason for it."

"Well, I'm sure of one thing. Luke will treasure your love no matter when, where, or how you tell him, but I do see your dilemma. Just don't wait too long. I've never thought it wise not to share what's on your heart. We aren't promised tomorrow, you know."

Sunday, November 16th

Aggie crept out of the little girls' room, peeked in on Ian, and then jogged downstairs. The children were still playing Uno while waiting for her to return. It was time to have a family meeting. That thought sent waves of panic over her. Times like that reminded her that she indeed had a family that she was responsible to lead. For a split second, the temptation to tell the children that they were going to new homes settled around her shoulders, but in the next, she shivered. Life without her children was unthinkable.

"Ok, when the game is done, I want everyone in the living room. We need to talk."

Laird tossed his cards in the discard pile and rose. "We can come now." Tavish, Ellie, and Kenzie followed suit.

"Vannie was winning?" The question was moot. Vannie had the same 'luck' with Uno that Kenzie had with Go Fish.

"It was my turn and I was going out. They knew it. I won regardless of default," the girl insisted.

"Ok, everyone needs to sit down and listen to me." Five pairs of earnest eyes, Vannie's clouded with concern as well, stared back at her from the couches. "Mr. Moss sent me a letter that your mother wrote me before she died."

"Can we read it?" The question stunned Aggie. She hadn't considered that they'd want to read it.

"I don't know. I'll think about it. Anyway, your mother was a very well prepared woman."

"Dad used to call her a better boy scout than the boy scouts." The choke in Laird's voice nearly tore at her heart.

"That sounds about right. Did you all know that your parents set up a few families that you know who agreed to become your guardians?"

377

"I thought you were our guardian?" Ellie's eyes widened — afraid.

"I am, but your parents set it up so that if I couldn't do it, there were other people ready to step in."

"You said families. So we'd have to go to different homes?" Vannie's face was as expressive as Aggie's usually was.

"Yes. They couldn't find anyone who felt confident to take on eight children, but there were three families that were ready to take you in groups. They'd planned to make sure you saw each other often."

"Oh, I am so glad you came, Aunt Aggie. I can't stand that. Losing Mommy and Daddy and then everyone else." As unofficial spokesperson, it was clear that Vannie spoke for all of them.

"Well, that's what I have to tell you. I almost didn't. I don't want to, but it's better that you hear this from me than from someone else. The letter I got from your mom last week releases me as your guardian if I want that. Do you understand what that means?"

"You don't have to be our mom anymore?" Kenzie's grasp of the situation was surprisingly simple and accurate.

"That's right. I don't have to do it if I don't want to."

The child burst into tears. "I don't want another mommy. I just want you!"

Aggie's arms opened to wrap around the little girl as Kenzie flung herself at her. "I'm not going anywhere, Kenzie. I just wanted you to know that it was something your parents provided for. I wanted you to hear it from me and know that I am not going to do it. The story is going to get around a little town like this, and I didn't want you to think for a second that I would sign away my guardianship rights. I'm not going to do it."

Cheers erupted from all but Vannie. The young girl sat, silent, her brow furrowed and her eyes lost in thought. "Vannie? What's wrong, sweetie?"

"If you let the other families take us, you can have a regular life. You don't have to marry Luke unless you want to, and you could still see us. I think you need to think about it more. It's a long time, Aunt Aggie. Seventeen years of your life taking care of us."

"Ok, whoa. Listen to me, all of you. First, I'm not going to marry anyone unless I want to. If I marry Luke, it's going to be because that's what I want to do more than anything. Just like I'm not giving up guardianship of you guys because *that* is what I want to do more than anything. Do you understand that?"

All heads nodded, but Vannie's expression told Aggie that the girl wasn't convinced. "Were the Kovaks one of the families?"

"Yes." Aggie hadn't considered that the children would guess who had offered.

Laird spoke up eagerly. "Oh, I bet the Chessneys were one. He looked at Aggie for confirmation, and then guessed again. "So, the Kovaks, Chessneys, and maybe the Torres'?"

"Good guesses guys."

Vannie's head shot up. "Can we go play now?"

"Sure. I just wanted you to hear it from me first so you'd know the facts. You could have gone to live with other families, but you won't. You're staying here with me. Does everyone understand?"

As expected, Vannie didn't leave with the rest of the children as they rushed out the door in search of rakes for leaf piles. The timelessness of jumping in leaves tugged at Aggie's heartstrings. She'd seen children growing up much too quickly, but somehow, her children seemed to have missed most of it. Lost in thought over the cause, Aggie almost forgot that Vannie hadn't left the room.

"Aunt Aggie?"

"Hmm?"

"Don't you think you'll regret it?"

She tore her eyes from the window and forced herself to give Vannie all her attention. "Regret what?"

"Taking us all in." She rushed to continue before Aggie could answer. "I know we're family, and I know you love us, but it's a lot of work for a long time. You didn't choose to get married and have lots of kids. You just got it dumped on you."

"Vannie, listen to me. I prayed about this. Did you hear that? I prayed about this. I talked to Mr. Vaughn, Libby Sullivan, Luke, William, and Tina. I asked Mrs. Dyke what she thought. I prayed some more. I tried to imagine my life without you guys, and I can't do it. It'd break my heart to lose you now. Do you understand that?"

The young girl practically threw herself across the room and into Aggie's arms. "I'm so happy. I didn't want to go anywhere else, but it's so much—"

"It's just where I want to be."

"And what did Luke say? Is he ok with it now that he knows he doesn't have to have all of us to marry you?"

A small secret smile stole over Aggie's face. "Vannie, I think he'd have begged me to reconsider. He loves you guys like his own children."

"No wonder you love him so much."

"No wonder is right."

Luke says: Aggie? Are you there?

Mibs says: Hey! Sure am. Took the kids longer to get in bed tonight.

Luke says: Any particular reason?

Mibs says: Lots of prayers thanking the Lord for their wonder-aunt for keeping them and not splitting them up. Their prayers made me sound like a saint.

Luke says: Saint Aggie. Did saints get to marry or were only priests and nuns disqualified?

Mibs says: Who knows?

Luke says: I wasn't sure you'd tell them. Did it go ok?

Mibs says: I didn't want them to hear it from someone else. You know? Better that they get the facts straight up front.

Luke says: That's a very wise decision.

Mibs says: I wish they didn't have to know.

Luke says: How did they take it?

Mibs says: Well, Vannie is old enough to see what I have to give up to do it, and she really thinks I should consider it.

Luke says: That girl is wise beyond her years sometimes.

Mibs says: It just makes me even more determined to stay right where I am.

Luke says: So you've made a definite decision? There's no doubt at all?

Mibs says: No doubt. I made myself really look at how my life would be. I forced myself to imagine epidemics of flu, possible rebellion, years of fighting Geraldine Stuart, but when I imagined them gone, it felt horrible to be all alone. I missed them. Not seeing Vannie grow into the amazing woman I know she'll be, not being the first one to see Ian climb a tree, not having that daily lesson in how

Cari and Lorna are identical opposites… it broke my heart.

Mibs says: I just saw myself sitting there as an old maid and it was horrible!

Luke says: I see.

Aggie says: What do you see? I thought you supported me keeping things the way they are.

Luke says: It sounds as though you've decided that I am not something you plan to have in your future. I think I need to go, Mibs.

Mibs says: That's not what I meant at all!

Luke says: Aggie, you spoke of being alone— being an old maid.

Mibs says: Well, that's my reality today. You seem hurt.

Luke says: Well, truthfully, I was. I thought we'd agreed that us was a when, not an if. It hurt to be cut from the when.

Luke says: Ok, so I was a little over sensitive. And, let's face it, this messenger thing doesn't convey emotion all that adequately.

Mibs says: I'll say!

Luke says: And what is that supposed to mean?

Mibs says: Well, just that some things cannot be said over the messenger or in a room full of people.

Luke says: I'll agree to that. With this thing, I never get to watch your face so I can see what you are going to say.

Mibs says: Ok, on that note, I'm going to bed. Tina insists that we start packing for mom's next week. Why a whole week in advance, I don't know, but she seems to think it'll take a week to get us all packed.

Luke says: Did she decide to go up with you after all?

Mibs says: Nope. She's staying here and having Thanksgiving with Murphy and William. I think William has another single deputy that he's bringing along, but I don't think Murphy is too thrilled. She seems to realize that William has developed an interest in Tina.

Luke says: Oh, I feel for her.

Mibs says: Me too, but why do you?

Luke says: I know what it's like to watch someone you care for deeply appear to be caught up in someone else.

Mibs says: You do know that while I might have been blind to your feelings for me, I was never interested in William. Right?

Luke says: Well, I do now, but at the time, it was extremely difficult to watch. Ellene must be hurting.

Mibs says: I'm sorry. I never wanted to hurt anyone.

Luke says: I'd say you've turned out to be worth the wait.

Mibs says: I hope so. I know you have.

Luke says: Have what?

Mibs says: Been worth the wait.

Luke says: What wait?

Mibs says: If you are that dense, then it's your problem.

Luke says: Do you have something you're trying to tell me? *grins*

Mibs says: Not on this thing. Goodnight, Lucas. I'll see you next week.

Luke says: Goodnight, Gracie.

Winnie's Pumpkin Butterscotch Cookies

Preheat oven to 325°

<u>Ingredients</u>

4 cups- flour
2 ½ - teaspoons baking powder
½ - teaspoon ground ginger
2- teaspoons ground cinnamon
1- teaspoon salt

- - - - - - *- - - - - -

2 ½ - cups brown sugar
4- large eggs (room temperature)
2- teaspoons vanilla extract
1 cup vegetable oil (light olive is perfect)
2- cups canned pureed pumpkin (1 15 or 16
oz can)

- - - - - - *- - - - - -

2- cups butterscotch chips
1 ½ - cups of pecans or walnuts as preferred/available.

Prepare cookie sheets by layering with parchment paper.

Mix together:

First set of ingredients in a bowl, stirring well or sifting. In a larger bowl, mix eggs and sugar until creamy, then add the remaining ingredients and mix well. Mix butterscotch chips and nuts gently into batter. Stir in dry ingredients until just moistened (as you would in making muffins). With an ice cream or cookie scoop, place mounds of dough on the cookie sheets approximately two inches apart and bake for 15-18 minutes or until a toothpick inserted comes out clean.

Makes approximately three dozen cookies. Serve with mulled cider for a great fall treat.

The games are getting old and the day is growing closer...

KEEP AWAY

Chautona Havig

In the hubbub of wedding preparations, Christmas celebrations, and a house full of lively children, Aggie is feeling overwhelmed and underappreciated. Add to that two puppies who are growing faster than she can replace chewed shoes and fix dug fences, it seems like things just can't get any worse. Then, as she should be enjoying the most exciting time of her life, she's faced with her worst nightmare.

386

[1] *The Awakening Chorus*, Words by Charles Gabriel (1905)

[2] *Fill Thou My Life*, Words by Horatio Bonar (1866)

[3] *Habakkuk 2:20*, Tune by William James Kirkpatrick (1838-1921)

[4] *God Will Take Care of You*, Words by Civilla Martin (1904)

[5] *Guide Me O Thou Great Jehovah*, Words by William Williams (1745)

[6] *Take Time to Be Holy*, Words by William D. Longstaff (1882)

[7] *Angry Words*, Words by Horatio R. Palmer (1867)

[8] *Thank you, Lord*, Words by Seth and Bessie Sykes (1931)

[9] *Twilight Time*, Words by Buck Ram (1944)

[10] *Heller in Pink Tights*, Universal Pictures (1960)

[11] *To the Work*, Words by Fanny Crosby (1869)

[12] *No, Never Alone*, Words by Ludie D. Pickett (1897)

Made in the USA
Lexington, KY
26 May 2013